DYNASTY OF SHADOWS

VINCENT STOIA

Copyright ©2023 Vincent Stoia

All Rights Reserved. No part of this publication may be reproduced, distributed, or transmitted in any form or by any means, including photocopying, recording, or other electronic or mechanical methods, without the prior written permission of the publisher, except in the case of brief quotations embodied in critical reviews and certain other noncommercial uses.

For Cousin Mike,
who made it happen

1

Changan, China. 805 A.D.

Lei Lei did not like the market but she went there twice a week. She was seven years old now, and according to her mother that was old enough to help with the shopping. If that was true, Lei Lei thought, then why couldn't she hold the money? Mama seemed to think "helping" just meant carrying armfuls of dead chickens.

It was early morning, but the market was already full. That was no surprise. This place was always packed with people no matter when Mama decided to do the shopping. They were walking through the butcher section of the market, and everywhere Lei Lei looked she saw dead animals. There were tables lined with chunks of pork and people walking past with sacks of fish. There were baskets full of snakes and pots full of turtles. There were pigs' heads hanging from metal hooks. There were organs from…who knew what? The smells from all those different meats mixed together to form another smell, something Lei Lei thought of as the *nasty meat smell*. She was used to it but still she hated it.

At least she wasn't at home. Home was bad right now. Mama and Papa hardly spoke. Lei Lei hadn't noticed it at first – they had always been quiet at home – but now silence was the only thing she noticed. Her parents only spoke late at night, when they thought she was asleep. That was when Mama whispered words like *whore* and *bitch*. Lei Lei didn't know what those words meant, but they were terrible words. They had to be.

"Lei Lei."

Lei Lei looked up to see Mama staring down at her.

"I'm going to buy some pork from Mr. Wen. Wait here."

Lei Lei nodded.

Mama stayed put, arms crossed and mouth turned into a frown. "Do not move from this spot. I don't want to see any of your footprints in the mud around you. Not even one."

Lei Lei nodded again.

"There are bad things happening in this city, Lei Lei. Awful things. So many children…" Mama appeared ready to say more. Instead her angry frown melted into a look of almost helpless sadness. "So just stay here."

"I will, Mama." Lei Lei hoped this was the end of the conversation. She had never seen her mother's face like that before, and it scared her.

She got her wish when Mama turned and began pushing her way to Mr. Wen's stall.

Lei Lei looked down at her feet, happy that the mud would show she had kept her promise. Then her breath caught in her throat. The ducks! If they were already near Mr. Lin's stall, it was time to see the ducks! She had been so busy daydreaming she had almost missed the only good thing in this whole smelly place.

The duck vendor's stall was on the other side of the street, but Lei Lei could barely see it through the forest of legs in front of her. That was all right. She knew this place so well she could find it with her eyes closed.

Lei Lei looked to her right. Mama was standing at the pork stall and haggling with Mr. Wen. They were both stubborn people, so Lei Lei knew they would be busy a good while. There was enough time to visit the ducks.

Lei Lei pulled her arms close to her body and began to fight her way across the street, thoughts of muddy footprints gone from her mind. Legs and hips knocked her around as she walked but she didn't notice. She was used to it and besides, it was time to see the ducks.

She broke through the crowd and there they were. Mr. Lin kept them in a wooden cage next to his table. There were…Lei Lei counted…eight of them today. Seven of them were dark brown but one was whiter than a cloud. They all were quacking away, probably excited by the people around them.

Lei Lei grinned.

Some of the market children didn't like ducks because they looked clumsy and a bit stupid. Lei Lei always tried to make them understand: that was what made the ducks so wonderful! She loved their wide beaks and those stubby legs that ended in big, silly feet.

They even made a funny noise. Lei Lei had been coming here for as long as she could remember, and that *quack quack* still made her smile every time.

She reached into her pocket and found a few pieces of grain. Mr. Lin used to give Lei Lei some of his own grain to feed to the ducks, but Mama had put a stop to that. It was all right for Lei Lei to feed the ducks, she said, but she shouldn't waste a hardworking vendor's supplies doing it.

Lei Lei never understood that. Weren't the ducks going to eat it all anyway?

Lei Lei stood up straight and waited for Mr. Lin to notice her. She always asked his permission to feed the ducks. Mama insisted on it.

But Mr. Lin was busy talking to a customer. It seemed like an important conversation too, because his voice was loud and he kept waving his arms as he spoke. So far he hadn't even glanced in Lei Lei's direction.

Lei Lei waited for what felt like a lifetime. Mr. Lin didn't look ready to stop any time soon.

She looked back over her shoulder. Mama was still arguing with Mr. Wen, but sooner or later she would pay him and take her pork. Time was running out.

Well, just this once she could feed the ducks without asking Mr. Lin. She was in a rush and besides, Mr. Lin always just smiled and said yes. Lei Lei liked Mr. Lin. He was nice.

Lei Lei took one step toward the ducks, and stopped.

A monk was kneeling a near the cage. He was holding a basket and bowing to the passersby. Most people ignored him, but now and then someone stooped low and dropped a copper into the basket. Every time the monk received money he responded with a deeper bow and a blessing of thanks. Like a lot of monks, he wore a dark cloak. His was too big, though. Lei Lei thought it looked big enough to fit a giant. Next to him was a worn satchel bag. It was just about the oldest, ugliest thing Lei Lei had ever seen.

Lei Lei watched the monk. What if he saw her feeding the ducks and yelled at her to go away? Usually the beggar monks minded their own business but some of them were snoops. They thought that just because they were older they could tell you what to do. Adults were like that sometimes.

Lei Lei decided it was better to wait for Mr. Lin after all.

She was doing just that when she saw something move in the monk's old satchel bag. Lei Lei made a face. It was probably a rat. They were awful things – little monsters with black fur and pink tails and evil red eyes. They were everywhere in the city, especially around the markets. This one had probably gone into the monk's bag because it smelled food there.

The shape was struggling toward the front of the bag. Lei Lei took a step back.

Then a head poked out of the bag, and Lei Lei shrieked in delight.

It was a baby duck! It was smaller than her hand and it had fuzzy yellow hair instead of feathers. Its eyes were black circles and its head was almost bigger than its body. It took two clumsy steps, seemed unable to balance its giant head, and fell down to one side.

Lei Lei giggled.

The monk glanced at the duck and muttered something. He pushed the animal back into the bag.

Lei Lei frowned. The monk was smart to keep his pet in the bag. After all, this place was filled with busy people and someone might step on it. But she had hardly gotten a look at it.

There was more movement near the front of the bag. Lei Lei squinted and stepped forward. The duck had come out once, hadn't he? He might come out again (Lei Lei felt certain the duck was a boy). Who would want to stay in that old bag, anyway?

Sure enough, soon a little beak poked through the bag's opening, and out came the duckling.

Lei Lei took another slow step forward. Could a little duck like that eat grain? She did not know.

The monk muttered something again. He put a hand on the duck and pushed it back toward the bag.

Before Lei Lei could stop herself, she cried one word: "No!"

The monk looked up at Lei Lei and frowned. "Is something the matter, child?"

Lei Lei felt her face burn. Her father always told her to respect the monks. They were close to Heaven, and they could do things normal people couldn't. Some even went a hundred years without food or water just to prove their love for the gods. And this one had caught her snooping! What would he do if he got mad at her?

The monk kept staring. "I am out here under the hot sun praying for coins. Why is a child looking at me like I'm a street performer? Surely you've seen a monk before?"

Lei Lei only nodded.

The monk glanced down at the duck. "Or maybe you're looking at this infernal thing. Do you know I tell him a hundred times a day to stay in his bag, and a hundred times a day he pokes his beak out and goes walking? He has even less respect than spying children. What do you have to say about that, child?"

Lei Lei said the only thing she could think of. "I knew it was a boy."

The monk smiled, and his face transformed. "A boy he is! I bought him in the east market just two weeks ago. He will keep me company while I beg, if only I can make him behave. He just won't listen. What do you think the problem is, child?" In one motion he scooped up the duck and held it out to Lei Lei.

Lei Lei stepped forward and examined the duck. She was less than an arm's length away, but the duck didn't seem to mind. It just sat in the monk's dirty palm and looked up at her. "He doesn't like the bag."

The monk raised his eyebrows. "No?"

"No. If you want him to stay in one place, you shouldn't keep him in the bag. He'll just want to wander around even more. I would never want to stay in a bag like that."

The monk chuckled. "I take your meaning, child. You have a way with animals. And did you know your father murdered a prostitute?"

The monk dropped the duck and grasped the front of Lei Lei's tunic. His other hand shot out and covered her mouth. Lei Lei felt rough fingers digging into her cheek. She smelled sweat and dirt.

Lei Lei tried to pull away and scream but the hands on her were too strong. She felt a painful, sickening tug as the monk yanked her forward.

Now fear came, hot and fast. Lei Lei understood. This was not a monk. It was a *mogui* – a wandering demon. They could change into people when they wanted to, could look like your mother or your brother to fool you. Everyone knew what they did to little children. They took them away to dark caves and put them in boiling water, cooked them like meat until they were ready to be eaten.

Lei Lei screamed into that dirty palm and fought harder. Something moved in front of her and the world went black. One thought came to her as she struggled. *The sack is over my head!* She tried to scream again but no sound came out.

Strong arms held her close, squeezed her so tight she could not move. Her feet left the ground and she suddenly wanted to vomit. Another thought came to her: *We're moving.* Then terror overwhelmed her and she could not think at all.

In the space of a few heartbeats, both Lei Lei and her captor were gone. All that remained in that spot by the road was a small yellow ducking that pecked at the ground.

2

Ming De Wei stood in a wide hallway of the Imperial Ministry, the building that housed the beating heart of Changan's omnipresent bureaucracy. Serious looking men in their forties and fifties rushed past him in both directions. Most of those men wore the long, immaculate robes of mandarins – officials charged with running the empire's daily affairs. Ming followed those men with his eyes, noting that the senior officials in their purple robes never spared him a glance. The junior mandarins, identifiable by their blue robes and youthful faces, sometimes favored him with the slightest of nods.

Ming wore woolen pants and a gray tunic. It was the best outfit his tutor's salary could justify. As he watched the important men hurrying by in their expensive robes, Ming wondered if his clothes looked as frayed as they felt.

Feeling like a criminal holding a murder weapon, Ming reached into his pocket and squeezed the small wooden object inside it. He fancied he could feel the dried flecks of blood creeping under his fingernails, but surely that was a trick of the mind. He had cleaned every spot of blood from the object just that morning.

Ming tapped his foot on the floor, slowly at first and then faster. The rapid *pat-pat-pat* sound reminded him of a heart beating too fast. He looked up at the high ceiling with its network of crisscrossing wooden beams, tried to slow his thoughts and found he could not. He tapped his foot faster.

He had known that returning to this building would be a challenge, of course, but he hadn't expected it to be *this* hard. The high polished walls seemed to watch him, to whisper that he no longer had business in this world.

Yes, came the whispers. *Yes, you were once in the Gold Bird Guard. Yes, you were once the Sorcerer, the steward of secret sins. But that was a lifetime ago. Now you are just an underpaid tutor with two young children and a dying wife. And is that anything less than you deserve?*

Ming tapped his foot harder, but he could not quite feel himself doing it. His foot seemed numb, far away. His arms and legs felt too light. He put a hand on his chest. His heartbeat was fast and shallow.

Was it one of his fits?

Ming closed his eyes. *Not now. It cannot happen now.*

He opened his eyes, felt the fear receding and allowed himself a bit of hope. Perhaps he had fought the fit off. Even if a fit did come, however, he was determined to push his way through it. He had done it before.

A pair of Gold Bird Guards strode past Ming in lockstep. Their white robes and long swords were as alike as their empty expressions. If either of the young men recognized Ming as a former officer in the Emperor's police force, they didn't show it.

Across the hallway an office door opened and a plump man in a red mandarin's robe stepped out. When the man saw Ming his eyes rounded in surprise and quickly became neutral again. The man crossed the hall and stood next to Ming. His head only reached Ming's shoulder. "Good afternoon, Ming. What are you doing in the Imperial Ministry without an escort?"

Ming swallowed hard. It was a trick he had taught himself years ago. He imagined forcing the fit into his belly, where it would strangle and die. "Good afternoon, Zhou. It couldn't be helped. I had to speak with you. I'm assuming you already know there was another one?"

"It makes four children now." Zhou motioned to another pair of stone-faced Gold Bird Guards hurrying past. "They're deploying forces throughout the city. Won't do much, though."

Ming agreed with Zhou. Sending Guards to the streets could soothe a nervous public, and it could prevent groups of angry men from forming into mobs of vigilantes. But these Guards with their stern faces and notched arrows could do little to find the killer. The madman had proven to be very cautious. "Zhou, I need to speak with you. It's about the killer and it's urgent."

Zhou was straightening out his mandarin's robe. When he heard Ming speak his arms dropped to his sides. "Is it about the madman's…connection to you?"

Ming's hand went to the outside of his pocket. He gripped the solid object through the cheap fabric of his clothing. "Yes. This morning –"

The door across the hall opened again to reveal a tall, reed-thin man in his early twenties. Ming had seen the young man several times before. His face was hard to forget. He had a deep dent the size of an egg in his forehead.

The tall man crossed the hallway in two long steps and bowed to Zhou. Then he looked at Ming and nodded.

"Good afternoon, Hai Tao." The words were tight in Ming's throat. He never felt comfortable around eunuchs. They were everywhere, of course, especially in government buildings. Some of them worked closely with the Emperor and enjoyed intimate access to the throne. Others tended to the Emperor's concubines, the logic being they posed no threat to the women. Some, like this particular eunuch, were taught to read and made scribes. Most, however, lived lives of menial labor. Even Hai Tao worked in the palace kitchens several nights a week, according to Zhou.

Ming wanted to pity them. After all, almost all of them were sold to the government as children…sold and then cut. They were victims. Still, Ming always had trouble looking them in the eye.

Zhou, never one to miss a signal, understood that Ming would not share his news with an outsider present. "I've got a criminal trial right now. The fool commandant who will adjudicate the case does not tolerate tardiness. Walk with me?"

"Of course."

Zhou looked at the silent young man before them. "Hai Tao, stay five paces behind and don't listen to what we're saying."

The eunuch Hai Tao bowed.

Zhou and Ming started down the hallway. They were both in their late thirties, but while Ming more or less looked his age, Zhou had a childlike face that would probably stay with him for life.

Ming could feel his heart hammering at his ribs. The immediate threat of a fit was gone, but the danger felt close, like a black serpent lurking beneath the still surface of a lake. "So this murder was the same as the others?"

Zhou trusted his eunuch, but he still kept his voice low as they spoke. "Yes. A child disappears, stays missing for a few days and then turns up dead in the city. This time it was a girl named Lei Lei. Her mother was haggling for some meat in the West Market and didn't realize she was missing until later. That was four days ago. A vendor found the child this morning."

"Beaten to death?"

"Yes."

Ming winced.

"We don't know much else yet," Zhou said. "The girl's father is a third level mandarin. Some kind of connection to military logistics. I've met him once or twice. Smart man but he's never going to rise past fourth or fifth level. Too much time in the Pleasure District and not enough effort hiding it." Zhou chuckled.

"What was the father's name?"

"Jin Lei Jin"

"Jin Lei Jin." Ming looked at his feet as he walked, trying to stimulate his memory. The name did not feel familiar, but surely Ming had some connection to the man. Why should this fellow be any different from the other victims' parents? "We can assume I assisted him while I was in the Guard. I will try and remember for you."

They rounded a corner and started down a wider hallway. The wooden floors were smooth underfoot, the walls so polished Ming could see his reflection in them. Ming said, "The dead girl was holding a carving of Leigong in her hand?" Leigong was the Thunder God and the punisher of hidden sins. If you committed a crime and got away with it, you spent the rest of your life waiting for Leigong to strike you down.

Zhou gave Ming a hard look. "Ming. You're not in the Gold Bird Guard anymore."

"I know that," Ming said. "I just –"

"And you're not supposed to know about the Thunder God carvings. *No one* outside the government is. I felt I had to let you in on that information because of your connection to this mystery. But you cannot speak about it, especially in public. If anyone finds out I told you, I may be killed myself."

"All right." Ming didn't have to press the question further anyway. So far every dead child had been found clutching a statue of the Thunder God. This was clearly the work of the same man, so there had to be a statue with the Lei Lei child as well. Ming glanced back at Hai Tao. The eunuch was five paces behind them, hands clasped and eyes dutifully pointed at the floor. "But I suppose the child was clutching a note in her other hand? A note pertaining to me?"

Zhou said nothing, and for Ming that was confirmation enough.

They passed two Guards flanking a low door. One of the Guards made eye contact with Ming and nodded. Ming nodded back. He wondered what his former comrade would think if he knew Ming was responsible for the wave of terror gripping the city. Ming did not let the concern show on his face. He was used to hiding his thoughts.

"Here," Zhou said.

They stopped in front of an office with a closed door. Three Gold Bird Guards coming the opposite way stopped at the door a beat later. In front of them was a man dressed in clothes so dirty they were almost rags. The grime on his face was thick, but not sufficient to hide the cuts and bruises. Wounds from the interrogation, Ming supposed.

The man wore wooden leg cuffs and a cangue – a large wooden block that closed around the neck and made even walking a trial.

"Wang Yi Bo," Zhou said as the man was escorted past. "Accused of murdering a musician outside a brothel last week. I'll be presenting the case against him."

Ming waited until the Guards led the prisoner into the office. "Did he do it?"

"Well, he's a rapist," Zhou said. "That much we know for sure. He has violated four women that we know of, but they were all commoners so nothing came of it. I want men like him out of my ward." The area Zhou oversaw was called the North Hamlet, but locals had another name for it: the Pleasure District. Most mandarins would have killed to oversee an entire ward of the city at Zhou's age, but Zhou hated dealing with the hookers and the pimps and the drunks. He didn't seem to care who knew it, either.

"And the murder?" Ming asked.

"It's possible he did it," Zhou said. "Witnesses saw a man of his description running from the kill scene, and I know he was in the area that night. Regardless, I will use it to get him for the rapes."

Ming didn't ask anything else. Plenty of men like Zhou used such tactics. If you could not convict a criminal for his own crimes, you convicted him for something else. Ming himself had never gone that route as an investigator. He found it distasteful. He would never say that to Zhou, however. His own past with the Gold Bird Guard being what it was, Ming had no business giving moral lectures. "What will happen to him after the conviction?"

"They'll probably strangle him," Zhou said. "If they find him abhorrent enough they may choose beheading instead, but I doubt it."

Ming nodded. Strangulation was the standard punishment for murder. Decapitation was reserved for the worst crimes, and fear of it was often enough to prompt a confession. Going to the grave with an intact body was a sacred obligation, dying in pieces a terrible sin. Most people preferred the agony of the wire over the taboo of beheading.

Zhou looked up at Ming. "I'm sorry. You came here for something urgent and you haven't even had the chance to tell me yet."

"Let's meet after you're done here." Ming squeezed the small wooden object in his pocket and threw a sidelong glance at Hai Tao. "There's been a development, Zhou. Everything we suspected is true. I'm being targeted by a mass murderer."

3

As the sun dropped behind Changan, turning the city's rooftops a shimmering gold, Ming and Zhou sat in a nameless ale house in the Alley of the Jingling Harness.

It was the hour when most people had finished work for the day, and the proprietors had spared no effort coaxing drinkers in from the street. The mob of men around their table stood shoulder to shoulder, their voices loud and thick with drink. To Ming's left, an Arab slid thin swords down his throat, peppering his act with lewd jokes he shouted in heavily accented Mandarin. Every comment on the phallic nature of his prop drew raucous laughter and a hail of coppers. Paid hostesses mingled with the men, playing drinking games, putting hands on shoulders and giggling at every jest they heard. From a place Ming could not see, a woman plucked her zither and sang sad, beautiful words about a lover killed in the South.

A server with blue eyes and golden hair placed two porcelain cups on their table. Ming took a deep swig of ale and sighed as it went down his throat. Alcohol was one of the only things that calmed his nerves, but as a tutor he could rarely afford to drink it. In some ways that was probably a blessing, he supposed. One could certainly consume too much of it. "Congratulations, Zhou. Today you did away with a rapist."

Zhou looked into his cup. "I did. Justice was done, but what did it accomplish? Three years of overseeing the North Hamlet. Three years of trying to clean out the drunks and the illegal pimps. And what has all my work achieved?"

"You'll never get rid of them all," Ming said. Most of the brothels in Zhou's ward were legal, but plenty operated without the proper licensing. The authorities took such breaches seriously – unregistered businesses did not pay taxes – but no amount of bearing down ever seemed to work. When the government closed one illegal pleasure house, two more popped up the next evening. "Your ward attracts a certain type of people, and those people don't change."

Zhou took a swig of ale and wiped his mouth with his forearm. "You're right. It's just a pity I realized it too late. When I was appointed to oversee the North Hamlet I told my superiors I would make it a respectable place, and they could see I meant it. They probably couldn't believe how naïve I was."

"Even so you've shown your abilities," Ming said. "People know you've got good ideas."

"You're right again." Zhou pointed a thin finger at Ming. "I won't be chasing whores and pimps forever. At some point I'll become a fifth level mandarin. It's just a question of when."

"I believe you." Ming wasn't humoring his friend. If anyone could rise to fifth level at such a young age, it was Zhou. He simply would not stop trying until it happened.

"All right, Ming. Tell me what this development is."

Ming reached into his pocket, grasped the item there and placed it on the table.

The color drained from Zhou's face. He opened his mouth to speak, swallowed hard and tried again. "Tell me that is not what it looks like."

"It is."

The object on the table was shorter than Ming's hand, and it was exquisitely crafted. It depicted a stout being with the body of a man and a bird's beak. Small wings extended from its back and its eyes were hardly larger than needle pricks. In one hand, the fiend held a shield. In the other was a short, thick hammer. All the statue needed to reach perfection was a layer of paint. The real god was said to have blue skin.

"Leigong." Zhou was whispering, but Ming had no trouble hearing him over the din of the pub. "The Thunder God."

"It was outside my student's home this morning, in a box with my name on it. The damn thing was smeared with blood." Ming snatched the object and shoved it back into his pocket, feeling again like a murderer smuggling a bloodstained blade. "I thank my ancestors the student's parents didn't look inside the box. They just handed it to me. They were quite curious, though."

Zhou's eyes stayed fixed on the outside of Ming's pocket. Finally he wrenched his gaze away. "Did the package have your real name or your…eh…your working name?"

"My name," Ming said. "It was addressed to Ming De Wei, not the Sorcerer."

"So the madman really does know who you are."

"Yes. And to be honest it's a relief at this point. This whole time the killer has been throwing accusations at the Sorcerer. Well, to be fair they were true accusations – and we never knew if he had discerned my real identity. At least now we know he has."

A passing server placed a bowl of sliced camel meat on their table and moved on without breaking stride. It may have been the same woman who had brought their drinks, but Ming could not be sure. People from the west often worked in ale houses, and Ming had trouble telling one from another.

Zhou put a piece of camel in his mouth. "Ming, if the madman knows your real name, surely he can discover where you live."

Ming nodded. "I have hired someone to look after my family while I'm away – no, I can pay the man myself, but thank you. He isn't the most fearsome bodyguard, but if he sees something he will make noise and scare off any intruder. It's the best approach because it's quiet. I don't need a battalion of soldiers surrounding my home and upsetting Li Juan. She's bad off enough as it is."

"Li Juan." Zhou sounded apologetic as he said the name. "How is she?"

Ming studied the dirt under his fingernails. "Lately she hardly has the strength to get out of bed."

"I'm sorry, Ming."

"Thank you." Ming did not know what else to say. Everyone was sorry. Family members, friends and doctors all extended their sincerest sympathies. But condolences did not cure disease. "I know there was another note with this latest child's body, Zhou. What did it say?"

"It's not good," Zhou said.

Ming folded his hands on the table and waited.

Zhou cleared his throat. "It said, 'This child's father impregnated a prostitute and then killed her. He would have been executed for his crime but the Sorcerer concealed it." Zhou studied Ming. "Does anything about the message seem familiar?"

"Of course it does." Now that Ming had heard the note, the memories were rushing back to him. "Jin Lei Jin was one of my last tasks before I left the Gold Bird Guard. The killer's accusation isn't entirely accurate. Jin Lei Jin didn't kill the prostitute himself. He hired a Uyghur to do the job for him. The Uyghur was caught and he confessed."

"And then you took over."

"That's right." Ming paused to let the memories coalesce. "They were going to convict Jin Lei Jin and strangle him in the West Market – both him and the Uyghur. I convinced the Uyghur to say he committed the killing on his own as a crime of passion. Then I got the mandarin overseeing the case to show leniency in return for the confession. I didn't know the woman was with child, though. I thought it was just about keeping the infidelity a secret."

"What did you give the Uyghur for his confession?"

"Gold," Ming said. "I don't remember how much. They gave him sixty-six lashings with the thick rod and banished him from the empire. But he left with enough in hand to start a small empire of his own."

Zhou smiled. "The Sorcerer casts another spell."

Ming did not smile back. "So the madman has killed yet another child of one of my former associates. And yet again he has left a note with the victim accusing me of covering up a crime." Ming often wondered why his strange adversary chose the victims he did. Ming had washed away countless sins during his time as the Sorcerer, and many were far worse than those mentioned by the killer. Why did the madman fixate on these particular people?

If you only knew, my insane friend. If you only knew the first magic I performed as the Sorcerer.

Unbidden, images formed in Ming's mind, like demons lurching from a dark cave.

The road that snaked beyond the city walls, thinning to a path as it dove deeper into the forest. The sudden clearing, the sad little shack atop a hill. The smell of blood strong in his nostrils as he pushed the door open. The victims, parents and their adolescent son, beaten so badly Ming and the other Guards could only tell their sex from their bodies. Then all thoughts cutting off as the dead boy rolled onto his back and began to groan.

And later, finding the truth about that family, realizing the scandal it would bring down on the city…

Ming felt a swell of panic and choked it back.

"Ming!" Zhou was waving his hands in front of Ming's face. "Ming, are you all right?"

Ming started. "Sorry. I'm fine. What were you saying?"

"I said why do you think this man is killing the children instead of the people he's accusing? You hate this Jin Lei Jin because he killed a prostitute? All right. Then you just kill him. You don't have reason to hurt his daughter."

"I haven't the faintest idea." Ming put a slice of camel in his mouth and winced. It was much too salty. "Anyway, Zhou, let's talk about you. Have I told you that you're a fool?"

Zhou smiled in a way Ming could not read. "Only a dozen times since I informed you of my decision."

"Well, you're a fool. Zhou, you actually volunteered to lead the investigation! If you fail to find the killer, whom do you think the government will blame?" Ming could still hardly believe his friend's decision. Asking to take on a hopeless cause like this one? That was like putting your head on the executioner's stone.

"Certainly my superior would agree with you," Zhou said. "The crown has been pressuring him to stop the killing. When I offered to take over the hunt, he was all too happy to agree."

Ming knew Zhou's superior from the old days. The man's name was Commandant Chen, and he had the charisma of a dead fish. "You played right into his hands."

That strange smile was back on Zhou's face. "I doubt that. The landscape is simple for me now. If I can find the madman, Chen will try to take all the credit. If I cannot, he'll try to put the blame on me. But it won't work. I am going to *solve* this crisis. And when I do, I'll see to it that *I* get the credit. When this is over the Emperor himself will probably thank me. I just told you I plan to be more than a fourth level mandarin, didn't I?"

"You'd better enlist the help of a god," Ming said. "Perhaps Zhong Kui." Zhong Kui was the Middle Kingdom's most revered deity. He hunted demons and protected mortals.

Zhou put his arms on the wooden table and leaned forward. "I don't need Zhong Kui. I need you. Ming, it's time for you to join this investigation."

Ming leaned back in his chair. He had never felt so weary in his life. "I suppose there's no stopping it now, is there?"

"I don't see how there could be." Zhou did not appear to share Ming's distress. "For weeks we have suspected the madman knows your true identity. That abomination in your pocket confirms our suspicions. It's time to get involved."

Ming said nothing.

"Don't look so distraught." Zhou pushed his ale aside. "We can use you. You have a…a sense for understanding people that cannot be taught.

Also, there's money in this. I've been given a stipend and I pay my private investigators well."

Ming's spirits rose. He couldn't help it. A little security in these lean days as a tutor would be a blessing. Still, he looked for flaws in Zhou's thinking. He was in the mood to be contrary. "The moment I accept payment, the authorities will know my name. How long until they figure out I am the Sorcerer these messages are talking about?" Plenty of people in law enforcement and the city's elite knew about the Sorcerer. They whispered about the man who could cover up any crime, no matter how disgraceful it was. But Ming could count on one hand the number of people who knew he was the man himself. Ming had never tried to gain credit for what he did. Such work was best carried out anonymously. "Surely you've thought that if people know who I am, they could blame me for the child murders."

Zhou waved a distracted hand, as though shooing the point away. "What are the chances that anyone handling the madman's notes could read them?"

Ming frowned. His friend was asking questions to which they both knew the answers. "It's close to impossible."

"It's almost *certainly* impossible." Zhou began to count off on his fingers. "Gold Bird Guards, the people who found the bodies, the workers who *moved* the bodies…surely they cannot read. For all they know those notes were prayers the children carried around at the behest of their parents. Those more senior men who have read the notes will not make the connection between you and your former occupation. I can see to that." Zhou was talking faster now. The ale was already making his eyes glow. "And when the killer is caught and I'm promoted, you can come back to the Gold Bird Guard full time. You're ready."

"I will never return permanently," Ming said. "I will help you track this man down because I have to. But as soon as he is caught I will be done."

"The fits are still bothering you?"

"Yes, but they have receded since I left the Gold Bird Guard last year." During his time in the Guard, Ming had consulted a government physician who linked his condition to screw worms – creatures the length of a human forearm that lived below the heart. They came in male and female pairs, the physician said, drinking their host's blood to survive. The physician had recommended a potion of alum and cinnabar as a cure, but Ming put little faith in remedies as likely to kill as they were to cure. Besides, Ming was not blind to his condition. He knew the greatest trigger was stress. "I'm not fit for that world anymore. I don't know that I ever was."

"It's time to let go of your guilt, Ming. Your work as the Sorcerer was distasteful but it was necessary."

Ming knew his friend was right. Ordinary people needed to have faith in their leaders. They could not know city officials were just as likely to be rapists or thieves or murderers. Faith in leadership was the thread that bound society together. If it wasn't strong, the seams would give and the world would descend into disorder. Like most people in the capital, Ming harbored a near superstitious dread of chaos. It was worse than the most destructive earthquake.

Ming did not do his ugly work to protect criminals. He did it to protect everyone. It was as necessary as the granaries and the city walls.

But why did his breathing feel so shallow? Why did his heart gallop until he felt sure it was going to fail? "I will join your investigation and together we will stop the killing. But that's as close as I will come to law enforcement ever again."

Zhou put up his hands. "All right. I'll desist for now, but we'll talk about it again. When I want something I can be determined."

Ming offered a weak smile, spotted a server and called for two more cups of ale.

4

The next morning Ming awoke with a headache.

He lay still, his eyes following the cracks in the brown ceiling. Finally he sat up and stretched his legs out in front of him, wincing as his knees popped like kindling in a fire. The room began to spin, so Ming waited patiently for it to stop. He longed for bamboo soup with boiled chicken eggs. Nothing was better for a hangover.

When he felt ready he stood up and stretched again. He rubbed his eyes and glanced around his home's common room. The light brown walls were made of rammed earth and its floor was uneven. Its two windows were covered with paper. In the center was a large dugout fireplace with a kettle hanging above it. There used to be several pieces of thick, polished furniture, but Ming had sold most of it off a bit at a time. Now they only had an old table and a barbarian bed – a foreign-made chair that could be folded when not in use.

The sleeping arrangements had changed as well. Until recently, everyone in the family had slept around the fireplace. Last month, however, Li Juan's illness had begun to accelerate. Sleeping around two noisy children got to be too much. So Ming put a bed in their tiny back room and that was where his wife slept.

Ming did not like to look in the direction of that room. He did not like the whispering voice that stirred in his mind when he saw that closed door.

The voice observed that a small, poorly lit room was the ideal place for his dying wife. Was he not storing her in a convenient space until she finally expired? Ming told that voice that it was his wife's idea, that now more than ever she needed peace and rest. Those arguments were enough to push the whispers from his mind...most of the time.

Both of the children were already sitting by their dugout fireplace and eating bowls of congee. Ming smiled. Most children couldn't be trusted to cook on their own, but his were the brightest in the world. His daughter Hui Fen was nine. Wei Sheng, his boy, was just five.

Ming squatted by the fireplace. "Is your mother up?"

Hui Fen said, "No. She's still in her room."

"Did the thunder keep you awake?" Ming vaguely remembered a storm trying to pull him from sleep all night.

"No," Hui Fen said again.

Wei Sheng was trying to get the congee in his mouth but most of it was on his chin. "*Baba,* there was a snake in front of the house yesterday."

Ming frowned. Snakes were a plague in the city. They usually nested in the tiles that topped most homes, but they also hid in bushes and even under wagons. "Were its eyes round or were they slits?"

"They were little circles."

"Well, that's good. And what did you do?"

"We..." Hui Fen hesitated, trying to remember her father's instructions regarding wild animals. "We backed away slowly. It just turned around and went away."

"That's good," Ming said again. "Snakes are dangerous. You remember that snakes are dangerous, don't you?"

Wei Sheng and Hui Fen both nodded dutifully.

Ming looked back over both his shoulders. He lowered his voice to a conspirator's whisper. "They're more dangerous than you think." He pointed at his son. "When I was your age, a snake swallowed me whole."

Hui Fen giggled and pointed a stubby finger at Ming. "Liar!"

Ming gave them a hurt look. "So your father is a liar, is he? Is that what you think too, Wei Sheng?"

The boy nodded without hesitation.

Ming scoffed. "I'll have you know it's a true story. I was looking at a big snail on a tree, when suddenly I heard a sound behind me." Ming made a low hissing noise.

The children giggled. Wei Sheng covered his face and watched Ming through the gaps of his fingers.

"I turned around and there was the biggest bear I had ever seen!"

Hui Fen said, "Snake, *Baba.*"

"Right. Snake. It was thicker than a tree and twice as long. And it was looking…right…at me!"

Hui Fen rolled her eyes, but Wei Sheng was looking at Ming with undisguised fascination.

Ming glanced back over his shoulder again. "It reared up and got ready to attack. Do you know how fast one of those things can strike you?"

"No," Wei Sheng said. His eyes, larger than saucers now, never left Ming's.

"Well, they can strike you…like this!" Ming shot his arms out and tickled both of his children on their stomachs. They howled laughter and tried to crawl away. He held them down and continued his attack.

"Baba!" Hui Fen giggled. "I'm going to spill my food!"

"All right." Ming stood up. He knew other people loved to tut their disapproval when they saw him playing with his children. Most parents expected unquestioning obedience from their offspring and reacted harshly to anything else. The crown even had laws to ensure piety toward parents. Ming never understood any of that. If you were going to spend years raising a child, why not enjoy it? "Clean up your bowls."

"But *Baba,*" Wei Sheng said. "Did the snake really swallow you?"

"Swallowed me whole."

"How did you get out?"

"Sorry. That's a story for another day." Ming went to the door that led to their tiny back room. He looked at his children, put a finger against his lips and mouthed *quiet.* Then he entered his wife's room and closed the door behind him.

Li Juan was lying on her back with her eyes closed. The blanket was flat against her thin body. After staring for a long moment, Ming could see her chest rising and falling.

He considered waking her up and decided she needed her sleep. She wouldn't have an appetite for breakfast anyway. Ming turned to leave.

"You were out drinking last night, Husband."

Ming turned back around. Li Juan was still on her back, but her eyes were open and her face was turned toward him. "Yes."

"With Zhou?"

"Yes," Ming said again.

"Any talk of a new wife?"

"If there is he didn't tell me." Privately, Ming was already certain his friend was not interested in marriage. Zhou had already divorced once by citing excessive jealousy, one of the allowed reasons for ending a marriage. His parents died not long after the divorce, so there was no one left to pressure him into matrimony. Still, most men would have tried for a second wife. If you didn't have a son to worship you after your death you became an *e gui*, a hungry ghost that wandered the world of the living. That was a fate nearly everyone strove to avoid, but it didn't seem to bother Zhou.

"Are the children eating?" Li Juan asked.

"They started the fire and cooked the congee all on their own. How are you feeling?"

Li Juan rested her head on the stone pillow and looked back at the ceiling. "Weak."

"I could bring you some congee. It's ready now."

Li Juan nodded to a small jug next to her bed. "Just water."

Ming poured a cup of water and placed a hand on his wife's back to help her up. He felt bones pushing through her skin as she moved.

Li Juan took a short sip of water, turned away from the cup and lay back down. "Your tutoring starts soon."

"I canceled the lesson. I have to tell you something."

Li Juan turned her head toward Ming again.

Seeing the cords stand out on his wife's neck, Ming felt an unseen dagger slip into his belly. "Zhou has hired me as a private investigator. I'm going to assist him until the madman is caught." Ming saw the look on his wife's face and continued quickly. "Just advising, looking at clues, making theories. No danger. Zhou thinks I have a knack for this sort of thing. He's going to pay well for it."

"That's good, then. What will you do if the fits get to be too much?"

"I will quit."

"Even better."

"Anyway, I'm meeting Zhou soon. Maybe together we can learn what's happening." Ming tried a smile, but it felt weak. Li Juan didn't know about the madman's interest in her family, and that deceit left a sour taste in Ming's mouth. Most men he knew would never consider sharing information with the women in their families, but Ming's marriage was different. He and Li Juan made their decisions together. But this time he chose to leave her ignorant. He knew all too well what stress and fear could do a person's wellbeing, and Li Juan's health was already weaker than wet paper.

But the sour taste still lingered on his tongue.

Li Juan reached out and brushed her fingers over Ming's knuckles. "Is my sister here?"

"No, Li Hua isn't here yet."

"Can you wait until she arrives?"

"Of course."

"Thank you. And remind her the children are not to play in front of the house."

"I already have. You don't need to worry."

"Yes, I do. There's been another murder."

Ming made a noise. "Your sister told you."

"Why shouldn't she? Ming, I may be dying but I still have to protect my children."

Ming groped for something to say and found nothing.

Li Juan closed her eyes. "I'm going back to sleep. You have to prepare to meet Zhou. I love you. Off you go."

"All right," Ming said. "I'll see you this evening."

Ming wasn't sure if Li Juan heard him or not. Her breathing had already taken on a slow, shallow rhythm. Ming's eyes drifted to his wife's face. It seemed that every day a little more color left her. More and more, her skin was taking on the sheen of unburned wax.

She already looked dead.

They had been together for more than twelve years, and those twelve years had been good. Their fathers had arranged the marriage, of course. Ming had not been excited to spend his life with a woman he had never met. He had entered the arrangement like a man starting a business partnership, his mind focused on the practical goal of making sons. But to his surprise he fell in love with her almost right away, and with the arrival of their children she became the cornerstone of his entire world.

And now she was getting ready to leave him.

Ming turned and walked out of the room.

• • •

Wang Wei sat on his stool, ten coppers in his hand and a smile on his face.

The man standing in front of him did not smile back. "So you will be out here until I return this evening? You can promise me that?"

Wang Wei's smile grew until all eight of his teeth were visible. "Of course, Ming. I'll just do my sharpening here instead of out back. Neighbors won't appreciate the noise but they won't dare say a thing to me."

"Thank you." Ming turned and headed down the dirt road, stepping over a basket overflowing with rice. He squeezed between two oxen pulling a cart weighed down with slabs of pork and vanished from sight.

Wang Wei's smile faded. He closed his fist around the coppers and stood up. Ming De Wei was an arrogant shit. That was true of all Gold Bird Guards, and Ming's being retired changed that not one bit. He clearly didn't think much of Wang Wei. He had only given him this "job" because their homes were across from each other.

Wang Wei spat in the dirt. Sit out here and watch his neighbor's home all day? Be ready to confront anyone who looked suspicious? Did Ming really think he had nothing better to do with his time? Still, if Ming was stupid enough to part with his money, Wang Wei was smart enough to take it. Besides, Ming was just being paranoid, like everyone else in the city. What were the chances that the madman would come here, of all places? It was like worrying you might be hit by lightning.

Wang Wei turned and headed for his workshop. He had knives to sharpen.

5

As changed the sky from blue to slate gray, Ming and Zhou made their way through the muddy streets of Changan. There were few shops in this part of the city. Most of the homes they passed doubled as little workshops, where the residents built things to sell elsewhere or made simple repairs for money. Here a woman sat on a stone porch weaving a basket. There a man hacked a piece of bamboo into long poles. Perhaps his customers would use those poles as transport, tying bundles to either end of the sturdy, buoyant wood.

Ming and Zhou drew a lot of stares from the people they passed. Ming supposed they made an odd pair – the mandarin in his bright robes and the peasant in his tunic. Besides, they were not known in this part of town, and these days people were always wary of outsiders.

Zhou stepped over a puddle of mud, pulling up the low hem of his robe. "I'm sorry to have yet another conversation with you while I'm walking. When you're a mandarin in this city, sitting down is a rare luxury."

"How much time do you have?" Ming asked.

"I've got a meeting in the Ministry soon. Walk with me there. I'll be in meetings until late – another glorious element of a mandarin's life. But we can meet tomorrow and make a more coherent plan."

"I can do that." In fact, it was ideal. Ming planned to spend the day walking through points of interest in the murders. When he was an investigator – before he became the Sorcerer – he found that visiting places of import gave him a better understanding of the crime.

Zhou stepped around a boiling pot and scowled. Men like him were rarely comfortable in the city's narrow side streets. "For now let me make sure you have all the pertinent information. You already know more about these killings than most, thanks to the information I let slip. Tell me everything you know. I have gone over the facts so many times I can't keep them ordered in my mind anymore."

Ming swatted at a fly buzzing around his face. "The first abduction was in front of a temple. The boy was eleven years old. His parents went to the Gold Bird Guard. They checked wells, abandoned buildings and every other spot where he could have been trapped or killed. Nothing. Four days later his body was found in the southeast ward, right after a big afternoon thunderstorm. The bastard just left him out in the rain."

"That's one point that bothers me," Zhou said. "How could no one have seen him dispose of the body?"

"There was a thunderstorm, Zhou. Everyone would have been indoors."

"But the storm did not destroy the document left in the child's hand," Zhou said. "Every character on it was legible."

Ming kept walking, eyes forward, hands behind his back. He had caught the expectant tone in Zhou's voice, and he didn't like it.

Zhou glanced around. The nearest person was a woman gutting a fish, her knife moving along the body with fast, expert strokes. She was watching them with a suspicion that bordered on hate, but she was too far away to hear anything. All the same, Zhou kept his voice low. "The note said 'This boy's father killed a man over a game of mahjong. The Sorcerer concealed his sin and saved him from justice.'"

His eyes still straight ahead, Ming nodded. "I remember that. He was a monster of a man and deserved execution."

"So he wasn't punished at all?"

"There was a complaint filed against him and logged in the Imperial Archives, if memory serves. That was the extent of it."

Zhou nodded. The Imperial Archives housed the government's official records. One could find information on anything there: budgets, government projects, diplomatic relations and more. A large part of the Archives was dedicated to old criminal cases, both solved and unsolved. Even if authorities didn't pursue a criminal complaint, they wrote down the details of that complaint and filed it away. Most of it was an obscene waste of time and money, but it just never stopped. Documenting information was an obsession in the city. There were times when Zhou honestly wondered if some poor scribe was charged with writing down the Emperor's bowel movements. "All right, what do you know about the second victim?"

A child cut across their path, running at full speed and hitting the ground with a stick. Ming needed a moment before he understood. The boy was chasing a rat. "The second victim was also a boy. He disappeared just three days after the first body was found. He was also left in the rain. Father was a cavalryman named Chen Shi Huang."

"When you concealed a crime for him, it was early in your career as the Sorcerer, correct?" Zhou knew these facts already, but he wanted to keep Ming talking.

"That's right. He was at a battle out west, in Henshui, I think. They looted a town and he got rich. Lots of civilians died, though, and he couldn't handle it. He was going to tell everyone the truth of what happened, that it was more than just a glorious battle. Too many dead innocents for glory and all that. But the government couldn't have him impugning the names of our brave soldiers. No one wants their heroes to be monsters."

"So they sent you," Zhou said.

"Easiest job I ever had. He agreed to keep his mouth shut as long as I sat there and listened to him tell me everything they did. I think he wanted to unburden himself more than anything."

"Was he ever in danger of prosecution?" Zhou asked.

"Only if he talked, and he didn't. In the end all that came of the Henshui business was an official reprimand against the army for all the looting."

"Lodged in the damn Archives, no doubt."

Both men fell silent. To Zhou, the sounds of the city became very loud. The hammers pounding wood into place seemed to scream at him. The snorts and whines of animals crowded out his thoughts. How many children had they passed on their short walk? Fifty? Any one of them might be snatched from under their parents' noses and murdered. And it could happen at any time.

Finally, Ming spoke. "The third victim was a nine-year-old girl named Xiu Rong. The note left with her body said, 'This child's father falsely accused two men of murder and had them executed.' You know my history with that man."

Zhou did. He started to say more, but cut himself off when he saw Ming's face. Bright patches were standing out on his cheeks. They were blood red, looking all the more sinister against his friend's suddenly pale skin.

Ming coughed, paused and coughed again. He could feel a fit coming on him now, fast and strong. That was troubling enough. Worse was Zhou's expression. Even in the midst of his worst fits, Ming usually managed to look as calm as a man relaxing in the sun. Over the years, that skill had become a perverse source of pride for him. But judging by the way Zhou was watching him, he wasn't fooling anyone right now.

As always, Zhou's first impulse was to ask his friend what was wrong. This time he ignored it. Either Ming would say what was bothering him or he wouldn't.

Ming did say. But when he spoke, his voice was hardly a whisper.

Zhou put a hand to his ear. "What's that?"

Ming cleared his throat. "I said all this death is happening because of me."

Ming picked up his pace, his long legs gracefully dodging the pools of mud. Zhou tried to keep up but he soon gave up and stopped. He stood in the mud, watching until his friend turned a corner and disappeared from sight.

6

That evening, business was slow in the White Swan Alehouse.

Meng Chun, the pub's owner and only worker, wiped the wooden counter and cursed under her breath. Now was the perfect time to drink, but her pub was quieter than a monastery. She had only one customer. He was sitting in a corner and sipping his ale as though he meant to make that one cup last all night.

Two revelers passed along the muddy street outside. The men's voices, slurred with drink, floated in to Meng Chun. They were having a good-natured argument about which of them was the better hunter. It was the sort of banter Meng Chun heard nearly every night. But neither of the drunks so much as looked through her pub's open door.

Perhaps it would be better to close early.

Meng Chun put the rag down, planted her hands on the small of her back and stretched. She looked around the old room and couldn't stop herself from smiling. Even during the lean times she was proud of her business. The ceiling was so low her tallest customers had to stoop and only one of her four tables had all its legs. Revelers often emptied the bladders on her outer wall, creating a stench she would never get used to. All the same, this place was *hers*.

Meng Chun had operated this little bar in the Pleasure District for more than twenty years. She and her husband An Lin opened it a week after they married. The first several moons had been hard going, but things picked up after An Lin died. Then Meng Chun was free to run the pub her way – the *right* way. Now, in a part of town where most drinking houses didn't last a year, she was still in business after two decades.

The man in the corner raised his cup. "Another."

Meng Chun nodded and took a clean cup from a shelf. So her customer was a faster drinker than she had thought.

As Meng Chun opened the ale barrel and filled the cup, she thought about An Lin. Her dear, dead husband had just never listened to reason. She suggested reducing prices once a week to attract more customers, and he declared the idea madness. She proposed providing free snacks – pistachios, snails, whatever – and he complained about the price. She wanted to walk through their ward and tell people about the pub. They could let everyone know what they sold and where they were located, and it wouldn't cost them a single copper. An Lin had laughed in her face.

Her husband's goals were simpler: gouging every last copper from anyone who walked through their door. *No Sir, I'm afraid you had four drinks, not three. I'm sorry Sir, but you most certainly did* not *give me ten coppers. I only have six in my hand, see? If you can't produce the other four I'll have to summon the Gold Bird Guard.*

And the drunk customers? Meng Chun sneered as she closed the barrel and wiped foam from the cup. That was when An Lin really got brave. He added phantom drink to their bills, pawed through their satchel bags when they went to the privy, and even cut bracelets from their wrists after they passed out.

With An Lin, it was always about making as much profit as possible as fast as possible, and prudence be damned. Meng Chun had tried so hard to make him understand. If you operate that way you might get a few extra coppers from a customer. You might even get a lot, if you were clever and shameless enough. The problem, of course, was that you could only do it once. Angry customers did not come back. Worse, they told their friends. No matter how many times Meng Chun tried to explain it, An Lin did not listen. He could never see past that little pile of coppers in front of him.

Within no time An Lin had alienated all the neighborhood drinkers. Most people who showed up just wanted to yell at them. During the evenings, when other pubs were so full the patrons had to stand, Meng Chun and An Lin had only each other for company.

Still An Lin could not see it. On the rare occasions when a new customer did come in, he was back to his old tricks.

They had come within a half year of total ruin, and Meng Chun was terrified. She had nowhere to go. She had already married out of her family, and she doubted they would take her back in. She and An Lin would end up begging on the street.

So Meng Chun had taken the only option that was left to her. She knew finding killers for hire wouldn't be hard. The important thing was to find people responsible enough to do it the right way. After all, she couldn't simply have them storm in here and stab An Lin to death. It had to look like something else. Eventually she hired a brother and sister from the West Market. People called the brother Toad and the sister Blossom. Everyone in the market knew those two wouldn't think twice about knifing someone for the right price.

It was the biggest risk Meng Chun had ever taken. Had investigators found her out, they would have wrapped a wire around her neck or perhaps even cut her head off. But she need not have worried. Toad and Blossom's work was nothing short of perfection. They killed An Lin and made it look like he had walked in on a robbery. All these years later, Meng Chun hardly thought of An Lin at all, except to remind herself how necessary his death had been.

Meng Chun handed the customer his cup. "Take your time, Sir, but I'm going to close when you finish."

The customer accepted his drink and placed it on the table. "All right. Thank you."

Meng Chun smiled, headed back to the counter and started putting away cups. *That* was how you dealt with customers. A little respect and consideration meant a lot to them. If that man was a local he might well become a regular.

Meng Chun took a small lock box from behind her counter and opened it. Normally she didn't count the day's earnings with a customer present, but she felt safe doing it tonight. The man at the table seemed harmless, and he certainly wasn't drunk. Besides, she kept a small dagger behind her counter.

She dumped the coppers out and began to count them, only half paying attention. She could do this task in her sleep. She just stacked the coppers into piles of ten and then counted the piles.

Sometimes she felt scared. After all, escaping the authorities was simple business, but you couldn't hide your crimes from the gods. They would send her to *diyu* – to hell. She might spend a hundred years hugging the white-hot pillar or climbing the mountain of knives. The hall of mirrors scared her the most. That part of hell was reserved for people who got away with their crimes in life. Demons grabbed you by the face and forced you to stare into a mirror at your true self. Who knew what would look back?

Meng Chun had one advantage, one thing she could use to save her from eternity in *diyu* – she could read. It was a point of immense pride with her. She knew only two or three others who understood characters. More than a matter of pride, it was a means of salvation.

Her confessions took the form of little scrolls, papers so tiny they were smaller than her pinkie finger when rolled up. Once a week she wrote out her confession. After that she placed the incriminating scroll on the inside of her forearm and burned it. Over the years, the scars had combined into one giant disfigurement, a puff of waxy, red and white skin that stretched from her palm to the inside of her elbow.

The gods saw her penance. They saw how she hurt herself, and the characters she wrote told Heaven *why* she was hurting herself. They would understand, and eventually she would leave hell and return to this world. She'd probably come back as a rat or a pig, but so what? In a thousand or ten thousand years she would be a person again.

Meng Chun looked at the counter and frowned. Less than fifty coppers. It was all thanks to that damned mandarin who had taken over the North Hamlet. He had taken it upon himself to clean the ward up and make it respectable. He was cracking down on everyone. Even successful people like Meng Chun found it hard to run a business with a man like that around.

The pub's front door opened and Meng Chun looked up. "I'm sorry. I'm about –" She wrinkled her nose.

It was as though thinking about that mandarin had summoned him. The man himself was standing in the doorway, arms folded over his thin chest. A Gold Bird Guard was behind him.

The mandarin walked into the pub and smiled. "Good evening, Meng Chun."

Meng Chun did not smile back. "Evening, Zhou."

Zhou glanced at the lone customer, who did not look up, and then walked to the counter. "No business tonight?"

"Not much," Meng Chun said. "The killings have everyone nervous. No one wants to be outside after dark." Of course, that wasn't the main reason. *Zhou* was main reason.

Zhou sat on a stool and rested his arms on the counter. He did not look at the coppers by his elbow. "Yes, the killings. That's actually why I'm here."

"Oh?"

"Yes. As you know, this section of the city contains a great deal of undesirables. Transients, beggars, whores and the like. A lot of them come in here. Have you seen anyone suspicious?"

"No."

"No one at all? What about conversations? Have you overheard anything that might be of use to me?"

"Sorry."

Zhou studied her. "You wouldn't say a word even if you knew, would you? The killer could dump another dead child right here on the floor and you would pretend not to notice…just so you could avoid helping me."

Meng Chun picked up a cup and began to clean it.

"I am in charge of the North Hamlet now." Zhou looked around the pub like a king surveying his domain. "It is my responsibility to make it an upstanding place. If I believe a business attracts the wrong kind of people, I have to put pressure on that business's owner and correct the problem. There is no second choice. Now, with these killings, I have to put even more pressure on the locals in order to find the culprit. We must all work together to stop this insanity. Again, there is no other choice."

Meng Chun knew the correct response was more silence. What would arguing get her? But something made holding her tongue impossible. It was that pitiful stash of coppers sitting on her bar. She had put twenty years into this place. That was a hard task for anyone, but she was a woman! That made it twice as difficult. And now she had to deal with a man like this. It just wasn't fair. "The North Hamlet is your steppingstone, Zhou. You believe that someday you will be a commandant or a general or perhaps the leader of the Gold Bird Guard. You want to show the palace what you can do, and that means cleaning up the Pleasure District. The problem is that in the process you're pushing out people like me – honest and hardworking people who have spent their lives building something. You've already put plenty of good people out of business and you clearly do not care. You are a plague on the North Hamlet, Zhou. Do you really believe anyone will cooperate with you?"

"I'll ask you one more time, Meng Chun. Have any customers struck you as suspicious? Specifically I'm thinking of vagrants, people with no families."

"No."

Zhou leaned forward. His elbow knocked a pile of coppers to the floor. "If you *do* see anyone suspicious, you'll tell me."

"I will."

Zhou looked like a man watching a poorly done magic trick. "Very good." He hopped down from the stool and made for the door, stopping only to study the lone customer in the corner. Zhou did things like that a lot. He always seemed to take stock of his surroundings.

The customer rested his head on his fist, blocking any view of his face. That reaction did not seem to surprise Zhou, and it certainly didn't surprise Meng Chun. Most people avoided the authorities when they could.

Then Zhou disappeared through the door. The guard nodded to Meng Chun and followed his boss out, closing the door after he left.

Meng Chun resisted the urge to spit on the floor. She looked at her customer. "Closing up, Sir. Your total is eight coppers."

The man nodded and produced a worn satchel. Meng Chun squatted to pick up the coppers the bastard Zhou had knocked over.

When she heard the man's voice, it was close. "That mandarin is right to get rid of the undesirables, you know."

Meng Chun stood up. The man was standing on the other side of the counter.

"Eight coppers, please," Meng Chun said.

The man was holding his satchel, but he did not open it. "Someone has to punish immorality. Otherwise what happens? People can get away with anything."

Meng Chun nodded somberly. "True. There is so much vice in the world."

The man nodded back at her. "You are part of the problem. You murdered your husband and no one's the wiser."

This is a dream, Meng Chun thought simply. *It has to be. He could not have said what I just heard.* "My husband was murdered by thieves."

"He was murdered by people you hired," the man said. "They were assassins, not thieves."

"Get out," Meng Chun heard herself say. "Get out now or I'll summon the Gold Bird Guard."

The man smiled. "I must admit I didn't know what to do with you. I believe the best way to punish a sinner is to take their child, but you are not a mother."

Meng Chun kept her eyes on the man's face. *When he smiles he's actually quite handsome.*

She reined her mind in. She needed to think through the sudden rush fear, to go back over what this man had told her. Something he had said was very important – and it was even more ominous than the knowledge he had revealed about her past. But what was it? Meng Chun tried to recall it and could not.

The man looked around the pub in much the same way Zhou had a moment ago. "I even thought of leaving you be – just too much trouble." He turned back to her, and his smile twisted into a leer of hate. "But what kind of person kills her spouse? Kills her own spouse and *lies* about it?"

Meng Chun thought about her dagger. In her twenty years of operating this place alone, she hadn't used it once. But it was right there behind the counter, not an arm's length away. She wanted to look down at it. "What do you want? Money? I have very little of that these days." She heard the hopeful tone in her voice and hated it. She sounded weak. She sounded afraid.

Her strange visitor said, "Leigong has no need for money."

"Leigong is the Thunder God," Meng Chun said. She had been hoping this was blackmail, but now that hope was dying. This man was touched. There was no reasoning with a man like him.

"That's right," the man whispered. He reached into his satchel. "The Thunder God. The punisher of secret crimes."

"What do you –" Meng Chun's voice faded to nothing. Understanding came to her, and her fear exploded into terror.

Children. That's what he said before. He told me he has taken children. And children are being murdered throughout the city. The man who kills children is right here, standing in front of me and staring at me. I am alone in the night with a madman.

The man was watching her closely. Meng Chun was suddenly certain he was listening to her thoughts. He smiled again. "You know who I am."

"Yes."

His smile stayed in place, but his eyes were gray stones. "You know that the Thunder God is the punisher of hidden sins. Therefore you know why I am here."

"Yes."

"Put your hands on the counter. Just like this." He placed one hand flat on the grainy counter wood.

Meng Chun did as she was told.

"Tell me," the man said. "Why am I here?"

Meng Chun looked in the man's gray eyes. "You are here because I killed my husband. I paid two people to murder him and disguise it as a robbery."

The gray eyes did not move. "And for twenty years you have concealed your crime. You have congratulated yourself for your cleverness and patted yourself on the back. But Heaven does not forget. You have a reckoning with the Thunder God."

With her right hand, Meng Chun reached for the dagger behind her counter. She moved faster than she had in a long time, and an instant later she had it.

Her mind was screaming at her again. *He's leaning close he's right there take a swing at his neck it could work he knows how could he possibly know it was twenty years ago so how could* anyone *know and I did the right thing I would do it again if I had to it was the right thing.*

She swung the blade forward. His neck was still right there – the perfect target.

Meng Chun felt pressure on her left hand. A distant part of her realized the madman was holding her hand against the counter. There was movement in the side of her vision, and a loud, flat noise: *thunk!*

Then the pressure doubled, trebled, became so heavy it felt like something was crushing her hand.

Meng Chun's arm stopped in mid swing. The dagger fell from her fingers. Somewhere, a world away, she heard it hit the floor.

Slowly, the pressure on her other hand was receding, was giving way to something else. It was still pain but now it was sharp, burning. Perhaps an animal was biting her fingers.

Meng Chun looked down. The man's left hand was holding her wrist down. His other hand was holding a knife. The knife's blade was buried deep into her cheap wooden counter.

But that wasn't important. The important thing was *her* hand. Something was wrong with the shape of her hand. The angle of her fingers wasn't right. Meng Chun looked closer. So that was it. The angle was wrong because her fingers were no longer attached to her hand.

She pulled her hand from the man's grip. He did not stop her. She held her hand close to her face, studied it. Four small stumps, round and flat, extended from her palm. Tiny geysers of blood shot from them in a steady rhythm. Only her thumb was intact.

Meng Chun watched as the blood spread from her wrist down to her elbow. There was so *much* of it. Who knew a body contained that much blood?

Movement. There was movement somewhere in front of her. She looked up, curious.

The man was walking around to her side of the counter. He stopped in front of her. Gently, he wrapped his fingers around Meng Chun's deformed hand and moved it down toward her waist.

"Leigong is the Thunder God." The man's voice sounded far away, as though it was coming from another room. "Leigong is the punisher of hidden sins. It is time to meet him."

More movement, a flash of metal. Then Meng Chun's neck exploded in pain. It was bright, strong, terrible.

Clarity returned with the pain. *I am being murdered. I am being sacrificed to the Thunder God.*

She opened her mouth to scream. But something was inside her neck, and she could make no sound.

Meng Chun reached out with her remaining hand and tried to claw at her killer's gray eyes. This creature wore a mask. It wore a mask that covered its real face – the face of the Thunder God. She wanted to see it.

He moved his head back and her fingers closed on empty air.

The last of Meng Chun's strength left her. The world was receding into a gray fog, and when her head snapped hard against the old wooden floor, she felt nothing.

7

The next morning, Zhou attended a meeting at a small office in the Imperial Ministry. The office belonged to Commandant Chen, an aging functionary who worked directly for the city governor.

Chen was Zhou's superior, and he had obtained his status through family connections. A law stated that any son of a mandarin could inherit a position one rank below his father's. Men like Chen had only to reach out and accept the power that was offered to them.

Chen had spent his career walking the corridors of authority, but he did not have the vigor of most powerful men. Zhou did not know if the fellow was fifty or seventy. His purple mandarin's robe was bright and clean, but he somehow made it look as worn as he was. His office, a square cell with no windows, was bare save for the code of laws inscribed on one wall. All offices had the laws in plain view so officials could study them while resting.

Two other mandarins were present. Zhou had learned last night that these men had volunteered to hunt the killer, just as he had. As things turned out, Zhou was not leading *the* investigation. He was leading one of several. Perhaps even more were happening elsewhere throughout the city. Yes, pressure from the crown to stop the killings was growing strong indeed.

Zhou was angry when he learned other investigations were underway. He did not begrudge these other mandarins their ambitions, but he should have seen this ahead of time. Of course other men would seek the prestige of catching a monster.

Just like Zhou, the other two mandarins were in charge of their own wards. Zhou had met them several times but he did not remember their names. One of them was short, even shorter than Zhou. The other was tall and thin. Zhou thought of them as Tall and Short. Zhou remembered only one relevant thing about either of these men: Tall had been convicted of removing his mourning garments sometime in the twenty-seven months when he was required to grieve his father. The penalty for such an offense was three years of penal servitude…and yet here the man sat, not a hammer or shovel in sight. Zhou decided to be wary. Chances were Tall had some kind of valuable connection.

As he always did in these meetings, Zhou made sure his face was as neutral as a mask made of wood. Being expressionless was an important skill for an official. A man did not reveal his feelings in a setting like this.

True to form, Chen's only greeting to his visitors was an order to sit. Now he was reading a scroll as though he were alone. Zhou had a feeling the old man enjoyed it – making people wait was a suitably petty display of power.

After an age Chen put the paper on his desk. "There was another killing. This time the victim was in your ward, Zhou."

Zhou felt his insides go cold. Another one! That meant five victims in less than two moons.

Tall said, "I wasn't even aware a child had been taken, Sir."

"This time it was not a child. This time it was…" Chen rummaged through his papers. He found one and held it close to his face. "A business owner in the North Hamlet. Her name was Li Meng Chun. A Gold Bird Guard on the night patrol found her."

Zhou's insides went from cold to freezing. Meng Chun! He had been in her pub just last night! "How do we know this was the work of the same man, Sir? The other victims were all children. They were taken and held for long periods of time. Couldn't this have been something else?"

Chen glared at Zhou. Like most incompetent leaders, he couldn't stand even a hint of disagreement. "A carving was in one of her hands. There was also a note next to her other hand. This time it wasn't *in* her hand, mind you, but that's because her fingers had been cut off."

"This is very odd," Zhou said. Odd indeed! None of it felt logical to him. He would check with Ming as a matter of due diligence, but he was certain his friend had never even heard of Meng Chun. The Sorcerer had helped a great deal of wealthy and powerful people, but surely he had never bothered with a useless pub owner in the Pleasure District.

And yet here she was, as dead as anyone else.

A feeling Zhou could not name stirred his belly. If Meng Chun was among the madman's victims, it stood to reason she had some kind of dark secret. Zhou was *very* interested in knowing what that secret was. For ages he had been trying to force the stubborn pub owner out of the North Hamlet. She was a nuisance, someone who cared about her business but not the overall condition of the ward in which she lived. She had fought almost every one of Zhou's reforms. She was impeding progress, and she needed to go.

Since taking over the North Hamlet, Zhou had gotten rid of more than a dozen troublesome business owners. His means of expelling them was simple but effective: he just looked into their past until he discovered a dirty secret. Then he approached his target and gave an ultimatum: leave quietly, or I will throw open your closet and show your skeletons to the world.

It was a risky tactic because it was illegal. Even a mandarin couldn't slip into someone's home and paw through their possessions. Now that Zhou had Hai Tao, however, he simply had the eunuch do the investigating for him. That made things a lot safer. Hai Tao was very young but he was smart and loyal. He would probably not get caught but even if he did, he would never implicate Zhou.

No, spying wasn't ideal, but it was a necessary risk. In a place like the North Hamlet, information was a powerful weapon. After all, *everyone* in that ward had a secret.

Everyone except Meng Chun, it seemed. She had owned a pub in the city's seediest ward for twenty years, but she had no demons. At least, that's what Zhou had come to believe. Hai Tao had slipped into her home three times and looked for evidence of some wrongdoing. He had poured over everything in her home, putting it all back just right so she wouldn't know she was being investigated. He had followed her, asked around about her and offered bribes for incriminating information. It had all come to nothing.

But it seemed Zhou and his eunuch had missed something. What could it be?

Zhou leaned forward. He couldn't help it. "What did the note say?"

Chen said, "I will read it in a moment. Now if there are no more interruptions, I will continue with the business at hand."

"My apologies, Sir." Zhou felt his cheeks growing hot. Sometimes dealing with the bureaucracy made one want to scream with frustration. Men like Chen always had their priorities backward. They were meant to work with subordinates, but keeping underlings in their place was always more important to them. No wonder the city couldn't solve its current crisis.

Chen folded his hands on the table. "So far, murders happened in each of your wards." He looked at Short. "Mandarin Shi, the first two abductions were in your ward, seven and five weeks ago, respectively." He turned to Tall. "Mandarin Ling, the next two happened in your ward. The first was three weeks ago, and the next …what was her name?"

"People called her Lei Lei, Sir."

"Lei Lei. She was kidnapped a week ago and her body was found in the city four days after..."

What followed was a recounting of the murders, an exercise as tedious as Chen himself. They had similar conversations after every murder. They were just covering old ground, and it was a colossal waste of time. Initiative was needed to catch the killer, not more conversation.

Now Tall was speaking, recounting information everyone in the room already knew.

At least this lull in productivity gave Zhou a chance to sniff the air. Careful not to draw attention to himself, he watched Chen. The Commandant was hanging on Tall's every word, his eyes wide and hopeful. That did not surprise Zhou. Everyone knew the murders were putting Chen out of favor with the crown. His attempt to shift the blame onto his subordinates wasn't working, and word had it the Emperor himself had begun asking questions. Why can't you stop this madness? How much longer shall I wait until I replace you with someone who *can* stop it? How many more of my subjects have to die?

Zhou found those questions intriguing. How many more murders *would* the Emperor tolerate? How many until the king finally got rid of this old fool?

Yes, those questions were very intriguing indeed.

Zhou often imagined himself sitting where Chen was now, drafting new policies for the good of the city. He would *listen* to his people, unlike most of these old fools who only heard what they wanted to hear. He would appoint competent underlings and work with them. He would make good, practical changes for the city. Most important, he would never let his ego get in the way.

"Zhou!"

The voice startled Zhou from his thoughts. He realized everyone was looking at him. "My apologies. I was lost in thought."

"Tell us about this Meng Chun woman."

"There isn't much to tell. She was in her late forties and she owned a reasonably successful pub in the North Hamlet."

"Yes, we know she owned a pub," Chen said. "She must have loved you, then. You and your…campaign of purity."

"Yes, Sir." Zhou bristled at the mockery in Chen's voice. Like most officials, Chen viewed Zhou's attempts to clean up the North Hamlet as incredibly naïve. On that point, even Zhou had to admit the old man was right.

"And when did you last see her, Zhou?"

"Last night."

Commandant Chen's mouth dropped open. Short and Tall drew in identical gasps of surprise.

"Mandarin Zhou," Chen said. "Why did you not tell me that before?" Chen's fist was clenched so hard his knuckles were white.

"I only found out about her death a moment ago," Zhou said simply. *Serves you right for never letting anyone else speak up, you ass.*

Slowly, slowly, Chen's hand relaxed. His thoughts were easy enough to read. He was beginning to hope Zhou might have some information that could save him. "All right. Tell me everything."

Zhou opened his mouth – and then his voice died in his throat. He had seen the killer! The murderer of children, the man the whole city was hunting…he had been right there, at the pub's corner table. Zhou had walked right by him! He had looked right at him!

Zhou struggled to keep his mask of neutrality in place as he relived last night in his mind. Yes. Chances were excellent that man was the killer. Chen had said the evening patrol of the Gold Bird Guard found Meng Chun's body. That patrol would have passed Meng Chun's pub very soon after Zhou left it. That meant the man was alone with Meng Chun right around the time she was killed. Besides, hadn't he turned away when Zhou was studying him?

The man had managed to conceal his face from Zhou. However, Zhou had seen other things. In his mind, he pictured the man's old satchel and black, shapeless cloak. The man wore his hair in a simple bun tied at the back of his head. And he was tall – that was clear even though he had been sitting down. Not a treasure trove of information, but certainly useful.

Zhou had walked right by him. What would his colleagues think? What would the North Hamlet think? Mandarin Zhou, the enemy of vice, didn't find anything amiss when he was standing right in front of the city's most wanted man.

Zhou cleared his throat. "I didn't see a thing."

The excitement drained from Chen's face. "Nothing at all?"

"Nothing. When we went to the ale house, the only person there was Meng Chun."

"We?"

"Officer Wen and myself. No one else was there. Meng Chun's business had been slow recently."

"We should call Officer Wen in here. Perhaps his information will be more useful."

"I assure you, Sir, that Officer Wen saw nothing." Zhou knew he might be making a colossal mistake. After all, if someone did ask Wen, he would talk about the man in the corner.

Chen was not ready to relent. "Nothing else. You're certain?"

"Yes." Zhou's voice was even, calm. He was doing the right thing. If he spoke the truth right now, Chen would respond with a flurry of useless questions. He would probably send an army of men to Meng Chun's pub, and that would just create hysteria. No, it would be better if Zhou followed up on this information himself. That way he could ensure there would be no mistakes.

Chen made no attempt to hide his disappointment. "I'll read the note left with Meng Chun's body, then." He reached under his desk and produced a small white piece of paper. It was curved at the edges, probably because it had been rolled up for some time. The bottom of the note was covered in an ugly brownish-red stain.

Zhou swallowed hard. That was Meng Chun's blood.

Chen held the note up to his face. If being so close to a bloodstained document bothered him, he did not show it. "It says, 'Twenty years ago this woman hired two people to murder her husband and disguise it as a robbery.'"

"Madness!" Zhou breathed. He saw Chen's glare and shut his mouth, but he supposed the shock was still on his face. Self-righteous Meng Chun had been a murderer – a murderer of her own husband! Had Zhou known that, he wouldn't have needed leverage to force her out. He could have simply arrested her. But he had never once suspected she was capable of such a thing.

Chen dropped the note on his desk. "Zhou, I'm assuming you had no notion of Meng Chun's past."

"None, Sir. But please rest assured I'll contemplate its significance. Perhaps if I could borrow the note –"

"No. I want a report on this Meng Chun by the end of the day."

"Yes, Sir. I'll have my eunuch write it."

Short raised a stubby finger. "There was no mention of a Sorcerer in this note. I find that odd."

Zhou did too, but he didn't say so.

"Odd?" Chen's face because a grotesque mixture of a smile and a sneer. "I find it odd that you attempt to understand an insane mind. Analyze the facts, Mandarin Liu." Chen's anger gave way to an indulging patience. "Evidence and witnesses are the only way to apprehend a man with no logic."

Short bowed his head.

Zhou's eyebrow moved, but only the most astute observer would have recognized it as a sign of disagreement. Don't try to understand the murderer? Simply dismiss his mind as beyond a sane man's reckoning? Don't even *consider* another approach? Sometimes Zhou wondered if Chen's complacency was itself a symptom of insanity.

Chen smoothed out the sleeves of his robe. Dressing down a subordinate appeared to put him at ease. "On to the next piece of business. On my recommendation, the crown has issued a decree. We are offering a reward. Ten thousand coppers for information that will lead to the killer's capture."

Zhou put his hand up. "Sir, we're going to *pay* for assistance from the public?"

"That's right," Chen said. "It was my idea, and it's a good one. There are two million people in this city. That means two million sets of eyes. Somewhere, someone has seen something."

Zhou felt a tug of unease. That *was* a shrewd idea…and if it worked, Chen would be a hero. Zhou, on the other hand, wouldn't get a scrap of recognition. "But what kind of example does this set? We'll be rewarding people for a sacred duty. Pretty soon the peasants will want compensation for tilling the fields and feeding the cities."

"That's right," Tall said. "Plus, a reward could lead to all kinds of fake accusations. Our investigators may spend ages sifting through false reports."

Zhou nodded eagerly. He felt his unease growing into panic. There would surely be plenty of false reports. But there might be a real report or two as well. It just wouldn't be right if Chen benefitted so greatly from his first good idea in years. "Commandant Chen, I urge you to reconsider. It –"

"I will not reconsider," Chen said. "Messengers have already spread the news throughout the city. Ten thousand to the person who provides information that brings about the killer's capture. Meeting over. Dismissed."

• • •

Zhou burst through the doors of Commandant Chen's office, ignoring the goodbyes from Tall and Short. He walked past Hai Tao, his eunuch assistant, without slowing down.

Hai Tao fell into step with his master. "Is everything all right, Sir?"

"No. Everything is not all right. A fool has gotten the first good idea of his miserable career, and it could be a gold mine for him."

Hai Tao walked faster to keep up. "I'm afraid I don't know what you mean, Sir."

"It doesn't matter." Zhou spoke more to himself than to Hai Tao. "It doesn't matter because I'm going to solve these murders myself. Chen can't get the credit because then he will be promoted. If that happens, the city will never change."

Hai Tao was speaking again, but Zhou did not listen. He was due to meet Ming soon, and they had a lot to discuss. Why was the madman suddenly changing his targets? Why did he use a knife this time instead of a blunt object, and why did the latest note make no mention of the Sorcerer? Better for Zhou not to tell anyone what he had seen last night, not even Ming. It was a detail no one needed to know. Zhou could simply figure out another way to let Ming know that the killer was tall, and that he went about in a black cloak.

Zhou headed down the Imperial Ministry's front steps, holding up his robe to avoid tripping. Until now the madman's actions had been consistent. To Zhou's ordered mind, that made the challenge seem surmountable. But everything was changing now, and the killer's movements felt as random as leaves on a windy day.

Even worse, things seemed to be accelerating.

Zhou strode across the Ministry's wide courtyard, praying Ming would find a way to catch a ghost.

8

Later that day, Ming and Zhou took on a new partner in their hunt. This was not their decision, and neither of them liked it. The man who forced his way onto their team acknowledged that his method of approaching them was unorthodox. On that point, Ming disagreed. Blackmail was a common tactic.

Ming and Zhou were in a restaurant called the Golden Lotus when the newcomer approached them. The Golden Lotus was tastefully designed with a view toward tranquility. Its floors were smooth wood, its walls draped with tapestries of gold and purple. Round, red lanterns hung from the ceiling. Its high windows were positioned to admit as much sunlight as possible, and there was even a stone pool by the entrance. In a city that never stopped moving, the Golden Lotus provided a welcome refuge to its patrons.

That serenity was shattered every midday, when dozens of mandarins descended on the restaurant from the nearby government offices. Customers who had been enjoying a relaxing meal suddenly faced a deluge of officials in bright robes of varying colors. Before the daily onslaught a conversation could be whispered; during the storm, people next to each other shouted to be heard.

Ming and Zhou were meeting when the chaos was at its peak, but they were lucky. Their table was near a back corner and somewhat removed from the madness.

Ming was in the midst of a delicate proposal, and he chose his words carefully. "What I am trying to say, Zhou, is that I might work better independently."

"Independently," Zhou echoed. "Without me."

Still Ming picked his way forward slowly. The problem wasn't that Zhou might be offended. It was that Zhou always had to oversee every aspect of the work that concerned him. He did not like to surrender control. "What I am telling you is that fewer and fewer people are willing to talk to the government about the killings. There is no progress and that is making people angrier, less cooperative."

Zhou's face hardened. "It is the sacred duty of every citizen to assist the authorities. They will comply with investigators or I will see them punished."

Ming wanted to pounce on that point. *You see? That hard head of yours is exactly what lost you the cooperation of the North Hamlet. It's no wonder they hate you. You favor a hammer when a feather touch is needed.* He decided to change his approach. "I cannot operate with the authorities over my shoulder, Zhou."

Zhou perked up. He didn't have the finesse needed to work with commoners, but he was sympathetic to any gripes about bureaucracy. "They are like weights tied to your back."

"Yes," Ming said a little too quickly. "Let me work alone, without government interference."

"It is true that the officials will get in your way," Zhou mused. "And as for interviewing citizens, I must concede that I lack the…eh, common touch."

"Your mandarin's robe can intimidate regular people. My white tunic is less threatening." Ming knew he was openly pandering now, but he forgave himself. He wanted to work alone.

As Zhou considered Ming's proposal, their visitor appeared. Standing by their table, hands clasped respectfully at his waist, was a middle-aged man the size of a mountain. He had the straight black hair of a local, but his brown-tinged skin and rounded eyes suggested at least some foreign blood.

The man bowed, his massive shoulders working beneath his expensive tunic. "Greetings." His voice seemed unnaturally soft. "My name is Li Jian Guo, but everyone calls me Dragon."

"Yes," Zhou said. "I know who you are. The cavalryman turned independent thief catcher."

Dragon smiled, making his short beard crinkle. He sat down next to Zhou without waiting to be asked. Ming had a moment of panic when he thought Dragon might flip the bench and catapult his friend across the restaurant.

Dragon folded his hands on the table. The middle finger on his left hand was missing. A scar, hardly thicker than a hair, dropped from the bottom of his right eye to the corner of his mouth. "Ming and Zhou. I know who both of you are as well. I would like to help you in your investigation."

"We're not looking for assistance," Ming said. He had worked with private thief catchers in the past and he considered them trouble. They were too unpredictable, too beholden to their rewards.

Dragon did not look offended. "I have an impeccable record. No fugitive has ever gotten away from me."

"Thief catchers don't have to turn in reports to the government," Zhou said. "They simply bring in their captives and collect their reward, no questions asked. How do we know your record is impeccable?"

Dragon shrugged. "I suppose you don't. But you do know I am excellent at my work. The sheer volume of my profits speaks to that."

Ming did not know if that was true. Bounty hunters traded in bravado, after all. "Why does the best thief catcher in the city need us?"

"The government has resources I do not. I pay assistants and I've got dozens of friends throughout the city who are happy to do me favors. But I don't have a tenth of the manpower Mandarin Zhou can summon with one raised finger." Dragon nodded respectfully to Zhou. "And you, Ming De Wei, were a first-rate investigator during your time with the Gold Bird

Guard. During the first part of your career, anyway." The large man appeared ready to say more, but instead he went silent.

Ming did not know what to make of their odd visitor. He had happily interrupted two strangers – one of them a mandarin – and yet every word from his mouth dripped honey. "Li Jian Guo –"

"Dragon."

"Dragon, what precisely are you proposing?"

"You don't know how you're going to catch him," Dragon said. "You have no idea, in fact. No one does, because the man is like a shadow. I can help you, and all I want is my share of the reward."

"No," Zhou said.

Dragon's mild eyes settled on the mandarin.

Zhou looked like a toddler next to Dragon. Perhaps he was aware of the comical difference in size, because he slid farther down the bench. "This is the most important investigation in living memory. I need qualified men, not a half-blood warrior who makes his living catching rapists and sheep thieves."

"I am indeed a half-blood. My mother was from a village of goat herders some three hundred *li* west of here. My father was a frontier soldier, I think." If Dragon took offense to Zhou's insult, his eyes did not betray it. "Those are rough lands out there, and the lessons they teach have made me equally rough. I'm as qualified as any man you'll find in this city. Besides, you're clearly willing to seek help outside the government." Dragon gestured toward Ming. "You hired him."

"Ming was a former investigator in the Gold Bird Guard," Zhou said. "He has ten years of experience. I'm sorry, but the answer is no. Leave us now, please."

Dragon sighed. "Another approach, then." He looked like a man forced to give sad news to a friend. "I know who you are, Ming. You are the Sorcerer."

"The Sorcerer is a myth," Ming said. "Someone conjured up by the city's elite and law enforcement."

"No." That apologetic look was still on Dragon's face. "The Sorcerer is a real man, and right now he is staring daggers at me from across this table."

"Be very careful, Li Jian Guo," Zhou said. "This talk is putting you at great risk."

"How so?" Dragon looked honestly curious. "I am not threatening to blackmail anyone."

"It is blackmail all the same," Ming said.

"I am only telling you what I know. When I learned that every dead child had a note about the Sorcerer, I was intrigued. My assistants did some digging and learned the Sorcerer's true identity. But I told no one, even though there are people who would surely pay for that information. The Sorcerer has made enemies over the years. I can be discrete."

"But you won't be if we refuse to hire you," Ming finished. "You will tell the world I am the Sorcerer – which I am not – and as a result I could end up murdered before sundown."

"I am only being forceful with you because I need you." Dragon looked at Zhou. "And this is more than just a play for money. Mandarin Zhou, I want to stop the terror. I can help you catch him."

"How?" Zhou asked.

Dragon smiled again, but now there was no kindness in it. He looked, Ming thought, like a cat rolling its shoulders before it strikes. "I have a way. Let me in and I'll help you lay a trap."

• • •

"It is not logical." Ming clenched his fists to show Dragon just how obstinate he was. It was a poor performance, though, and he suspected Dragon knew that. If anything affected Ming's behavior, it was an excitement building in his belly, an eagerness that threatened to expand until it blew him apart.

The restaurant had reverted to its usual state of tranquility. In one corner an elderly man sipped tea from a stone cup. A young woman swept the front walk, her hips swinging invitingly beneath her tunic as she worked. The three men at the rear of the restaurant noticed none of it.

Dragon waited until a boy finished pouring his tea. "I did not happen upon my information by chance. I have this lead thanks to exhaustive investigation."

"Two million people live in Changan," Zhou said. "That's only counting those within the city walls. The rabble outside the walls adds unknown thousands to the population. And here you sit, telling us that among these countless, shifting masses, you have identified the madman's next victim."

"It is not as random as you believe it to be, Mandarin Zhou." Dragon nodded politely toward Ming. "It became easier to narrow the list of targets when I learned he was the Sorcerer."

"When you claimed to learn I was the Sorcerer," Ming said.

"All right. How many wealthy people did you – did the Sorcerer – save from prosecution? The Sorcerer worked for seven or eight years, by my estimation. Let's say he assisted fifteen people per year. That is a rough number, but close enough for our purposes."

Ming was nodding now, in spite of himself. He could see where Dragon was going.

"Based on those numbers, we can estimate two hundred people have been helped by the Sorcerer. Now, that may seem like a high number when trying to find the killer's next target – an impossibly high number. But how many of those people have children? How many of those children are young enough to be in the killer's…eh…preferred range?"

"How many?" Zhou asked. Ming was fast losing the ability to conceal his excitement, but the mandarin's face was as impassive as a stone tablet.

"Twenty-six." Dragon looked pleased. "I don't pretend to think we have found everyone who has had dealings with the Sorcerer, but I do believe we have come close."

Zhou's face remained expressionless. "We?"

"As I said, I have people throughout the city to help me. Some I pay. Some owe me favors."

I wonder how many are simply scared of you, Ming thought. "I thought you wanted our help because you don't have the manpower."

"The people I...employ are not soldiers," Dragon said. "They are excellent eyes and ears, but they wouldn't be much help in catching a madman."

"So," Zhou said. "Tell us what these eyes and ears have found."

Dragon took a long drink of tea. Just like Zhou, he did not reveal a trace of emotion. "My people around the city have been watching the homes of those twenty-six families. Before you asked, no one noticed them."

"How can you be sure?" Ming asked.

"They are the kind of people who go unseen for most of their lives. Some make a career of it. Others are simply beneath the notice of most people. Yesterday around sundown, one of my people saw something: a man was outside one of the homes we were watching. He was observing the home from an abandoned building across the street."

"*Which* home?" Zhou asked.

"It belongs a trader named Chang Li Jun."

Ming remembered the name. So Dragon really had done some investigating. "Did this person see a face?"

Dragon shook his head. "He saw the man from behind and didn't dare go for a closer look. But he saw some things of use. The man wore a cloak – baggy and black. His hair was in a bun, and he was tall."

Ming saw the color rise in Zhou's face. Finally, the composed official was betraying his excitement.

"This was yesterday?" Ming asked.

"Just before sundown."

"If what you are saying is accurate," Ming said, "your inaction may well have led to the death of another child."

"No. My people are watching every entrance to the home, every road that approaches it. If a cloaked figure comes close to the home's outer walls, they will scream to wake the dead. But I need your help. My people can alert the family but as I said, they cannot apprehend anyone."

Zhou looked Dragon up and down. "But surely you could subdue this man."

"If I had the opportunity, yes. But that area is too big for me to cover by myself. Six roads converge on the home and there are four entrances. If you help me cover the house – every approach and every exit – we will catch him. All I need is men who are trained and armed. We get him and I receive my share of the reward. I will not ask for more, despite the fact that I was the one who provided this crucial information. The prestige I'll gain from catching him will be invaluable."

Zhou threw his hands in the air. "So you would have us spend days outside this home. Countless Gold Bird Guards lying in wait for an unspecified amount of time, all in the *hopes* this man will show."

That predatory smile returned to Dragon's face. "Wrong. I have a very good idea of when he's going to show: tomorrow at midday."

• • •

The Chang family had no connections to the government. The patriarch of that family did not grow fat and rich accepting bribes or pocketing money earmarked for public projects. Chang Li Jun made his fortune through that ancillary trade which is as old as commerce itself. He was a smuggler.

Opportunity for men like Chang lay not in the eastern ports but to the west, where the roads crawled over the horizon. Silk went west, travelling thousands of *li* over mountains and past bandits until it reached men who could not name the country from which it had come. Out west the hunger for silk was ravenous. That demand suited China's leaders quite well, because they were equally covetous of the west's strong and sturdy horses.

There was one restriction on the Chinese end of the trade: no live silkworms were to leave the empire. Punishment for violating that restriction was death. For centuries the blockade worked, and China grew fat off its monopoly. Then two missionaries smuggled live silkworms through China's nets, and the Chinese grip on silk was broken.

In Ming's time silkworms could be found in many places beyond the empire's borders, but the demand for live specimens from China was still high. Chang was happy to oblige. To smuggle his goods past customs agents, he copied the tactics used by those two long dead missionaries. He hid the silkworms in his smugglers' walking sticks.

The worms slipped out of China, and the money flowed back to Chang.

There were a lot of successful smugglers throughout the city, but not all of them were wise. Chang was wise. He stayed in business just long enough to make his fortune, and then he got out.

Chang Li Jun's contact with Ming came later, when he forced himself on a woman in his ward. Rape was rarely punished, but the young woman came from wealth. Her family lodged a complaint against Chang, and it looked as though he might pay for his crime with his head.

As Ming watched Chang's home from a noodle shop across the muddy street, he relived his first impressions of that distasteful fellow. A fat man. Hair thinning on top. Looked sixty but was probably closer to forty. Not scared by the idea of punishment, as most clients were, but offended by it. A woman was his to take, no different from gold or a cup of ale.

Ming had saved Chang, just as he had saved most of the others. He convinced the woman's family of the scandal that could ensue from accusations of a sexual nature. How could they prove that it was rape and not consensual? Even if they *could* prove it, what about the gossip? People would whisper no matter what. They would joke and snicker. How would they marry their unfortunate daughter off then?

Such arguments often worked against rape accusations, and Ming's gambit was no exception. The complaint against Chang was already official, so no one could stop it from being filed in the Imperial Archives. But there were mountains of such complaints in the Archives and Chang's case was soon forgotten.

Next to Ming sat Dragon, dressed not in his expensive robes but the simple whites and grays of a commoner. Dragon's sword, almost the size of Ming's leg, was on the table, hidden by a white piece of cloth.

Ming looked at the sky. "If he were coming, he'd be here by now."

Dragon downed a cup of tea in one gulp and released a watery belch. "Relax, Ming. I told you the son leaves home every day at the same time. I wouldn't expect our man to show until the last possible moment."

Ming leaned closer to the window and scanned the buildings outside. Many of those structures concealed Gold Bird Guards, all out of uniform, all watching for a tall figure clad in black. Ming saw no sign of them but their presence gave him comfort, like the weight of a blade against his hip.

Zhou was up there somewhere. Ming hoped his friend could resist controlling his Guards' every movement.

Dragon burped again and scratched himself. Ming suspected that with the mandarin elsewhere, he was getting a look at how the true Dragon behaved.

"You've got the best vantage point possible." Dragon picked something from his teeth. "The boy leaves from that door right there. Plenty of alleys along his route, plenty of spots where a person could jump out. If he attempts an abduction, it will likely be here."

"Chang is a fool to let his son out alone in times like this," Ming said.

"He assumes no one would dare cross him. A lot of men like him think that way."

Ming kept his eyes straight ahead. "If you tell the city I am the Sorcerer you may as well hang yourself, because I will come for you." He turned to look at Dragon. "My wife is dying and if something happens to me my children will be alone. I'll cut your throat for that."

"I know you hate me," Dragon said. "And that's all right."

"Of course I hate you. You're a blackmailer and a cretin. You traffic with the worst people to get what you want. You're one of the squirming insects one sees after kicking over a rock. I saw plenty of men like you when I was in the Gold Bird Guard."

"You saw men like me?" Dragon's eyebrows rose in a tell of mild surprise. "Did you see them while you were protecting rapists and murderers?"

Ming said nothing.

Dragon took a long swig of his tea. "You and I are not all that different. We both operate outside the law when it suits us."

"The Sorcerer worked for a greater good," Ming said. "The men he protected meant nothing. To hell with them all. But the offices they represent, the tiers of society they hold – they are sacred. Imagine the chaos that would ensue if people knew their leaders were impure."

Dragon coughed a mouthful of tea onto his cheap white shirt. He wiped the tea from his mouth and gave Ming a toothy grin. "Come with me to an alehouse outside the city walls sometime. Ask the locals about the purity of our leaders. I only ask that you let me watch."

Ming shook his head. Men like Dragon weren't so different from children. They believed their world was constant, as unchangeable as the moon or the tides. They did not appreciate that others hovered over them, controlling every aspect of their lives and keeping them safe. "You operate outside the law, but you do it for money. Do you know the Sorcerer did not accept a single copper for his work? That alone should tell you where his heart was."

"And his motivation justified everything he did?"

"Yes."

"Let me ask you this." Dragon turned to face Ming. "Forgetting your duties, forgetting the sanctity of the order you claim to protect, what do you regret?"

"You ask that question as though you're sure I must regret something."

"That's right."

The images came to Ming then, curses whispered on stinking breath.

Three bodies in the shack, the floor covered in blood. The boy groaning, beaten so badly it was a wonder he could make any noise at all. That same boy in Ming's barracks, bandaged and wounded but alive, wanting to be alive. Ming letting the child stay, despite the disapproval of his comrades. Ming sleeping on the floor of his barracks so the boy could have his mat. Later, Ming understanding the child could not stay, understanding he knew too much. The scandal would be monstrous. The boy begging not to be sent away. Ming turning his back to the screams as the wagon trundled off, its unlucky cargo still crying inside it.

"Regrets don't change anything." Ming knew that was an empty statement. Worse, he felt sure Dragon knew it too.

A flurry of horrified shouts pulled the men from conversation. Ming looked at the store's entrance to see the elderly owner flailing his arms and stomping his bare feet. Moving past him without a second glance was a man wearing only pants and a layer of grime so thick it turned his skin black.

The visitor bowed to Dragon, sending off a stench that kicked Ming in the face.

Dragon handed a fistful of coppers to the enraged store owner. The man nodded once, glared at his intruder one more time and vanished into a back room.

Dragon took out another copper and passed it between his fingers. "What is it, Guang?"

"We saw something," said the man named Guang. "It was person dressed in black, like a beggar monk."

Ming felt a hot rush of excitement. "Where?"

"East of here, maybe one thousand paces. Mandarin Zhou told me to report it to you."

Ming smiled to himself. He would love to see Zhou dealing with a man like Guang. "You're the one who spotted him?"

"That's right. It was very fast, though. It felt like the moment I saw him he blended into the shadows."

Dragon's fingers traced the edge of his sword. "He's close."

Guang stayed put, sallow eyes on Dragon.

Dragon handed Guang the copper. Then he fished several more coins from his pocket and handed them over as well. "Back to your post."

The coppers disappeared into Guang's pocket and Guang disappeared from the store.

● ● ●

It happened at midday, just as Dragon had predicted. The door to the Chang family home opened with a protesting groan and there went the boy, kicking a stone ahead of him as he walked.

Ming's eyes tracked the child, shifting to every hiding spot he passed. Some of those spots concealed Guards, but many did not. Ming imagined a being hiding in one of those black holes, a watcher who knew he was being watched. He imagined that mind calculating the time it would take to rush from the shadows, gather up its prize and disappear into another pool of black. He imagined the spite at being hunted, the decision to simply stab the child in the street and run.

Then Dragon pointed, like a man who has spotted some mildly interesting animal. "Here he comes now."

Ming looked. At the far end of the street, a man dressed in black was coming toward the boy. A hood covered the man's face. Ming could hear his own blood.

Dragon's hand was on his sword. "Nobody move." He whispered as though the informants and soldiers could hear his orders. "Nobody damn well move until we know it's him."

The boy apparently noticed the black figure too, because he began drifting to the opposite side of the road. He kicked his rock once more and walked on without it. They were thirty paces apart now. The figure in black gave the boy no interest, showed no sign he had even noticed him. But Ming wondered if the man wasn't walking just a little slower.

Fifteen paces. Now Ming could see that only one of the man's sleeves had an arm in it. Either the monster was missing a limb or he was concealing his other arm beneath the cloak. They were going to cross paths next to an alley. It was the perfect spot to grab a child and disappear into the city. Ming wanted to know if a Gold Bird Guard was hiding there. He wanted to know if the madman would charge the boy straight on, or pass him and then double back.

Then things began to happen very fast.

The black figure took a long, lurching step forward. He looked like a novice sailor walking on a ship in heaving waters. The boy saw this and slowed, inching forward now, on the opposite side of the road. The figure took another stagger-step toward the boy, straightened up for an instant and moved toward him again.

The boy kept picking his way forward, his gaze never leaving the black figure. His back was to the alley now.

Dragon stood up. He grabbed his sword, sending the white cloth to the floor in lazy zigzags.

Ming was on his feet. "He's asking the boy for help. Then he'll scoop him up and rush him through the alley before anyone can stop it."

Ming thought of Wei Sheng, his boy, only five years old. Then he hopped through the store window and was running, his feet kicking up clouds of dirt on the old road. Behind him Dragon cursed, and Ming heard heavier footsteps join him.

The black figure was going directly for the boy now, all pretense of anything else gone. Ming's mind created snatches of conversation as he ran. *Help me, Son. Something is happening to me and I need your help. No, stay right there and wait for me. Stay there, with your back to that alley.*

Ming was fifty paces from the boy now. He heard stirring from the windows around him, low voices registering surprise. He saw the boy crying as the black thing extended its one long arm, moving for the child like a fiend come from hell.

Then Ming slammed into the figure at full speed. He heard a muffled grunt of pain and surprise before the world began to spin.

The next thing Ming felt was pain, somewhere high on his body. His shoulder. Something pressed against his back and he realized he was on the ground. Voices. Adult, male. Some were panicked, some angry. Another spoke with the calm tones of authority. Ming recognized that voice. It was Zhou.

There was crying, too. Not from pain but fear. The boy. The boy was safe.

Ming sat up and rubbed his eyes like a child rising from a nap.

"Ming." Dragon's voice. "Ming, can you stand?"

Ming nodded. A giant hand enveloped his own and hoisted him to his feet. Ming shook off the last of his confusion. There were perhaps a dozen people on the road, all of them male, most of them young. They were dressed as commoners but held government issued weapons. Zhou was there too, wearing his red mandarin's robe as always.

The men stood in a rough circle around something Ming could not see. He moved forward, wincing at the pain in his shoulder. Zhou saw Ming and ordered the Guards to step aside.

The man's black cloak was off him now. Someone had rolled it up and put it under his head like a pillow. He was shirtless. His eyes, foggy and sightless, studied the sky with stupid indifference. Ming saw with numb interest that the man did indeed have two hands. Both of them covered the gash that started on his left side and crossed his belly in an obscene smile. Gray and red innards oozed from the wound like vomit.

"It's a Guard." Zhou's voice made Ming jump. "We had him hiding out behind a temple. I don't know his name."

"En Lai," said another Guard. The young man's face was black with rage. "His name was En Lai."

"Why didn't he call out for help?" Ming asked.

Dragon knelt and placed a finger on the dead man's mouth. "This is why. Someone sewed his lips shut."

Ming knelt next to Dragon, wishing he could turn his face away. En Lai's lips were pursed together and pouted out, almost as though he meant to give someone an affectionate kiss. Tiny loops of stitching sprouted from the tops of his lips like hideous grass. Dried blood surrounded the ragged punctures.

Ming pointed to the side of the Guard's face. It was an angry, purplish red. The cheek was sunken and misshaped. "Beat him senseless first so he couldn't fight back or even call out. Closed his mouth up and waited for him to come back around."

Zhou leaned over them, holding his robe so it wouldn't touch the corpse. "Then he cut the man's stomach open and sent him on his way." He tried to say more, but he put a finger to his mouth and stepped back.

Ming's heart was slamming in his chest. He stood up too fast, and silver stars winked in his vision. "Why…" He swallowed hard. "Why do this? Why not just run when he knew we were waiting for him?"

Dragon brushed the dead man's hand with the tips of his fingers. "Retribution. He's punishing us for trying to apprehend him."

A flurry of cries erupted as a woman emerged from her home and ran toward the frightened boy. The boy ran for the woman, who wrapped the hem of her dress around him like a shield and spirited him from the grisly scene. Ming wondered if the boy had seen the body. He hoped not.

Dragon removed the black cloak from beneath En Lai's head. He covered the ruined body with it. Then he took off his own shirt, revealing a mat of thick, black hair. The shirt went over En Lai's face.

Zhou's eyes passed over the watching Gold Bird Guards. In every face he saw churning anger. He leaned close to Ming and spoke in a low whisper. "Now a Guard is dead. We all need to find shelter, because soon it's going to start raining shit."

9

Night came to Changan. Ming and Dragon sat in Ming's tiny courtyard, under the jumping glow of torches. Inside the children slept on their mats, while Li Juan lay on her back, creeping ever closer to a different kind of sleep.

Ming walked to the courtyard doors that opened onto the street. He gave them a push to make sure they were closed, then looked over the wall to check for anyone who might be nearby. The doors felt flimsy. The wall seemed so low a child could jump over it. This whole damn place felt exposed. Vulnerable.

Ming sat on a stone bench next to Dragon. His nerves were shattered. More than ten commoners had seen the dead Gold Bird Guard in the street today. So far, no one had made the connection between the murder and the madman taking the children. It was just another street killing, the witnesses were told. Ugly, yes, but no different from the robberies and revenge murders one hears about from time to time.

The lie seemed to be holding so far, but Ming did not believe it would survive much longer. How many robbery victims had their bellies cut open? What kind of thief sewed a man's mouth shut? On top of that, there were nearly a dozen Gold Bird Guards who knew the truth. Sooner or later one of them would talk. Ming had seen it countless times before.

Dragon's eyes were red at the bottoms. His skin beaded with sweat beneath the torchlight. "Thank you for bringing me into your home, Ming."

"Don't feel too welcome. You've proven we can use you in our investigation, but that does not make us friends."

Dragon tilted his head toward the courtyard's outer door. "That's the only security you have here? It will not be enough if our friend comes calling."

"I pay a neighbor to keep an eye on the house while I'm working."

"I could have some of my people stay nearby if you want," Dragon said. "They can't fight, but –"

"But they will scream if they see anything. No thank you. We need to decide what our next step is going to be." Ming shifted in his chair. This morning had been a rush of excitement as they laid their trap, as the Guards crept into their hiding places. Then the madman had made fools of them all, had cut one of their own open and slipped away, losing nothing but his old cloak.

How old was the dead Guard? He couldn't have been past twenty.

A deep, steady drumbeat began its slow, monotonous cadence. The man hitting that drum was several streets over, by the gate that led to this ward of the city, but the *bom-bom-bom* still shook the ground under Ming's feet. The drummer would strike six hundred times before the gates closed, giving subjects ample time to return to their wards before curfew. Anyone not in their ward after the drumbeat ended faced twenty blows with the thin rod.

"I wish I could know this man's mind," Ming said. "I don't just mean his interest in the Sorcerer. And why the carvings of Leigong? Why kill the children instead of their parents?"

Dragon crossed his tree trunk legs and stared into the torchlight. Watching him, Ming thought he must have been a good cavalry officer. He had that mix of authority and fraternity that inspired loyalty among the rank and file. At least he could appear that way when he wanted to. "I think you already have answers to those questions. I think you want see if I will agree with you."

Ming didn't bother arguing. They both knew Dragon was right. "It's revenge. Well, justice might be a more accurate word. This man leaves carvings of Leigong with the children because the Thunder God is the punisher of hidden sins. And *all* the parents had sinned and got away with it."

Ming threw a sidelong glance at Dragon, waiting for some reference to the Sorcerer. The big man stayed silent.

Bom-bom-bom. To Ming it sounded like the slow heartbeat of a sleeping giant.

"Surely this man sees himself as an agent of justice," Ming continued. "He worships Leigong, perhaps even sees himself as the Thunder God's agent in this world. But again, why the children? Why not the parents?"

"You already know that answer, too."

Ming looked back to the wooden door in front of him, the door that could be broken open with two or three kicks. He thought of his cheap home, its walls of rammed earth the only thing between his sleeping children and the outside world. Yes, the security here was weak, and it created in him a panicky terror. "He does it to bring maximum suffering to the parents."

Dragon nodded, and both men fell into a somber silence.

After a length of time he could not measure, Ming said, "I wish there was more we could do right now."

"We have plenty of work ahead of us," Dragon said. "Tomorrow I want to revisit the abduction sites. I want to speak with people and look for witnesses."

"So do I. But that seems so…so passive. I hate waiting for this fiend to make his next move."

"Unfortunately we will have to, Ming. But I don't think we'll be waiting for very long."

Ming looked at Dragon, his eyes questioning.

"Think about it, Ming. Things are changing. This man, whoever he is, he is growing bolder. He took the first child in front of a temple. Not very dangerous, if you are observant and patient. But the last time he took a child he did it in a crowded market. He probably decided he would go unnoticed in the noise and the bustle. That is a logical calculation, but it's a big risk all the same. And today he could have run. When he saw us he could have slipped away unnoticed, leaving us none the wiser, making me look like a fool for having wasted your time. Instead he chose to sneak up on an armed man and murder him in the most horrific way imaginable, just to send us a message. You can bet he watched, too. Somewhere, he was watching us and laughing."

Ming thought of the killer, a being still without a face, watching his victim stagger down the road in a black cloak. Bold indeed. "You're saying his boldness will be his undoing."

"That's it precisely." Dragon stood up and dusted the seat of his pants. "I'll come here tomorrow morning and we'll visit the abduction sites. But mark my words, Ming. He's going to make a mistake. When he does, we must be ready to pounce."

10

Ming asked, "What time of day was the boy abducted?"

The monk rubbed his shaved head and looked up at the sky. He looked about thirty and had a ruddy, healthy face that had seen its share of sun. He had introduced himself as Big Jin, and it wasn't hard to see why. He was positively the largest monk Ming had ever seen. Those shoulders and barrel arms gave him an air of menace that clashed with his mild face. He was holding a wooden broom; in his giant hands it looked like a child's toy. "Just after lunchtime."

Ming and Dragon were standing in front of a temple in the east ward. As Taoist temples went it was simple, but it was still beautiful. Its red, tiled roof slanted down at a sharp angle and curved up gracefully at the edges. The roof was held up by bright red columns that looked as smooth as the surface of a still pond. On either side of the front door, two stone lions kept a silent vigil.

This was where Min Sheng, the first child, had been taken. It was the ideal spot for an abduction – on a little side street, at least one hundred paces from the nearest large thoroughfare. The building across the street looked abandoned.

All anyone knew for certain was the child had been playing in front of the temple when someone took him. His father had been inside, speaking to the monks.

Dragon was standing a respectful distance from Big Jin, his arms behind his back. "No one saw anything?"

"No one."

Ming was taller than most men, but standing between these two giants made him feel like a dwarf. "Does anyone occupy the building across the way there?"

A long pause. A shake of the massive head.

Ming was beginning to think this monk was feeble. Perhaps his parents had left him at this temple when he was young. It wouldn't be the first time such a thing had happened. "Did you ever see anyone lurking around there? It wouldn't have to be on the day of the kidnapping. We're also thinking of the week or so leading up to it."

"No."

"Do you think anyone else saw something?"

"No."

Ming frowned. "How can you be sure? Have you spoken about it to the other monks?" Ming was a Buddhist and he didn't know much about Taoism. To him it was a strange and foreign religion. Its pantheon of gods and creatures confused him. One thing he knew, though, was these monks spent more time at prayer than they did at conversation. It could well be feasible that one of them saw something and didn't think to mention it to anyone else.

"I'm sure." Big Jin frowned back at Ming, suddenly looking less like a disinterested monk and more like an angry god. "Nobody saw."

Dragon smiled. "Brother, could we take a look around your temple and perhaps speak with your master?"

"Why?"

"Well, we're investigating these murders, you see, and we need all the information we can find. It would be a big help to us."

Big Jin put the broom down. "Wait. I'll get the master." He shuffled into the temple, stooping as he passed through the door.

Ming looked up at Dragon. "Why do you want to go in there?"

Dragon glanced around. "Are you a Taoist, Ming?"

"Buddhist."

"Well, I'm a Taoist. I've spent a great deal of time among the monks of my religion. They may strike outsiders as reserved, but they're not above gossip when they're among their own. If we get the chance to speak with someone else in that temple, perhaps I can –"

Before Dragon could finish, the temple doors swung open. Big Jin stooped through the doorway and held one of the doors ajar. A slight man in his sixties came out behind him and bowed. Ming took note of the man's purple robe. Laws restricted the clothing of commoners to white and gray, but prominent subjects were sometimes allowed more colorful dress.

The man's face had the expression of one who has found a dead rat in his home. "I am Master Fan. Big Jin tells me you want to take a look inside?"

Dragon bowed so low he almost doubled over. "Yes, Master Fan. We're just doing everything we can to stop the killing. We're not acting out of suspicion, of course."

The hostility on Fan's face ebbed but did not vanish. "Of course. We want the killings to stop as much as anyone does. I trust you are here in an official capacity?"

Ming said, "We are private investigators hired by the government."

"This way, gentlemen." Fan turned and headed into the temple, the giant close behind.

Ming and Dragon followed.

• • •

Ming tried to keep his whole body still, tried to move his eyes and nothing else. He did not like being in temples. The incense was like poison, filling his lungs and pushing the air from his body. The walls in this particular temple were painted bright gold, and the sun coming in through the window made them brighter still. Most people probably found that beautiful, but to Ming it was just overpowering.

Somewhere, at the end of the long wooden hallway, a man was pleading to his gods in a voice that edged ever closer to screams. After a moment of listening Ming understood. A monk was begging the deities to release trapped souls from hell.

Ming took a deep breath, held it, let it out. *I cannot have a fit right now.*

Master Fan was looking at Ming. "Are you all right?"

"Just tired." Ming was surprised by the question. He wondered if his acting was poor today or if the monk just had a keen eye.

Dragon looked at a small statue on that rested on a stone column. "That is beautiful."

"That is Wen Qu," Master Fan said. "The God of Literature."

Ming examined the statue. It depicted a man sitting on a chair of polished wood. The man had a beard fashioned from a material Ming could not identify and his robes were flowing blue and gold. Smaller versions of the same man sat around his feet. Overhead, the tapestry of a fierce dragon kept watch.

Ming glanced down the hallway. Both walls were lined with statues of stone. He saw Xi Wang Mu, the Queen Mother of the West, revered by many as the creator of all humans. He saw Tu Di Gong, God of the Soil and the Ground, with his gray beard and friendly, smiling eyes. The row of gods disappeared into the gloom, giving Ming the queer certainty that if he started down that hallway he would walk forever, a lost soul wandering under the gaze of stone deities.

Master Fan cleared his throat. "How may I help with your investigation?"

"To start with," Ming said, "how well did you know the family of the child that was taken?"

"Quite well. His father is a devout man and he comes here every week. He has always struck me as somewhat troubled. Well…temperamental might be a better word. He believes there are demons within him that push him to rage. He has come here for years seeking spiritual counseling. I have given it to him because, well, he is a generous donor."

Ming said, "Did his son always come with him?"

"Often, but not always."

Ming glanced at the temple's entrance. The doors had been propped open, giving them a clear view of the street in front. "So if a person were following the child, he would soon realize that out front would be a good spot for an abduction."

"I suppose."

Dragon said, "Did anyone hear or see anything strange on the day Min Sheng was taken?"

"Not a thing."

Ming tried to hide his frustration. The monk was being stubborn. "How can you be certain? Did you ask them?"

"As a matter of fact, I did." Fan turned toward Ming. "I spoke to everyone and asked if they had seen or heard anything. None of them had. You are not the only person who is appalled by the killing of children, Sir."

Ming bowed. "I'm sorry. How many monks live in this monastery?"

"Sixteen, including myself."

"How do they come to be in your service?" Dragon asked.

Master Fan smiled. "There are many paths to the Path."

Dragon burst out laughing, but Ming did not see what was funny. "You mean not all of them chose this life?

"Correct," Fan said. "Many of them did, but about half the men here were orphans. Now and then someone asks us to take a homeless child in. We do it if we can."

In Ming's opinion, that was the least these temples could do. Many religious organizations were exempt from paying taxes, and their people did not do the government labor required of most subjects. On top of that, many of the bigger monasteries – both Taoist and Buddhist – swam in donations from wealthy people looking for blessings. He said the most diplomatic thing he could think of. "You must be a savior to the people you take in."

"Some of them certainly need us. Big Jin – the man you met at the door – his parents turned him out when he was nine years old because he was feeble. He spent years wandering the streets, begging and stealing to survive. His situation is typical. He does labor around the temple. In return we provide food, shelter and education."

"Education," Ming echoed. He looked toward the entrance again. Big Jin was still out there, sweeping away at that same patch of ground by the road. It was hard to believe such a man had academic training.

"Oh yes," Fan said. "Our converts are introduced to religion at a very young age, but we do more than just indoctrinate them. Everyone here can read and write, although some are more proficient than others."

"Impressive," Dragon said.

Ming nodded. It was impressive. Other that government workers, he knew almost no literate people. His eye fell on a shelf of texts and he was surprised to see several books on Buddhism among them. "Why do you have the writings of rival religions here?"

"Preparedness," Han said. "On occasion the throne sponsors debates between scholars of the different faiths. I must know Buddhism's false testimony if I am to refute it. But I don't suppose your investigation requires you to ask such things?"

"I suppose not," Ming said. "Dragon, do you have any more questions?"

"No." Dragon bowed. "Thank you, Master Fan."

"You go first," Ming said. "I'd like a private word with Master Fan."

A shadow passed over Dragon's face. "Ming –"

"Go have a look at that building across the street. I'll be there in a moment."

When Dragon was gone, Ming turned to Master Fan. "I want to ask you about something that is not related to our investigation."

Fan's eyes were wary. "What is it?"

Ming bit his lip. His decision to speak with Fan alone had been spontaneous. Now he didn't know how to say what was on his mind. "I am a Buddhist. Everyone in my family is Buddhist. My parents hated Taoism. My father used to say Taoism is an imposter religion that hinders the real faith."

A smile appeared at the edges of Fan's mouth. "He was not the first or the last of your faith to say that."

"No. Of course not. I'm sure that right now he is not happy to see me consulting with…with one of you."

"And what do you want to consult with me about?"

"My wife. She's very sick." The words felt thick in Ming's mouth. "She started getting weak a year ago. She has lost weight and her skin is always pale. Just lately she doesn't have the strength to get out of bed, or the will to try."

"I am sorry to hear that," Fan said.

A pair of monks passed through the corridor, talking softly. Ming waited until they were out of earshot. "Thank you. Master Fan, I know a little about Taoism's ideas regarding health. Health is related to virtue, is it not?"

"That's correct," Fan said. "The Three Corpses reside in every person's body – one in the belly, one in the stomach and one in the head. Once every sixty days they ascend to Heaven and file reports on whatever sins we have committed. Heaven then doles out the appropriate illnesses as punishment."

"I was also raised to believe that morality affects one's health," Ming said. "The Buddhist teachers tell us sin creates unhealthy karma, which then causes illness. The logic therefore is that only unrighteous people get sick. Does that mean my –"

"There is no faith I know of that explains why good people grow ill, Ming. I for one do not believe every person who contracts a disease is a sinner. If I did, I would have to imagine my own parents suffering in the afterlife right now."

"What if the sick person has been stricken not for their own misdeeds, but for those of a loved one? I have committed grave sins in my life, Master Fan. I believed in a greater good I was serving, but I sinned all the same. Could the gods be punishing me by taking my wife?"

"I do not believe the gods act on such a…personal level, Ming. And after a lifetime of study I still can't pretend to understand every word in our sacred texts. I wouldn't say this in front of the people who donate money to our temple, but I don't feel we *have* to understand the texts. Not every single word, anyway. I think it's better to see those texts as more of a...guide."

"A guide," Ming said slowly. "In a few moons my children will have no mother. She is only thirty-two. What guidance can a religion give to make sense of that?"

"I don't know," Fan said. "But if I find out you will be the first person I tell."

• • •

Dragon was waiting for Ming outside the temple.

Ming put his hands up, like a person surrendering. "I was as respectful as a novice monk addressing his master. You have my word."

Dragon jerked a thumb back over his shoulder. "I had a look in the building across the street."

"And?"

"And I think the killer hid out there. He would have had a perfect view of the temple but no one would have seen him from the street."

"Did you find anything more tangible?"

"As a matter of fact, I may have. Come."

Ming followed Dragon into the building. The front room was full of desks and chairs. Perhaps this had once been some kind of office. The furniture was falling apart from neglect, but it stood in precise rows. Ming found the place strange and a little eerie. Why would the inhabitants make this room nice and neat before leaving it to crumble?

Dragon smiled at Ming. "See anything interesting?"

"Nothing at all. But you're grinning like a child so I must be missing something."

Dragon walked over to the front wall. There was a hole in it about seven feet off the ground, and a chair right below the hole. "You're missing this. This chair is the only out of place piece of furniture in the whole room. I am not a gambler, but I'd bet the killer stood on this chair and watched the temple through that opening in the wall."

"I don't see how you could know that, Dragon."

"Look at the wall a little more closely."

Ming leaned over and examined the wall. It was made of rammed earth that looked old but strong. "I don't see –"

Then Ming did see it. Most of the wall was brownish gray, the color of dirt that has spent a long time in dry air. But the section of wall right below the hole was a deeper, healthier looking brown.

Dragon pointed at the dark brown patch. "That spot wasn't part of the original building. Someone added it. The hole here used to be much bigger until it was fixed."

Ming rubbed his fingers along the smooth dirt. "Do you think the culprit fixed it?"

"It makes sense," Dragon said. "Who else? All he did was fill in the bottom two thirds of the hole. If he hadn't done that he'd have been exposed while he watched the temple. After he fixed it only his head would have been visible from the street. He would have been much harder to spot."

"You seem very confident in this theory."

"While you were inside I spoke to that fellow Big Jin. He looked at the hole in the wall and he believes it used to be much larger. He spends ages tending to the front yard there, so he would know."

Ming brushed the dirt from his hands. "Let's say you're right. Let's say the killer did this work."

"I think he did."

"All right. But so what? How does this information help us?"

"Ming, do you remember the flood three summers ago?"

"Of course."

"We had at least fifteen days of rain. The river overflowed and half the damn city was under water."

"I remember."

"I wasn't here. I was out west serving in the cavalry. That's where I got this scar." Dragon touched the mark under his eye. "We were charging a group of archers –"

"Dragon, why are we talking about the flood?"

"Was your house damaged in it?"

"Half our outer wall was swept away." Now that Ming spoke of the flood, he remembered all of it. The smell of damp had lingered in their little home for a month afterwards. "We're lucky we didn't lose our entire home."

"And after the waters subsided, what did you do? How did you fix the wall?"

"I was still in the Gold Bird Guard," Ming said. "I just hired a mason to come and repair it." Ming almost laughed. Were there days when he could pay for such a service? Were there really days when his first thought was *I'll bring someone in to fix that?* Now, in a life when a cup of ale was a luxury, such extravagance felt obscene.

Dragon clapped his hands. "Exactly! You hired someone. Could you have fixed the wall yourself? Could you have chosen the right materials, mixed them the right way, and then used them to repair the wall?"

"You're saying that whoever fixed this wall knew what he was doing."

Dragon tapped the darker part of the wall with his finger. "This is fine workmanship. Aside from the slight difference in color, you can hardly tell anything was done at all."

Ming leaned in for a closer look at the wall. "So the killer is a mason of some kind?"

"Maybe. We're certainly not looking for a peasant. Think of what we know. We have notes left with the victims. That means that the killer is literate, which eliminates a huge pool of suspects. Now there is a strong possibility that the killer has substantial craftsmanship skills."

Ming felt a vague stirring of excitement. It was tempered by the image of a guard on his back, belly cut open and lips sewn shut.

Dragon said, "There's something else. I found it on the floor in there."

"What is it?"

"Not here. Let's find a place where we sit and talk."

"All right."

They stepped out of the abandoned building and back onto the street. Big Jin was still in front of the temple. Did he just sweep the same spot all day?

Ming pointed toward the closest thoroughfare. "Come on. I know a good congee shop nearby. Let's see what you've got."

11

Mr. Lin sat behind his booth in the West Market and watched the shoppers stream past. Now and then someone broke from the human flood and approached him, their eyes on his rows of ducks. On another day Mr. Lin might well have chatted with one of them until sunset, but today he hardly spoke a word to anyone. Whenever he made a sale his only feeling was relief at being left alone again.

He put his face in his hands. It was so hot today. He was in the shade and he fanned himself constantly, but that did nothing. The sun seemed determined to melt him.

But he was used to the heat in this market. He had first started trading here when he was twenty. That was more than fifty years ago.

No one called Mr. Lin by his first name, and that was how he liked it. There were precious few benefits of old age, especially for people with no children. No one would take care of him when he became too frail to work; he wouldn't even have anyone to keep him company. But at least most young folks treated their elders with respect.

He figured he may as well enjoy it.

Unable to stop himself, Mr. Lin looked at the duck cage to his right. Agony hit him like a punch to the stomach. If only he had looked over at the cage on *that* day.

Because of him a child had been taken and beaten like a stray animal. Whoever killed Lei Lei had known she came to feed his ducks several times a week. That monster had used Mr. Lin's ducks as bait, had hidden out like a spider waiting to trap a fly. Mr. Lin had been just a few paces away when it happened. He must have been chatting away with his customers like he always did, ignoring Lei Lei in her final moments of terror.

Had she looked at him and cried out for help?

Mr. Lin covered his mouth and bit back a cry.

I want Yu Sheng. I need *him.*

Slowly, slowly, he drew his palm away from his mouth. Even the thought of Yu Sheng was enough to calm him. Mr. Lin hadn't seen Yu Sheng for almost fifty years, but certain feelings stayed with a person for life.

Yu Sheng's family had lived across the road from Mr. Lin's, a lifetime ago. Their families' ancestral tombs were next to each other, and Mr. Lin often walked to the cemetery with Yu Sheng. Those walks quickly became the highlight of Mr. Lin's day. It wasn't long before he was peering across the street and waiting for Yu Sheng's front door to open.

You're heading to the cemetery now too?

Their trips to the cemetery grew longer and longer. Usually they spent a few moments praying to their ancestors and a much longer time alone in the nearby woods. Mr. Lin's favorite part was always after. He loved lying on his back, feeling his arm on Yu Sheng's, feeling the forest dirt on his skin.

Their parents found out. To this day Mr. Lin did not know how. It happened on an autumn afternoon. Mr. Lin had been gripped by a vague sadness all day because it was to be their last meeting that year. Soon it would be too cold, and it wasn't safe to meet indoors.

When they emerged from the forest, talking and laughing, their parents were waiting right there – all four of them. Had Mr. Lin and Yu Sheng been prepared they may have fended off the accusations. But surprise and guilt were all over their faces, and denial would have been pointless.

Mr. Lin's parents were devastated. How, his father wanted to know, could a man do this to his elders? Didn't he know the shame he was putting on his ancestors?

No wonder you haven't married.

His father had shouted that over and over again like a curse, his voice laced with bitterness.

No wonder you haven't married. You're not going to have any sons. There will be no one to worship us after we are dead, and you will share that fate. You are weak. You are a blight upon this family.

His mother had been worse. She had only said one thing, her voice level and calm: *If you do it again I will hang myself.*

Mr. Lin did not doubt her threat.

And that was the last time Mr. Lin ever spoke to Yu Sheng. They could have arranged something, of course. They could have met after dark or left Changan. Hell, they could have left *China*. Leaving the empire was one of the Ten Abominations, and the penalty would have been beheading. But the empire did not span the entire world. Perhaps they could have gotten away. They could have settled near each other in some distant city. They could have even lived together, posing as brothers.

In the end it was impossible. Fleeing would have meant leaving their ancestors' burial plots, and that was out of the question. You did not abandon your ancestors unless your life was under threat. Even then the morality of such a measure was questionable. A pious man worshipped the dead of his family. Mr. Lin often noted, with more than a little bitterness, that he felt a stronger connection to his dead relatives than he did to his living ones.

They had spent the next two years avoiding each other, both of them slaves to parents' threats. Then Yu Sheng just…died. He went to bed one evening and did not wake up. He wasn't even thirty.

Mr. Lin's parents had nodded knowingly when they heard the news. See what happens when you violate the natural way of things? It was for the best, really. Thank goodness their own son had listened to reason and abandoned such reckless behavior.

The six moons after Yu Sheng's death were the worst of Mr. Lin's life. During the days he had to hide the grief, had to put on a mask of indifference toward that unspeakable tragedy. The only freedom came at night, when his parents were asleep on the other side of the fireplace. Then he was free to cry soundlessly into the darkness.

Mr. Lin looked down at his hands. Here he was, so many years later, still wishing for Yu Sheng when life got difficult. Well, things were worse for a lot of people. Certainly Lei Lei's father would agree with that.

Something bumped his table, making it jump. The sound startled Mr. Lin from his thoughts. He looked up, a vacant greeting on his lips. Then he saw the pair standing over him and felt a sudden urge to pinch his nostrils shut.

The two people in front of Mr. Lin's stall had the manners of vagrants, but they both carried a smugness that one never saw on the destitute. The older brother was named An Guo, but everyone called him Toad. Mr. Lin thought the nickname was an insult to toads everywhere. Toad couldn't have been fifty yet but he was already down to eight or nine teeth. Blossom, his younger sister, was with him. She was probably in her mid-forties, but the scores of pockmarks on her face made her look ten years older.

Both siblings had taken great pains to address their striking ugliness. Blossom, a clear adherent to the trend of a bright yellow forehead, always went about with a thick golden substance slathered above her eyebrows. Toad had a winding serpent tattoo that stretched from his thumb to the bottom of his neck.

Toad took a step forward, his arms across his chest. "What're you up to today, Lin?"

"The same thing as always." Mr. Lin swept a hand over his row of dead ducks, his face carefully indifferent. Were Toad and Blossom here to make their collections? They had already gathered their "management fee" from the vendors this week, but sometimes they doubled up. Toad and Blossom had family in the government, a rare prize in the despised merchant class. They had used their connections to turn the West Market into their own little empire, and within that empire their word was law.

Blossom said, "Been here all day then, have you?"

"That's right. Nice, fat ducks today. Twelve coppers for half a bird, twenty for a full one. Interested?"

Toad picked up one of Mr. Lin's ducks by the neck, stared at it and then dropped it back on the table. "Where was the girl kidnapped?"

Mr. Lin paused. At first he didn't know what Toad was talking about. "What?"

"The girl," Blossom snapped. "The Lie Lie child who was taken from here." She waved a thin arm at nothing in particular, making the bracelets on her wrist rattle.

"Lei Lei," Mr. Lin said.

Toad nodded. "That's the one. Word has it she disappeared right around here."

A man at the next stall was looking at a slab of pork. When he heard Toad he looked up, his eyes circles of shock.

Mr. Lin pointed to his right. "Over there. On the far side of my duck cage."

"We should take a look," Toad said. He and Blossom hurried over to the spot Mr. Lin had indicated. Toad probed the ground with his boot, as though trying to extract evidence from the dirt. Blossom was whispering into her brother's ear, throwing an occasional glance at Mr. Lin.

Toad nodded now and then, his face idle and his eyes still scanning the ground. What were they doing? Even the empty-headed Toad had to know they couldn't solve a crime that way.

A moment later Toad said something. He and Blossom walked back to Mr. Lin.

Toad tapped the small lock box on Mr. Lin's table. "Open that."

Mr. Lin scooted back in his chair. "Excuse me?"

Blossom pointed a skinny finger at Mr. Lin's chest. "Open it or we'll call the Gold Bird Guard!"

Mr. Lin, a man who prided himself on almost endless reservoir of patience, finally bristled. "My personal effects are in there. I will not open it."

Blossom bared her teeth. "You open that right now! You do it or –"

Toad raised a hand, quieting his sister. "We want to know more about what happened to the Lei Lei child. You were right here when she was taken, right?"

"I was sitting in this chair," Mr. Lin said. "At least I think I was."

Blossom looked hard at Mr. Lin. "What do you mean, you *think* you were?"

"I mean that no one knows exactly when the child was attacked. If I don't know that I can't know where I was when the incident took place, can I? But yes, if it happened when the authorities think it did, then I was right here. I must have been."

Blossom put her palms flat on Mr. Lin's old table and leaned in close. The cloves in her mouth, meant to combat the taboo of unpleasant breath, only increased her stink. "You weren't talking to her? Everyone knows you like to play with the neighborhood kiddies."

As Mr. Lin stared at Blossom, his head full of confusion, he noticed something – they were drawing a crowd. The man who had first heard them and looked up in shock was still watching them. Six or seven others were now there as well. Talk about the killings must have drawn their attention.

Toad noticed it too. He looked around and raised his voice. When he spoke he could almost shake the ground if he wanted to. "This is the thing, Lin. The authorities have a theory. I was talking about it with my uncle last night. He's a mandarin –"

"Seventh level," Blossom cut in, giving the crowd a meaningful look.

"Seventh level. He told me the authorities think Lei Lei knew the abductor. After all, she was taken from a crowded market. If she didn't know the man who took her, she probably would have run away when he approached her."

Mr. Lin thought that over. "It makes sense."

"I *know* it makes sense," Toad said. "You see, our uncle has tasked us with canvassing this area. They are desperate to find the killer…so desperate they've even offered a reward for him."

"Ten thousand coppers," Blossom whispered, staring at Mr. Lin. Her eyes somehow looked black and bright at the same time.

A larger crowd was gathering now, attracted by Toad's booming voice. When Toad revealed the incredible sum there was a chorus of *oohs* and *aahs*.

Blossom placed a scrawny hand on Mr. Lin's lock box and threw it open. "So let's see what you've got here!"

Mr. Lin grabbed the lock box and shut it with a bang, making Blossom yank her fingers back. "That is my property and I won't have you two rifling through it like a pair of bandits. Why don't you tell me just what you're doing here?"

Blossom was staring death at Mr. Lin. Toad put a hand on his sister's elbow and eased her back. She went, still staring.

Toad raised his voice even more. Now he was so loud half the damn market could probably hear him. "All we're doing is investigating the murders of children. It is the duty of every loyal subject to oppose crime. We are looking for information and this man won't give it to us."

Mr. Lin stood up. "I don't care who your uncle is. I am a responsible citizen. I pay my taxes and I worship my ancestors. When I was able to I did my compulsory labor for the government. I won't be bullied."

For a blessed moment Toad and Blossom looked cowed. They weren't used to resistance, and their only response to Mr. Lin's defense was an exchange of nonplussed glances. Perhaps they might even give up and leave him alone now.

Then a wiry, sweat-covered man emerged from the crowd and fixed his eyes on Mr. Lin. "You knew the girl and she was taken right here. The law says they have a right to help investigate any crime. Open it."

Mr. Lin heard murmurs of agreement from the crowd. Finally he put up his hands. This was still a mystery to him, but the sooner Toad and Blossom got what they wanted, the sooner they would leave him alone. "Go ahead."

Toad attempted a smile, but it looked more like a smirk. "We'll do that, Mr. Lin."

Mr. Lin stood up and pushed the lock box across his table. Then he took two long backward steps.

Toad turned away from Mr. Lin's stall and looked at the crowd. More than fifty people were watching now. "This morning we spoke to Lei Lei's father. As many of you know, her mother hanged herself after learning of the murder."

A shudder ran through the crowd of onlookers. Suicide was a taboo topic. People who killed themselves became wandering demons, taking their rage out on the living. Speaking of such demons might well attract their attention.

Mr. Lin cleared his throat and looked out at the crowd. "What does this have to with me?" After hearing Toad's booming voice, he was certain he sounded like a sick old man. "I am a simple businessman. I have done nothing to deserve this…this harassment."

Blossom wagged her finger at him. "An old man who never married? His parents are wandering ghosts because of him. What kind of person could be that irresponsible?"

Before Mr. Lin could respond, Toad spoke up. "We asked the child's father what she had on the day she was taken. He didn't know, of course. After all, what wealthy man keeps track of the countless things his daughter wears?"

A few of the onlookers smiled.

Toad's voice dropped. People farther away stood on their tiptoes and strained to hear. "He gave us the only piece of information he could. His daughter always wore a white bracelet on her left wrist. Mutton fat jade. He gave it to her on her fourth birthday and it was her most prized possession."

Blossom looked down at the ground, her face somber.

But the crowd was more concerned with the mutton fat bracelet. Mutton fat jade, so named because of its color, was more valuable than the green variety. There were more murmurs, this time speculation about the bracelet's value.

"And this is the thing," Toad said. "When the body was recovered the bracelet was gone."

Mr. Lin's unease grew. Toad's speech was too smooth, too rehearsed. Clearly they were throwing suspicion on him, but why? They had no reason to suspect him of anything. Yet here they were, attacking him with complete confidence even though they knew a false accusation was punishable by flogging.

Mr. Lin's unease exploded into panic. They were setting him up!

His eyes moved to the lock box. *They put something in there. Had to. The bracelet. Toad is talking about the bracelet and he wants to open my box because that's where it is. They slipped the bracelet in there and they want to find it with all these people watching.*

The crowd of spectators began to part. Two Gold Bird Guards were forcing their way through the sea of people. They broke through the crowd and stepped into the clearing. One of them was around forty and the other was hardly more than a boy. The older man was short and thick, the kind of man built like a bulldog. The younger one was tall and thinner than a board of wood.

They both looked at Mr. Lin, their faces void of expression.

Mr. Lin pushed the fear down. He would not be coerced by a pair of thugs. He raised his voice again. It wasn't as loud as Toad's, but it no longer felt frail. "I knew the child Lei Lei, it is true." He waited until everyone was looking at him before he continued. "I knew her family as well. They are good people. But my knowing one of the victims does not give others leave to harass me. I have plied my trade in this market for fifty years. Everyone here knows I am a man of good repute."

A few familiar faces in the crowd nodded.

Blossom wagged her skinny finger at him again. "I tell you there is something wrong with a man who does not marry. What kind of person is content to let his parents wander the world forever?"

"I never wanted to be tied down by marriage, so I never married. I worship my ancestors the same as –"

Then Blossom's finger was in Mr. Lin's face again. "He's the one! That's him! He's the *killer!*"

Mr. Lin wanted to scream back at her, but he held his tongue. He marveled at his own his calm. Here he was being accused of murder – of murdering *children* – and he felt as relaxed as a man strolling through a field. It was time to make his play. "I have nothing to hide. Come. My home is in the alley behind me. Bring the Gold Bird Guard and have a look in there if you like."

Something in Toad's mask of arrogance seemed to crack. "That's not...we don't need to take such a drastic step."

"Oh, but it's my pleasure." Mr. Lin allowed himself a bit of hope. They may have planted something in his lock box, but he was fairly confident they hadn't gone into his home. "It's just fifty paces from here. The Guards are most welcome to search it. I'll wait outside."

"Enough of this!" Blossom pushed Toad out of her way. In one motion she threw open the lock box and thrust her hand inside.

Mr. Lin opened his mouth to shout, to tell this terrible woman she was not a member of the Guard and had no business rummaging through his things.

But it was already too late.

Blossom's eyes grew wide in theatrical shock. She drew out the bracelet and held it high above her head. "See," she shrieked. "Here's the bracelet!"

In the space of a breath, the crowd became a mob. Onlookers who had been watching with rapt interest became a sea of faces twisted with rage. Hands reached out for Mr. Lin, grabbing at his clothes, his limbs, his hair. The two Gold Bird Guards pushed them back, and Mr. Lin's frantic mind conjured an image of madmen trying to stop the tide with a pair of brooms.

Then more Guards appeared like magic and fought their way to the front of the crowd. Most pushed back against the wall of people. Several others made for Mr. Lin.

Blossom saw the Guards and waved her arms. She pointed in Mr. Lin's face. "There he is! The killer is right there! We found this in his lock box! Arrest him! We found him and the bounty is ours. *Arrest him!*"

Mr. Lin swatted Blossom's finger away. "Lying pig!" His limbs shook with rage. "This will never work. All you did was steal a bracelet and slip it into my things. Your story will unravel in a day and you'll be flogged for lodging a false accusation."

Fear flickered across Toad's face. Then it vanished as quickly as it had come. "We have proof. You'll have to explain how a dead child's bracelet found its way into your possession."

"I can explain it."

The Guard built like a bulldog shoved Toad away and looked at Mr. Lin. "You will come with me."

Mr. Lin pointed at Toad and Blossom. "They are framing me for the bounty. How hard would it be for them to place that item in my things?"

Toad feigned indignation. Blossom just watched Mr. Lin, her eyes singing with triumph.

The Guard took Mr. Lin's wrist. "The authorities will decide all of that. You will walk with me or we will drag you."

Mr. Lin let the Guards lead him away.

All around him the world was in chaos. The Guards pushed the mob and the mob pushed back. Curses were hurled against Mr. Lin and his ancestors. Threats were made on his life. People cried in relief, thanking the gods that the monster was finally caught. Blossom screeched at the Guards and demanded the bounty.

Mr. Lin heard none of it. Feeling like a man in the grip of a nightmare, he let the Gold Bird Guards rush him from the market to the nearest barracks.

12

Around the time Gold Bird Guards were escorting Mr. Lin from the West Market, Commandant Chen's scrawny fist slammed down on his desk. "A dead Guard now!" He brought his fist up high again, as though it held an invisible hammer. *"A dead Guard!"* Down came the fist once more.

Zhou sat across from the old man, hands folded demurely in his lap. Next to him were the venerable Short and Tall, both of whom looked ready to lie prostrate on the floor and beg Chen's forgiveness.

Zhou himself couldn't help feeling a swell satisfaction, although he would never dare show it. The crown no longer saw the commandant as the man who had failed to catch a monster. Now it saw him as the man who had lost a *Guard* to a monster. The fact that Zhou had overseen the operation mattered not at all. Chen had approved it, and that was all the crown cared about. Clearly the old man's play to shift blame onto his subordinates had failed. One needed only to look at the man's trembling hands to know that.

Chen jabbed a finger at Short. "You. What are you doing to prevent further abductions in your ward?"

Short's face was neutral, but Zhou noted that his knuckles had gone white. "We have doubled Gold Bird Guard patrols day and night, Sir. The men have been instructed to be on the lookout for anyone who appears…uh…suspicious."

"You've doubled Gold Bird Guard patrols," Chen intoned. His voice had a bitter, mocking edge. "And how about investigation? What have you done on that front?"

Without waiting for Short to answer, Chen looked at Tall. "How about you? More double patrols?"

Tall said, "We are doing everything we can, Sir. We've followed all your instructions so I am sure we'll succeed."

Zhou sniffed. Any competent leader would have purged sycophants like these two ages ago. What good were men who lacked the courage to speak their minds? When Zhou thought of how the city was run, of how no official dared contradict his superiors, he felt sick to his stomach.

That was why he was beginning to believe the city's crisis wasn't all bad. If there was one benefit to the tragedy unfolding around them, it was that frauds like Chen were finally being exposed. Here was a man who had inherited his position, who wasn't fit to clean out stables. He had no business being a Commandant. Zhou had known that for years, and now the rest of the city was seeing it as well.

Chen swung his gaze to Zhou. The rage was gone from his face. In its place was a knowing sneer. "And what is my best mandarin doing? What steps are you taking to stop this madness?"

"The same as my colleagues." Zhou nodded to Short and Tall. "If anyone so much as looks at a child the wrong way in the North Hamlet, you can be sure we will know about it. Sir."

"You certainly proved your mettle yesterday," Chen said. "You lost a Guard and the killer slipped effortlessly through your grasp."

Zhou shrugged, a gesture shocking in its informality. "The man is crafty."

Chen glared at Zhou. He appeared to have another biting remark waiting behind his teeth. Then the fire left him and he flopped into his chair. "This has been a nightmare. For the city and for its keepers."

Mostly for you, Zhou wanted to say.

"If we cannot find this man soon," Chen said, "the repercussions will be disastrous."

Tall straightened up in his chair. "I am still confident the reward we are offering will lead to this man's capture. We –"

There was a knock on the door.

"Enter," Chen shouted.

The door slid open. A man stepped in and bowed, his face wary. "A message from the palace, Commandant Chen."

"What is it?"

The messenger cleared his throat and unrolled a scroll. "The authorities have arrested a vendor in the West Market. They suspect him in the child killings."

The room went silent.

Commandant Chen stared at the messenger. "On what evidence?"

The messenger looked down at the scroll. "It goes back to the fourth child who was taken – Lei Lei. One of her possessions was found among the vendor's things. It was a mutton fat jade bracelet that belonged to the child."

"How did the authorities know to investigate this man?" Zhou asked.

"Two other vendors from the market turned him in." The messenger unrolled more of the scroll and read the bottom. "It appears they're going to get the reward for finding the killer."

Chen walked around from behind his desk. "Let me see that." He snatched the scroll from the messenger. He held it close to his face, his hands trembling as he read. Finally he looked up and pounded the desk with his fist again. "This says the vendor's stall is less than ten paces from where the child was taken! Gentlemen, I believe this is it."

Short shouted out in celebration. Tall clasped his hands and prayed.

Zhou allowed himself a smile. The evidence *did* seem damning. If this man worked where the child was taken, and if he had the child's bracelet, then the evidence was damning indeed. Even if the vendor wasn't the right man, a mutton fat bracelet was an excellent lead. Perhaps it could be traced back to the real culprit.

So the terror might well be over. Zhou tried to widen his smile. An end to the death was a blessing for the city. And yet…it came with a price, didn't it? The killer's capture meant Chen was going to survive this crisis. Only a moment ago the old Commandant had been a picture of desperation. He had fretted like a man awaiting the executioner's wire. Now he looked like he had received a royal pardon.

Zhou realized with a rush of misery that it was even worse. *Chen was going to get credit for catching the murderer*. After all, the messenger had said two people were likely going to receive the reward, and the reward had been Chen's idea. He was going to be a hero to the whole city. The Emperor himself might even congratulate him.

After the celebrations faded, Chen dismissed the messenger. Then he turned to his men. "We need to investigate this man, this…" He looked down at his scroll. "This Lin fellow. We need to go back to the abduction spots and look for witnesses. Now that we know what the madman looks like, we can find out if anyone spotted him around the times the other children were taken. I've got to speak with other colleagues. Return here after the midday meal. I'll give you more detailed instructions then. For now, the meeting is over."

• • •

Zhou left Chen's office and walked down the corridor, his hands clasped behind his back. All around him mandarins were hurrying by in both directions. Zhou knew from the colors of their robes they all outranked him. That wasn't a surprise – some of Changan's most important men had offices in this wing of the Imperial Ministry.

As Zhou walked, he tried to emulate the senior men around him. He tried to cultivate their air of authority, to look as though he belonged among them. But his red robe betrayed his rank. No one so much as glanced in his direction. To them he was little more than a servant.

But how many of *these* men had earned their prestigious ranks? How many of them had fought their way uphill with merit and dedication? How many had undergone the crucible of the Imperial Exams, huddled in a windowless cell and writing answers that would determine the rest of their lives? Half? A third? Fewer than that?

And it was all because these men were the sons of mandarins, while Zhou was the son of a butcher. Their way had been lit by golden sunshine. Zhou had crawled along a path of shit because he came from the despised merchant class. It was more than unfair. It was a travesty.

Zhou rounded a corner, thinking of how Commandant Chen had celebrated. The old fool had been relieved almost to tears. Now, as Chen's euphoria ebbed, that relief was probably giving way to anticipation. Who knew what rewards he would reap for this?

And he had been so *close* to ruin.

Zhou was so lost in bitterness he didn't notice the door in front of him swing open. He didn't see a man emerge with a scroll under one arm. Zhou and the other man spotted each other just in time. They both pulled up and stopped.

The man was wearing the gray garments of servant. He looked at Zhou. When he realized he had nearly collided with a mandarin, his skin went scarlet. "I am very sorry, Sir. I –"

Zhou dusted off his robe, as though mere conversation with a servant might dirty it. "If you paid attention to where you were going you wouldn't have to be sorry." Zhou saw the man's fear and felt grim satisfaction.

"I'm terribly sorry. If –"

"I know you. You delivered a message to Commandant Chen's office a moment ago."

The man bowed. "Yes, Sir." Like most servants, he avoided eye contact when speaking with superiors.

"I imagine you're still spreading your good cheer throughout this building?"

"Yes, Sir," the man repeated. He glanced to his left and then looked back at the floor.

"What is it?" Zhou asked.

"Sir?"

Zhou took a step forward and looked up at the man. "You look…I don't know. Uneasy."

"I'm sorry, Sir. I'm only trying to show the proper respect." The messenger's eyes stayed fixed firmly on the floor.

Zhou watched the servant. He couldn't read people as well as Ming could, but he had done his share of interrogations. He could usually sense when someone was being evasive. "Something is on your mind. And my feelings are telling me it has to do with these messages you're delivering."

"I'm afraid I don't understand, Sir."

"Yes, you do. Something is bothering you." Zhou felt a strange burning in his stomach, as though his insides were on fire. He got that feeling now and then, usually when he was about to uncover a key lie in an interview. He didn't know why he should have that feeling right now, but he had it. And he trusted it. "Tell me."

Looking miserable, the messenger said, "It doesn't make sense."

"What doesn't?"

"This Lin fellow – the accused." The messenger met Zhou's eye for the first time. "He must be seventy years old."

"Seventy?"

"Yes, Sir. Also, I deliver messages to the West Market quite often. I've seen the people who turned him in for the reward. They're fixtures over there. They're…" The messenger's voice dropped to a conspirator's whisper. "They're gangsters, Sir. About as trustworthy as a pair of vipers."

"You don't believe we have the right man." Zhou was speaking more to himself than to the messenger. "You think we've made a horrible mistake."

The messenger's only response was to look more miserable. It was a logical reaction. He was, after all, openly challenging the judgment of his superiors.

"Don't worry," Zhou said. "This conversation remains our secret."

"Thank you," the messenger mumbled.

"But what about the bracelet?" Zhou asked. "They found the girl's bracelet among the man's things."

Before the messenger could speak, Zhou answered himself. "They put it there. Planted it themselves to set Lin up. Perhaps they stole it from the girl's father and hoped he wouldn't remember if she was wearing it when she died."

The messenger shifted on his feet and kept staring at the floor.

Zhou smiled. "It's all right. I already promised I won't speak of this conversation to anyone." He jabbed a finger in the man's face. "And neither will you."

"Of course not, Sir."

"Good," Zhou said. "Then go."

The messenger bowed and hurried off like a rabbit running from a wolf.

Zhou turned and watched the man go. Sometimes the servants were the smartest people in the room. That young man with the frightened eyes saw what all the mandarins – including Zhou himself – had been too excited to understand. The evidence against this Lin fellow was as weak as a brittle piece of kindling. If the authorities had nothing further, their evidence was weak indeed.

And Chen was almost certainly trying to take credit for the arrest already. But if Chen was *wrong,* then what would the damage be? What would happen if this whole affair was exposed as a farce?

If that happened, Chen would be finished. The same would be true of his lackeys, Tall and Short. But if Zhou were the lone voice of reason, the one man courageous enough to speak the truth…

The windfall would be enormous.

Zhou slapped himself on the forehead. He was supposed to meet Ren Shu! He had been so focused on today's developments that he had almost forgotten. Well, if he headed to the boarding house now he wouldn't be late. Spending time with Ren Shu was just what Zhou needed right now. It would help him relax and think things through.

Zhou turned and made for the exit, his mind alive with new possibilities.

13

Later that day, when the sun had already traveled a good ways across the sky, Zhou threw on his robe and glanced out the boardinghouse window. The sun was farther along than he had expected. He had lingered here too long.

Ren Shu was still on the bed, a blanket draped over his thin shoulders. "There's no need to rush out of here. Miss Ling won't be anxious to kick her two best customers out."

Miss Ling ran the little boardinghouse Zhou and Ren Shu used three times a week. It was the perfect spot for them – down a narrow alley and across from a windowless building. Miss Ling was the perfect owner as well. She was a widow with two small children to mind. As long as her customers paid their bill, she was too busy to care what they did in her rooms.

Zhou began to tie his belt. A mandarin's clothes were painfully intricate, and putting them on was no small affair. "I've got to be back at Chen's office soon. We're going to discuss this man, this Lin fellow." Before that, though, Zhou meant to make another stop. If he left right now he would have enough time.

Ren Shu hugged his legs close to his chest. "Please, gods, let him be the right man. These killings are a travesty."

Ren Shu was twenty-two years old, fifteen years Zhou's junior. He had come to the capital from Chengdu last year to prepare for the Imperial Exams. He and Zhou had met in one of the city's libraries. After Ren Shu passed the exams – and Zhou knew he would – Zhou meant to get him a posting here in the city. It was all a terrible risk for a man as methodical as Zhou, but he saw no other course he could take in life.

There were times – not many but some – when Zhou thought back to his marriage with Fen Fang. When she had confronted Zhou about his secret, he was shocked to learn she had already known of it for some time. Her manner in that awkward conversation had been measured, rational – so much so, in fact, that it pained Zhou. And in the end, their separation was just as civil. They had agreed that Zhou would register the divorce on the grounds of Fen Fang's excessive jealousy. She could have revealed Zhou to the world and ended his life, but that may have brought dangerous questions about her own conduct. As Zhou later learned, Fen Fang had been unfaithful too.

Zhou finished his belt and got to work on the top part of his robe. "You're right. The death needs to stop."

Ren Shu said, "It's hard to believe such a person could exist right here in the city. Imagine! Killing a child and then leaving a statue of a god with the body! It's –"

"Quiet!" Zhou's voice was suddenly angry. "I wasn't supposed to tell you that and you *cannot* repeat it."

"I'm sorry." Ren Shu sat up in bed. "Do you think Lin really is the killer?"

"He had the child's bracelet. That is damning evidence." Zhou kept working on his robe. Everything about it had to be just so. The sash had to be the right width and the skirt had to be tied so that it almost brushed the ground. Like all citizens, mandarins were subject to punishment if they flouted the dress regulations.

Zhou pulled his tunic a bit too far out of his sash and cursed. Now he would have to start the top half of his outfit all over again. He was so preoccupied that he almost didn't notice Ren Shu staring at him.

Zhou let go of his robe. "What is it?"

"You haven't answered my question. Do you think Lin is the killer?"

There was no use in trying to mislead Ren Shu. He had an uncanny knack for reading people. He was a bit like Ming that way. "Maybe yes and maybe no."

"But you're leaning toward no. I can tell."

Zhou shrugged and resumed the tedious task of dressing himself. "The truth is I *don't* know. But my superior believes we've got the killer. He believes it with absolute certainty. The people need to feel safe. Arresting someone for the crime will achieve that."

"Not if it's the wrong man," Ren Shu said. "If you accuse this man and it turns out you're mistaken, think of the scandal!"

I have, Zhou thought. He forced himself not to smile.

"What are you up to?" Ren Shu asked.

"What do you mean?"

"Zhou, if you mean to use this for yourself..."

Zhou faced the window and kept tugging at his robe. He knew his face was neutral, but he still didn't want Ren Shu looking at it. Yes, Ren Shu had Ming's gift for reading people. He might make a great investigator in the Gold Bird Guard very soon.

A hand fell on Zhou's shoulder, making him jump. He turned to see Ren Shu standing behind him. Zhou hadn't even heard him climb out of bed.

Ren Shu's face suddenly looked older. "I know you, Zhou. I know you're sincere in your desire to solve a lot of the city's problems. But you're also very ambitious. Sometimes your sincerity justifies your ambition. Sometimes, but not always. Not this time."

Zhou pulled away and turned to a mirror on the wall. He started to work on his hair. Putting your hair in order when you were a mandarin wasn't as cumbersome as arranging your clothing, but it was close. "So what is your point?"

Ren Shu's warped and shifting reflection watched him through the mirror's bronze surface. "Zhou, there are times when it is all right to maneuver for advancement. There are times when it's all right to use politics for your own gain. That's cynical thinking, but it's the way of things. But Zhou, this isn't one of those times. These killings are a curse on the city. Your job is to lift that curse. If you try to play this to your own advantage, terrible things could happen."

Zhou finished his hair and turned around. "Your opinion of me is that low? I mean to help find the killer and restore calm to the city. Nothing more."

"I don't —"

Zhou kissed Ren Shu and picked up his satchel. "I'm going to be late. Same time two days from now?"

Ren Shu smiled, but the smile did not reach his eyes. "Of course."

Zhou nodded and hurried out the door.

14

"This is a mistake," said the old man.

Zhou eyed Mr. Lin through the cell's wooden bars. "Anyone in your position would say that."

They were in a Gold Bird Guard barracks in the southwestern corner of the city. The building was ringed with Guards. Mr. Lin was in a basement, the door of which was manned by four more Guards. There was a real fear that people might storm the building and lynch him. It wasn't a groundless concern. Several people had followed Mr. Lin's escort from the market to the barracks. Now word was spreading fast, and the men guarding the barracks found themselves facing an angry, growing crowd.

Zhou had already gotten what he came here for. One glance was all he needed to confirm the messenger's suspicion – this man was not the killer. He was much smaller than the person who had been in Meng Chun's pub.

Mr. Lin stood up and wrapped his fingers around the bars. "Those two planted Lei Lei's bracelet. How hard would it have been to steal it and slip it among my things?"

"You mean Blossom and – what is the other one's name?"

"Well, everyone calls him Toad."

"Toad. Why would they do such a thing to you?"

Mr. Lin hit a bar with his palm. "For the reward! They're both gangsters. They think they can do whatever they want just because their uncle is a mandarin. No offense."

"Of course. What about the theory that the abductor knew the child? That is logical, is it not? After all, how else could he have gotten so close to her? Wouldn't she have screamed?"

"Lei Lei was a friendly child, Sir. She was far more outgoing than other girls her age."

Zhou took a step forward and lowered his voice. "Let me ask you something. Why do you think people are so eager to believe you are the killer? There is a mob outside baying for your blood, after all."

"I suppose I fit their image of a deviant, at least in some ways. I live alone, I never married, and..." Mr. Lin trailed off.

Zhou already knew what Mr. Lin was. He had seen it the moment they started talking. He often recognized other men who were like him, but probably not always. "The throne is reviewing your case right now. I for one believe in your innocence, and I'm going to fight for your release. I came here to tell you that."

"That's wonderful. Thank you, Sir." Mr. Lin smiled at Zhou with pathetic gratitude.

Zhou stepped back from the bars. "I'll give the jailer some coppers and tell him to feed you."

Mr. Lin made a noise. "I've worked since I was a boy. I can look after myself. But thank you."

"Suit yourself," Zhou said. "I'll be back when I have news."

**

When Zhou left the barracks he saw right away that the crowd had indeed grown. There had been several dozen people when he entered the building. Now there were at least one hundred.

The crowd was ugly. It emitted a deep, steady drone that reminded Zhou of a hornet's nest. Zhou could sense every set of eyes drilling into him. The hostility was so thick it made the air feel heavy. He supposed it was natural for people to turn their anger on him. In their eyes he was another official who had let the killings continue for too long. Now they believed the government had the murderer…had him and was protecting him.

"Master Zhou!"

Zhou turned to see Hai Tao fighting his way forward through the crowd. The eunuch stopped and bowed. "Commandant Chen dispatched me to find you and relay a message."

"What is it?"

"Your meeting with Commandant Chen is postponed until tomorrow," Hai Tao said. "Today the Commandant is meeting with Governor Han."

Zhou pursed his lips. "That is strange."

Hai Tao's brow furrowed, making the dent shift strangely on his forehead. "Does this pose a problem, Master?"

"It does. I need to speak with Commandant Chen sooner than that. He must know that they have arrested the wrong man." Zhou started walking, with Hai Tao close behind. The crowd parted reluctantly for them.

Hai Tao was only one pace behind Zhou, but he had to raise his voice to be heard over the sea of angry shouts. "Master, why do you think Lin is innocent?"

Normally Zhou didn't discuss official matters with servants, but he sometimes indulged Hai Tao. The eunuch was a smart young man. "He wasn't…the evidence is not at all sufficient." He elbowed a man out of the way. "The government is jumping to conclusions because they are desperate to end this tragedy."

The crowd was getting thicker even as they walked. More people seemed to be arriving every moment. Zhou squared his shoulders and tried to fight his way forward, but he felt like a fish swimming against the current. He slowed to a walking pace.

Hai Tao reached forward and pushed the nearest people away in one easy motion. Their pace picked up again. "But how can you convince anyone of his innocence, Master? Can he prove he was elsewhere during at least one of the murders?"

They broke through the fringes of the crowd and stepped onto open ground again. To Zhou, it felt like stepping from a hot room into the cool autumn air.

Zhou stopped and fixed his robe. It had been tousled by the crowd. "He can't prove that. I already asked him."

"Then what is to be done? I can't see how his innocence can be proven. Master, may I speak frankly?"

Zhou turned toward Hai Tao. "Go ahead."

"I just came from the Imperial Ministry. Commandant Chen is already saying publicly that Lin is guilty. If you say otherwise, you will be openly defying him."

Zhou threw up hands. "What can I do? I cannot remain silent if I think an innocent man is going to be executed."

"Chen will take it as a challenge. He'll see you as a threat."

"I don't have a choice."

"Yes, you do," Hai Tao said. "You could take the safe option and let them kill this man. You could quietly distance yourself from efforts to convict him, so that if he does turn out to be innocent the repercussions against you would be minimal. Instead you've decided to take a gamble and speak out. If you free Lin and he turns out to be innocent, you'll be a hero. Commandant Chen, on the other hand, will look like a fool before the entire city."

Zhou almost laughed. He should have reprimanded his servant for being so familiar, but Hai Tao had articulated his thoughts with perfect accuracy. In the eunuch's next life he might well be a mandarin. "You're wrong, of course. I want only to protect an innocent man and save my superiors from a tragic blunder."

Hai Tao bowed. "I apologize, Sir."

"I don't need you right now," Zhou said. "You can rest before your evening duty." Like most eunuchs, Hai Tao didn't have only one job. He was on call for countless officials who needed scribes, servers and even laborers.

"Are you certain, Master? I could help you think things over."

"It's all right. I need to find Ming and Dragon."

15

"More drinks?"

Ming and Dragon nodded in unison to the white-skinned serving girl, who immediately turned and wove her way through the restaurant's stout wooden tables.

Dragon felt his swollen belly. "Have we really reached our third round of drinks?"

"Are you surprised? We've been here since late afternoon." Even as Ming spoke, dinner patrons were trickling through the front door. "Let's see it again."

"All right." Dragon reached into his pocket and produced the object he had found across the street from the temple.

The object in Dragon's massive hand was clearly fruit, but Ming had never seen anything like it in his life. It was about the size of a man's thumb. The skin looked like it had once been dark purple, but too much time in the air had made it a shade lighter. The meat, which was white, had gone dry and wrinkled. Ming could tell this was a piece of a larger fruit. Someone had sliced this part off with a blade.

Ming poked it with his finger. It felt like dry leather. "Have you ever seen anything like this before?"

"Yes."

"Where? This is not a Chinese food."

"You're right, but remember I've spent most of my life out west. First as a child and later in the cavalry."

Ming poked the strange fruit again. "They fed you these in the military?"

"They fed us rice and stale carrots. I mean that I saw these a lot once, when we were on a campaign against the Tibetans. I never saw them *growing,* mind you. I just took them off the bodies of dead enemy soldiers."

Ming studied Dragon's oval-shaped eyes. "You fought your own people?"

Dragon grunted. "The Tibetans are not my people. Not everyone beyond the frontier is the same, Ming."

The serving girl put their drinks on the table. Ming eyed the thick, cream-colored liquid sloshing about dragon's cup and finally decided to ask. "What you've been drinking all night...it's milk?"

"Fermented mare's milk. One of the many gifts my people have bestowed upon yours." Dragon held out the cup.

When the thick cream touched Ming's tongue, his first thought was Dragon had poisoned him in the cruelest way possible. Then, as the bite of sour milk surged through him, he decided death would have been a better fate. He would have related these feelings to Dragon, but the coughs and gags stole his powers of speech. Regardless, Dragon would not have heard, distracted as he was by his own bellowing laughter.

After a moment that felt like an hour, Ming found his voice. "You are a cruel man."

"It's an acquired taste."

Ming swallowed his ale in two gulps. He did not believe that vile taste would ever leave his tongue. "So what does this food you found mean? We're looking for a Tibetan?"

"Tibet is more than one thousand *li* from where we now sit." Dragon lowered his voice. "But this is an important discovery. This kind of food is rare, even out west. When I was in the cavalry, everyone wanted to find a live one of these. Do you know why?"

"Why?"

"Because the wealthy people all love them. They probably just love them because they're rare, like a status symbol. They pay unthinkable sums for them."

Ming chuckled. "And you all thought that if you could find a live one, you would be able to bring the seeds back and start your own farm."

"That's right." Dragon didn't seem to see the humor. "You bring one back and extract the seeds from it. A person who could grow these would never have to worry about coin again."

"So you're saying very few people in the city would have this. It's like a rare piece of jewelry." That was not a bad theory, Ming supposed. Changan's elite were ravenous for anything deemed exotic, from Persian pistachios to frogs boiled live in taro.

Dragon tapped the dried piece of fruit. "You're correct. This is exclusively the food of the rich. You'll only find it in the homes of high-level mandarins and wealthy merchants. I would wager it's also in the palace."

"I suppose someone who worked for a wealthy person would also have access to this food," Ming said. "It could have been stolen by a cook."

"True. Here's what I think. Whoever was waiting in that building for the first child had this with him. Perhaps this piece was one of several he had. It may have been a long wait, right? He must have been snacking on these when he dropped one."

Ming said, "We don't even know if this belonged to the culprit. It could be anyone's."

Dragon shook his head. "Think about what that building looked like. It had old furniture and so much dust you could hardly breathe. Who else would go in there? Besides, this fruit is stale. It's been sitting in the open for some time."

"Since the time the boy was taken," Ming said. "But if it's as rare and expensive as you say it is, he wouldn't drop it."

"Well, probably not under normal circumstances," Dragon said. "But if he was in there waiting for his chance to grab the child, maybe he dropped it as he rushed out."

"All right. It might be worthwhile finding out how a person could obtain this food. I'll see if Zhou can help with that."

A voice said, "Help with what?"

Ming and Dragon both looked up. Zhou was standing by their table, hands clasped at his waist as always.

Dragon asked, "How did you know we were here?"

"I didn't. I've been looking for you for half the evening."

"We found something," Ming said. "Something important."

Dragon was nodding. "It might help us find him, Zhou."

"They've arrested someone," Zhou said. "That's why I was looking for you. You haven't heard?"

Ming slammed his hand down on the table. "That's fantastic!" He picked up his mug and took a long swallow, savoring the ale as it went down his throat. He doubted a drink would ever taste that good again.

Zhou found a chair and pulled it up to the table. "May I?"

"Of course," Dragon said. He ordered Zhou a cup of ale.

Zhou folded his hands on the table. "The arrested man's name is Lin. He's a duck vendor in the West Market."

Ming said, "What is the evidence against him? A witness?"

The serving girl arrived with Zhou's ale. Zhou took the cup without looking at her. "No. His stall is right next to the spot where Lei Lei was taken. He couldn't have been more than fifteen paces away when the abduction happened."

"All right,'" Dragon said. "His stall is there. What else?"

"Two things. First of all, the child's bracelet was apparently found among the man's possessions. The girl's father has already said it looks like Lei Lei's. Second, authorities are operating on the theory that the abductor knew the child. Otherwise it would have been harder for him to get close to her."

"The bracelet *looks* like Lei Lei's?" Ming thought it over. "That's very weak."

"I went to the place where they're holding Lin and spoke with him," Zhou said. "He is claiming two people in the market planted the bracelet in his things to implicate him. He says they're just after the reward."

Dragon sat back and took a pull on his vile drink. "Guilty people often say that evidence was planted to hurt them. Is there anything else we should know about Lin?"

"Just one thing so far," Zhou said. "He is seventy years old."

Ming's eyes went wide. "*Seventy* years old? They're saying a grandfather is behind all of this?"

"Unlikely," Dragon said, "but not impossible."

"Perhaps." Ming did know plenty of older people who were in better physical condition than he was. Why, the woman living next door to his family was past eighty, and she carried buckets of well water back to her home every day. Once Ming had offered to help her, and she told him to stop being ridiculous. Still, a man of seventy abducting children and killing them? A man that age bludgeoning a Gold Bird Guard senseless and then cutting his stomach open? It was difficult to believe. "It's not impossible, but…it already feels wrong." He turned to Zhou. "You don't believe this Lin is the killer, do you?"

"No," Zhou said. "I don't. But I worry we won't have the chance to investigate for ourselves. I think the crown is so desperate to stop the killings they are willing to believe almost any scenario."

"Have you spoken to them?" Ming asked. "Expressed your doubts?"

"Not yet. I was supposed to meet with Commandant Chen today, but he's in a meeting with the Governor. My guess is they're talking about how to convict Lin. I doubt they're bothering to question the case against him very much."

"Gods." Dragon made a fist the size of boulder and rested his chin on it.

Ming looked at his ale. Suddenly he didn't feel so thirsty. "A man who might well be innocent is going to be strangled. That's what's going to happen."

Zhou nodded. "Probably."

Dragon jabbed his finger at them. "Not if we don't allow it."

Speaking slowly, Dragon told Zhou about the fruit they had found. He explained that it was a rare food, so rare that very few people had even seen it. He described the hole in the building across from the temple and the skill needed to fill part of it in. He explained that only a tall man could have looked through the remaining part of the hole. He closed by saying that in their estimation, the killer was most likely a wealthy person, or someone who worked around wealthy people. The man was tall, he had access to rare foods, and he was skilled with his hands. Most unique of all, he was literate.

A small smile appeared on Zhou's face. "I work for wealthy people."

"Believe me," Ming said. "We are watching you."

Ming and Zhou laughed, but Dragon was not in the mood for jokes. His eyes didn't leave Zhou. "We need to find out where these fruits are sold and who buys them. Can you help us?"

"All right. I'll have my eunuch ask around tomorrow."

"Good," Dragon said. "Also, we may need access to the Imperial Archives to obtain information on some of the victims' families. Can you get us in?"

Zhou gave them a doubtful look. "I can try, but I wouldn't be too hopeful. Only officials and their servants can get in there."

"The information stored there would be a big asset," Ming said. *Gold mine* was probably a better description. They needed to know about the victims' families and their secrets, but people were always reticent to part with sensitive information. The Archives, with its volumes on crime and business and everything else, would not feel the same reluctance.

Zhou thought for a moment. "How about this? I'll try to get you in. If I fail – and I probably will – you can tell me the information you need. I'll pass that along to my eunuch. He'll read the scrolls, copy down important information and hand it over to you."

"Can't he just bring us the scrolls?" Dragon asked.

Zhou smiled. "Sorry. Nothing is allowed to leave the Archives."

"All right," Ming said. "Thank you." He tried to conceal his disappointment. If the eunuch really did have to copy the scrolls down, it would waste a lot of valuable time. "What do you know about Meng Chun?"

"That old pub owner? Only that she brilliantly evaded blame for her husband's murder." A shadow of anger crossed Zhou's face.

"Wait," Ming said. *"Murder?"*

"Correct." The disgust stayed plain on Zhou's face as he told them what he had learned about Meng Chun. "I never knew a thing about it. I was investigating her, but –"

"Why were you investigating her?" Dragon asked.

"An unrelated matter. Suffice to say she was a problem and I wanted leverage in case I had to force her out of my ward. I had my eunuch Hai Tao go into her pub – which was also her home – and look for something we could use against her. She didn't possess a thing that would incriminate her for murder or anything else. That's what we had concluded, at least."

"All right," Ming said again. "We'll worry about Meng Chun later. There's more you can do tonight, Zhou. You should go to the Imperial Ministry and request an emergency meeting. Explain that we may be able to exonerate this vendor, or at least lessen the suspicion on him."

"I'm already planning to do that." Zhou glanced at the drinks on the table. "Before you two get too deep into your cups, I need something else from you."

"What's that?" Dragon asked.

Zhou reached into his satchel and produced a blank piece of parchment. "A letter. Address it directly to the Governor and explain what you've discovered. Point out the weaknesses in the government's evidence against Lin. I will go to the Ministry tonight to speak with whoever I can find, and tomorrow I'll return with your letter. You're both experienced lawmen. Your support will lend credibility to my cause. Respectful language, please. The men who will read your letter are stubborn, and they don't react well to criticism."

Ming wanted to slap Zhou on the back. There was a reason his friend was so successful. He always seemed to find the best approach to a problem. "It will be ready first thing tomorrow. Don't worry. Stubborn or not, your superiors will understand."

Dragon grinned. "That's right! Now get out of here!"

Zhou offered a thin smile in return. "I'll do my best. Let's get together tomorrow morning at the Red Sun Restaurant. I'll send a messenger to tell you when we should meet." Before anyone else could speak he stood up, gave them an exaggerated bow, and headed for the exit. His mug was still full.

As Ming watched his friend go, he began to feel something he did not like. It was relief. When Zhou first told them about the arrest there had been joy, certainly. But beneath that, in a part of his mind where the base thoughts flourished, there was something else. Jealousy. Someone *else* had caught the murderer. Ming wouldn't have the satisfaction of doing it himself. He wouldn't get to look that man in the face and tell him he never should have fooled with the Sorcerer.

But now they were back in the hunt.

We still have a chance to catch this man ourselves.

Ming looked at Dragon and guessed he wasn't the only one with those feelings.

"Come on," Dragon said. "We have a letter to write."

• • •

Zhou walked through the dark city, his eyes pointed at the muddy ground. He passed a vendor trying to lead his donkey through the street. A pile of sacks was loaded onto the animal's back, tied down and ready for transport. The beast, however, seemed content to stand in the muck and stare straight ahead. The vendor used his lash and every curse he could conjure as motivation, but the animal's only response was a bored swish of the tail. Two Gold Bird Guards watched from the side of the road and laughed.

Zhou just glanced at the scene and went on his way.

He thought of poor Mr. Lin, sitting in a cell and waiting for the wire to go around his neck. There were similarities between Zhou and the old man. Part of it was sexuality, of course, but there was more. They were both victims. Zhou was talented and ambitious, but his good ideas were crushed by the capital's relentless bureaucracy. Now that same monster meant to claim Mr. Lin's life. It demanded a sacrifice, hoping against all logic that it would somehow end the chaos.

It wasn't fair.

As Zhou walked, he took a fan from his pocket and cooled himself. The air was hot, oppressive. On nights like this he felt like he was walking through water. Well, the Imperial Ministry wasn't far.

He had implied to Ming and Dragon that no one in the government would want to hear that Lin might be innocent. That was…an embellishment. Zhou had only contempt for most officials, but he knew some who would hear him out. The best course now was to seek those men out and explain why Mr. Lin could not be the killer. At least some of them would listen. It was unlikely they could save Mr. Lin, but there was a chance.

Zhou stopped at a corner and fanned himself again. If Mr. Lin was released, then what? They would all be back at the beginning – floundering and baffled, their humiliation compounded for having arrested the wrong man.

Also, Mr. Lin's release would outrage Commandant Chen. Zhou smiled. At least there was that.

But then, Lin's salvation would be a blessing for the dimwitted Commandant. After all, if Mr. Lin *was* executed, Chen's euphoria would be short-lived. As soon as the next child was taken the Commandant would look like a buffoon.

Zhou started walking again. So there it was. By saving Mr. Lin, they would also be saving Commandant Chen from a grave mistake. It was a part of the bargain that couldn't be avoided.

Black anger stirred in Zhou's stomach. He let it come, made no effort to stop it. It was cleansing somehow, like bitter medicine. The reward for doing the moral thing was more of the same: laboring in obscurity under the dullard Chen.

Zhou thought of Tall and Short. He thought of the way they kowtowed to Commandant Chen as though the old fart were Confucius. They supported Chen's every move, so if Mr. Lin died, they would be finished along with their boss.

Zhou was going to save them all from ruin, and they didn't even know it.

Well, this debacle would help Zhou in one way. If he managed to get Mr. Lin released, everyone would see he had been right all along. After the next child was killed, the whole city would know Mr. Lin was innocent (Zhou would have to tell the old man to have an alibi at all times so no one could suspect him again). Commandant Chen would still hold a grudge against Zhou, but all in all, Zhou would look smart. People would know that during the hysteria, he was the one voice of reason.

That would have to be payment enough.

The giant, sloping roof of the Imperial Ministry came into view. Zhou picked up his pace, hoping Commandant Chen was still in his office.

• • •

As it turned out, Zhou got his wish.

He spotted Chen at the far end of the Ministry's longest corridor. The old Commandant was standing outside his office. His back was to Zhou, but those hunched shoulders were impossible to mistake. And who was there with him? Why, those two pillars of public service, Tall and Short.

From his end of the hall, Zhou could see that the three men were deep in conversation. Short had a contented look on his face. Tall was grinning like a drunk man in a brothel.

Zhou gritted his teeth as he walked. What was that conversation about, and why hadn't he been invited to join it?

Short looked up, saw Zhou approaching and said something. Chen turned and motioned for Zhou to join them. The three men waited for Zhou, standing like soldiers at attention.

Zhou reached them and bowed.

Chen said, "Mandarin Zhou. I see my messenger found you. That's good. I have important news."

"No, Sir. I didn't even know you had a messenger looking for me. I came on my own. Gentlemen, I have something important to tell you."

"Later," Chen said. "In my office – all three of you."

• • •

As Zhou took his seat across from Chen, he realized it would have been wise to bring Ming and Dragon along with him. Ming was a former Gold Bird Guard and Dragon was a renowned thief catcher. They would have given Zhou's arguments more credibility. Well, it didn't matter. Zhou was a better speaker than both Ming and Dragon. Besides, even a doddering fool like Chen would have to acknowledge the flaws in the evidence against Mr. Lin.

Zhou cleared his throat. "Sir, I –"

"I have an announcement," Chen said. "Despite the late hour I deemed it necessary to tell you all now. Starting next week, I will no longer be Commandant."

"A pity." Zhou tried to appear neutral but even he could tell he was putting on a poor show. In truth, Zhou would have been less shocked if he had looked up and saw the sky turn green. No longer Commandant? So the old man's incompetence had finally done him in. Amazing. Perhaps some men were so inept that even the city's bureaucracy could not protect them.

A new thought surfaced in Zhou's mind. *I am Chen's most logical replacement.* Unable to stop himself, he began a frantic mental inventory of his career's achievements and blunders. Had he done enough for a promotion? Had he angered too many men? Had he groveled enough, or perhaps too much? Once again Zhou became certain his face was betraying his thoughts. A man could only conceal so much.

Chen smiled, creating a network of lines on his face. "The Emperor has seen fit to promote me to Assistant Governor." He gestured to Tall. "Mandarin Ling will be taking my place as Commandant."

"I see," Zhou said. He recognized that voice as his own, but it sounded as though it belonged to someone else. "Congratulations." He turned to Tall. "To both of you."

Tall said something that sounded like an expression of gratitude, but Zhou did not hear it. He could form only one thought: *I am in shock.*

Slowly, slowly, Zhou felt the realization setting in. Chen wasn't being dismissed. He was being promoted. And Zhou wasn't going to take his place. He had been passed over in favor of a man just as stupid as Chen. All of his hard work, all of his plans to help the city had come to nothing.

"Zhou!"

Zhou started as though he had been slapped. "Yes?"

Chen was watching him, his gray eyebrows drawn together in anger. "You said you had something important to tell me."

Zhou took an extra moment – no more – to gather his thoughts. "It concerns the child killings. In particular I came to speak with you about Mr. Lin."

Chen settled back in his chair. "Go on."

Zhou took a deep gulp of air, held it, let it out. "Mr. Lin is not the killer."

The room went quiet. It was as though some god had descended from Heaven and stopped time in that sad little office. Zhou could feel Tall and Short watching him. He waited for Chen to explode.

But the old man's face remained blank. "Really? Why?"

"The case against him is shoddy, to say the least."

Tall cleared his throat and leaned forward. "Lin has a previous connection to one of the children." Zhou noted that Tall's voice had already taken on the arrogant tones of high authority. "The child's bracelet was found in his lock box. The child was taken just a few paces from his stall. These things mean nothing?"

"Those are not –"

"Enough," Chen said. "We all know what the evidence against the vendor is. Believe it or not, we have examined its so-called flaws, Zhou. We have already decided that according to what we know, Lin must be guilty. Tell me. Have you anything else to support your opinion? Have you discovered something new – something that might make us reconsider?"

Zhou glanced around. Short was sitting quietly with his hands folded in his lap. The small man had clearly decided to stay out of this conversation. Tall's face was distant as well, but Zhou could feel an ocean of hostility beneath that still demeanor. Tall was betting that this case would advance his career immeasurably, and Zhou was interfering. He would probably slit Zhou's throat to stop him from meddling.

Zhou looked at Chen. Why wasn't the Commandant showing anger at this challenge? The answer came to him through those smug, satisfied eyes. *I am going to be one of the most powerful men in the city*, those eyes said. *It's already been confirmed. So go on. Challenge me if you like. Amuse me.*

Chen rested his chin on the heel of his hand. "I am sure you have more." He sounded like a patient father indulging a child's fantasy. "A new piece of evidence? A witness? *Some* kind of information or insight that will undermine the government's case against Lin?"

Zhou thought of the odd piece of fruit Ming and Dragon had found. He thought of the man he had seen in Meng Chun's pub – the man who was much larger than Mr. Lin. He thought of Dragon's beggar, the man named Guang, who had spotted the killer and could confirm the man's height. "No, Sir, I have nothing else. I only wanted to come here and voice my disagreement formally. I want to make it known that I believe Mr. Lin to be innocent. We should not stop the investigation for other suspects. We are making a grave mistake."

"All right," Chen said. His smile was still in place. "Noted."

"I am also going to write a formal letter. I'll deliver one copy to you and one to the palace. It will outline all of my misgivings."

"You do that, Zhou. Was there anything else?"

"No, Sir."

• • •

When Zhou stepped out of the building, his first thought was that the night had somehow grown darker. It was as though the whole city had been doused in black ink. A strange notion, to be sure, but he couldn't resist the feeling that it was real.

Zhou headed down the building's front stairs, his steps fast and light. He had an odd sensation, one he had never known before. He felt like he had been carrying a giant stone on his back for his entire life, and he had just now managed to set it down. The feeling was…wonderful. He wanted to whistle but he stopped himself. That was unbecoming of a mandarin.

For years he had worked in silence, had toiled to make his corner of the empire a better place. And what had it gotten him? Anonymity and frustration. The bitter drama had climaxed tonight with the ultimate humiliation: watching Chen rise to the post of Assistant Governor, and watching an undeserving whelp get promoted to take his place.

As he stepped onto the street, Zhou picked up his pace. That feeling was growing. An invisible burden had been weighing him down throughout his entire career – his entire *life* – but now he was free. Freedom came with a simple understanding: only fools followed the rules. If you never reached out and took the things you wanted, you were doomed to remain a fool for life.

A passing Gold Bird Guard looked at Zhou and nodded. Zhou smiled and nodded back.

Being a leader meant making choices. The greater good was what mattered. How could that greater good be protected when the world was run by men like Chen?

The answer was simple. It could not be protected.

The city was desperate for fresh leadership, but it would not change on its own. Responsible men had to make change. To *force* change. Commandant Chen and his lackeys *had* to go. But of course, they would never go willingly.

They would have to be forced to resign. That meant humiliating them in front of the entire city. And Zhou knew how to do that.

As things stood now, Chen and the others would suffer embarrassment when the city finally saw that Lin was not the killer. But that mistake would not be enough to ruin them. They couldn't just be blamed for accusing the wrong man. The disgrace would only be severe enough if they *executed* the wrong man. Then, after another child died, they would be held responsible for convicting and killing an innocent person. They would never survive such a scandal.

But Zhou would not be blamed. If he continued his campaign to free Mr. Lin, then he would look wise while his enemies looked like fools...dangerously incompetent fools.

Zhou would have to navigate a rocky course. He would need to appear to fight for Mr. Lin's innocence, while secretly working to see a wire go around the old man's neck.

Mr. Lin would have to pay a tragic price. It really was unfair. But it was all in the name of progress, of the greater good. After Mr. Lin was gone, Zhou would see to it that he did not die for nothing. Mr. Lin's death would enable Zhou to usher in an era of reform. Countless people would benefit.

It was the only way.

Zhou picked up his pace. He needed to get home and think things over. As he turned a corner and his house came into view, he started to whistle.

16

The next morning, just before the sun rose, a young man stood by the city gates and raised two wooden sticks high over his head. He began the monotonous drumming that always reminded Ming of a giant's heartbeat, and he would not stop until he struck his drum three thousand times. At the sound of his drums, gates all over the city opened and people prepared for another day.

There was a visible change in the city that morning. Streets which had been all but deserted the day before were now mobbed. Folks who had gotten used to hurrying from place to place now took their time and enjoyed the summer weather. Those who had been throwing furtive, suspicious glances at one another now greeted strangers with hearty claps on the back. It was as though China had won a long and costly war.

In the West Market vendors were hurriedly setting up, bracing for the inflated crowds they hoped would come.

Blossom stood at one of the market stalls, a small painting in her hands. The painting showed a giant of a man holding a short, gray sword. Small demons surrounded him, but the fiends looked more like servants than enemies. The artwork was simple yet competent, something Blossom would expect from a painter's first-year apprentice.

Blossom squinted at the man in the painting. He was clearly a deity, and he looked familiar. She had seen that thick beard and those tiny, menacing eyes many time before. "Who is this, Lee?"

The vendor named Lee was standing behind his stall, but he looked like he was sitting down. At his full height he only reached the shoulders of most women. Age had taken some hand in that. Lee was at least ten years older than Mr. Lin. "That is Zhong Kui. He's the slayer of ghosts and the protector of the common people. He –"

"I know who Zhong Kui is!" Blossom dropped the painting on the table. "The work was so poor I couldn't recognize his face."

Lee mumbled something and looked down.

The paintings, all of which depicted gods, were spread out on Lee's table. Blossom found it disorienting see so many deities staring up at her. "You painted all of these yourself?"

Lee's face brightened. "I did. You would be amazed at how hard it is to obtain the right colors." He picked up a painting that was all reds and yellows. "Artisans create these colors by extracting them from vegetables. It's a difficult process and they charge accordingly, but I've always been willing –"

"Hush!" Blossom hated dealing with Lee. Just like everyone else in the market he was afraid of her and Toad. But even that fear didn't stop him from jabbering on like an adolescent girl when the mood struck him. Well, soon enough she wouldn't have to deal with Lee at all.

Blossom felt something tickle her ankle. She looked down to see a brown rat sniffing her foot. She cursed and kicked at the little beast, sending it scurrying off. She watched it go. It was a pity she didn't have something to throw at it. She hated the damn rats. By this time of morning most of them were gone, but a few of the bolder ones were still out. They darted from one hiding spot to another, looking for scraps of food. Soon, after more customers showed up, even the most brazen pests would retire until dusk.

Blossom would have liked to come here later in the day, when she wouldn't have to deal with the vermin. But she preferred doing her most sensitive business in the mornings. There were fewer snooping customers to worry about.

She picked up another painting. This one was clearly Ji Gong, the beggar god. The drunken monk was fanning himself and grinning. Blossom dropped the painting onto the table. She didn't like the god's smiling eyes. He seemed to be laughing at her secrets. "You owe us money, Lee."

Lee hurried around to the front of his stall and stood before Blossom. He bowed so low his torso was parallel to the muddy ground. He stayed in that position as he spoke. "I am sorry, Blossom! Business has been slow. I think the murders have made people less willing to come here."

"Plenty of hardworking folks weathered the storm just fine." Blossom raised her voice. She wanted the other vendors to hear her. *"They* haven't given me excuses."

Lee stood up straight. He tried to meet Blossom's eye but couldn't quite do it. "I'll work twice as hard. I'll stay up late and paint more – the most beautiful pictures you've ever seen."

Blossom sneered. "Paint more of your garbage? I wouldn't trade a stick of firewood for this." She picked up the picture of Ji Gong, tore it down the middle and dropped both pieces in the mud.

Lee cringed at the sound of his painting being ripped. He made a motion to pick the pieces up, then pulled back and hung his head.

Blossom took a step closer to Lee. She wasn't taller than many people – physical intimidation was her brother's job – and she enjoyed looking down at the short man. She raised her voice a little more. "My brother and I only collect a fee of fifty coppers per week. In return –"

"You also take the vendors' wares whenever you want," Lee muttered.

"In return, we keep the market running smoothly and we keep the thieves away. It is a fair trade. We are the only ones who can provide this service, because we have connections in the government." That lie had been Toad's idea. He was a fool in most things, but when it came to manipulation he had a low cunning. At first Blossom had called it madness. Who would believe they had a seventh level mandarin in their

family? But Toad had insisted it could work. People believe anything if you present it to them with absolute confidence, he had said. And he was right. After ten years, no one had even asked for their phantom uncle's name.

As Blossom continued her speech, she noticed something unusual. Some of the nearby vendors had stopped unpacking. They were watching her, hands on their hips or arms across their chests. A few had even walked up for a closer look.

Blossom pressed on, her voice still slightly raised. "Our obligation is to ensure safety and stability."

Somewhere in the growing crowd, a spectator issued a single, sharp laugh.

Blossom pretended not to notice. "If a vendor can't fulfill his part of the bargain, it creates problems for the entire market." She gave Lee an ominous look.

Lee knelt down and picked up the pieces of his painting. He wiped the mud from them, placed them carefully on his stall and finally met Blossom's eye. "I have been paying you and your brother for years. Then you raised your fees without warning. I had no way of preparing."

That's the idea, Blossom wanted to say. It was time for Lee to go. He had been here since the last dynasty, and what did he provide? Just useless gossip and endless excuses for late payments. Even worse, he was taking up one of the best spots in the market.

Blossom and Toad had already accepted an outside bid for Lee's spot. It came from a pork vendor eager to start his new business. He was only twenty-one years old, and he had that youthful mix of ambition and foolishness. He had agreed to the obscene sum of four thousand coppers.

Blossom and Toad both knew they had been testing a lot of people's patience these days. After all, they had only recently gotten Mr. Lin arrested for killing the children. He was well-liked in the market, and putting those murders on him had stirred up resentment. A part of Blossom even worried that they had gone too far this time. In the end, though, it would work out. She knew how to handle these fools.

But then, at least thirty of those very fools were watching her right now. Trying to appear casual, Blossom looked the crowd over. She saw sweaty, wiry men wearing cotton pants and no shirts. She saw women in dirty dresses, tools and brooms in their hands.

And they were all staring at her.

Blossom ignored them. These merchants were like children. You didn't show them a speck of weakness. If they sensed you were on the back foot you were finished. "Mr. Lee, I have looked the other way long enough. If you can't provide everything you owe by tomorrow, we will have to sell your spot to the highest bidder."

Before Blossom even finished speaking, angry sounds began to rise from the crowd. Some people were pointing at her and scowling. A few had even stepped forward.

"I can pay you one hundred," Lee blubbered. "The rest I will get for you soon. Give me until the next moon to catch up. I'll do it. I swear to you on my ancestors."

Blossom shook her head mournfully. "I'm afraid I have to insist. Unless someone is willing to give you a loan?" She gave the crowd a curious glance.

Suddenly no one seemed willing to meet her eye. Blossom smirked at them. Merchants were hardheaded people and they never parted with money willingly.

She turned back to Lee. "My brother and I will be here tomorrow morning. If you don't–"

"Out of my way!" The high, rasped voice shot out from the middle of the crowd. "Out of my way! Go on! Move!"

Blossom felt a surge of loathing. She recognized that voice.

A woman stepped out of the crowd and drew up next to Lee. This woman was even shorter than Lee, and she was older than time itself. She smiled at Lee, revealing all eight of her teeth. Then her smile vanished as she looked up at Blossom. "Good morning, Blossom."

Through a supreme effort of will, Blossom kept the snarl from her face. "Morning, Yu Shuan."

Yu Shuan planted her cane in the mud. "What's this about, then?"

"You know precisely what it's about," Blossom snapped. She loathed Yu Shuan more than any other vendor in this whole miserable market. Yu Shuan thought that just because she was ancient she had the right to meddle in the affairs of others. She was always standing up to Blossom and Toad, telling them to relent, to give the other vendors a break. "Mr. Lee here is taking advantage of my brother and me."

Lee looked hurt. "I'm not –"

Yu Shuan raised her hand, and Lee's voice cut off immediately. "You raised his fees without warning. Of course it is difficult for him to cope."

A few people in the crowd murmured their agreement.

"We had no choice." Blossom regretted the words as soon as they left her mouth. *Why* did they have no choice? Weren't they always working to give the impression of absolute power? "With the recent killings our job has increased ten-fold in difficulty."

That was the wrong thing to say, given Mr. Lin's popularity in the West Market. The crowd's rumbling grew louder.

Yu Shuan stared at Blossom, her hands still on the cane. "You mean the murders for which you accused that poor Mr. Lin? I imagine the reward is enough to cover your extra labor."

Most of the heads in the crowd began to nod. A few people shouted their agreement.

Blossom looked at the tiny old woman with the mob at her back. This was even worse than she had feared. She had never seen the merchants this worked up before. In spite of herself she took a backward step. Her bottom bumped against Lee's stall. The angry people sensed her fear and moved in closer. She was suddenly certain they meant to carry her off and lynch her.

She felt the first stirrings of real panic.

We've pushed them too far. Just yesterday we set up Mr. Lin. Today we are forcing out another old man, and these people have had enough. On the heels of that came an even more ominous thought. *They're too angry to be afraid anymore. What happens if you hit a dog one too many times?*

As if in answer, something small and brown flew out of the crowd and struck Blossom in the face.

Blossom squawked in pain and surprise. She looked down at the object that had landed by her feet. She picked it up and stared at it. At first she was too surprised to recognize it. Then, as the shock ebbed away, she began to tremble with rage.

Someone had thrown a shoe at her!

Something else was different. When Blossom realized what it was, she gnashed her teeth with hate. The crowd was laughing at her. They were jeering as though she were a juggler who had dropped her pins. Some of them were pointing. Even little Lee was tittering like a child. Their anger was gone, replaced with mocking derision. Somehow that was worse.

Blossom threw her head back and screamed. The laughter faltered, then bubbled right back up.

"Wait until my uncle hears about this!" Blossom's voice rose to a grating screech. "You all just wait! After he's done you'll be begging me to let you back into this market! You'll all be on the street before the next moon!"

The crowd's only answer was more laughter.

"Sister. Sister!"

Blossom turned toward the voice. Toad was fighting his way through the crowd, his eyes wide and confused.

Blossom spun on Toad. "Brother, they're laughing at me! We have to punish them all! Remember every face in this crowd so we can tell our uncle!"

Toad broke from the crowd and reached his sister in two long steps. "What is happening?"

"I don't know! I was just talking to Lee and then all of this started." She pointed at the jeering crowd.

"Sister, some Gold Bird Guards came to see me. We're wanted at the Imperial Ministry. About the reward."

"The Ministry? Yes! The *Imperial* Ministry!" Blossom raised her voice, but even she had trouble hearing it above the laughter. "You hear that, you miserable peasants? We're wanted at the Ministry. We're going to tell our uncle all about this. You just wait!"

Toad tugged her arm. "They're waiting for us. Come *on!*"

Blossom went with her brother, still seething at the laughter that chased her out of the market.

• • •

Soon Blossom and Toad were standing in one of the Imperial Ministry's basement offices.

When Blossom was a child, she sometimes stood outside buildings like this and imagined life behind their thick walls. She had always pictured wide hallways, polished floors and bronze statues. Slaves waited by every door, jumping to action whenever a mandarin snapped his fingers.

Glancing around the windowless room, Blossom realized her ideas couldn't have been more wrong. This place felt less like an office and more like a storage room.

In lieu of sunlight the room had a dozen candles. Even with the candles burning the shadows were dark and thick. The sole decoration was a giant portrait of some long-gone Emperor. Blossom could feel the dead man looking down at her, studying her.

Two men were in the room with Blossom and Toad. One man was sitting behind a small wooden desk and looking at a scroll. Well...in Blossom's opinion you couldn't really call that kind of person a *man*.

The eunuch had introduced himself as Hai Tao and sat down without another word. He hadn't invited Blossom or Toad to sit, even though there were two chairs right in front of them. He was making them stand in order to humble them. Blossom displayed her own power often enough to know when someone else was doing it.

The second man stood behind Hai Tao. He was a short, prim looking fellow in a red mandarin's robe. The man had not introduced himself or even said hello. He was standing as still as a statue, his hands clasped at his waist. Only his eyes moved. They shifted back and forth between Blossom and Toad.

Hai Tao made no effort to conceal his scroll's contents, probably because he knew neither Blossom nor Toad could read. After an age he put down the scroll and looked up at them. In this sunless room, that strange dent in his forehead looked black. "It says here you're the ones who discovered the bracelet in Lin's lock box."

"That's right," Toad said. He leaned forward, placed his hands on the desk and stared at the eunuch. "We found the killer and we're here for the reward."

Blossom wanted to smack her brother on the back of his stupid head. They were not in the West Market, and Hai Tao was no vendor struggling to make his way in the world. Intimidation would not work with someone like him. It would only make him angry. She said, "The notices around the city promised a reward for the killer's capture."

Toad nodded. "Ten thousand coppers."

The eunuch said, "How did you find the bracelet?"

"It was in Lin's lock box," Toad said.

"I know that." The eunuch looked impatient. "I am asking how you knew to check there."

Toad stared at the eunuch and then turned to Blossom. He opened his mouth, paused and then closed it again.

"We saw him looking at it," Blossom said. For the second time she wanted to slap her brother. The eunuch had asked a simple question, and what a reaction! Toad may as well have come out and said *we're lying*. "He was sitting at his stall one day and admiring it in the sunlight. The lock box was sitting open on the table next to him."

Fortunately the eunuch seemed to accept Blossom's answer. He nodded and made a note in his scroll. "And how did you know the bracelet was an item of significance?"

"What do you mean?" Blossom asked.

Hai Tao put down his quill and folded his long fingers. "I mean it is entirely normal to have a jade bracelet. I have one myself. See?" He pulled back his sleeve and showed them the green circlet around his wrist. "Why did a simple bracelet arouse your suspicion?"

Blossom bit her lip. She had expected questions, of course, but this was more like an interrogation. The eunuch was quick, too. Even more troubling was the man standing motionless behind the eunuch. Blossom sensed he was committing every detail to memory, maybe to use against them later. Perhaps he was a torturer. Everyone said the crown employed specialists who knew all kinds of ways to brutalize criminals. Was this man thinking of a special punishment for their perjury?

I have to think fast, Blossom's mind blared. *If I don't say something soon, my idiot brother will speak and condemn us both.*

She glanced at Toad. She could tell he was coming up with some fumbling lie. Oh no…he was opening his mouth!

Blossom spat, "Lei Lei showed it to me!"

All three men looked at her.

"I work in the West Market," Blossom said. "My brother and I both spend a lot of time there. Perhaps you knew that."

"Oh, I do," the eunuch said. "We have heard all about you and your…imperial connections." His eyes danced with mocking amusement.

Blossom wanted to take a deep breath but she forced herself not to. "Yes, we're there all time. We have, uh, interests there. I know all the vendors – their names, the locations of their stalls, and what they sell." That part at least was true.

"Me too," Toad said proudly.

Blossom spoke quickly so her brother couldn't say anything else. "Lei Lei and her mother came to the West Market all the time. I was very friendly with the child. She showed me her mutton fat bracelet once. It was very valuable so I remembered it. When I saw Mr. Lin with it, of course I became suspicious." Most of that was fiction, but so what? The only people who could contradict Blossom were Lei Lei and her mother, and they were both dead.

"So we decided to look into it," Toad said.

Blossom considered her brother's statement and decided it was harmless. Should she say anything more? Probably not. If you explained too much then you looked like you had something to hide.

The eunuch made another note on his scroll. "Is there any other information you can give us?"

Blossom and Toad both said no.

Hai Tao placed his quill on the desk. "Tell me about these connections you have. Everyone in the West Market says you're related to a seventh level mandarin."

Blossom cleared her throat. "That's, ah…things get mixed up in the gossip and the confusion of the market. Information gets twisted all the time."

"Twisted," Hai Tao said. "I wouldn't describe it that way. I think you made the connection up and hoped no one would think to question it. Is that about right?"

Blossom stomped her foot. "No! We –"

"It's true," Toad moaned. "We need to look important out there. What else can we do?"

Blossom gaped at her brother. She couldn't believe what she had just heard. How stupid could one man be?

The eunuch picked up his quill again. "Very well. I have the testimony of two gangsters from the market – two people we can very easily prove as liars. They only came forward after the reward was posted and their evidence is a joke. Do you know the penalty for perjury? You're sent 833 miles from home and cannot return on penalty of beheading. Perhaps we'll add several years of compulsory labor for your insolence."

The man behind Hai Tao stepped forward. Blossom jumped. She had forgotten all about him.

The man looked down at Hai Tao. "I'll take it from here."

Hai Tao rose from the chair and stood behind it.

"No," said the man. "You're dismissed."

Hai Tao bowed and immediately headed out of the room.

As the eunuch walked away, Blossom saw a shadow of anger pass over his face. It must be terrible to be a servant. He was clearly furious at having to leave, yet his only option was to obey without comment. And to bow.

Blossom wanted to yell a taunt after him. Served him right for being so uppity. A eunuch's role was to serve the empire, not harass hardworking citizens.

The small man waited until Hai Tao closed the door behind him. Then he sat down behind the desk. He motioned to the empty chairs. "Please."

Blossom and Toad both sat down.

The man said, "My name is Mandarin Zhou. You two are petty gangsters, and you're both full of shit."

Blossom wagged her finger at Zhou. "Now see here. I am a legitimate trader and I won't –"

"No," Zhou said. Most people were taken aback by Blossom's abrasiveness, but he didn't seem to notice it. "I know for a fact you're both full of shit. Weren't you listening to my eunuch? I can prove you've been lying about having an uncle in the government. I also know you planted that bracelet in poor Mr. Lin's lock box. I have proof."

Before Blossom could speak, Toad put his hands over his face and cried out. "How did you know?"

At that moment, Blossom wanted to murder her brother.

Zhou smiled. "Because you just told me."

It took Toad a while, but he finally began to understand he had been duped. He even seemed to grasp how simple the trick had been. He bunched his fists and glared like an angry child, but at least he had the presence of mind to stay quiet.

Zhou tapped the scroll with his finger. "I have enough here to seal your fate. And my eunuch was right. We can beat you, send you away and make you slaves, all without anyone raising a single word in your defense."

Toad moaned again.

Zhou looked at the ceiling, his eyes musing. "Perhaps we'll send you to Lingnan." His bored gaze settled on his guests. "You know what it's like there, don't you?"

Blossom did. The mere mention of such a place was enough to make the hairs on her arm stand ramrod straight. Lingnan was a poisonous land cooked by the sun and ravaged by typhoons. The snakes chased you until you no longer had the power to run, and then they struck their death blow. The air itself was poison, a miasma so toxic its very smell meant a slow and agonizing end. But the worst were the savages, the mindless animals that attacked civilized foreigners on sight. People said the barbarians peeled flesh from their victims while they still lived because fear enriched the taste of meat. Blossom believed all of it.

"I could have you in a wagon by sundown," Zhou said. "Before the next moon, you could be picking thorned plants from the ground and hoping you can eat them without dying. How does that sound?"

Toad's wailing grew louder with each word, but Blossom suddenly felt her fear fading. Something about this man's approach seemed…exaggerated. No, that wasn't the right word. It seemed rehearsed. "I think you want something."

Zhou didn't look surprised. "I want this man Lin convicted of the child murders. And for that I need credible witnesses."

"You have already said you don't believe our story." Blossom spoke slowly, listening to each word as it left her mouth. Was the mandarin laying some kind of trap?

"That's right," Zhou said. "I don't believe it."

Blossom usually disliked evasiveness, but she hardly noticed it now. She was too intrigued. "You know he's innocent. You know and you still want him executed. Why?"

Zhou said nothing.

Blossom decided she didn't need to know for now. "If you want a conviction, we can get one for you."

Zhou made an exaggerated scoff. "No you can't – at least not if you follow your current plan. The word of two degenerate gangsters might be enough for an arrest, but soon the scrutiny will start. People will ask why they should believe the likes of you."

"The bracelet –"

"You stole the bracelet and planted it among Lin's things," Zhou said absently. "Lin will say that over and over, and people will believe him. After all, he might be a lowly merchant but you two are even worse. You're criminals. People will start to see that the entire case against Lee is more than just weak. It's suspicious."

"Then what can be done?"

"If you follow my instructions then Lin will be executed and you will escape punishment for perjury."

Blossom sat back in her chair. Now that she knew Zhou was a criminal she felt more comfortable. "That's not enough. I want more."

"You can forget about the reward," Zhou said. "People will say you set Lin up for the money, which is the truth. The first step is to *renounce* the reward. That will secure some credibility."

Toad sat up straight. "Oh no! We're not leaving without our money."

Blossom and Zhou ignored him.

Zhou picked up his quill and wrote something on the scroll. "You can at least read numerals, I assume? Cooperate and I'll compensate you myself. But I require complete secrecy."

Blossom looked at the figure. "That's less than half the government's reward."

"It's in addition to clemency for perjuring yourselves."

"Not enough."

Zhou spread his hands. "I am not a wealthy man."

"To give me what I want you won't have to be," Blossom said. "We'll take this amount and your promise of clemency. But I want something else, and it won't cost you a single extra copper."

"Tell me."

Blossom thought of the people who had chased her from the market just that morning. Now the memory of their laughter brought her a grim satisfaction. She leaned forward, looked Zhou in the eye and began to speak.

17

While Blossom schemed with Zhou, Ming watched Physician Lu examine Li Juan. The doctor was a small man dressed in a billowing silk robe that looked wholly unsuited to his profession.

Lu pressed three fingers against Li Juan's neck.

Ming said, "Physician Lu, what do you–"

Lu put up a hand for silence. Finally, he took his fingers from Li Juan. "Your wife's pulse is weak. It is a wonder she can rise from her sickbed at all."

"I *can't* rise," Li Juan said.

Lu did not look at Li Juan. "How much saliva does she have?"

Ming read his wife's face for an answer. "The normal amount."

"That is good," the little doctor said. "The jade liquor waters the organs and enables *qi* to flow more freely. And the volume of her monthly discharges?"

Li Juan laid a hand on Lu's shoulder. "What is the relevance of that question?"

Lu looked at Li Juan's hand as though he did not know what it was. Physicians were not used to familiarity from any patients, let alone women. "Excessive monthly bleeding dries out the brain. Your levels?"

Something like a smile formed on Li Juan's thin face. "My bleeding has lessened to almost nothing, Physician Lu."

Ming wished he could bury his face in his hands. Zhou had been kind to arrange for a physician visit for Li Juan. Even better, this man was no shaman or Taoist priest preaching about demons and sin. Lu came straight from the Office of Supreme Medicine and his craft was secular. Like all those in his field, he had taken the oaths to show compassion and to heal the sick as best he could. But it seemed this particular healer put more effort into another oath: never fraternize with patients.

The stone-faced doctor lean in close to Li Juan. "Red," he muttered. "Skin too red."

Watching the doctor examine Li Juan, Ming found himself thinking back to his childhood trips to the temples. Father had been a devout man who took his only son to pray on an unbending schedule. They went to Buddha on the fifth and tenth day of every week. But even as a boy, Ming had harbored doubts about praying to stone idols. The gods alone chose whom they heard, and no amount of supplication could change that. By the time Ming reached adolescence, his suspicion had become a certainty – praying to those serene faces of stone gave a person comfort, but beyond that it did nothing.

Worshippers lying prostrate before stone idols of Buddha. People begging in prayers so loud they were almost screams. Nervous husbands watching rude doctors perform exams. You could indulge any number of magic tricks to sell yourself the illusion of control, but in the end fate always collected its due.

Pain slid into Ming's gut like a dull blade. He felt tears pressing the backs of his eyes and turned away.

Lu felt Li Juan's temples, his sleeve drooping so low it nearly brushed the bed. "Give the woman rhubarb. It loosens blood in the vagina and the womb."

"Physician Lu," Li Juan said. "As we told Mandarin Zhou, we asked you here to help with the pain."

Lu turned to Ming. "You allow your wife to speak quite freely, don't you?"

Li Juan's hand went back to Lu's shoulder. "The pain, Physician Lu?"

Lu wrinkled his nose. The doctor seemed to take Li Juan's touch as a provocation. Ming thought the man was likely right.

"Pine tree," Lu said at last. "The resin eases discomfort and the tree's evergreen properties extend life. With proper living, a person can reach one-hundred-and-twenty years of age."

Li Juan said, "It is a shame, then, that I have not lived properly."

"Of course," Lu said, "a large part of health is related to piety. In this case, the issue of concern is a woman's subservience to her husband. That you haven't learned that principle is a shame indeed."

Li Juan's smile returned, and it was brighter than the last one. "I'm told excessive fornication exhausts one's energy. Do you recommend my husband and I stop fucking?"

Physician Lu blinked. He looked at Ming, as if seeking advice. Ming raised his hands and let them fall to his sides. Then the doctor hurried from the room, tripped over his long robe and was still off balance when he stumbled through the front door.

Ming watched the door slam home. "He might file a complaint against you."

"I'm not concerned with legal troubles these days." Li Juan lay back on her stone pillow. "How is your investigation coming along?"

"Li Juan." Ming felt tears threaten again, and this time he made no effort to stop them. "Li Juan, you are the bravest woman I have ever known."

"The case, Ming."

"It is all so slow." Ming sat by the bed. "The man we are looking for is elusive."

Li Juan grinned. "He vanishes like a bird and slithers unseen through the grass like a snake." Ming had once described a fugitive to her that way, and she had teased him for his flowery language ever since.

"Your husband has the soul of a poet," Ming said. "When will you realize how much you've been blessed?"

"You will catch him, though." Li Juan spoke with the cool, unassuming optimism she always had. She didn't predict good things. She believed in them the way people believe dawn will come. Even her illness hadn't changed that. "You'll catch him and then you'll return to the Gold Bird Guard. Full time, like before."

"I'll…what?"

Li Juan's eyes, half closed and ringed red, turned to Ming. "You don't have a choice. You cannot support a family on a tutor's wages. You tried and for that I am grateful. But it's not enough. Just promise me you will let Zhou give you a *safe* job. That will help with the fits, don't you think?"

Ming said nothing, and Li Juan smiled again. Here was another one of her traits: she always knew when her husband had acquiesced, even if he didn't answer her.

Li Juan's eyes closed. She placed a hand, brittle and dry, on Ming's. "Ming. Take me to the carnival."

Ming traced a finger along the back of his wife's hand. "It has been a while, hasn't it? The last time we went was just before Hui Fen was born."

Eyes still closed, Li Juan nodded for Ming to continue.

Ming looked at the ceiling and remembered. "Dusk has arrived but no one is worried about going home. They've lifted the curfew for the celebrations. The air is clean. It smells beautiful, the way the city smelled to me when I was young.

"You and I are walking down Heaven's Ford Street, your hand around my elbow as you tease me for my expensive clothes. The street is lined with trees. Cherry, elm, locust and others I pretend to know but could never really name. I point to the trees and give them my own names, always adamant that I'm correct. I'm so good I could be a palace gardener."

Li Juan laughed. It was a sharp, hollow lurching of the chest.

"There are tents too, tents beyond counting for the dancers, the singers and the storytellers. All the entertainers are out now, cavorting for the crowd and bringing waves of laughter as they mug for coins. We hardly glance at them, because now I'm boasting of how impressive my own skills are, how I've got the build of an acrobat and the grace of a dancer. You pinch me hard on the arm but you're laughing.

"We make our way down the street. The people around us are just decorations, sounds and sights for our pleasure. It's really just us in this beautiful world of song and shifting colors. I look down the tree-lined street and wish it went on forever."

Li Juan's head was to one side, her shallow breathing steady. Ming watched her, waiting to see if she would ask him to continue, but she did not stir.

Moving slowly, Ming lay down on the thin bed next to his wife. Fatigue was heavy on him now, and sleep came fast.

He dreamed of a creature with blue skin, a god that stole children from the night.

• • •

Ming grumbled. Someone was shaking him.

"Wake up, *Baba!*" A whisper.

Ming blinked the sleep from his eyes and turned toward the voice. "Hello, Hui Fen."

He put one hand over his mouth and with his other he pointed to the door. Hui Fen turned and headed out of the room, feet sliding soundlessly over the floor. Ming followed, closing the door softly behind him.

Hui Fen smiled up at him. A lot of children had crooked teeth, but hers were straight and white. Ming was immensely proud of that. "*Baba,* you were asleep forever!"

"If I've been asleep forever, this must be the afterlife," Ming said. "I take it you're one of my servants?"

Hui Fen giggled. "No!"

Ming put a finger to his lips and looked up at the ceiling. "Let's see. To start with, I want three casks of wine and a nice meal – something expensive. How about bear's head?"

Hui Fen's giggles turned to laughter. "I'm not your servant."

"Well, all right." Ming stretched his arms. "How long was I asleep?"

A woman's voice said, "Not so long."

Ming turned. Li Hua, his sister-in-law, was sitting by the fireplace and stirring a pot of congee in lazy circles. "Your friend's not here yet, Ming. Sit down and have some congee."

Ming accepted the bowl and ate a spoonful. "Thank you for being here again. I know it's a lot of work for you."

Li Hua nodded and pointed to the closed backroom door. "How is my sister?"

"Asleep." Ming did not know what else to say. He looked down at his bowl, suddenly not feeling hungry, not even wanting to smell food.

As he pushed the congee around his bowl with listless strokes, Ming noticed something. Wei Sheng was happily wrestling with his aunt's leg, but Hui Fen was motionless. She just watched him, her eyes heavy with concern beyond her years, her lower lip shaking. She looked, in fact, to be on the verge of breaking down.

She's getting old enough to understand. Not everything, but some things. Wei Sheng does not sense that his mother is going to die, but Hui Fen does. Maybe it's more than just a sense. Maybe she understands all of it. It's time to start watching what we say in front of her.

Three sharp knocks shook their front door.

Hui Fen jumped to her feet. The misery on her face had already given way to excitement. "I'll get it!"

Before Ming could intervene, his daughter flew across the room and slid the door open. "It's a man. A big man!"

"Ming?" Dragon's voice floated into the common room. "Ming, are you in there?"

Ming walked to the front door and glared at his daughter. "Impudent little girl. Answering the door like the man of the house now? Off with you!"

Hui Fen ran away, giggling.

Dragon was standing in the doorway with a confused smile on his face. "A daughter answering the door? Can't say I've seen that before."

"She could get away with bloody murder here and she knows it. Come in."

"Actually, I should wait out here." Dragon lifted his foot and showed it to Ming. "Everything below my knees is soaked with mud. Last night's storm turned the streets into little rivers."

Ming looked at Dragon's feet and wrinkled his nose. They were positively black with muck. "That's all right. Come in and leave your shoes on. Do your best to leave some tracks."

Dragon gave Ming another confused smile and followed him into the house.

Ming gestured toward Dragon. "Please meet Li Jian Guo. He is my partner in investigating the...the recent events. He goes by Dragon." Ming clucked his tongue silently. He had almost introduced Dragon as his friend. "Dragon, sit and have a bowl of congee."

Without being asked, Li Hua got to her feet and opened the metal pot over the fire. She began to ladle congee into it.

Ming glanced at his children. Wei Sheng was hiding behind his aunt's leg and peeking out at Dragon as though he were an angry monster. Hui Fen was standing in the middle of the room and staring at him with unabashed fascination. Ming supposed Dragon was probably used to that reaction from children.

Li Hua handed Dragon a cup of tea and placed a bowl of congee at his feet. Dragon gave her a slight bow, sat on a chair and turned to Ming. "Zhou sent a messenger to my home this morning. The message said –"

"I thought you couldn't read."

"I mean the messenger related it to me. He told me Zhou wants to meet us at the Red Sun at lunchtime. He also said Zhou has a meeting with Governor Han."

"Governor Han? Our friend Zhou is becoming an important fellow."

"The message was vague." Dragon picked up the wooden bowl and ate a spoonful of congee. "It just said he was pleading our case to the Governor."

"Of course," Ming said. An ambiguous message was no surprise. Zhou wouldn't want the messenger to know anything important. "This is good news."

"It's very good. Zhou is taking the initiative instead of sitting idle." Dragon wolfed down his congee and finished the tea in one gulp. He noticed Ming smiling at him. "Military men learn to eat fast. Shall we?"

They stood up.

Hui Fen ran to Dragon and tugged at his tunic. "Mr. Dragon? You're about the biggest man I ever saw! It was…" She paused, trying to remember the line she'd been told so many times. "It was…nice meeting you."

Dragon smiled. "It was nice meeting you, too."

"I have raised such a polite daughter," Ming said. He picked up an old rag next to the fireplace and tossed it to Hui Fen.

Hui Fen caught the rag out of reflex and looked at Ming questioningly.

Ming pointed at the mud on the floor. "I've told you more times than I can count not to answer the door. You can think about it while you're cleaning up that mud."

They left the house before the protests got too loud.

18

Zhou thought, *I'll never feel dignified in my office again.*

Governor Han's office was the most impressive room Zhou had ever seen. It was three times larger than Zhou's office, and the decorations alone looked more valuable than most people's homes. Clay soldiers stood in each corner, watching like silent sentries. There was a wall-size painting of a pagoda overlooking a snowy valley. A large wooden desk was the room's centerpiece, and on that desk sat a jade dragon made of the brightest, prettiest green Zhou had ever seen.

There were also two Gold Bird Guards in the office. They were just like the Guards in Zhou's corner of the Imperial Ministry, but their armor was a bit brighter, their chests a bit broader. They stood against the walls to Zhou's left and right, as still and silent as their clay counterparts.

More impressive than all that, however, was the little old man sitting behind the desk and picking his nose. The fellow was entirely bald save for a few wisps of gray hair that clung to the sides of his head. His skin was so dry it was cracking and red in places. He probably hadn't cut his nails in a year. Anyone who saw him on the street might well have dismissed him as a beggar.

But looks could be deceiving.

People called Governor Han the Snake. Some said he had gotten that name because of his duplicitous nature. Others claimed it was because he struck fast and hard at his enemies. Zhou suspected there was truth to both theories.

The Snake had a direct hand in all the daily functions of Changan, a city of two million people. When he first became Governor about three thousand years ago, he turned his attention to the city's crumbling walls. Within a year the old walls were knocked down, replaced with thick, impressive barricades three times the height of a man. There were countless other stories about Han's efficiency, about his ability to hammer at any problem until a solution was formed. In Zhou's opinion, this little old man could well be the most competent administrator in the Empire.

But there were other stories about the Snake – stories best told in whispers. Those stories were about political enemies strangled in brothels, about men stabbed in their beds while they slept. The most well-known rumor came from Han's younger years, before people started calling him the Snake. According to that story, Han had spent the better part of a year feuding with his most ambitious peers. Finally everyone managed to reconcile, and Han organized a wine-laden banquet to celebrate the bright future. Every one of his former enemies received a white flower, which Han insisted they attach to their clothing as a reminder of renewed friendships. Late in the evening thugs crashed through the doors, and everyone who wore a white flower was cut down.

Zhou could not verify that story, but it felt safer to assume it was true.

The palace had ordered Han to adjudicate the case against Mr. Lin. Ultimately, this dirty little man would give the Emperor his opinion on Lin's guilt or innocence. After that, the Emperor would decide for himself. That was likely to be a formality, though. The Emperor would almost certainly accept Han's ruling.

Governor Han. The Snake himself. And I'm sitting across from him, watching him pick his nose.

Zhou wanted to steal a glance at Commandant Chen. The old piss pot was right next to him, looking entirely at ease. That was not surprising. After all, Chen was used to being around powerful men.

Governor Han finished mining his nose. He examined the spoils on the tip of his finger and flicked them away. "Right. We're here to discuss the case against Lin, the man accused of the child murders."

Zhou's palms began to sweat. He swallowed so loudly he felt sure it was audible in the next room. When he was plotting at home last night, it was easy to think of this as a game. Sitting here with the Snake, he felt that illusion shatter like a vase thrown against a wall.

If I'm found out they'll strangle me in the West Market.

The Snake turned to Chen. "You. Commandant Chan."

"Uh, Chen, Sir."

"Chen. You believe we've got the right man?"

"I do, Governor. The Lei Lei child's bracelet was in Lin's lock box. He still has not given a credible reason for it's being there."

"You interrogated him?"

"Yes, Governor. The palace tasked me personally with finding the killer." Chen paused, waiting for some reaction from the Snake. When it became clear he would never get one, he continued. "I therefore interrogated the suspect quite thoroughly."

"I trust," Han said, "that you used the sanctioned techniques?"

"I did. I tested his ears to ensure he could hear my questions and checked his face for redness. I listened for rapid breathing and made sure his eyes were clear."

Zhou wanted to roll his eyes. The techniques Chen listed were indeed part of the standard interrogation method, but they only worked if the interviewer was competent. A man like Chen might have government texts committed to memory, but he lacked the innovation to use them effectively. And the saddest part of it all was the city had hundreds of men like Chen. Perhaps thousands.

Han said, "Have you gotten a confession?"

"No. Not yet."

"Torture?"

"Not yet."

Han nodded. "And you arrested him because of information given by two witnesses, correct?"

"Yes, Sir. They saw Lin talking to the child on numerous occasions, even though he had no reason to do so. *And* they noticed him looking at the child's bracelet. After the killing, I mean. They saw him sitting at his stall and staring at it with a strange look on his face."

Zhou frowned and exhaled loudly.

The Snake said, "Anything else?"

"One more thing. We are operating on the belief that the abductor knew the child. Otherwise he could never have gotten close to her. She would have screamed and run away. And we know with certainty that Lin and the girl were well acquainted."

"I see." The Snake looked at Zhou. "You. You are Mandarin Zhou, correct?"

"Yes, Governor."

"You fought very hard to be in this meeting."

"I did, Governor." That was true enough. As a fourth level mandarin, Zhou had no business in this extravagant office. He had exploited every one of his connections for access, claiming all the while his conscience would not let him rest.

"You believe in Lin's innocence," Han said. "That is why you're here?"

"Yes, Sir. My conscience would not let me rest."

"Tell me why you have doubts," the Snake said.

Zhou cleared his throat and prepared to commit treason. "First of all, Sir, the evidence we have against this man is quite weak." Treason wasn't the only risk Zhou was taking. He was also crossing Chen, his superior. If Zhou did not depose Chen, he would have an enemy who wanted nothing more than to see him bleed to death in the dust.

"A victim's bracelet among Lin's things is not weak evidence," the Snake said.

"It's not damning evidence either – not by itself. I can think of ten ways it could have gotten there."

"Such as?"

"He could have found it on the street. Any commoner would pick up a bracelet made of mutton fat jade if –"

Chen said, "Who would drop such an object? Even a child –"

Governor Han swung his gaze on Chen. "You do not interrupt another mandarin during a formal interview. It is highly disrespectful of the process. Do you understand?" In that moment Han really did resemble a snake, some man-sized serpent with slitted eyes and a forked tongue, about to strike across the table and devour Chen.

Poor Commandant Chen withered under the Snake's glare. "I am sorry, Governor Han."

When Han turned back to Zhou, his face was mild again. "Continue."

"Sir, my point is that we really have very little evidence against this man. In my eyes a bracelet is far too coincidental. I even find it rather suspicious."

Han glanced down at a scroll on his desk. "You're referring to the witnesses? Toad and Blossom? You think they may have planted the bracelet to set up Chen and obtain the reward?"

The Snake is no fool, Zhou thought. "I certainly believe it is a possibility. The accusers are of, uh, low moral standing. I asked around. They're known in the West Market for extorting the vendors and pushing out the people they dislike. They even tell people they're related to a seventh level mandarin. That is a complete fabrication. They say it to intimidate the locals."

Zhou was finding this harder than he had expected. He was openly arguing for one outcome: the exoneration of Mr. Lin. In reality he needed to create the opposite result. What if his false arguments were too effective and he freed Mr. Lin? Even worse, what if he said the wrong thing and this old serpent that looked like a man sniffed it out? He wished he had thought to eat bat brains before coming here. The physicians claimed nothing was better for boosting the memory, and Zhou agreed.

"Anything else?" Governor Han asked.

Zhou made himself focus. "Only that I believe we should not rush to judgment, Sir. If it turns out this man is innocent, we will have committed a grievous error. And when the public sees that error we will look…bad." He swallowed hard again. He had almost said *we will look like fools.* Implying that the Snake might look foolish could not be a good idea.

Han turned back to Commandant Chen. "Your response to that?"

Zhou looked at Chen. This was the moment that would decide everything. He had told Toad and Blossom exactly what to say when they went to the Commandant's office. He had warned them again and again not to deviate from the plan at all. Once again, Zhou scolded himself for trusting a pair of thugs. What if they betrayed him? What if Chen simply hadn't believed them? Who knew? The old man might be smarter than Zhou believed.

Zhou saw Chen smiling triumphantly and knew there was nothing to fear. The old man had taken the bait offered by Toad and Blossom.

"Your honor," Chen said. "I have news that will cast this entire issue in a different light."

"And what news is that?"

Chen's smile widened. "The accusers have waived their reward."

Zhou expected Han to be surprised, but the Governor's face did not change. "Oh?"

"Yes," Chen said. "They were offended when I asked if they were doing this for money. Without any urging from me, they volunteered to forego the ten thousand coppers. The woman told me it was a question of honor."

Zhou tried to look impatient, as though anxious to refute that point. When Han invited him to speak, he said, "Sir, these two people are not terribly smart. My guess is when they hatched this scheme they did not understand the gravity of their crime. Now they do understand it, and they're afraid of a perjury accusation. They're desperate to give up the money and save themselves. And I remind you again that an innocent man is going to pay for their chicanery with his life. An *innocent man.*"

Han was unmoved. "Passing up ten thousand coppers is an enormous gesture for a commoner. That gives their testimony credibility. There is more evidence to consider, but I am probably going to tell the Emperor we have the right man and the terror is over."

Zhou wanted to jump from his seat and raise his fists in the air. He was winning! He was going to secure Lin's execution while appearing to oppose it! All he needed now was for the killer to murder another child. Then he could shake his head mournfully and say *I tried to tell you.*

Zhou watched the Snake making notes on his scroll. The talk about him was true. He really was an intelligent fellow. But he should have known better. Intelligent or not, he had bowed to the pressure and trusted evidence that was clearly flawed. Well, when this was all said and done he was going to look bad, too.

An image came to Zhou's mind. He saw himself as an older man. He was sitting where the Snake was right now. Zhou saw himself conducting meetings and passing down decisions. He saw himself attacking problems and cutting through the bureaucratic nonsense that was stifling the city's potential. He saw younger mandarins around him, men who learned from him that cooperation and flexibility were always better than pettiness and nepotism.

Zhou took a deep breath. *One step at a time. If your ambition gets too big too fast, you'll trip up.*

Governor Han put his quill down. "Dismissed, gentlemen."

Zhou and Chen stood up and bowed.

• • •

They entered the hallway together. Just as in Zhou's section of the building, the corridors here were teeming with important men walking to and fro. The only difference was these men were older and looked to be in less of a hurry.

Chen waited for the Snake's office door to close. Then he turned to Zhou. "You're going to regret doing that, Mandarin Zhou. Your eyes got too big, and now I have no choice but to pluck them out."

Zhou did his best to look abashed. "I was only doing what I felt was right, Sir."

"You were trying to discredit me, to usurp me."

Quite right, you doddering old fool. "I assure you that was not the case."

Chen waved his hand like a man shooing away a mosquito. "Your time comes soon." He turned and headed down the giant corridor, his robe billowing behind him.

We'll see, Zhou thought. He began walking in the opposite direction. The first part of his plan had gone flawlessly. Now he had to deal with Ming and Dragon. It was still important that they solve this mystery, but they couldn't do it until Mr. Lin was in the ground. Only then could Zhou have the double victory of catching the killer and making Chen look like an ass.

Zhou smiled as he walked down the building's front steps. The thought of Chen's humiliation really was pleasing. Why, just now the old fool had grinned as he promised Zhou's demise. Zhou could not wait to grin back at the bastard, to say something cutting as Chen felt the full weight of his disgrace. *Tell me again what you were going to do?*

It would be especially lovely if Chen figured out that Zhou had duped him. Unfortunately, the old man was likely too stupid to see the whole picture. Well, perhaps Zhou could simply tell him.

But no, this wasn't about personal grudges. It wasn't even about Zhou's advancement. It was about making the city a better place, about doing away with stuffy traditions.

It was for a higher cause.

Zhou hurried out of the Ministry's courtyard and made his way along the thoroughfare. He shook off the dreams of glory and focused his mind. He had an appointment with Ming and Dragon at the Red Sun Restaurant soon.

Zhou thought of the letter he had asked Ming and Dragon to write. Sitting at home last night, he had realized that requesting that letter was a lapse in judgment. It had the potential to free Lin, so it was a threat.

But Zhou had already discerned a way to solve that problem. In theory his play was a risky one, but Ming and Dragon would never know. After all, Zhou was their only source of information on activity in the Imperial Ministry. After manipulating Governor Han and Commandant Chen, Zhou knew he could handle a couple of thief catchers. He hurried down the street, feeling like a man in control of the world.

19

The Red Sun Restaurant was packed to the walls. The tables were lined with benches on which people sat shoulder to shoulder. Some who couldn't claim a spot on a bench settled for knee-high footstools instead. The least fortunate diners stood against walls or pillars, holding their bowls close to their mouths. Servers weaved through the chaos with expert skill.

Ming and Dragon had managed to secure spots on benches. They were better off than the footstool people, but not by much. Ming was squashed between two other men, his arms pinned tight against his body. Dragon was sitting across from Ming. People pressed up against him as well, but they may as well have been pushing a boulder. The giant didn't appear uncomfortable in the least.

Ming looked down at his congee and wondered why he had even ordered it. He still didn't have a trace of an appetite. He was just too nervous.

Zhou was due to show up any moment and collect their letter. Ming knew they had written out an excellent argument. Refuting the evidence against Lin was child's play. But would anyone even read it? The government wanted desperately for the terror to be over, and in Ming's experience that desperation could lead to willful blindness. Some mandarin or commandant might accept the letter from Zhou, put it aside and forget all about it. If that happened, Lin would be finished.

Lin's death would be tragic enough, but the consequences wouldn't stop there. The real killer would also benefit. If the government executed the wrong man, a scandal would consume the city. Dealing with that scandal would distract everyone from catching the *right* man. The madman might take three more little ones before the city could regroup and start a new investigation.

And of course, faith in the city's leaders would be shaken to the core.

Ming asked himself how the Sorcerer would have handled this. Would he have planted some sort of evidence exonerating Lin? Or would he have turned a blind eye himself, believing Lin had to be executed for the sake of civil order? He had no idea. More and more, the Sorcerer felt like a separate person to Ming, a stranger whose motives could not be fathomed.

Dragon finished the last of his food. "Not hungry?" He eyed Ming's bowl.

Ming pushed his bowl across the table. "Here."

As Dragon inhaled Ming's food, he pointed to a spot in the crowd. "Look. There's Zhou now."

Ming turned. Zhou was working his way through the ocean of people. His bright mandarin's robe made him look out of place in this restaurant full of common folk. The rigid look on his face only increased the effect. He seemed terrified that some ruffian might grab him by the shoulders and berate him for no reason.

By the time Zhou arrived at their table, he looked so uncomfortable that Ming had to smile.

Dragon gestured to the packed benches. "I would invite you to sit, but…"

"It's all right." Zhou frowned at the chaos around him. "I can't stay. I just came to tell you my meeting with Governor Han did not go well. He indicated he's leaning heavily toward naming Lin the killer."

Ming said, "You mean he's going to say that to the Emperor?"

"It appears so," Zhou said. "And the Emperor will likely accept whatever Han tells him."

Dragon slammed his bowl down on the table. The loud *bang* was lost in the restaurant's bustle. "This is madness! Will no one in this damned government listen to reason?"

Ming looked over his shoulder, suddenly grateful for the loud noise around them. In theory a man could criticize the government. In practice it could cost him his head. "But you'll be able to deliver our letter to Han before he makes his final decision?"

"I believe so." Zhou put his hand out, palm up. "Is the letter ready?"

"Just a moment." Ming opened his satchel and rummaged through it.

Dragon said, "Zhou, perhaps we should go with you when you call on Han. We can support your arguments and help answer questions about the investigation."

"I'm afraid that wouldn't be a good idea." A pained look crossed Zhou's face. "You see, men like Governor Han are used to dealing only with…a certain kind of people."

Dragon took a long drink of tea and belched through his teeth. "What does that mean?"

Ming chuckled. "It means Han doesn't like unwashed peasants like you and me, Dragon." He found the letter and handed it to Zhou. "Isn't that right?"

Zhou bowed his head as he accepted the letter. "I'm afraid so. My understanding is that Han *never* speaks to…er…commoners."

Dragon was not amused. "You could talk to him first. If he is as intelligent as people say, he'll listen."

"I would rather you two continue your investigation," Zhou said. "Let me deal with the bureaucrats."

Ming nodded. "He's right, Dragon. We wouldn't be much use to Zhou in the Snake's office."

"All right," Dragon said slowly. "If that's how you both feel I won't argue."

Zhou looked down at the letter in his hands. "Will *this* be of much use?"

"That depends," Ming said. "Are your superiors so deluded that they will turn away from the truth and cover their ears?"

"Are they actively courting catastrophe?" Dragon added.

Zhou snorted. "No, but sometimes it seems like they are."

Dragon stood up and put his hand on Zhou's shoulder. It seemed that if he squeezed he could pierce skin and break bone. "What else can we do? How can we convince them?"

"I just told you. You can keep going with your investigation." Zhou pulled free from Dragon's grasp. It seemed to make him uncomfortable. "You've already been sidetracked too much."

Dragon reached into his pocket and produced the strange purple fruit they had found yesterday. "Has your eunuch discovered anything about this?"

Zhou stared. "That. Right."

Dragon's large hand closed around the fruit. He stuffed it back into his pocket. "You didn't even check, did you?"

"I forgot," Zhou said. "I'm sorry."

"Today." Dragon pointed a meaty finger at Zhou. "Find out today, Zhou. Who sells this fruit? Where do they sell it? Who buys it? We need to know it all."

Zhou began to shift on his feet. "I'll try, but you need to understand that I'm going to be quite busy today. I am going to visit some of the more levelheaded officials I know and try to garner more support. Plus I have other obligations. Mandarins have to…" Zhou saw the way Dragon was looking at him and trailed off. "All right. I'll send Hai Tao out today."

"Zhou," Dragon said. "Is your eunuch competent? Do you trust him with these tasks?"

"Absolutely. He's only been with me for a few months but he's proven reliable. In the meantime, what is your plan?"

Ming said, "We need to discover how the madman learned the secrets of such powerful people. We're going to interview the victims' parents today."

"That's good," Zhou said. "In that case I will leave the experts to their work. I will meet you tonight at the Green Ale House, right after my shift ends. You know where that is?"

"Sure," Dragon said. "Right by the Imperial Ministry."

"That's right." Zhou bowed, turned and headed for the exit.

Ming watched his friend squeezing through the crowd. He certainly was in a hurry to leave. He had seemed different, too…distracted. Well, they were all under a great deal of strain. He turned to Dragon. "Are you ready to find some rich people and ask uncomfortable questions?"

"Ming," Dragon said. "Will these people recognize the Sorcerer?"

"No. They know they were saved from disgrace by someone in the government, but they have no idea who that someone was."

"Will they recognize you at all? Remember you from the investigations?"

"Some might," Ming said. "But to them I was just another Guard. Nothing of note."

"Whom should we speak with first?"

"Let's start with Guang Fu, the cavalryman."

"A cavalryman," Dragon said. "I will be useful in that conversation. Let me take the lead?"

"All right."

"We need to find out everything we can. But remember the most important question: how did the madman learn Guang Fu's secrets?"

Ming stood up. "It's a shame Zhou can't come with us. Monks and shopkeepers might be willing to speak with private investigators, but the wealthy elite? They may say we don't have the authority to question them."

"Doesn't matter. We have the *air* of authority. Look at you, Ming. You left the Gold Bird Guard a year ago but you're starting to carry yourself like one of them again. I'd wager you feel it yourself."

Ming realized Dragon was right. He *was* starting to feel like his old self again – not the Ming from his Sorcerer days, but from his earliest days in the Guard. It was in the way he moved, in the way he felt faster, stronger. He glanced down at his body, half expecting to see a set of armor on his chest. "I hope you're right. But if we do get any resistance, just find something heavy and break it."

"I'll do that. Let's go."

20

Lee stood behind his stall and tried to size up the man across from him. This customer looked like the serious type, the kind of punter who had a budget he held sacred and would not break. On the other hand, he had been examining that painting in his hands for some time and he seemed to like it. Some bargaining might be possible, but just a little.

The man looked down at Lee's other paintings. "Why do you have so many pictures of Zhong Kui?"

"Because," Lee said. "He is the protector of the common people. The other gods sit in Heaven and watch us like a child watching ants. But not Zhong Kui. He gets involved in our affairs and kills any demons who threaten us."

"It's very nice."

Lee smiled. Just that morning he had promised the witch Blossom he would paint more. He had already started to deliver on that promise. He had just finished the Zhong Kui painting, and it was his best work in ages. Why, it was hardly dry and he was already close to selling it. And this was only the beginning. This week he would work every night, would work until his eyes were sore and his fingers ached.

There was no other choice. Some vendors were saying they had finally driven off Toad and Blossom for good, but Lee did not believe it.

The gangsters would come back. When that happened, there would be a reckoning. Lee knew he had better be ready to pay what he owed.

The customer held the painting out at arm's length and squinted at it. "I could use something like this. For my daughter, I mean. She needs protection."

Lee nodded somberly. "The dead are everywhere. Whenever a son fails to venerate his ancestors there are more spirits that do not rest."

"I mean protection from the murderer."

Lee nodded again. "Crime is rampant in this city. It is a plague." He was the world's most agreeable man when it was time to make a sale.

"No." The man placed the painting back on the stall and looked at Lee. "I am talking about the child killings. The real villain may still be out there."

Lee sat down and began to tidy up the paintings on his table. Like most people in the market, he did not believe Mr. Lin was guilty. But one did not contradict the city's investigators, especially in the presence of strangers.

The man picked up the painting again. "Forty coppers."

Lee barked a single shrill laugh. It was a calculated noise he had made countless times in his life. "Sir, you cannot be serious."

"Oh, but I am. What price are you asking?"

"Seventy-five."

The man grinned. "It's too early to ask me for such a price. You see, I haven't been to an ale house yet. Perhaps if I were drunk…"

Lee decided that he liked this customer. Even better, this looked like a sale. People usually didn't stay this long unless they meant to give you their business in the end. "How about this? I'll charge you fifty, but –"

Lee's voice was cut off by a high, shrill yell. It came from somewhere to his left. Every head turned in that direction, as though they were all controlled by invisible strings.

Lee's vision was getting worse by the year, but there was nothing wrong with his hearing. Whoever had screamed was a woman, and she sounded familiar. It had to be another vendor.

Now Lee heard a different voice. The new speaker was male, and he had the calm, assured tones of authority.

The woman answered with more screaming.

This time Lee recognized the voice. It was Yu Shuan, the old woman who had saved him from Blossom that morning.

Lee cupped a hand to his ear. He heard Yu Shuan say, "But you *can't!*"

Lee's heart sank. The authorities had probably come to cause trouble. It wouldn't be the first time. Sometimes the government sent Gold Bird Guards to extort money. Other times it seemed they just wanted to remind merchants they were despised.

He turned to his customer. "I'm sorry. We'll have to conclude our business another time."

"We can conclude it now," the man said. He counted out fifty coppers and placed them on Lee's stall.

Lee was never one to turn down money. "My thanks." He scooped up the coppers and handed the man his painting.

A large crowd was forming near Yu Shuan's stall. Lee stepped out from behind his stall and began elbowing his way forward. It was no easy task. More and more people were gathering to see the spectacle. Finally, huffing and sweating, Lee came to the edge of a rough circle that had formed around the combatants.

Yu Shuan was standing in front of her fruit stall. Her hair was disheveled and she was panting in great heaves. The lychees and jujubes she sold were scattered on the ground around her, making Lee think of colorful toys some careless child hadn't picked up.

Two Gold Bird Guards were speaking to Yu Shuan. They were both young, and they seemed to fear Yu Shuan as though she were an angry tiger.

Yu Shuan planted her hands on her hips and glared up at the closest Guard. "I pay my taxes and I break no laws. Why are you doing this to me? I even gave my only son to the Emperor. He was killed in the army."

Lee made a silent gasp. He didn't know that.

The closer of the two Guards unrolled a scroll and held it up like a shield. "The authorities have decreed –"

"Speak up, boy," Yu Shuan shouted. "Let the others hear your *decree.*"

The other Guard jabbed a finger in Yu Shuan's face. *"Quiet!"*

Lee and the rest of the crowd started to grumble. Yu Shuan might be a pushy old lady sometimes, but she stood up for people. Why, just today she had pulled Lee from the fire.

The Guard holding the scroll cleared his throat. "The authorities have decreed that those behind on their permit payments must settle their back fees immediately or face eviction."

Terror churned in Lee's gut. Like most people in the West Market, he was always a bit behind on his permit fees. After all, he paid an additional management fee to Toad and Blossom every week. The authorities often hassled merchants about paying up, but in the end they settled for a fraction of what they were owed. Now, however, it seemed they were demanding everything. Lee couldn't come close to paying all of that.

Then again, *no one* would be able to pay all their back fees at once. The government couldn't possibly evict everyone from the market…could they?

Yu Shuan poked the first Gold Bird Guard in the chest, bringing a ripple of laughter from the onlookers. "Who is behind this, boy?"

As Yu Shuan spoke, the crowd opposite Lee began to part. Another, older Gold Bird Guard stepped into the circle. At least a dozen more Guards behind were him. The new Guard crossed his arms and looked levelly at Yu Shuan. "There was a complaint. It alleges that most of you vendors are behind on your payments. The authorities have looked into it, and it's worse than the usual problem of being behind by a few weeks. This time we can't let it pass."

Yu Shuan seemed to sense that she couldn't bully this man as she had the two younger Guards. When she spoke again, her voice was more subdued. "Who made the complaint?"

A female voice said, "I did."

More movement in the crowd. Blossom and Toad stepped into the clearing. Blossom stared down at Yu Shuan, her face smug and satisfied.

"I went to my uncle and told him that not a single vendor here is paying permit fees on time."

The older Gold Bird Guard raised his voice and looked at the crowed. "I'll say it again. We know many of you vendors have been disregarding your financial obligations to the crown. We have all your records right here and we will deal with everyone individually. Those of you who cannot meet your obligations must be ready to leave the market immediately."

Lee saw Blossom say something to Yu Shuan. He could not make out what the witch was saying, but he could hear the gloating tone of her voice. Yu Shuan stared up at Blossom and said something back.

Blossom scoffed and turned to the crowd. "I warned you all, didn't I? I told you just this morning that our uncle wouldn't abide a bunch of vendors making trouble. You have only yourselves to blame."

Toad crossed his arms and grinned like the idiot he was. "Yeah!"

Lee's panic grew. *They may not be able to push everyone out of the market, but they can evict the people who have crossed them. That includes me.*

Blossom said something to the officer in charge. The officer nodded and shouted a command. The other Gold Bird Guards jumped into action.

Lee spun around and made for his stall. He did not have a great deal of cash but he did have one very valuable possession: a jade carving of the god Zhong Kui. It had been in Lee's family for three generations, and it was worth at least fifty of Lee's paintings. Some would have deemed it foolish to keep such a treasure here in the market, but Lee did not. He liked to have the statue where he could keep an eye on it.

If Lee really was evicted, that statue would be the key to his survival. He could sell it and live on the money while he figured things out. The idea of parting with a family heirloom was a horrendous one, but Lee knew his ancestors would understand.

Lee fought his way through the crowd, elbowing people aside and muttering distracted apologies. Everyone was moving now, and the mob tossed him around like a small boat in rough seas. Lee hardly noticed. He needed to hurry. If the wrong Guard found the statue, Lee would never see it again.

The crowd finally spat Lee out in front of his stall. He grabbed the lockbox in which he kept the statue. Sweat stung his eyes and blurred his vision as he tried to worry the crude thing open.

He felt tears threatening. What would happen to him? He had worked in this market for most of his life and he had no other skills. Hell, his wife died twenty years ago and his only daughter died five years after that. Where would he go?

At least the money for this statue would buy him some time if the worst came.

Going to make it. Have to hide this statue in my clothes and pray they don't search me.

"Hello, Lee."

Lee stood up and turned around, his hands empty. "Blossom."

Blossom was standing in front of Lee's stall. She was flanked by two Gold Bird Guards. "I asked my uncle to look up your records."

"All right."

Blossom put her hand out, palm up, to one of the Gold Bird Guards. The man placed a scroll in her hand.

Blossom opened the scroll and looked it over. "Hmmm. It says here you're quite behind on your payments, Lee. More than three moons, in fact."

Lee crossed his arms. He wanted to tell Blossom he knew damn well she couldn't read, but he restrained himself. "I could have met those costs if I didn't have to pay protection fees to you and your brother as well."

"You heard the announcement," Blossom said. "We're here to collect what you owe."

"What are you going to do, Blossom? Empty out the entire market?"

"Just the dead weight." Blossom grinned, exposing her brown teeth.

Lee took a step forward and looked up at Blossom. "How did you manage this? This behavior is outrageous even for you. What officials are you and your brother in bed with?" Lee never spoke to anyone this way, but he was too angry to stop himself. Just a moment ago he had been in the middle of a sale and tending to the dull affairs of his life. Now Blossom was going to tear that life from him. And why? Because he had been pulled into this morning's confrontation?

"I have given you enough chances over the years," Blossom said. "You and the rest have shirked your responsibilities for too long. I had no choice but to tell my uncle about it."

Lee opened his mouth to protest, and then closed it with a *snap*. Amazement took hold of him. "Blossom. What is your uncle's name?"

One of the Gold Bird Guards furrowed his brow and glanced down at the skinny woman.

For just an instant, Blossom showed a trace of fear. Then her face darkened with anger. "Two thousand coppers!" Her voice rose to a trilling shriek. *"Now!"*

Lee knew he should have been miserable with fear, but he felt himself smiling. "What was he again, Blossom? A seventh level mandarin? A general in the Army of Divine Strategy? Maybe you're related to the Emperor himself!"

"Arrogant bastard!" Blossom whacked one of the Gold Bird Guards in the chest, making him jump. "He can't pay! Turn him out! You have your orders, so do it!"

The two men walked around to Lee's side of the stall. One of them said, "She's right. You owe two thousand. Can you pay?"

At the sound of the Guard's voice, Lee's giddy rebellion vanished. He felt the reality of his new life pressing on him. "No. I can't even come close."

The Guard's voice dropped to a whisper. "So maybe you don't give us everything. Give us *something,* just a bit to stave your creditors off until things calm down. You might still get out of this."

Lee smiled and patted the Guard's hand. "I appreciate your concern. But do you really think she is here for money?"

"No." The Guard stared at the ground. He was at least forty, and the scars slashed across his face said he had seen his share of fights. But right then he looked like a boy wearing his father's uniform. "No, she isn't."

Blossom stalked over to Lee. "Two thousand coppers. Let's have it."

"I cannot pay."

"A pity." Blossom beamed at Lee. "In that case we've got no choice but to turn you out on your worthless ass."

Lee glanced around his stall. He had never thought he might end his life as a pauper, but now that future was staring him in the face. He knelt down, picked up his lock box and put it in his satchel. "I am going."

Blossom pointed at the satchel. "What's in *that?*"

Lee started pushing through the crowd.

Blossom screeched, "Wait!"

Lee stopped. He wanted to pull the satchel close to his body but he didn't. "What is it?"

"You know what." Blossom extended her hand again. "Being unable to pay the full amount doesn't free you of your obligations. You still have to pay what you can."

"The contents of this satchel represent almost all the money I have," Lee said. "Without this I will be destitute."

Blossom grinned. Her hand did not move.

"Blossom, you can go to hell," Lee said.

Blossom turned to the Guard next to her. "Confiscate that bag."

The Guard started forward.

The Guard with the facial scars shouted an order, and the other man stopped immediately.

Blossom spun on the Guard. "What are you *doing?* You're under orders to move these people out."

The scarred man said, "That's right. I am under orders to move out those who cannot pay their back fees. I received no orders to collect punitive fees from those who don't pay."

Lee started to back away.

"Lee, don't you go anywhere," Blossom shouted. "I'm not done with you. Don't you *dare* leave."

Lee turned and started walking, ignoring the shouts that followed him. What else could Blossom do? Kill him? If he couldn't make a living he would starve on the street anyway.

He hurried through the market, clutching his satchel as though it were a magic talisman. As he moved he heard a volley of shouts, followed by a loud crash. Lee turned and saw a stall lying on its side. Pieces of bread rolled away from it in all directions. A guard was standing next to the stall and shouting at a female vendor.

All around Lee the same chaos was unfolding. How had this happened? What sudden power had Blossom and Toad found?

Lee realized he did not care. Life as he had always known it was over. As he found an alley and started down it, he felt the first tears come.

• • •

Blossom and Toad stood at the edge of the market and watched the chaos. They both wanted to move in for a closer look, but they restrained themselves. Walking among the vendors right now would be unwise. Blossom could imagine them dragging her into an alley and quietly slitting her throat.

Blossom's gaze drifted over to the Gold Bird Guard with the scarred face. The ugly bastard was standing just twenty paces away. He was also watching the mayhem, the corners of his mouth turned down in disgust.

Blossom tore her gaze from the Guard, but soon she was staring at him again. That man had defied her. She had told him to confiscate Lee's bag, and he ignored her! He knew full well that he was supposed to follow her every order. That was part of her price for giving the false testimony Zhou wanted. She was to have total authority over this undertaking. She reminded herself to get the Guard's name before this was all over.

Toad was holding a jug of wine. He had only started on it a few moments ago but it was almost empty. He took another drink and wiped his mouth with the tunic of his sleeve. "Sister, what're you staring at?"

"The self-righteous Guard over there."

Toad squinted. "The scarred one? What'd he do?"

"I told him to take Lee's bag and he refused. He let the old man go!" Even thinking about it was enough to make Blossom's skin feel hot.

"Some people just don't have the skill to work with others," Toad said. Wine always made him philosophical. "What can you do?"

"I'm going to make Zhou dismiss him."

Toad was tipping his jug back again. He stopped mid-tip and frowned. "We can't tell him to do anything. He already paid us half the reward and this is the rest of our price." He looked over the market and grinned. "I think it's a fair deal. With this deadwood swept away, we'll have a hundred new people bidding to get into the market."

"It's not going to end with this," Blossom said. "Think about it. Zhou has gotten into bed with a pair of criminals."

"You mean us." Toad giggled.

"Yes. Us. We know he is conspiring to get Lin executed, and we can hold that secret over him for the rest of his life. Brother, we're going to have a mandarin at our beck and call!"

Toad looked up at the sky and hashed it out. Finally his face lit up with understanding. "Right! Because we can sell him out whenever we want to." Then the smile turned to confusion. "But if we betray him, won't we be executed too?"

"I don't think he would risk that kind of disgrace. Either way, you let me handle it."

"Sure." Toad threw back the last of his wine.

When Blossom turned back to the market, she saw a tiny figure fighting its way through the mass of bodies. Blossom squinted. Her eyesight was poor, but even at this distance she recognized the figure as Yu Shuan. The old woman was carrying a giant bundle in her arms, and she was coming right toward Blossom.

As Blossom watched Yu Shuan struggle to carry the last of her things from the market, a smile formed on her face. It served the old bat right for meddling all these years. She had never stopped butting into the affairs of others, despite Blossom's repeated warnings. Yu Shuan only had herself to blame for this unfortunate turn.

Yu Shuan stopped in front of Blossom. Beads of sweat were tumbling down her wrinkled forehead.

Blossom's grin widened. "Where are you heading now, Yu Shuan? I trust you have somewhere to go?"

Yu Shuan looked Blossom up and down. For a moment her face hardened and she looked ready to give a rebuke. Instead she turned and walked away without a word.

Toad giggled again. "She's not so smart now."

Blossom nodded. "Sore loser."

Toad held out his jug to Blossom. "Here, Sister. It's time to celebrate!"

Blossom opened her mouth to say no, but the word died before it left her lips. She looked back at Yu Shuan. The old woman was turning down a side alley that led out of the market.

Toad was studying Blossom. "What is it, Sister?"

"I just had an idea. You'll see." Blossom took the jug. It *was* time to celebrate. They had taken risks most people wouldn't dare contemplate. Now they were reaping the first rewards for their bravery. Things were good, and they were only going to get better. She took a long swallow, wincing as the sickly-sweet liquid slid down her throat.

When she turned to watch the Gold Bird Guards clear out the rest of the market, she was smiling again.

21

Zhou loved coming to the Imperial Archives. This was the only place in Changan where a man could turn his attention to study and escape the interfering nonsense of officialdom. There was no one here to tap you on the shoulder, no endless bureaucracy to contend with. In fact, aside from the silent Guards and attendants, the only people here were mandarins hunched over their work. In Zhou's opinion, the Archives' silence was as valuable as its ocean of scrolls.

Zhou also loved the Archives' design. The high walls and ornate paintings gave study a dignity that was sadly lacking elsewhere in the city. Over Zhou's shoulder, a woman in a long gown smiled at herself in a mirror. Zhou always worked under that painting. It was so lifelike he believed one day those smiling eyes would look up from the mirror and settle on him. Whoever built this place clearly understood that China owed its glory not only to the farmers and the builders, but also to the learned men who guided them.

Coming here always reminded Zhou of the days when he was preparing for his exams. To call those times stressful would be a wild understatement. The pressure on a young man studying for the tests was crushing. The candidate's family spent a fortune preparing him. They hired tutors, procured study materials, and sent him to places like this. It was the family's investment in the future.

But it was a gamble.

If the young man passed the exams, he would likely find work in China's massive bureaucracy. His family would be comfortable for life. Because sons of mandarins got favorable postings, future generations could be secure as well. But if the boy failed, he would pass into obscurity and all the family's support would have gone for nothing.

The system was not a sympathetic one. Only about one in one hundred candidates passed. Zhou had passed, however, and over the years he had learned to forget the misery of that time and look back on it with fondness.

Zhou looked down at his table. In front of him were two open scrolls. One of them was the letter Ming had written in Mr. Lin's defense. Zhou was writing on the other one. He dipped his brush into a bowl of ink and wrote his letter's last few characters. Then he picked up both letters and read them.

Zhou's version began with a spirited defense of Mr. Lin and moved on to a scathing attack against the prosecution. But a practiced eye would note that it provided no solid evidence in Mr. Lin's favor. It left out mention of the odd fruit Dragon and Ming had found. And of course, Zhou didn't mention that he himself had seen the killer and knew the madman was much larger than Lin.

Zhou's letter ended with a long lecture on the government's moral responsibilities. That part was going to be essential after Mr. Lin's innocence came to light. It was written evidence that only one man had the courage and foresight to speak out amidst the hysteria.

Zhou put his name at the end of the new letter. He reminded himself to burn Ming's letter as soon as he had some privacy.

Zhou wanted more time to refine his letter, but that wasn't possible. Just this morning he had gotten a shock – Lin's trial had already started in secret, and it was to end later today! So far, the "trial" had probably just consisted of the Snake sitting in his office and pondering the facts. But today was to be different. This was the day when Lin would be allowed to speak in his own defense. It was scheduled to happen in Han's office later today. Both Zhou and Chen were going to attend.

Zhou hadn't shared any of this news with Ming or Dragon. As with the revised letter, the accelerated trial was a detail they did not need to know.

The thought of Lin speaking directly to Han made Zhou nervous. The old vendor might persuade the Governor of his innocence. Zhou could not permit that to happen. He had an idea that might hush Lin up, but it would mean taking his biggest risk so far. Just thinking about it made Zhou's hands shake. In fact, if he didn't get going right now he might lose his nerve.

Zhou gathered his things and headed for the exit.

• • •

Mr. Lin was beginning to talk to himself. He had first noticed it when he heard a low voice muttering strange, nonsensical things. At first he thought a Guard was doing it. Only later did he recognize the voice as his own. He was trying to stop, but now and then he caught himself slipping again.

He was no longer sure of how long he had been imprisoned. There were no windows down here. His only way of counting the days was by following the number of times they emptied his chamber pot. Mr. Lin estimated they threw out his waste twice a day. If that was correct, then every second time meant the passing of another day.

By Mr. Lin's count, three days had passed. It felt like thirty.

So when the basement's door swung open and Mandarin Zhou walked in, Mr. Lin's heart almost leapt from his chest. "You're back! I thought you had forgotten about me."

Zhou said something to the Guard. The Guard bowed, hurried off and returned with a stool. He placed it in front of the cell.

Zhou sat on the stool and smiled at Mr. Lin.

Mr. Lin smiled back. He was very lucky to have the support of such a powerful man. "Thank you for coming."

"Of course. How are you doing down here?"

"I'm losing my mind. This whole place smells of piss and shit and I haven't seen the sun since I got here. I've probably lost my stall in the market and everyone thinks I killed those poor –"

"I don't think you'll be down here much longer," Zhou said.

Mr. Lin bit his lip and tried to stay calm. "Why?"

"Your trial is already going on. You've got a good chance of being exonerated and walking free."

"I didn't know it had started."

"It has." Zhou leaned forward and stared at Mr. Lin through the bars. "Everyone gets to speak at his or her own trial. What are you planning to say?"

"The truth." Mr. Lin already knew he would have the chance to speak at his trial, but he hadn't thought about what he would say. He feared that too much preparation would make his words sound rehearsed and fake. It was better to give a natural account of his position and answer any questions they asked. Years of dealing with customers had honed his charm, and he knew how to be persuasive. He was confident he could make a good case…but less confident anyone would listen.

Zhou pulled his chair a little closer to the prison bars. "Telling the truth is admirable, but it raises a daunting concern. They will surely ask you to confess, and if you do not they have the right to use torture. You could endure three separate beatings and each time they are allowed up to two hundred lashes. I worry about the damage it would do to a man your age."

"But if I endure all three torture sessions without confessing, they have to let me go."

"That is true," Zhou said. "But it won't matter if you die."

"Look where I am. I'm already dying."

Zhou lapsed into a long silence. Mr. Lin, who made his living reading faces, did not know what the mandarin was thinking. "Mr. Lin, I have a suggestion you're not going to like."

"What is it?"

"I suggest," Zhou said, "that you waive your right to speak at your trial."

"You're joking."

"I am not. Every defendant has the right to speak in his or her defense – the right, but not the obligation. You can inform them you wish to say nothing."

Mr. Lin jumped to his feet, knocking his chair to the floor. "The entire city believes I took those children and…and beat them to death! You think I'm going to stay quiet? Have you lost your mind?" He had never dreamed he would speak this way to a mandarin, but right now he did not care. He was too upset.

Zhou didn't appear bothered by the outburst. "Do you know who the judge in your trial is?"

Mr. Lin picked up his chair and sat down again. "A functionary charged with overseeing the city's sewers or something similar, no doubt." Such officials also handled criminal trials. It was part of their job.

"No. Your trial is being adjudicated by Governor Han." Zhou glanced over at the guards and then looked back at Mr. Lin. When he spoke again, his voice was hardly a whisper. "People call him the Snake."

"You're telling me," Mr. Lin said, "that one of the most feared men in the city is *my judge?*"

"Yes." Zhou appeared confused by Mr. Lin's surprise. "The entire city wants your head, Sir. Did you really think they would leave your trial to a meaningless bureaucrat like me?"

"But still," Mr. Lin said, "the Snake? Wouldn't a man like that be too busy to concern himself with me?"

"A situation like this is bigger than anyone's concerns."

"Gods. The Snake himself." Mr. Lin wanted to hide in the corner of his cell. He wanted to fashion his blanket into a noose and wrap it around his neck. How could he plead his case before a man like Governor Han? The Snake might sentence him to death for wearing the wrong clothes or speaking out of turn. But then, he was facing almost certain death anyway, wasn't he? Why should he care who oversaw his trial? "I still don't see why I should waive my right to speak."

"Most officials have poor tempers, especially when dealing with commoners," Zhou said. "That's doubly true for a man like Governor Han. He has a poor disposition *and* he never deals with regular people."

"The relevance of all that escapes me."

"The Snake insists on strict adherence to etiquette. Breaches of that etiquette will be sure to infuriate him. If he's too angry he may lose his patience and order an execution on the spot. Now, I don't wish to offend you, Sir." Zhou started to say more and then trailed off, an apologetic smile on his face.

"You're worried I'll say the wrong thing and throw the Snake into a rage," Mr. Lin said. "Because I'm a commoner and an unrefined merchant."

Zhou offered another abashed smile. "Forgive me. Yes."

"I cannot argue with your assessment of me, Mandarin Zhou. But I don't care." Mr. Lin tapped himself on the chest. "I don't care if I have to plead my case before the Emperor. I am going to speak on my own behalf and reveal all this as the farce it is."

Zhou said, "You need to be careful, Mr. Lin. Things could end up going very badly for you. I mean worse than just an execution."

"What could be worse than execution?"

"They could behead you instead of strangle you."

"No," Mr. Lin said slowly. "No, they would never do that."

Zhou leaned forward again, and his eyes narrowed. "They'll cut your head off," he whispered. "You'll go to your grave in pieces. It is your obligation to return your body, this sacred vessel, to your ancestors intact. They'll see to it that you can't."

Mr. Lin sat up straight and put his hands on his knees. Go to his grave with his body not intact? The idea was terrifying. There were worse disgraces a person could endure, but not many. Losing one's head would surely bring horrific torment in the afterlife.

But then, Mr. Lin had made up his mind about the afterlife a long time ago. Chances were he was already going to *diyu* – to hell. He did not have a son to worship him. His parents were already in the next world, so they knew he had never really abandoned his desires. They were probably cursing him from the afterlife every day. On top of all that, he was a merchant and therefore loathed by society.

So yes, hell was likely his fate no matter what. What difference would it make if he died with his head attached or not? "No. I'm not going to waive my right to speak. I don't care what the dangers or the consequences are. I will not be called a murderer of children and remain silent."

Zhou was quiet for a long time. He just watched Mr. Lin through the bars. Finally he broke eye contact and stood up. "If that is how you feel, then so be it."

"Are you still going to help me?"

"Of course." Zhou brushed the front of his red robe. "I just don't know how effective my help will be if you insist on taking this course. You are sure I can't change your mind?"

Mr. Lin thought of how it would feel to answer Governor Han's questions. Like everyone in the city he knew all the stories, had heard the whispers of betrayals and murders. It would be terrifying to stand accused before such a man, to feel those eyes on him. But remaining silent would be worse. "I'm sure."

"All right," Zhou said. "You still have my help, but do not expect a good outcome."

With that the mandarin turned and left the room.

Mr. Lin stood until the door closed behind Zhou. Then he sat down on his stiff bed and waited.

• • •

The Gold Bird Guard seated outside Governor Han's office was tall and lined with muscle, but he looked terrified.

Zhou stood over the young man's desk and glared. "I am not going to ask you again. Tell Governor Han that Mandarin Zhou is here to see him. Tell him it's an emergency. I am already scheduled to see him later in the day for Lin's trial."

"Yes, Sir," the Guard said. "Later in the day. Until then Governor Han is not to be disturbed."

Zhou cursed and made for Han's closed office door. Imagine! Some assistant telling a mandarin where he could and could not go. It was incredible.

With the Guard on his heels, Zhou pushed the door open. "Governor Han!"

Han was sitting behind his desk, head down and shoulders slumped. Zhou saw the Governor straightening up and understood right away. The great man had been sleeping. A knife of fear cut through Zhou's bravado.

I just charged into the Snake's office and interrupted his nap!

Zhou saw real terror on Han's face. Maybe he thought this was an assassination.

Then Han recognized Zhou, and his shock turned to disbelieving anger. "What are you doing here?"

A part of Zhou was happy the young Guard had tried to stop him. It gave the whole affair a more dramatic effect. That would be useful if he survived this meeting. "Governor Han, I need to speak with you."

All of Han's sleepiness had evaporated. His sharp eyes focused on Zhou. "Mandarin Zhou, this had damn well better be an emergency."

"It is." Zhou swallowed. If he didn't convince the Snake this was a matter of heaven and earth, he would be lucky to walk out of here having lost his job and nothing else. "It concerns Lin's trial."

The Snake regarded Zhou with that flat gaze of his. Then he looked at the Guard. "Get out. And the next time an intruder tries to force his way into this office, one of you had better end up dead."

The Guard bowed. "Yes, Sir." He turned, almost tripped over his own feet, and scurried out of the room.

"All right," Han said. "Go."

Zhou made a point of sitting down even though he hadn't been invited to do so. That kind of brazenness showed confidence. "Sir, we are going to execute an innocent man."

"So you said before. I trust you haven't come just to preach at me?"

"No. I've written a letter." Zhou placed his scroll on the Governor's desk. "It outlines Mr. Lin's defense, as well as my own reservations. I felt I had to show up early so you would have time to read it before the trial resumes. I'm sorry, but I will go to any lengths to stop this madness and save an innocent man."

Han did not touch the letter. "Zhou, these things have their own process. If Lin is innocent he will have the chance to tell me himself later today."

"Sadly, Sir, Mr. Lin has waived his right to speak in his own defense." As Zhou waited for Han's reply, the walls seemed to watch him.

"Old fool," Han muttered. "He should cut his own head off and save us the effort."

"Sir, I won't take any more of your time. All my concerns are, as I said, in this letter. Will you read it before the trial starts?"

"No. You and Commandant Chen are due here for a meeting quite soon. I don't want to see you until then. And the next time you wish to speak with me go through the proper channels. If you ever charge into my office again, I'll cut out your tongue."

Zhou stood up and bowed. He fought the impulse to press his point more. That would try the Governor's patience – never a wise move. Besides, he had already achieved his goal. "Thank you, Sir."

• • •

When Zhou stepped into the hallway, the young Guard looked up at him in wonder. "You just stormed into the Governor's office."

Zhou was still irritated with the Guard for trying to stop him, but his success with the Snake had left him feeling expansive. "There are times when a person can't wait for procedure." He wagged a stern finger at the Guard. "Sometimes a man has to do what he knows is right, regardless of the consequences."

The Guard barked a nervous laugh. "You're lucky. I don't think you know how lucky you are. Men like that…" He lowered his voice and glanced at the closed door. "Men like that, they can have your throat cut just because they didn't sleep well last night. Those are the ways of people in power."

"Well," Zhou said. "Maybe those ways are going to change."

• • •

Soon Zhou was back in Han's office, sitting next to Commandant Chen. Zhou's thoughts were teeming with reasons to doubt himself and his plans. Every one of those doubts felt entirely plausible. This was a complicated undertaking, after all. Perhaps he had made some blunder that would allow Lin to escape with his life.

Governor Han folded his hands on his expensive desk. "Normally these trials last three days, but circumstances have forced me to accelerate the process. I spent yesterday reviewing the evidence. Today would have been Lin's chance to speak with me personally, but he has elected not to do so. Therefore no more analysis is necessary. I have found Lin guilty of murder. The sentence is death. Strangulation, not beheading."

Zhou felt an enormous weight leave his shoulders. It was really happening. Now that Han's verdict was official, everything else would fall into place. As soon as the next child was killed, Zhou would look like the only wise man left in the government.

He just needed one more piece of good fortune from this meeting.

Governor Han turned to Zhou. "Mandarin Zhou, although your technique lacks convention, I admire your efforts. You put your career at great risk for your principles."

Zhou bowed, his face a picture of disappointed resignation. "Thank you, Governor."

Han looked at Chen. "I'm going to let you handle the execution, Commandant Chen. Any thoughts on how you'll do it?"

Zhou held his breath. If Chen said what Zhou hoped he would, things would go a lot easier.

"I can think of two imperatives," Chen said. "First, let the execution take place right away. Today would be best. Second, I am going to have the condemned man gagged. Otherwise he could well say the wrong thing and stir the onlookers to riot."

Zhou wanted to smile. It was common to gag prisoners who might speak out before execution, and Zhou had been hoping Chen might take that course today. It would be much better if Lin were gagged. Zhou didn't fear a riot…but he *was* concerned Lin would rave about scheming and treacherous mandarins.

Now there was one less thing to worry about.

"May I repeat one more time," Zhou said, "that Mr. Lin is clearly an innocent man. I am telling you both here and now this will end in disaster for us."

"Noted," Han said. "Commandant Chen, carry out the execution today. Do it in the usual place, under the willow tree by the West Market. Meeting over."

22

"Where is this place?" Dragon asked.

"It should be nearby," Ming said. "Lei Lei's father recently moved to a house in a lane right off Snake Alley. And in case you weren't sure, this is Snake Alley."

They were walking down a narrow and muddy street that cut horizontally through the West Ward. Stalls and storefronts lined both sides of the street. There were baskets full of slithering snakes and plates with sliced snake meat. There were old women selling jars of snake blood and other old women selling jars of snake bile.

The ladies called out to Ming and Dragon as they walked past. Snake meat for energy, snake blood to cure boils. Nearly all the vendors declared their wares helped men perform with their wives every time. Ming tried not to take the sales pitches personally.

Both Ming and Dragon were in poor humor. They had set out this morning hoping to interview the parents of the victims, but so far their efforts had come to nothing. The only parent they had even located was Guang Fu, the former cavalryman accused of looting a city out west. He had watched them through a crack in his door, eyes expressionless in his sallow face. Dragon had managed three words before the door slammed shut. Hunts for the next two sets of parents had been just as fruitless.

The only remaining parent was Jin Lei Jin, father of the Lei Lei child.

Dragon pointed. "Is that the lane right there?"

Ming squinted. "Do you mean that little alley?"

"Yes."

"I suppose it must be." Ming had been expecting a wide road. Dragon was pointing at an old dirt path that looked like it never got swept.

Dragon's face was showing the same doubt. "As far as I can see it's the only lane that runs into Snake Alley. It has to be that one, right?"

"Let's go find out."

They rounded the little turnoff. The path – it could not really be called a lane – was about sixty paces long and came to a dead end. Bits of refuse dotted the ground, and bushes were encroaching on it from either side.

Dragon pointed again. "There."

Ming looked. At first he saw nothing. Then he noticed the tip of a roof poking up from a tangle of foliage. He took a step forward and saw a short staircase leading up to a tiny porch. So a house was there, but the bushes were swallowing it whole.

They fought their way through the brambles, pushing past the thin twigs that reached out and poked them. After some spirited cursing they stopped in front of a sad little dwelling that was more a shack than a house. The place looked older than the Middle Kingdom itself. The top of the front door frame was sagging and at least half the roof tiles were gone. The windows of most homes were covered with paper, but these windows only had rotting spider webs.

"It makes no sense," Ming said. "Jin Lei Jin is a wealthy man."

Dragon peered through a window. "Nobody's home."

At the sound of Dragon's voice, the front door opened with a crash. A thin, bearded man emerged from the darkness and looked at them. His clothes were dotted with holes and frayed at the edges, but they were also straight and neat. His dirty sash was tied perfectly, synching his faded robe close to his body. His hair had grown a bit too long but it was tied into a perfect bun on top of his head. The bun came to a point that leaned lazily to one side. Ming searched his mind for the hairstyle's name and it soon came to him: the tall bindings style.

Ming said, "Good afternoon. We're investigators for the city government. We're looking for Jin Lei Jin."

The man only stared.

"Wrong house," Dragon muttered. Their strange host was probably a vagrant. The city was littered with old buildings that such people used for shelter.

As they turned to leave, the man said, "I'm Jin Lei Jin. Everyone calls me Jin."

Lies, Ming thought. Jin Lei Jin was a third level mandarin, not a squatter.

It was as though Ming had spoken his thought out loud. The man said, "I was a mandarin but they dismissed me. Are you here about the death of my daughter, the death of my wife or the death of the whore?"

Dragon didn't miss a beat. "We're here about the deaths of your daughter and of the prostitute. We think they're connected."

Jin nodded. "Because they found that note in Lei Lei's hand."

Ming frowned. Not even the victims' parents had been told about the notes. "How did –"

"I'm a mandarin," Jin said. "At least I used to be. With my connections, I was able to learn all the details about my daughter's death. Does that really surprise you?"

"No," Ming said. "I suppose not."

"I'm afraid I can't invite you in," Jin said. "Have a seat on the steps and try to keep the splinters out of your ass."

• • •

Both Ming and Dragon ignored Jin's invitation to sit, but Jin didn't seem to take offense. He just sat down on the step and produced a jug of wine. Ming caught the wine's scent in the air and tried not to wrinkle his nose. It smelled like rotting fruit.

Jin swallowed some wine, winced and took another swig. "I killed her."

Ming couldn't keep the surprise from his face. "Excuse me?"

"The prostitute." Jin used his sleeve to wipe a dribble of purple liquid from his chin. "Her working name was Swan. I never knew her real name. I'm not sure she knew it herself."

Dragon said, "If you killed this woman then why have you not been executed?" It was a question both he and Ming could have answered, but they wanted to keep Jin talking.

"I almost was," Jin said. "I was accused and imprisoned for days while I waited for my trial to start. But I managed to wriggle my way out of it. I wasn't exonerated, exactly. The authorities just…"

"Decided not to pursue the matter further," Ming said. *You're welcome.* It had taken Ming days to save Jin Lei Jin. Murder was a hard crime to conceal, even when the culprit was a mandarin and the victim was a prostitute.

"I avoided execution but I lost everything else," Jin said. "I had to pay a fortune to the brothel's madam. I lost my employment as well. That's why I'm living here now." He jerked a thumb at the ruin of a home behind him.

"Why did you kill the prostitute?" Ming asked. Keep him talking, keep him relaxed.

"She caught pregnant and claimed the child was mine," Jin said. "As if there was any way of proving that. I gave her money to shut her up, a tragic miscalculation on my part. She sensed my desperation and insisted I give her more. She even threatened to tell my wife if I didn't comply."

Dragon nodded. "So you killed her."

"Well, I had her killed," Jin said tonelessly. He took another swig of his disgusting wine. "I paid a Uyghur living in the North Hamlet to cut her throat. Some Gold Bird Guards caught the savage leaving Swan's brothel. Eventually he told them everything in exchange for his own life. Fucking barbarians."

Dragon made a noise. He crossed his arms, showing the thick mats of hair that went from his wrists to his elbows. To Ming it was clear that his large companion had foreign blood, but Jin either did not notice or did not care.

Either way, it seemed the wine was making Jin talkative. Ming was starting to suspect their host was a lot drunker than he looked. Time to ask the question. "Who else knew about your crime?"

"You want to know how the killer of my daughter learned of what I did."

Ming nodded.

"Well my wife knew because some interrogators from the Gold Bird Guard spoke to her. I suppose it was an open secret among a lot of mandarins as well, but those men didn't know the details. And they were smart enough to not ask questions."

"That's all?"

"That's all."

Dragon made another noise. Ming understood his frustration. They had spent all morning searching for this man, and it was looking like a waste of precious time.

"Everything else you already know," Jin said. "That Lin son of a bitch snatched my daughter from the market and beat her to death." For the first time, a real emotion surfaced on his face. His eyes turned a deep scarlet and his chin began to tremble. Then the moment passed and he was detached again. "My wife hanged herself a day later. Good riddance."

Ming wondered what the consequences would be if he pulled his foot back and kicked this man in the face. "I believe we have everything we need."

Jin looked up at them. "Do you know when they'll execute Lin?"

"No," Dragon said. "He hasn't even been found guilty yet."

Jin took another long drink. A few more drops of wine leaked onto his chin and gleamed in the sunlight. "I'm going to watch. I'm going to stand at the front of the mob and toast him right before they hack his head off."

Dragon's face contorted into a strange parody of a smile. "I'm sure you will."

• • •

Ming pointed into the writhing basket of snakes. "I'll take that one."

The ancient woman behind the basket snatched the serpent from its brothers and laid it flat on a cutting board. Then, before the wretched creature had a chance to struggle, she lopped its head off with a knife. *Thock!*

Ming looked at the dead beast and smiled. It was nice and fat.

Dragon pointed at another snake. "That one, please."

The woman grabbed the snake and repeated her grim ritual. *Thock!*

Once their meals were cooked, Ming and Dragon sat at a small wooden table in front of the woman's stall.

Ming tried a piece of snake. It was nice and tender. "Mandarin Jin. A man of great character."

"I saw plenty of men like him in the cavalry." Dragon spoke around the food in his mouth. "Entitled fools I wouldn't trust with a shovel. I would bet a thousand coppers he got his post because his father was a mandarin."

Ming knew from his past experience with Jin Lei Jin that Dragon was right. Jin's father had been a mandarin, so he received the lucrative job like a gift from Heaven. And he paid that good fortune back with murder.

Ming thought back to something he had said to Dragon a lifetime ago. *The Sorcerer worked for a greater good.* On the heels of that, like a bitter joke, came another thought: the picture of a half-drunk mandarin sitting on his porch and casually talking of murdering a pregnant woman. Ming hadn't known about the pregnancy. Would he have helped Jin if he *had* known? Ming realized with something like terror that he did not know the answer to that question.

The old woman placed two steaming cups of tea on their table and left without a word.

Dragon waited until the woman was back at her stall. "Powerful people. All of whom have dirty secrets, all of whom were saved by the Sorcerer."

Ming rested his chin on the heel of his palm. "Not all of them. There's one victim who doesn't fit into our puzzle."

"That pub owner, Meng Chun."

"Yes. Perhaps that was something else. Maybe someone just made it look like it was related to the child killings."

"The same thought occurred to me," Dragon said. "Someone owning a pub in that part of the city could have a lot of enemies. But no one outside law enforcement knows the killer is leaving the notes and the statues of Leigong behind."

"If the killer is in law enforcement then he could know everything," Ming said. "Regardless, I am more certain than ever of Lin's innocence. How in the world could a vendor from some market learn the secrets of the elite?"

Dragon swallowed his last piece of snake. "He couldn't. And can you imagine someone his age moving around the city, abducting children and depositing their bodies elsewhere? All the while escaping notice? It's nonsense."

"At the very least, we should be able to get Lin a stay of execution." Ming looked up at the sky. The sun was directly overhead. "I've got to go home and check on my family. I'll see you when we meet with Zhou tonight."

Dragon frowned, but he did not protest. He knew about Li Juan's health. "All right, but don't let that mind of yours mind rest. And remember that the madman may be watching you. Keep your eyes open and your hand close to your dagger."

• • •

As Ming walked home, he realized he was close to the market from which Lei Lei had been taken. On an impulse he decided to go there.

The market was unusually full for this time of day. The main road was packed with shoppers and the vendors were doing brisk business. Ming guessed that with the presumed killer captured, folks were more willing to venture out again.

Ming tried to focus his thoughts as he walked. A feeling had been building in him ever since he parted ways with Dragon. He was becoming more and more certain that all the pieces he needed to solve this riddle were already in from of him. Now he just had to fit them together.

The crowd grew thicker as Ming went deeper into the market. He began to weave his way through the throng, holding his satchel close to protect it from thieves. Soon he found himself before a shifting wall of people. They stood shoulder to shoulder and jostled with each other, as if trying to get a better view of something up ahead.

Ming gave up immediately. Fighting through that mob would be harder than scaling a castle wall. He turned left and wandered up to a stall holding neat stacks of expensive-looking plates. A young man was standing behind the stall and smiling at him.

Ming pointed west, toward the growing crowd. "Do you know what's going on there?"

The young man's smile was so steady it looked painted on his face. "I'm sorry but I don't, Sir. To my knowledge nothing important was planned here for today."

"Have I seen you here before?" Ming squinted across the table. "You don't look familiar."

The young vendor's smile grew. "I'm new here, Sir. Can I interest you in some plates or bowls?"

"No thank you." Ming walked away before the vendor could say anything else. He stopped in the middle of the thoroughfare and looked down at his feet. People muttered that he was blocking their way, but he did not care. He needed to think.

How was the madman discovering his victims' secrets? What kind of person could see into the intimate worlds of so many powerful people? As the Sorcerer, Ming knew how well the elites protected their shame. Discovering their misdeeds would be like slipping into a treasury, fillings one's pockets and slipping out again, all the while going unnoticed. It was a magic trick of incredible skill.

And yet someone had managed it four times. Five, if you counted the pub owner.

Still without a direction in mind, Ming walked through the market and tried to understand.

● ● ●

At the far end of that same market, Mr. Lin stood under the giant willow tree with a gag in his mouth and his hands bound behind his back. A crowd of onlookers surrounded him. Some fifty Gold Bird Guards faced that crowd, swords at the ready in case things got out of hand.

Mr. Lin's eyes passed over the crowd. He had been expecting jeering faces, faces twisted with hate. He had been expecting hands to grab him and claim him before the executioners could. But looking out at the crowd, he recognized many people from the market. Most of those people were looking at him with sympathy.

Which meant they thought he was innocent.

Of course, there *were* jeering people as well. Most of them were adolescent boys, the kind of people who stole coins from blind beggars and threw rocks at dogs. There were others – mostly parents, it seemed – who shook their fists and cursed his ancestors. They taunted him and said he was going to be an *egui* – a hungry ghost – because he did not have any sons to worship him.

It was hard to blame them. After all, they believed he was a killer of children. Besides, the people full of hate did not matter. Only the ones who believed in him did.

Mr. Lin was surprised at his sense of calm. He had expected to cry and shout, to grovel and fight…and certainly the fear *was* there. He felt it in the bottom of his stomach, and he could sense it trying overwhelm him. In just a moment they would wrap a wire around his neck and twist it tight. His eyes would bulge and his tongue would stick out of his mouth. The agony would last an eternity. He might even soil his pants.

Yes, there was plenty of fear.

Still, he was as close to peace as he could be, and he did not believe panic would conquer him. That would have to be enough.

Mr. Lin turned his head and looked at another section of crowd. Almost right away he saw Blossom and Toad. They were both staring at him, of course. Toad was grinning in that vacant, open-mouthed way of his. Blossom's eyes were locked fast on Mr. Lin's, her face beaming with victory.

Mr. Lin ignored them and kept looking. He was not surprised to see the mandarin Zhou standing with a group of Guards. The small man was looking down at the ground, up at the sky, at the crowd...at everything but Mr. Lin himself.

Zhou had betrayed him. Mr. Lin knew that now. Somehow Zhou had cheated him of his chance to speak out for himself. Likely he had done a lot of other underhanded things. After all, how else could gangsters like Blossom and Toad suddenly look like credible witnesses? That Zhou fellow had arranged it. Zhou must have concluded that Mr. Lin's death would benefit him somehow. Perhaps Mr. Lin should have foreseen that. Perhaps he should have known not to trust someone who spent his days immersed in palace intrigue.

Mr. Lin looked away. He only had a few moments of life left. Why waste them feeling bitter toward a man like that?

The crowd's hum of conversation suddenly died. It was as though everyone had received a silent command to go quiet at the same time. Mr. Lin had seen enough executions to know why.

Across from him, the crowd began to part. Two men were moving through the throng of people, but they did not have to push anyone. The onlookers shrank from them as though they bore some horrific plague.

The men stepped into the clearing. They were dressed like Gold Bird Guards but their uniforms were considerably older and more worn. One of the men was a foreigner, probably a Uyghur.

The foreign-looking Guard held a long, thin wire in his right hand. The wire was a loop with wooden handles on both ends.

Mr. Lin felt an upsurge of nausea and turned away. The panic he had been fighting threatened to explode again. Any moment now they were going to wrap that wire around his neck. They were going to twist it tighter and tighter, twist it until the pressure crushed his throat closed. Perhaps the wire would cut into his skin, making him bleed to death before he could suffocate.

Again he stamped the fear down.

Mr. Lin looked back at the two Guards. He could not help it. The Guard holding the wire was standing next to Zhou, nodding as Zhou spoke. Then both Guards turned and walked toward Mr. Lin.

The buzz of conversation grew again, grew until it became a solid wall of sound. Or maybe that sound was coming from within Mr. Lin's own skull.

Mr. Lin closed his eyes. He tried to picture the face of Yu Sheng, his lover from so many years ago. Other memories came – the sound of Yu Sheng's voice, the touch of his skin, the smell of his hair. They all swirled through Mr. Lin's mind, but they would not coalesce into Yu Sheng's face.

Panic rushed back at Mr. Lin. He was going to die and he could not remember Yu Sheng one last time. Being unable to conjure Yu Sheng made his panic grow, and that made remembering harder still.

The executioners stood on either side of Mr. Lin and placed the wire around his neck. Without ceremony they began to twist the handles in opposite directions, tightening the wire with each turn.

And still Yu Sheng's face did not appear. Mr. Lin thought of the temple where they prayed, the forest where they made love. Those things came to him with perfect clarity but Yu Sheng's face remained a gray shadow.

Mr. Lin was going to die as he had lived. Alone.

The wire pulled tight against Mr. Lin's neck. He felt the first real bite of pain on his skin, and with that, the shadows in his mind finally formed into Yu Sheng's face. Mr. Lin smiled. He held that image in his mind, willed it stay with him until the end.

The wire grew tighter. To Mr. Lin it felt like giant, unseen hands were strangling him. The pressure on his throat was grinding, incredible. He tried to take a breath but his throat was closed. His body tried to react with a fit of coughing but it failed, making his throat close even tighter.

The pain doubled, trebled. The world was receding into an ocean of fog.

And still Mr. Lin held the image of Yu Sheng. His last thoughts were of trips into the forest so many years ago, and the feeling of soft ground against his skin after love.

23

Twilight arrived.

Ming and Dragon stood outside the Green Ale House and watched people stream through the front door. Quite a few folks were already unsteady on their feet, even though full dark had not yet come. Many were singing songs and clapping each other on the back. It was as though some new holiday had been declared, but no one had bothered to tell Ming or Dragon.

Ming kept his eyes on the crowded the thoroughfare. "Zhou's late."

A drunk leaving the pub crashed into Dragon and mumbled an apology. Dragon sent the man on his way with a gentle push on the shoulder. "I take this as a reason to hope. Perhaps he's still in a meeting. Who knows? Maybe he's convincing them of Lin's innocence right now."

Ming spotted Zhou picking his way through the street. Even in the fading light his red mandarin's robe stood out in a crowd. "There."

Zhou bowed. "Good evening. Sorry I'm late."

"It's all right," Ming said. "How did it go? They'll at least *consider* the possibility of Lin's innocence? Perhaps wait a few more days before they give a verdict?"

Zhou became very still. "You haven't heard."

"Heard what?" Dragon asked.

"Lin was executed in the West Market today."

Ming stared at Zhou. All around, bodies continued to flow past. People shouted and laughed, jostled and cursed. Beasts of burden struggled through the mud, grunting under their heavy loads. To Ming, it was all happening in another world.

"It was this afternoon." Zhou gestured to the people around them. "That's why so many revelers are out tonight. The Emperor granted a carnival to celebrate the end of the terror."

Dragon opened his mouth, paused, and closed it again. He looked like someone trying to figure out a difficult riddle. "I thought the letter was going to secure us at least a few days."

"I thought so too," Zhou said. "But they started the trial in secret and rushed through it. Governor Han didn't even speak with any witnesses. I think they wanted to kill Lin as quickly as possible, to just have it over and done."

"That is completely illogical." Dragon's tone grew hostile as the finality of it all coalesced in his mind. "A child could have understood the arguments in our letter. How could you have failed to convince them?"

"Have you ever gone into Governor Han's office to protest?" Anger was creeping into Zhou's voice as well. "Have you ever looked the Snake in the eye and told him he's wrong? That is what I did today."

Ming cut in before either man could say anything else. "I'm sure you tried your best." The words sounded empty even as Ming spoke them, but he could think of nothing better.

Dragon ignored Ming. "Did you show the Snake our letter, Zhou? Did you explain the thinking we used to rule Lin out?"

"Yes," Zhou said. "I did everything in my power to stop the execution. Word had it the Emperor himself intervened."

"The Emperor always intervenes in these cases," Dragon said. "He has to approve every death sentence himself."

"But he usually just hears a summary of the crime and gives quick approval." Zhou took on the tone of a patient teacher addressing a frustrated student. "This time he probably told the Governor to resolve the situation immediately."

Dragon looked ready to say more, but then the fire left his eyes. He crossed his arms over his giant chest, muttered something to himself and went quiet.

"Zhou, I'm sure you tried your best," Ming said again. This time the words had even less meaning. He felt despair coming, heavy and thick. All day long he had been certain they could save Lin. And now Lin was just…dead. Sometime today, while they were running about the city, executioners were twisting a wire around the old man's neck.

Dragon looked up at the darkening sky. "This is going to be a catastrophe. When the next child is beaten to death and left in the city for someone to find…gods. Everyone in power is going to look like an ass."

"I suppose that's true," Zhou said sadly. "But that isn't our concern. The three of *us* know a madman is still menacing the city. It's our duty to find him."

Ming shook his head. "No."

Zhou cocked his ear toward Ming, as though he had trouble hearing. "What?"

"We shouted the truth at them," Ming said. "We told them the sky was blue and they wouldn't even look up to confirm it. Why should we worry about our duty when they won't give a moment's thought to theirs?"

Dragon was watching Ming carefully. "What are you saying?"

"I am saying I quit." The words gave Ming a dark satisfaction. "I have two children and a dying wife to look after. At least they let me know they need me."

Zhou placed a hand on Ming's elbow. "You two have made incredible progress in just a few days. If you keep at it a little longer –"

Ming pulled his elbow free. "Doesn't matter. I don't think anyone outside the three of us cares anymore. Well, the parents do, but that's it. The other citizens only know they've been scared and now it's over. The authorities are just happy to see it all go away."

Dragon stepped away from a group of drunks that had congregated behind him. "Ming, it's not *going* to go away. No matter how obstinate the rulers are the problem won't disappear until we destroy it. And the madman is after you, perhaps even your family."

"All the more reason for me to be with them." Ming was so exhausted he failed to notice had finally admitted to being the Sorcerer. "I had hoped to protect them by catching this man. Since that is not going to happen I had better stay with them."

"But Ming, it *can* happen." Dragon's eyes were desperate. "We're *close.*"

Ming bowed. "Dragon, I was wrong about you. I didn't want to work with you, but you've proven yourself a brilliant investigator. Zhou, thank you for giving me a chance to take back my old life. I think, though, that I'll have to be content as a tutor and a widower."

Then Ming turned toward the thoroughfare and disappeared into the crowd.

• • •

Zhou called after Ming. He stood on the tips of his toes and shouted his friend's name again and again. He just needed to get Ming back here. If he could speak with Ming face to face, he could convince him to continue the investigation.

He was certain of it.

Zhou called Ming's name again, louder this time. He waited. There was no sign of him. He called Ming's name again. And again.

"Ming! *Ming!*" Zhou's voice began to crack. How could Ming do this to him? If it weren't for Zhou's generosity, Ming would still be tutoring the city's brats for table scraps. And now Ming felt he had the right to just walk away?

Dragon put an arm around Zhou's shoulders. He looked like a father coddling his son. "Let him go."

Zhou stepped away from Dragon. He didn't like being comforted that way. It was patronizing. "The murderer hasn't been apprehended yet. The job is not finished."

"That's true," Dragon said. "But I don't think we're going to catch him now."

Zhou wanted to grab Dragon's tunic and start screaming. *It's not enough! Now that Lin is dead we have to find the real killer! That will double the glory. First I fight for an innocent man, and then I catch the real culprit. We're not* done *yet! How can you not see that, you fucking barbarian oaf?!*

Zhou turned away and kept watching the crowd. He felt black, impotent rage churning in his stomach. After all his success in getting Lin convicted and killed, failure was unthinkable. He had come too far to be defied by a tutor.

Ming did not reappear. Finally, Zhou crossed his arms. "I'm not going to pay him."

"You're not going to – what? You're telling me that after all the work we did you're going to cheat him?"

"I'm not cheating anyone," Zhou said. "If you walk out on a job, you don't get paid. Nothing could be simpler."

Dragon scowled. "Ming did everything he could to help you. You are *not* going to renege on your obligations to him."

Zhou knew one angry look from Dragon could shatter most people's courage in a heartbeat. But Zhou was not like most people. He was a mandarin on the rise. People should be wary of *him,* not the other way around. "The money is to be spent at my discretion. We had a deal."

"A deal to investigate the crimes. You never said payment depended on success."

"I'll think about it."

Dragon stepped forward and looked down at Zhou. "You'll think about it, and then you'll do it."

"We'll see." But the truth was Zhou had already made his decision. If Ming refused to come back, he would not receive a single copper. Why should Zhou pay a man who lacked even the most basic business morals? "Are you going to tell me you're outraged now? Do you not remember how you forced your way into all of this? And if memory serves, one of the first things you did – *after* you blackmailed us – was negotiate your portion of the reward."

Dragon snorted heavily and spat in the dirt. "Damn the fucking reward. The Emperor can toss my share into a river. This has grown past matters of money and you know it."

Zhou saw that Dragon was being honest. He really had stopped caring about his money. "What about you? Are you quitting as well?"

"I don't know," Dragon said. "I don't want to give up, but I'm not hunting some horse thief in the countryside. To tell you the truth, I need Ming."

Zhou made a show of looking around. "I don't see Ming here. Do you?"

"Stop it. I'll speak with him tomorrow. I'll do my best to bring him back, but I'm not hopeful."

"That's all right." Zhou felt a sense of calm returning. Perhaps this was just a small setback. Perhaps Ming could be brought back into the fold. But Zhou would have to see to that himself. Dragon lacked the finesse. "I should speak with Ming. I'll make him see reason."

Dragon jerked his thumb at the pub behind him. "Tonight I am going to drink all of their ale and maybe take out my anger on a loud patron or two. And no matter what Ming decides, I expect to see him paid. With that I will say goodnight."

• • •

As it turned out, the next person to see Ming again was not Zhou but Dragon.

Dragon stepped out of the Green Ale House with the slightest sway in his gait. How long since Zhou had left his company? Dragon counted on his fingers. He'd had…five cups of ale. Long enough for the little mandarin to be far away, at least. That was a relief. Zhou was sharp, but Dragon found something about him vaguely distasteful.

Dragon made his way down the muddy street, going nowhere in particular, making no effort get out of anyone's way. A few pedestrians grumbled as the giant stomped past, but no one confronted him. Surely that was wise. Dragon would not have reacted well to confrontation.

And look here. Another ale house was across the street, torches blazing and door open.

Dragon saw Ming as soon as he stepped into the building. His erstwhile partner was at a back table, shoulders slumped, head down. Dragon purchased two cups of ale, handed one to Ming and sat across from him.

Ming took a heavy gulp. "I finally revealed that I was the Sorcerer tonight. I'm not sure if you noticed."

"I expected you to deny it forever."

"So did I. You know my wife doesn't even know that part of my life?"

"Not at all?"

Another gulp. "She knows a bit, that I was involved in unsavory politics and so forth. But she certainly isn't aware of how deep my involvement went. Then again, who could say? Maybe she figured it all out ages ago and decided not to tell me. You know, it's been a long time since I've consumed so much alcohol. It's an impossible vice for a tutor."

Dragon wondered how much Ming had consumed tonight. "I never would have blackmailed you, Ming."

"You did, though," Ming said. "You looked right in my eyes and threatened to tell the world my secret."

"I am saying that I never would have followed through with it. It was bluster so you would take me on and give me access to Zhou's resources."

Ming rocked his cup gently, watching his ale slosh back and forth. "I was furious when you questioned my work. I lectured you about the greater good, about people needing faith in their leaders. Now..."

"Now Lin's body is stiffening outside the city walls and a killer is free. All thanks to our leaders."

"You asked me what I regret," Ming said. "You remember? In the noodle shop? You asked it as though you assumed I *did* have regrets."

"I remember."

"And you were right. The story of my regret also happens to be the story of how I became the Sorcerer." Ming wiped droplets of ale from his lips. "My first coverup. Do you want to hear it?"

Dragon did, but before he could say so Ming resumed speaking.

"A merchant came to our barracks and told us he'd heard screaming from a home outside the city walls. I rode out there with two other men. We found a little shack on the other side of nowhere, off a narrow forest path at the top of a hill. That place wasn't fit for a family of rats, and it certainly didn't suit the former mandarin who *did* live there."

"The mandarin squatted out there?" Dragon asked. "Took his family to a place where they wouldn't have to pay?"

"That's right. No landlord to worry about. No one to gawk at the disgraced official, either. I need to tell you about the blood in that shack. There was a pool of it, Dragon. I mean enough that when you stepped in it your foot sent out ripples."

"How many bodies?"

"Three. Two adults and an adolescent. All beaten to death, the woman so badly we only *knew* she was a woman from her body. But I recognized the man. He was an ex-mandarin who had grown to some infamy after killing his wife for an affair. The killing was legal, mind you. But it was ugly enough to force him from office. The other dead were his son and his new wife."

Dragon knew the law that had saved the mandarin. If a man discovered his wife was unfaithful, he had the right to kill her, provided he notified the authorities immediately afterwards. He had to kill the other man his wife had slept with as well. It was not legal to kill only one. "What happened after you discovered the bodies?"

"One of them began to groan."

"A survivor."

"The boy," Ming said. "He had been beaten terribly but he was groaning and even moving around. We cleaned him up and brought him to our barracks. We called in physicians who administered their medicines and bandaged him up. Then we just…"

"Waited." Dragon had seen enough injuries in his time. "You waited to see if he would pull through or not."

"I didn't think he would. But he held on, and soon he was up and around. I kept an eye on him, kept him company, that sort of thing. The men in the barracks joked that I had a new pet. They even gave him a nickname. Everyone called him Rabbit because he was so shy and jumpy."

"You had a kind commander." Dragon finished off his ale. "Not many would abide an injured boy in the barracks."

"He *was* kind, as commanders go. But he knew it couldn't last forever. He pulled me aside one evening and told me as much. Told me to send the boy away. I hesitated for as long as I could. But then something happened and I realized I really had to do something about that boy. He was a...a loose end, you could say."

"He told you something, didn't he? Some kind of secret."

Ming smiled. "You're quick, Dragon. He told us his mother hadn't been unfaithful to his father. His father had made up the affair so he could kill his wife and remarry."

"So who broke into the shack? Who killed the mandarin and his new wife?"

"Thieves, the boy said. Out there it's rife with outlaws and a mandarin wouldn't know how to protect himself."

"What did the boy want? I mean what did he hope to gain from telling you about his parents?"

"I think it went back to his mother. He just wanted someone to know she hadn't been unfaithful. Nothing more. That's when I saw the problem."

"A scandal."

Ming nodded "I imagined the whole city knowing one of their officials was a murderer. I still remember that feeling in my belly, the nausea that roiled around in there. I was raised to believe that our leaders are sacred, that they can't be questioned. When there's questioning, there's doubt. Then people start to grumble, and no one knows what could come of that."

Dragon disagreed, but he didn't say so. The people *always* grumbled. The problem was men like Ming and Zhou didn't always listen.

"I couldn't abide the thought of a scandal," Ming said. "It scared me in some deep way, like not knowing where my family's next meal would come from. So I sent the boy away. I gave him a small gift that I thought might make our parting easier, and I sent him away."

"Where?"

"A home for orphans."

Something in Dragon's face changed. Ming, normally an astute observer, was too lost in memory to notice.

"He begged me not to do it," Ming said. "He told me he could survive on his own. He'd been through more than I knew, he said. But I couldn't stand the thought of gossip spreading throughout the city, and I convinced myself I was helping him.

"Anyway, during all that a superior noticed my talent for concealing scandal, and I was on my way to becoming the Sorcerer. Every subsequent job felt easy. They were all child's play next to the memory of that boy being carted off in a wagon. So now you know the story of how I started that life."

Dragon, an orphan himself, was not inclined to comfort Ming. "There were other ways you could have handled it. You could have figured out a way to cover up the scandal and protect the boy."

Ming thought about making some whimsy remark, perhaps an ironic comment on sacrificing the one to save the many. Instead he caught a server's eye and called for more ale.

24

Blossom threw back the last of her drink and slammed her cup on the table. "Another!" She released a heavy burp, grimacing as the taste of vomit filled her mouth.

Toad grinned at her. He was already on his eighth cup and his face wasn't even red yet. "Can't handle it, Sister?"

Blossom tried to speak, but her mouth seemed to be filled with mud. She took a deep breath and gathered her faculties. "Shut your fucking hole."

Toad turned toward the kitchen. "One for me, too."

As she waited for her drink, Blossom sat back and looked around their little common room. She and Toad had the largest home in the West Market. In addition to this room, they had a kitchen and even a little bedroom. Blossom was especially fond of the bedroom, a luxury inconceivable to most. She slept in there, and Toad slept out here by the fireplace. Those sleeping arrangements would come in useful tonight. After Toad drank, his snoring shook the walls.

Blossom's eyes followed a network of cracks crawling up the wall opposite her. She grimaced again. Yes, they were better off than their neighbors, but this was still a hovel. Their rammed earth walls, once a deep and healthy brown, were now grayish yellow. The paper that covered their windows did little to fight the summer heat or the winter freeze. Whenever it rained, water invaded their home through a hundred leaks.

There was also the issue of security. Safety was a bigger concern than ever before, now that so many people surely wanted them dead. Like most homes, theirs was surrounded by a wall made of rammed earth. One could make a hole in that wall with just a pail of water and a bit of patience. Hell, their walls were so short a spry person could just scramble over them.

All of life's hardships were soon to disappear, though. Zhou was going to change everything for them.

The first fruits of their efforts had ripened earlier today, when they expelled half the market. New, more lucrative vendors had already bought up most of the vacancies. Others were bidding exorbitant sums for the remaining spots. They were making those bids to Blossom and Toad, of course. Their hold over this market had always been strong, but now it was backed by the authorities. Now the market was their private empire.

And that was just the start.

This afternoon, Zhou's eunuch had come by and paid them their fee. Before leaving he had declared their business complete. Blossom's only response had been a smile. Their business was *not* complete. They knew Zhou's dirty secret. They could blackmail him whenever they wanted something, and he would comply. He would give them whatever they demanded or they would destroy him.

Of course, at some point the real killer would strike again, and the whole city would know Mr. Lin had been innocent all along. That would not matter to Blossom and Toad. They would still have Zhou under their thumb, and *that* was all that mattered. Besides, no one could prove they had planted the bracelet and set Lin up. People might hate them a little more after Lin was proved innocent, but so what? They were already hated.

Yes, life was about to get a lot better.

"Another!" Blossom shouted again. She wasn't one to drink to excess, but tonight was a celebration. Besides, she meant to break her new servant in. "Quickly!"

The door to their kitchen slid open, revealing a woman hardly larger than a child. The woman pushed the door with her back, holding two cups of ale out at arm's length as though she couldn't stand the smell. As the tiny figure stepped through the door, she caught her toe on the threshold and nearly went sprawling. She righted herself just in time to prevent a spill.

Blossom hit the table with the heel of her palm. "Let's go, Yu Shuan!"

Yu Shuan waited until the ale stopped sloshing around in the cups. Then she placed both cups on the table and turned away.

Blossom wagged her finger. "No. Get back here."

Yu Shuan's shoulders sagged. To Blossom it was a beautiful sight. Why, just this morning Yu Shuan had led a mob that chased Blossom from the market. She had grinned while the other vendors jeered Blossom. She had stuck her finger in Blossom's face and given orders like a damn mandarin.

Let's see her do it now.

The idea to hire Yu Shuan had come to Blossom this afternoon. She had been watching the old woman struggle out of the market, delighting in the knowledge that she had nowhere to go. Then inspiration had come. Yu Shuan was far too proud to beg on the streets. She would do anything to avoid that humiliation.

So why not offer the dried-up old bitch a job?

Yu Shuan straightened herself up and turned around. "Yes?"

"Yes, *Mistress.*"

"Yes, Mistress?"

"Get a cloth and wipe down this table. You spilled ale on it earlier."

Toad, who knew full well that he was the real offender, guffawed. "Yeah. I seen better servers, I can tell you that. I guess it's easier to yell at people than work for a living, huh?"

Yu Shuan walked into the kitchen and returned with a cloth and a bucket. She began to wipe their old table down. Her face was a mask of determined dignity. She seemed to believe she could be their servant and retain a bit of her old self-respect.

Blossom watched the cloth go back and forth across the table. She rubbed her eyes, trying to bring a bit of clarity back to her vision. The truth was that Yu Shuan didn't *deserve* dignity. She had lost, had been outmaneuvered by a superior opponent. Now that opponent was gracious enough to give her work. But she still insisted on walking around with her back straight and her head held high.

It seemed the servant needed a lesson.

Blossom struggled to her feet, trying to ignore the ale sloshing in her belly. When she finally managed to stand she reached out and grabbed Yu Shuan's scrawny wrist. "Stupid bitch!"

Yu Shuan looked up, her eyes filled with fear. "What?"

"What? *What?* You spilled water on my dress. *Look!*"

"I'm sorry. I –"

"Why don't you tell me I'm being unreasonable?" Blossom pressed her fingers into Yu Shuan's wrist, bringing a strangled moan from the old woman. "Why don't you embarrass me in front of everyone again? Why don't you laugh at me, the way you did when some pig hit me with a shoe?"

Yu Shuan twisted and fought, but she could not escape Blossom's grip. "Let me *go!*"

"Still telling me what to do?" Blossom whipped her free hand out and caught Yu Shuan across the cheek. "Get out! *Out!*"

Toad put his hands on his little belly and threw his head back. He belted out reams of deep, rasping laughter.

Yu Shuan finally yanked her wrist free and stumbled backward. The part of her face that Blossom had struck was already a bright, angry red. She brushed her fingers over the growing welt and winced. Her eyes welled with water.

Blossom curled her hand into a fist. "Didn't you hear me?"

Yu Shuan looked up at Blossom. "I heard you."

"Then get out," Blossom said again. This time her voice was more subdued. She wanted to feel a great triumph, but it didn't come. This wasn't going the way she had planned. She had meant to savor Yu Shuan's servitude, to draw it out for days or even weeks. Instead she had lost her temper and ended it much too soon. "Now."

Yu Shuan folded her arms over her chest. She tilted her chin up and stared at Blossom. "You won't get away with this."

Blossom sat down. "People hit their servants all the time."

"You know I'm not talking about that. I'm talking about your maneuvering, your plotting. You have schemed too much and made too many enemies. Sooner or later something will come back to bite you. Perhaps the vendors you turned out will show up at the market one day and lynch you. Perhaps you have a secret partner who will betray you. Those things could well happen, but I think your undoing will be much simpler. The authorities will realize you framed Mr. Lin, and they'll kill you for it."

Toad slammed his cup on the table, sending a fountain of ale into the air. "Did not! We're heroes – me and Blossom both!"

Yu Shuan smiled at Toad. "Wait a week, maybe two. You'll be at the end of the market under the willow tree. They'll strangle you both for that you've done."

Toad jumped to his feet and stood over Yu Shuan. "I ought to break your jaw for talking like that."

Yu Shuan ignored Toad, but as she turned to leave she gave Blossom a wink.

Then she opened the door and melted into the hot night.

● ● ●

Later, as the rest of the market slept, Blossom lay on her back and looked up at the bedroom ceiling. She had finished six cups of ale that night, and she should have been in a deep slumber. Instead she had only managed a few winks of sleep before waking up suddenly. Now her body seemed to think it was the middle of the day. She didn't even feel drunk.

Blossom turned onto her stomach and grunted. The heat was thick and wet. She felt dirt sticking to her skin. How could anyone sleep on a night like this?

Her mind turned back to Yu Shuan. That smug bitch! She had walked out on them, had taunted Blossom before she left. And she didn't even ask for money. Yu Shuan preferred her dignity over begging for a copper or two. Somehow that was the biggest outrage of all.

A heavy crash from outside wrenched Blossom from her thoughts. On the heels of that sound came the screech of an outraged cat.

Blossom groaned. Life in the market brought all kinds of nuisances. During the day it was always noisy, with the vendors and the punters and the rest of the bustle. At night it was worse. Night was when the animals came. The rats poured over the street looking for garbage, and the felines came for the rats. At night the market was a world of scavenging and feeding, of stalking and killing. Blossom hated the scurrying rats and the sharp feline hisses. A person could live here for a lifetime and never get used to it.

Tonight it seemed the vermin were conducting their grim business right outside Blossom's window. She sat up and pawed at the floor. Soon her fingers touched cold metal. She felt her way along that metal until she found the hilt of her little dagger.

All she had to do was step outside and bang her knife against something. That would send the animals scurrying off.

Blossom lit a candle and slid a tunic over her thin shoulders. She crept toward the door, tented her fingers against its rough wood, and slid it open.

Toad was lying on his side next to the dugout fireplace. Blossom closed the door behind her, careful not to make a sound. If she roused Toad after he had passed out from drinking, he would get nasty.

She stopped. It was even hotter out here than it was in her room. Perhaps Toad had gotten it in his drunken head to light a fire before bed. No. It was the height of summer and even he wasn't that stupid. Besides, there were no glowing embers down in the fireplace.

Then why was it so hot?

The front door had to be open. A wall extended into their common room, blocking her view of the door, but Blossom was certain the heat was coming from there. Toad had probably gone outside to piss and forgotten to close the door when he came back in.

Blossom had the sudden urge to kick her brother awake and tell him to shut the door. But no, that wouldn't be wise. At this time of night, in his state, he might deal her a blow for doing that.

Besides, he was sleeping like a stone and it would take ages to wake him. She made up her mind to berate him for it tomorrow. She placed her candle on the table and turned toward the door.

When Blossom heard the noise, she recognized it right away. She had heard that long, heavy creak on her floor countless times.

It was a footstep.

The noise had come from the front door. It was the only part of the room she could not see, so it must have come from there.

Someone was in their house.

Blossom did not move. She tried to make her breathing silent. How much noise had she just made? She had been moving around the room, but she had tried to be quiet because Toad was asleep. Did the intruder assume *she* was asleep as well, or did he know she was out of bed? Was he listening, waiting?

Not he. She.

The thought slid into Blossom's mind like a thin, sharp blade. Of course. She knew who was here. It was her. It was the Blue Woman.

Blossom and Toad had grown up in this market, just a few hundred paces from the government's execution grounds. When they were children, the strangulations and beheadings were a free source of entertainment. They went to see as many as they could. By the time Blossom was an adolescent, those killings had become routine. After that they got boring, and today Blossom didn't remember any of them.

Except for one. Except for the Blue Woman.

Blossom was nine years old at the time. She and Toad had heard all about the prisoner. The condemned was a woman who had been found guilty of drowning her infant son.

A lot of people came out that day, drawn by the prisoner's hideous crime. Toad and Blossom stood at the front of the crowd with the other children, shouting for the Guards to bring out the murderer.

But when the woman was led into view, Blossom's voice trailed off to nothing. One thought had come to her: *She's so young!* On the heels of that thought came another: *She is innocent.* Blossom had no reason to believe that but she did. She believed it with a clear and simple certainty. *She will die for a sin that is not hers.*

It was as though Blossom had spoken her thoughts out loud. The woman turned and looked right at her. The sadness in her eyes was so strong that Blossom felt an unseen hand reach into her chest and squeeze her heart.

Then the woman smiled.

The woman who was about to die had looked at Blossom and smiled. Blossom, who had a talent for reading people even then, understood right away.

She's trying to form a bond with me. She wants one last human connection before she dies.

Blossom wasted no time responding. She picked up a rock and threw it as hard as she could. It was a lucky shot. It hit the woman just above her left eye.

Toad and the other children bellowed in triumph. They all followed her example, and the air grew thick with flying rocks. They struck the woman on her face, her legs, her belly. She bent down low to protect herself, but then the top of her head was exposed to the cruel rocks.

It continued until a Gold Bird Guard sauntered up and told them to give it a rest. The rocks stopped but the jeers did not.

And as soon as the woman found the strength to look up, her eyes were on Blossom again. Her face had become a mask of blood. Her lower lip was split by a deep gash. She was not smiling at Blossom anymore, but there was no hate in her eyes either. Instead her face was just…blank. Blossom remembered thinking the rocks must have struck all the sense from her.

But then why did the woman still stare at Blossom?

When the Guards strangled the prisoner, her tongue pushed out through her lips and her eyes bulged until they almost burst into mush. The whole time, Blossom was sure those bulging, bursting eyes were watching her.

Most strangulation victims turned purple, but this woman's skin became a deep, icy blue. Blossom had never seen anything like it. Her skin was the color of a clear sky on a cold day. The rest of the crowd must have noticed as well, because the jeering faded to an eerie silence.

The woman's head finally dropped to one side. It came to a rest all the way down on her shoulder because the tendons inside her neck were cut. By then the crowd was so quiet Blossom could hear wind pushing through the willow tree.

The crowd began to thin out, but Blossom stayed and watched the Guards load the body into a cart. The Guards pulled the body right past her. It was so close Blossom could have reached out and touched the dead woman's skin. Blossom saw the woman's bloodied face, her black and swollen tongue, her broken neck.

But the worst part was the wire. No one had bothered to remove the wire from her neck. It was imbedded deep into her flesh like a hideous necklace.

As the dead woman passed by, Blossom became certain her eyes would snap open. She would turn those sightless eyes on Blossom. In a low and creaking voice, she would ask why Blossom had thrown rocks at a person condemned to die. She would point a long, thin finger at Blossom, marking her for revenge.

Instead the wagon picked up speed and headed away from the market. Blossom watched until it disappeared around a corner.

As Blossom stood alone in the market, a name formed in her mind: the Blue Woman.

That was more than thirty years ago, but Blossom knew the Blue Woman had not forgotten. Over the years, Blossom saw her. Usually it was in the market. The Blue Woman would be standing far away, a still figure in the bustling crowd. She always just stood and watched, her head hanging to one side because her neck had been snapped by the wire.

Blossom never caught more than a glimpse of her. As soon as she noticed the terrible figure, it vanished.

The Blue Woman taunted her. She *wanted* Blossom to see her. She wanted Blossom to know she was always close, always waiting.

And now, finally, she had come.

The heat was so heavy Blossom was sure it would melt her. She clutched her knife but could not manage a strong grip. The handle was slick and wet in her hands.

She looked at the wall that blocked their front door, stared so hard her eyes hurt.

More movement behind the wall. Blossom sensed it more than she heard it. It was a strange shift in the stillness: limbs moving through the wet air.

Then came another sound Blossom recognized. It was the soft, gentle noise of wood settling against wood.

The front door was closing.

Blossom felt wild hope. Maybe it was just a thief who was leaving because there was nothing to steal. Maybe her imagination had gotten the better of her.

She heard another footstep.

The Blue Woman had come. Blossom was alone in this dark house with the Blue Woman.

Another footstep. Blossom tried to move but her body refused. Her mind screamed at her to run.

But run where? This house only had one exit.

A revelation hit Blossom with the force of a hammer. She wasn't alone! Toad was sleeping on the floor, less than five paces from her!

Blossom dove to the floor and scrambled toward Toad on her hands and knees. "Toad! Toad, wake up! There's –"

Her first disjointed thought was that Toad had spilled ale all over the floor. It must have been a full cup, because it was everywhere.

Then, as more sensations came to her, understanding set in. The liquid was thick and tacky. It had a strange metallic smell. It stuck to her hands and her knees. It sucked her old robe against her chest.

Blossom placed a hand on her brother's arm to turn him over. As soon as she felt his weight, she knew. It was like trying to move a giant bag of meat. She pulled harder and finally managed to turn him onto his back.

Another confused thought came to her. *This can't be Toad. This can't be Toad because Toad has eyes.*

Blossom wanted to look up at their cracked ceiling and tell the gods there was some kind of mistake. The dead man could not be her brother. Toad's eyes were small and close together. This man *had* no eyes. Where the eyes should have been there were deep, red gashes.

She looked down at her brother's chest. His tunic was black and wet. Holes had been torn into it.

Stab wounds, her mind whispered.

Blossom let go of Toad's arm. She crawled away from him, ignoring the sticky liquid that clung to her. After an eternity she found a corner, sat in it and pulled her knees tight against her chest. She stared at the dead man on her floor.

The dead man stared back with hollow eyes.

Another footstep.

Blossom stood up. Her legs wavered, but they held. "I know you're there. I know you're there so come on."

More footsteps. It seemed the intruder had accepted her invitation.

Just before the figure stepped into the weak light, Blossom saw everything. The Blue Woman's head lay to one side, lolling grotesquely on her shoulder. Her tongue, swollen and black, pressed through her lips like a serpent emerging from her body. Her eyes were masses of whitish yellow mush…but Blossom knew the Blue Woman could see her.

Blossom saw the dead thing reaching up to its neck, saw it digging its fingers into its own dead flesh. She heard the tearing of dry skin as it pulled the wire free. She heard more footsteps as the thing crossed the room, arms outstretched, hands holding the wire taut. Blossom felt dull metal against her skin as the Blue Woman wrapped the wire around her neck and began to twist.

Then the figure stepped into the room and the illusion was gone. Darkness still covered the intruder's face, but Blossom could see this was not Blue Woman coming for her revenge. It was just a man.

"You killed him in his sleep," Blossom said. "You stabbed him before he could fight back."

The man shook his head. Blossom sensed he was smiling. "I did his eyes first." His voice was a black whisper. "I did his eyes while he was still alive."

"Impossible. My brother is as strong as a giant. He'd kill you."

The only reply was another smile in the darkness.

"How could you have done that without waking me?" Blossom heard herself ask. "How can you kill that silently? No one has that much skill."

The man only watched her.

"We have money in the back room. Just today we received a sizable amount. I could –"

"I know about your dirty money." The voice became a low growl. "I know what you did to get it. Because of you the whole city believes my sacrifices are the work of an old merchant."

Blossom did not have to ask the man who he was. She already knew. "They'll know you did this. They'll know you're not dead and they'll be looking for you again."

The man said nothing, but Blossom sensed another smile.

"If you let me go I'll fix this." Blossom tried to look the black figure in the face and could not. "I'll go to the authorities and tell them I made a mistake."

The man extended his right arm. Blossom saw a short, thick knife.

"No hammer? No club? I thought you bludgeoned your victims."

"A hammer would be too fast. We have all night."

Blossom looked down at her brother. She looked at the holes where his eyes had been, at the wounds on his chest. She decided this man had told her the truth. He had waited until the very end to kill Toad.

The man started toward her. Blossom forced herself to act. She held her knife out, its tip pointing at the ceiling. She closed her eyes, gritted her teeth, and swung the knife toward her throat.

Somewhere, she heard one word: "No!"

Then some terrible animal was biting her, was tearing into her neck. She pushed harder, felt the cruel blade ripping through her skin and cutting into her throat. She was vaguely aware of more wetness on the front of her robe. Her hands were slick and hot. When she tried to breathe, a choking pain wracked her body.

And still she pushed.

Blossom opened her eyes. She saw a figure rushing toward her through the darkness, arms outstretched. Then rough, strong hands were at her throat. She tried to free herself of those hands but their grip was too strong, the pain too great.

Long, black fingers yanked the knife from Blossom's throat. There was another rush of pain, this one greater than the first.

Blossom watched a strange liquid spraying from her neck and thought *that's mine.*

The room began to pull away from her – slowly at first, and then faster. Strength left her limbs and she fell. She hit something hard. The floor. She looked up, saw a black shape standing over her. Somewhere, a world away, she heard a man whispering outraged curses.

She felt herself falling back, back into darkness. The figure staring down at her began to look smaller. *I beat you! You did it to my brother but you didn't do it to me! You didn't do it to me because I outsmarted you. I beat you!*

Hands reached for her. She felt someone grabbing her, shaking her. That brought the room slightly back into focus...and then all of Blossom's elation withered away.

The figure above her had changed. Its angular, masculine outline was now smooth and curved. It seemed to have longer hair. Its head was leaning so far to the side its ear rested on its shoulder.

Terror gripped Blossom. She reached out, touched the hands of the thing that was shaking her. She felt cold, dead skin and she knew. If the room were brighter she would see a being with blue skin.

I was right. She really did *come for me. She came because she knew I was going to die tonight. She knew I was going to die and I could not escape.*

Less of that strange liquid was spraying from Blossom's neck. The darkness returned, faster than before. Blossom fell back, back into that darkness forever.

And the Blue Woman followed.

25

"Quickly!" Hui Fen had many fine traits, but patience was not one of them. "It's your turn."

"I'll only do it if you keep quiet." Ming had lost count of how many times he'd spoken those words this evening. Counting wasn't easy thanks to the fog of alcohol covering his brain, and his daughter's prodding did not help.

Ming looked at the square of cloth spread over the floor of their little common room. On top of the cloth was a thin layer of soot from the fireplace. Everyone's fingers were dirty from tracing in the black powder.

Ming placed his finger in the soot and began to draw. He started with the legs, making four that were roughly the same length. The children laughed and accused him of making silly pictures on purpose. Ming didn't have the heart to tell them they were seeing the best of their father's artistic prowess.

He finished the legs and began to draw a long, fat body. "This is the hard part," he whispered. "All right. Now the nose."

Hui Fen brayed laughter. "That's not real!"

Ming looked up. "Not so loud. You were supposed to be asleep quite some time ago so don't test my patience. And don't be angry just because *you* don't know what the animal is."

"It's not an animal. That's like something from Heaven!"

Ming smirked. "You're just angry because you're losing. I guessed most of your animals correctly and I never questioned the caliber of your work. I guessed tiger, dog, *and* hawk."

"You didn't guess bear!" Wei Sheng put in.

"No, I did not guess bear." Ming thought his son's picture looked more like a serving plate with eyes, but he kept that opinion to himself. "I guessed the rest of them, though. You'll *never* guess this one." He put his finger back in the soot and finished his picture – such as it was.

"It's not real," Hui Fen said again. "It's big and it's fat and it has long, floppy ears. Its nose is hanging down from its face like a…" She trailed off, thinking.

Wei Sheng pointed at the picture. "Like a tree vine!"

Hui Fen giggled. "Right!"

Ming tried hard to look exasperated. "If you children only knew the places your father has been, the things he knows. These animals are real."

Wei Sheng's eyes went wide with amazement, but Hui Fen did not look impressed.

"It's true," Ming said. "There's a country to the west where they're everywhere. The kings ride them like horses and soldiers use them in battle."

Hui Fen made a noise, as if to suggest she couldn't believe her father could be so old and stupid. "Have *you* ever seen one?"

"Well, no," Ming said honestly. "But I know people who have. In fact, there's a man in the West Market who sells medicine made from their teeth. The next time we go there I'll show you."

Ming could tell his son believed all of it now. Hui Fen scoffed again, but Ming thought she was beginning to doubt her own doubt.

Wei Sheng looked down at the picture. "How big are they? Bigger than bears?"

"Much bigger."

Hui Fen said, "That's not true! No animal is bigger than a bear."

"You're quite wrong, my daughter. These are bigger. In fact, some people say they're taller than most of the houses in this city."

"*Impossible!*" Hui Fen's voice threatened to bring the house down around them.

"Quieter, please."

"Impossible!" Hui Fen's voice was lower but her scorn was not.

"Don't believe me, then. But your father knows more than you think. I've read all about these animals in the Imperial Archives."

Hui Fen's face was all suspicion again. "What's an…an archive?"

"It's a record kept by the government," Ming said. "Usually it's a very important record that only important people can see."

"Important people like you," Wei Sheng said proudly.

"That's right. Important people like me." Ming prepared to barrage his children with more nonsense…and then he trailed off.

"*Baba,*" Hui Fen said. "*Baba,* are you all right?"

"I'm fine." Ming smacked his lips, wincing at the lingering taste of ale. "Why would you ask me that?"

"You were just looking at nothing and making a strange face."

"A strange face? Like this?" Ming pushed his cheeks together and poked out his tongue. The little ones erupted into laughter.

There was a chorus of shouts for another face. Ming did not hear them. He stood up and crossed the room in three long strides. His satchel of papers was sitting in a corner. He brushed the soot from his hands, opened the satchel and dumped its contents onto their small wooden table.

There was a tug on his pant leg. Ming looked down. He had almost forgotten that other people were in the room.

It was Wei Sheng. "*Baba,* what are you doing?"

"Nothing. Get ready for bed."

Wei Sheng did not seem to detect the change in Ming's voice, but Hui Fen did. She took her little brother by the hand and led him to their sleeping mats.

Ming picked up a scroll from the table. He looked the scroll over, dropped it on the table and picked up another one. Something he had just said to his children was important. He had inadvertently touched on something relevant to the killings. But *what* had he said? He did not know.

He looked at more of his notes, hoping to see something that would help him remember.

Ming picked up another paper, and another. Each one was a mess of scrawled thoughts and theories. It was like trying to read a coded message. Finally he slammed a paper against the table hard enough to hurt his hand. "Shit!"

Ming noticed a strange stillness in the room. He looked up. Both of the children were staring at him. Wei Sheng appeared to be the verge of tears. Even Hui Fen looked scared.

Ming gave them a tired smile. "It's all right. Just something about work. Off to sleep now, the both of you. I'm sorry but you'll have to cope with the candles a bit longer."

Soon the children were stretched out on mats and dutifully pretending to be asleep.

Ming closed his eyes. This was the kind of behavior that brought on his fits. Even now he could feel his body tensing up, and that was a sure warning sign. The ocean of alcohol he had consumed tonight only made it worse. The heavy drone on his mind confused him, agitated him. He needed to calm his nerves. If he stayed this upset his throat would start to feel tight and then his chest would hurt. That couldn't happen. Not now. Because he was close to something.

Ming kept his eyes closed. When had this feeling come to him? He had told his children…what? He had bragged about having access to the Imperial Archives, about being an important person. The next thing he knew he was on the verge of a fit.

The danger of a fit was fading, but Ming knew one could still strike. He turned and made a weaving line toward a window. He pulled back the paper curtain and looked outside. The night was hot, the air heavy and wet. The darkness gave Ming a sense of peace that made thinking easier. He admonished himself to slow down.

Maybe the answer was in Ming's notes and maybe it was not. Perhaps it was buried somewhere in his mind, waiting to be unearthed.

Think. Give yourself a moment and think.

Throughout their investigation, Ming and Dragon had paid special attention to the crimes of the parents. Those crimes were the key, they reasoned, because they were secrets. The wealthy protected their dirty secrets like treasures. It was therefore a question of who had access to those secrets.

A rush of fear slammed into Ming's chest. He staggered back from the window frame, and then the panic was on him like a swarm of hornets. There was pain, pain everywhere, and with it a strange numbness that was somehow more terrifying. He lurched forward again and searched for the window, thinking vaguely that he may need to vomit. He groped but only found the wall. It was like the window had vanished. He tried to breathe and felt more pain deep in his chest. The world spun away from him.

This is it. This is the fit that finally kills me. But I can't die now. My children will be alone.

Ming tried to focus on the thought that had sent him flying into his fit. He reached for it, like a drowning man grasping for a rope.

Concentrate. Give your mind something to do. What did you say to your children that was important?

Slowly, slowly, the world settled back into place. Ming's heart was still galloping, but his throat opened just a little and he began to take in air.

The window was there in front of him after all. Seeing it brought Ming an absurd relief. He gripped the window frame hard.

It happened because I'm close. It happened because I'm going to find the answer.

And then Ming had it. He had told his children about the Imperial Archives.

The criminal complaint against Lei Lei's father had been logged in the Archives. Guang Fu, the soldier who had pillaged a city out west, was treated in a similar fashion. The government had reprimanded his unit for looting and then filed the shame away the Archives.

Ming thought back to Chang, the unsavory smuggler he'd saved from a rape accusation. He was able to rescue Chang, but not before an official complaint was made and handed in to the government. There was only one place such a complaint would have gone.

How had the madman discovered his victims' secrets? Why, he sat in the Imperial Archives and read about them. The Archives were the only place in which every parent's secret was accessible.

Ming made a noise that was something between a laugh and a scream. The madman was a city official. Only those people had access to the Archives. This was it. It was the great stride he had been waiting to take.

There was still a slew of suspects – investigators, mandarins, accountants, engineers and others all accessed the Archives daily. With a little effort any one of those people could seek the information he wanted and avoid notice. But Ming was not discouraged, because he knew a way of narrowing the search. It meant learning the significance of Meng Chun, the pub owner. Her death was now the key to this riddle, because her crime was not listed in the Archives. It couldn't be, because no complaint was ever filed against her. If Ming could learn how a childless pub owner fit into this story, he might eliminate all the suspects. All but one.

Who could access the Archives *and* learn Meng Chun's secrets?

Ming felt panic threatening to surge and ignored it. He would keep at this even if he could hardly breathe anymore.

Feeling a bit foolish but unable to help himself, Ming walked back to the table and swept his papers to the floor in a grand gesture. His notes had served their purpose. The same feeling was back. All the pieces were there in his mind, waiting to be put together.

In the weak glow of the candles, Ming began to assemble them.

26

Zhou also stayed awake late into the night. He was back in the Imperial Archives, a lone figure hunched over a pile of scrolls.

Zhou always felt this hall lost its majesty after the sun went down. At night the main room was lit by dozens of torches that bathed everything in an eerie, jumping light. The high walls that were so impressive during the day became the walls of some vast, empty tomb. The painting he loved to admire in the sunlight was almost invisible. Looking up at the vague outline of that smiling woman in her long robe, Zhou was certain she had transformed into a demon – some red, scaly beast with curved talons and a forked tongue. He sometimes feared that if he fell asleep she would crawl down the walls like a lizard and gather him up.

Tonight the dread was even worse than usual. Because tonight Zhou had realized he wasn't the only person with an interest the Archives.

He had come here just after dusk, determined to solve the crimes on his own. If Ming and Dragon lacked the resolve to finish what they had started, so be it. Zhou would pick up the slack and do it on his own. After all, he was cleverer than the both of them. He had already manipulated the bureaucracy, had positioned himself perfectly inside the government. He had even outwitted that master of intrigue, Governor Han. How hard would it be to track down an insane man? All he had to do was learn the significance of those secret notes. Where had the killer found such sensitive information?

At some point in the evening – he could not be sure when – Zhou had felt his insides go cold.

Everything was right here. In the Imperial Archives.

As they had done countless times that night, Zhou's eyes passed over the shelves, over the endless rows of scrolls. Those scrolls contained records on everything a man could imagine, including criminal complaints. And what did each dead child have in common? A complaint had been filed against the parents.

How else could a person learn the deepest secrets of so many powerful families? The answer was simple. There *was* no other way. The madman must have come right here, to the Imperial Archives.

Zhou looked at two Guards standing by the west exit. He waited for one of those Guards to smile, draw a knife and start toward him. But the men just stared straight ahead, like statues that breathed.

Zhou drew in a sharp breath and focused his mind.

Just as Ming had, Zhou turned his thoughts to Meng Chun. There was nothing about the pub owner in these Archives. How did the killer learn her secrets? How did *she* fit in?

Fortunately, when it came to Meng Chun Zhou did not need the Archives. He already knew about her business, her partners, her enemies and everything else. Well, perhaps not everything. He hadn't known about the murder of her husband. Still, Zhou had vast amounts of information on Meng Chun, thanks to –

That feeling was back. Zhou's insides were turning to ice. The feeling was stronger now, as though his body were about to freeze solid and shatter.

And then he knew.

Meng Chun did more than just fit into this mystery. She completed it, perfected it like a painter's final brushstroke in a masterpiece. If you thought about Meng Chun's history with Zhou, it all made sense.

But if Zhou was right, that meant…

A name came to Zhou. Could it be the right name? The killer's name? Zhou turned the possibility over in his mind, looked at it from every angle. Yes. Only one person other than Zhou had access to these Archives *and* knew Meng Chun's secrets. Zhou himself had sent that man to investigate Meng Chun several times. The man waited until Meng Chun was away, then slipped into her pub and looked for damaging secrets. He had finally told Zhou there was nothing to find.

But it seemed he *had* found something. He had found Meng Chun's dark secret and kept it to himself.

Zhou thought of the name again. This time it felt different, like a dark curse.

It was Hai Tao. It was Zhou's eunuch.

Zhou felt sweat pushing through his skin. What would happen when the city found out? The authorities might learn that Zhou had used Hai Tao as a spy. That could lead them to blame Zhou for the killings. They might even think he had *ordered* the killings. They could well wrap a wire around his neck.

Even if Zhou escaped punishment, his career would be over. He would be mocked as the city's most hopeless incompetent. He had spent weeks and weeks chasing a killer, never realizing the fiend was in plain view the entire time. The scandal would be monstrous.

For the first time in his life, Zhou understood what Ming meant when he talked about his fits. Zhou felt something growing inside his chest. He felt it growing larger, felt it expand until it threatened to fill his chest and strangle him.

Zhou choked it back. He was not Ming. He had not come this far to let fate cheat him at the last moment. He could get out of this. After all, no one else knew the truth. All he had to do was create his *own* truth. Hadn't he been doing that all along?

Zhou began to think of possible solutions. Every time he concocted a new idea he found a flaw and discarded it. But he didn't lose hope. The correct strategy *did* exist. There had to be a way of escaping this disaster unscathed.

When Zhou finally found the answer, he couldn't believe how simple it was.

• • •

Later that night, Zhou looked down at the object in his hands. It was a crude rendition, hewn from a piece of wood he'd found on the street outside. To carve it he'd used his little dagger. Such a blade was not optimal for this kind of task, and Zhou had almost cut himself twice.

This work left a lot to be desired, but it would do.

Zhou began to gather up his things, careful to keep his eyes from the silent woman who watched him from above.

27

The next morning, just after the sun came up, Zhou was waiting outside Governor Han's office. The office door was closed, but the young Guard had informed Zhou that Han was inside. That was not a surprise. Did the Snake ever stop working?

Zhou glanced both ways down the corridor. A few officials were already scurrying here and there, but the building was still very quiet. It wouldn't become busy for some time.

Zhou wondered again why he was here. Just before dawn, a messenger had arrived at his home and announced that Han wished to see him right away. The messenger didn't give a reason for the summons and Zhou did not ask for one. Surely the messenger didn't know the reason anyway.

The messenger's surprise visit had almost brought catastrophe. Because Zhou was not alone. Ren Shu was there, too. Zhou had stopped by Ren Shu's boarding house on his way home last night and invited him over. Ren Shu had declared the idea madness at first, but he finally gave in to Zhou's pleas. Fortunately, this morning Ren Shu had slipped out of sight before the messenger could spot him.

Zhou had already been planning to call on Han today. He needed to look the Snake in the eye and tell the biggest lie of his career – of his life.

If he failed, he would likely lose his head. If he succeeded, he would have to commit a sin far darker than anything he had ever imagined.

Commandant Chen was there too. The old jackass was sitting on a bench and looking over a scroll. Zhou did not know the reason for their summons, but clearly Chen had made a guess. Every now and then he looked up and gave Zhou a mocking smile. Perhaps he was expecting to see Zhou dismissed.

Zhou wanted very much to smile back. *Keep doing that. It will come back to you later.*

What would Chen's punishment be for this debacle? He would at least be forced into early retirement, and of course he would lose a great deal of face. And more could very well happen...perhaps a lot more. If the Snake got angry enough, Chen could face legal punishment. The old man might receive sixty lashes with the thick rod, with a few years of hard labor waiting for him after he recovered. He might even end up under the willow tree with a wire around his neck.

The massive door to the Snake's office opened with a groan, and a Guard poked his head out. "The Governor is ready for you both."

Chen puffed his narrow chest out and strutted into the office like a conquering general. Zhou made sure his mask of neutrality was on and then followed.

Governor Han was standing with his hands planted on his desk, his head dangling between his narrow shoulders. He glanced up and gestured to the two seats in front of his desk. "Sit." Then he half sat, half fell into his own seat.

Zhou sat down, never taking his eyes off Han. He had never seen the Governor so distraught. He could think of only one thing that would shake the old veteran so badly.

Han confirmed Zhou's suspicion. "There were two more murders last night."

Chen drew in a fast, sharp breath.

Zhou had been predicting this all along, so he decided it was best not to appear shocked. He tried to look upset instead.

Chen said, "Who...what happened?"

"The government's two witnesses against Lin." Han ran a hand over his bald pate. "They were both killed last night in their home."

Zhou flinched in spite of himself. Toad and Blossom! He had been expecting to hear of another child killing.

"Terrible," Chen said. "I am sorry to hear of it."

Zhou noted that the old commandant spoke slowly. Perhaps he was buying himself time to think. Zhou had to do the same. This was the golden moment he had been waiting for, the moment when the killer struck again. He had to play it perfectly. "What do we know?"

"What do we know?" The fatigue in Han's voice took on a bitterness that made him sound a great deal like Commandant Chen. "We know the terror is not over, even though we told the whole city it was. We know we have made a terrible mistake in executing Lin."

"Impossible," Chen blurted. As soon as the word left his mouth, a pained look crossed his face. He had spoken far too frankly to his superior.

But Han appeared too upset to care about outbursts. "These killings mean our real criminal is still alive. Either that or Lin has returned from the underworld to exact revenge on Toad and Blossom."

"Those two were gangsters," Chen said. "They could have been killed for any number of reasons."

Han looked at Chen. "I thought they were concerned citizens who just wanted to do the right thing."

"They *were* – at least in this instance." Flecks of spittle flew from Chen's mouth as he spoke. "I meant to say that most commoners make enemies now and then. I do not believe we should rush to conclusions. Not that *you* ever would, of course."

Zhou allowed himself a secret smile. Chen was digging his own grave.

"Perhaps," Han said, "you can explain why these two witnesses were killed on the very day Lin was executed?"

"No," Chen mumbled. He looked like a child being berated by his father.

"Perhaps you think it is a coincidence?"

Another shake of the head.

"Perhaps you can explain why both victims were holding statues of Leigong? Commandant Chen, we kept that information from the public! My personal feeling is that we accused the wrong man, and this has offended the real killer for some reason."

Zhou stole a glance at Chen. The commandant's face was motionless, but his mind appeared to be working fast under the surface. It seemed the old fool had finally realized his mistake and the consequences it could bring.

Han leaned forward and stared at Chen. His eyes narrowed and he lowered his head. Zhou half expected to see a forked tongue flick out between the old man's teeth. The Snake had arrived. "Chen. You campaigned tirelessly to see Lin condemned to death. You sat in that very spot and argued that we had found the right man. We trusted you. The *Emperor* trusted you."

If Governor Han looked like a viper about to strike, Chen suddenly resembled a wounded mouse. The old man squirmed in his chair and tried desperately to meet Han's eyes. He never quite managed it.

Zhou knew enough to keep his mouth shut and let his enemy suffer. He needed to do nothing else to fortify his position. Besides, he was enjoying this.

Han no longer looked disheveled or uncomfortable. Now that he was a predator again, all his uncertainty was gone. "If this becomes a humiliation we will hold you responsible, Commandant Chen. You will be blamed for bringing disgrace upon the Emperor himself."

Chen seemed to understand there was nothing else to say. In a rare display of wisdom, he kept his mouth shut.

Han said, "You are dismissed, Commandant Chen."

Chen shot up from his seat and bowed so low his forehead almost hit the desk. Then he spun around hurried out of the room.

Han waited until the door was closed. "He's done. The best he can hope for is retirement in disgrace. He's finished and he knows it."

Zhou sighed. "A tragedy."

Han watched Zhou for what felt like an age. Then he threw back his head and released a gale of high, rasping laughter. His face squinted into a hundred lines and his small hands curled into fists. His whole body shook with the effort.

As Han's laughter died down, he actually brushed a tear from his eye. "Come, Zhou. You've been waiting for that ever since this affair started – probably since before that. You knew we had this whole thing wrong and you used it to your advantage."

Zhou tried to look hurt. "I have only done my sacred duty, Sir."

Han nodded as though he had expected nothing else. "Of course. Your rather, eh, creative methods notwithstanding, I must admit you have shown foresight and courage. After all, you were the only one who saw our mistakes."

"Thank you, Governor."

Han settled back in his chair. "What would you like to see happen as a result of all this?"

"I would like to see the killer caught and the city safe."

"Anything else?"

Zhou decided to be honest. "And I would like to replace Commandant Chen."

Han pointed a knowing finger at Zhou. "Of course you would. And you want my job, too."

Zhou felt as though someone had put a knife to his throat. If the Snake saw him as a threat, he already a corpse. "I do not."

"I am seventy years old," Han said. "I'm planning to stay at my post for at least another five years."

"I see." Zhou could think of nothing else to say. He doubted Han could last that much longer, but who knew? If anyone could remain in office until the staggering age of seventy-five, it was this tiny man with the bald head and yellow teeth. After all, mandarins faced mandatory retirement at age sixty-nine, and Han had already gotten around that somehow.

"But I can't keep this job forever," Han said. "Soon I will have to find a successor."

"I consider myself the best candidate," Zhou said.

Han smiled. He looked more like a serpent than ever. "It's good that you forewent the sycophantic denials this time. Of course you want to sit in this chair someday. And I want to find a man who can rule this city effectively."

Zhou looked the Snake in the eye. "How can I prove myself to you?"

"By finding the real perpetrator and putting this whole damned affair down for good. But here's the thing." That bony finger wagged in Zhou's face again. "The city already thinks the real killer is dead. If the people realize we were wrong, it will be a disaster."

"So you want it done quietly," Zhou said.

"Correct. Find the right man and bring him to us. We will deal with him out of the public's view. That by itself won't guarantee you this position, but it will earn you more of my attention."

Zhou wasn't sure that attention from the Snake was a good thing. "What are you going to do with the killer when he's caught?"

"This man murdered four children and left them to rot in the streets," Han said. "He'll watch us peel the flesh from his body."

"And Chen?"

"He knows our dirty secret. I suppose that is more motivation for us to kill him, but I don't believe it will come to that. We will dismiss him and let him live out his days in shame. In return he will stay quiet. He knows the consequences if he does not."

Zhou decided it was time to make his move. "Sir, I believe I have identified the real killer."

Han only stared. It really seemed you could not shock him. "You have waited until now to tell me this?"

"I almost didn't tell you at all. You see, I only suspect that I have found the right man. I don't know for certain yet." Zhou nodded toward the exit through which Commandant Chen had just left. "I have seen what happens to officials who are not prudent."

Han said, "Tell me everything."

Now that Zhou was in the part of the conversation he had planned, he felt more comfortable. "In order to learn about each family, the killer needed access to the Imperial Archives. After all, complaints were lodged against someone in every victim's family – lodged and then filed away in the Archives. That is the common procedure, correct?"

"Interesting," Han murmured. "Plausible."

Zhou took a breath, held it an extra moment and let it out. "I believe our killer is an examination candidate from Chengdu. His name is Wang Ren Shu."

"Are you saying this boy used his status as a candidate to enter the Imperial Archives? That he then discovered the families' secrets in the Archives?"

"Yes," Zhou said. "No one would notice a young man walking through the Archives. People would assume he was studying for the exams."

"Still, reading such things in the open would have been quite a gamble."

"True. I suspect the young man felt the same way. Which is why I believe he may have smuggled the scrolls out of the Archives and read them elsewhere." Before leaving the Archives last night, Zhou had quietly removed files on two of the victims' families. Those files were now at the bottom of Ren Shu's satchel. That would be enough to shift the guilt onto him. Just to be sure, Zhou had planted something else with the files. It was abhorrent to hurt such a fine young man, but Zhou did not have time to formulate a different strategy. He needed to point suspicion away from Hai Tao immediately, and Ren Shu was the only person whose effects he could access. Zhou *had* to betray Ren Shu. If he didn't, all his work over the last few days would come to nothing.

"Your ideas are logical," Han said. "But how have you come to notice this Ren Shu?"

"I spend a great deal of time in the Archives myself. I see that young man there often, and his behavior is odd. Most of the exam candidates spend their time reading philosophy, law, and so forth. But I often see Ren Shu in the criminal complaints section of the Archives. He always seems to be…how can I say this? Looking over his shoulder. Then just last night I saw him slip a file into his satchel. That made me very suspicious."

"Perhaps the boy was just smuggling something out so he could study it for the exams," Han said. "Exam candidates often do such things."

"I don't believe so, Sir. You see, he was in the criminal records section when I saw him steal the scroll." Zhou felt his calm beginning to crack. He had spent most of last night planning what he would say to Han, but now he could remember none of it. "I asked an attendant to find me files on the parents of Lei Lei and Xiu Rong – two of the victims. He looked for quite some time and finally declared them missing."

Han's face remained as still as the side of a mountain. Zhou tried to guess what he was thinking and could not.

Finally Han said, "You really believe this Ren Shu is the guilty man?"

"I do," Zhou said. "But I have no proof yet."

"Then find proof. And Zhou, do it quietly."

"Sir, if there's nothing else I'll start on it right now."

Han picked up a quill and began to write. "All right then. Off you go."

28

It wasn't until Ming arrived on Dragon's street that he realized he had a problem. He didn't know which house was Dragon's.

Ming rounded the corner, stopped and looked. The street was really just a small lane lined with houses. They were jammed so close together some of their roofs touched. Several of them had neat little gardens in front, and a few of the nicer ones had small statues.

Fortune was with Ming that morning. Dragon was sitting in front of the third house on the left, smoking a pipe. He saw Ming and waved.

Ming hurried over to Dragon. "It's good you're out here. I don't know how I would have found you otherwise."

Dragon blew out a plume of smoke and grinned. "Couldn't stay away, could you?"

"Dragon, I know who the killer is."

Dragon's hand, which had been tapping fresh supplies into his thin wooden pipe, froze. He looked up at Ming. "Go on."

"We've been searching for someone who has access to secrets."

"Yes."

Ming told Dragon about the Imperial Archives, about that being the only place in which every family's secret could be unearthed.

"But what about Meng Chun?" Dragon brought the pipe to his lips. "No complaints were filed against her."

"Correct. So can you think of anyone who knew about Meng Chun's past *and* had access to the Archives?" Ming tried to slow down. He had only managed a few snatches of fitful sleep last night. He didn't know how coherent he sounded. "There is only one person. The man Zhou had tasked with *investigating* Meng Chun."

"Him," Dragon said softly. The pipe slipped from his lips and fell to the ground, kicking up little pieces of dirt. "You're right. It has to be him."

"And don't forget that strange fruit we found. He works in the palace kitchens. He probably just slipped it into his pocket one day for a snack while he was waiting outside the temple."

"Yes," Dragon said. "Ming, you've done it."

"All this time he's been right in front of us," Ming said. "It's Zhou's assistant. It's the eunuch, Hai Tao."

"We need to find Zhou."

"I don't know where he is," Ming said. "I went to his home before I came here but he wasn't there. He's not supposed to be working yet, either."

Dragon stood up and dusted his off hands. "Then let's go to Governor Han and tell him. Wait just a moment while I get my things. Then we can head to the Imperial Ministry."

29

Ren Shu sat in his boarding house room and tried to study, but his eyes didn't want to stay open. Even brewing a strong cup of tea and sitting in his least comfortable chair failed to help. He was just too exhausted.

When Zhou showed up here late last night and invited him over, Ren Shu could hardly believe it. Their routine was carved in stone. They met at the same boarding house at the same time every week. It was the safest way of doing things, and they had never once strayed from it.

But last night Zhou had begged Ren Shu to come over. He needed company, he said, and damn the risk.

Ren Shu had resisted at first. The danger was reason enough to say no. On top of that, the exams were just two weeks away. Even if he studied without rest throughout the next twenty days, he would still go into the tests feeling like an unready buffoon.

But in the end Zhou had convinced him, and they spent a very good night together.

Ren Shu turned a paper over and tried to focus. Almost immediately his thoughts began to drift again. That had been the magical part of it – spending the night together. Last night was the first time Ren Shu had gotten to sleep in the same bed as Zhou, to put his arm on him and feel the steady rhythm of his sleep. He'd never done that before with anyone. In some ways it was better than lovemaking.

Ren Shu had no illusions about the future. He knew his time with Zhou was running out. If he failed the exams he would go back to his hometown, and if he passed he could be sent anywhere in the empire. He would almost certainly end up far from Zhou. Besides, soon he would have to marry and make grandsons for his parents. That was a good son's first duty.

Sooner or later it would be over between them. Knowing that made last night even more precious.

The only problem was that now Ren Shu was exhausted. He was going easy on himself by studying Confucianism in government, his favorite topic. It didn't help. His eyelids were getting heavier with every turn of the page.

Well, maybe just a quick nap.

Ren Shu was heading toward his thin cot when he heard three loud, sharp knocks on his door.

Ren Shu opened the door. It was all he could do to keep his jaw from going slack with idiot surprise.

For the second time in less than a day, Zhou was standing outside Ren Shu's room. Only this time Zhou wasn't alone. Behind him were three of the biggest, ugliest Gold Bird Guards Ren Shu had ever seen.

Zhou's face had a look Ren Shu could not identify. It was a strange mix of fear and something else. Shame?

We've been discovered, Ren Shu's mind screamed. *We've been discovered and this is going to lead to some kind of public punishment. What will my parents say?*

Ren Shu decided to feign ignorance. "Yes?"

Zhou's strange, pained look seemed to ease. "Is your name Wang Ren Shu?"

"It is."

"We are here to search your possessions. If you resist, these men will use force."

Ren Shu could only stare at Zhou. What in the world was going on? He would have been no more surprised if Zhou had come here and proclaimed himself the new Emperor. "Zhou, what are you doing?"

Zhou pushed past Ren Shu and walked into the small room. He beckoned for the three Guards to follow. He pointed to each of them, giving out crisp orders. "You. Search the closet and the clothes. You check around the bed and you keep an eye on this boy. I'll search the rest of the place."

A massive Guard stood in front of Ren Shu. Of the three ugly Guards, this man was easily the ugliest. His forehead was almost as large as the rest of his face. He put a hand on the hilt of his sword and stared at Ren Shu.

Zhou began picking up papers and looking at them one by one. The Guards started pawing through Ren Shu's clothing, his desk, his trunk. One of them even put his ear to the wall and began tapping it. Ren Shu watched the man and tried to understand. Then his jaw went slack again. He was looking for hidden storage spaces!

Ren Shu tried to calm himself. There was nothing he could do to stop this search. Protesting would be as futile as trying to fight the three giant Guards. Instead he had to relax and keep his wits about him.

A new possibility occurred to Ren Shu. Maybe this wasn't the disaster it appeared to be. Perhaps he was in some kind of trouble he didn't know about. Perhaps Zhou had gotten wind of that trouble and was here to help. This might all be a ruse for Ren Shu's benefit.

But then, what kind of trouble could Ren Shu possibly be in? Aside from his indiscretions with Zhou, Ren Shu *had* no secrets. He spent all his time at study.

Ren Shu's eyes went to the two Guards going through his things. They seemed most interested in documents. Whenever they came across a paper they placed it carefully in a pile with the others.

Ren Shu looked at Zhou. He was standing by the luggage, going through one bag at a time. His face was set and serious. Not once did he meet Ren Shu's gaze.

Zhou picked up Ren Shu's old gray satchel and looked into it. "Ah!" He pulled out a scroll with a grand sweep and held close it to Ren Shu's face. "Can you explain this?"

Ren Shu squinted at the paper. It was hard to read because Zhou's hand was shaking, but it appeared to detail a murder accusation against a man named Jin Lei Jin. That name was familiar, although Ren Shu did not know why. "I don't know what that is."

"This is a government document." Zhou wagged the scroll as he spoke. "It concerns a criminal investigation. It should never leave the Imperial Archives. Perhaps you can tell me what you're doing with it?" Zhou moved his hand forward until the paper almost touched Ren Shu's nose.

A new realization came to Ren Shu, and it was more frightening than anything else that had happened in this terrible drama. *Zhou is holding the paper close to my face on purpose. He doesn't want me to look him in the eye.* Ren Shu saw with a heavy finality that Zhou was not enacting some elaborate ruse. Whatever this was, it was real. And it was deadly serious.

Ren Shu made his voice steady. "I have never seen that document in my life. Furthermore I do not understand why you are harassing me."

Zhou turned away and resumed pawing through Ren Shu's bag. He suddenly stopped, and his eyes grew wide. "And perhaps you can explain this?"

Zhou drew a small, wooden object from Ren Shu's satchel. He dropped the satchel and held the object out to Ren Shu.

Ren Shu's fear became confusion. The object in Zhou's hand was a carving. Whoever had made it was clearly not an expert. Someone had just hacked away at the wood instead of sculpting it. It almost looked as though a child had fashioned it.

Still, Ren Shu could tell the carving depicted a man. Well, it wasn't quite a man. The nose was so pointed it almost resembled a beak. It had two bumps on its back that might have been wings. It was holding a long, thin object in its right hand. The object looked a bit like a sword, but Ren Shu couldn't be sure. "I have never seen that in my life, either."

Zhou stuffed the strange carving into his pocket and turned away. "You are to come with us for questioning." He motioned to the two Guards searching the room. "You two, pack all the documents and be sure not to damage any." He jabbed a finger at the ugly Guard with the giant forehead. "You. Arrest Wang Ren Shu. Restrain him, gag him and put a sack over his head before you take him out of here."

"This is madness." Ren Shu spoke quickly as the Guard began to tie his hands. "You claim to find a document about a murder. Then you concoct a strange carving and ask me what it is. I have already told you I don't –"

Ren Shu closed his mouth. Black dread swept over him.

A document detailing a murder accusation. A document with the name Jin Lei Jin on it. Now Ren Shu remembered where he had heard that name. Jin Lei Jin was the father of Lei Lei, one of the dead children. Zhou was claiming Ren Shu possessed forbidden information about the girl's father. And there was the statue with the beak nose and the crude wings.

What secret about the investigation had Zhou once shared with Ren Shu? Every murdered child was found with a statue of Leigong.

Zhou was setting him up.

Ren Shu began to yell, to shout every curse his rattled mind could produce. He called Zhou a liar and a traitor and a coward. He swore on his ancestors he would overcome this and expose Zhou no matter the cost.

Finally, Ren Shu reigned his panic in. He had to list specific accusations against Zhou. He even needed to reveal their secret relationship, and he needed to do it now. This might be his only chance to speak out. He had to use it even though these Guards were his only witnesses.

Just as Ren Shu was ready say something more coherent, someone stuffed a cloth into his mouth. Ren Shu was so surprised he almost choked on it.

Ren Shu's last sight was the ugly Guard with the giant forehead. The Guard's eyes, dark and intelligent, were studying Ren Shu with keen interest. Then the sack went over Ren Shu's head and the world was dark.

30

Hui Fen pointed at the floor. "Tiger!"

Wei Sheng looked up and grinned. "Yes!"

Hui Fen grinned back. They had been practicing all morning, preparing for another game against their father. *Baba* had told them not to use soot when he wasn't there, so they traced invisible lines on the floor instead. They were getting good. They would beat *Baba* the next time they played, as long as he didn't make up any more imaginary animals.

Wei Sheng jumped to his feet. "Your turn to draw."

"All right." Hui Fen tried to think of a harder animal. She really wanted to stump Wei Sheng. He was smart but he needed to remember that *she* was smarter. She would always be smarter than him. After all, she was older.

"Come on!" Wei Sheng crossed his arms and frowned.

"Keep quiet, you two," Aunty said. She was sitting on the barbarian bed and drinking a cup of tea. "Your mother needs her sleep."

"I have a good one." Hui Fen put her finger to the floor and started to draw a long, curved line.

Wei Sheng squatted, rested his chin on his palm and watched.

They hardly noticed Aunty stand up. "I'm going out to the privy. Will you two be all right?"

Hui Fen gave her aunt an absent nod. She finished drawing the curved line and decided it was perfect. The best artist in the city couldn't draw a better shell. She started on the feet, tracing four curved little lines below the shell. In her mind she could see the turtle's smooth, sloped back and flat, clawed feet.

Wei Sheng's eyes lit up. "It's a rat!"

"No! Does a rat have a round back like this?" Hui Fen laughed indignantly as she started on the belly. It was amazing how silly her brother was sometimes.

Hui Fen began to talk about the bodies of rats. Did rats have curved beaks like the one she drew? Did they have tiny tails shaped like triangles?

Wei Sheng looked up and turned toward the door. "Someone's outside."

"You haven't seen half the animals I have," Hui Fen said. "Remember that big animal with the floppy ears *Baba* was talking about? Well I've seen one. I've even *ridden* one."

Wei Sheng slapped the floor with the palm of his hand. "Liar! Last night you said they weren't real."

Hui Fen finally heard the knocking. She got to her feet and headed for the front door. "Fine. Don't believe me. I was even going to show you one."

"You've never –" Wei Sheng saw where his sister was heading, and fear flashed across his face. "You can't open the door! Aunty's supposed to do that!"

Hui Fen stood at their front window, pulled the paper curtains back and peeked out. "It's all right. It's just a monk." She reached for the door.

"But you can't!" Wei Sheng was close to tears. He did not like it when his sister broke the rules, and now she was about to break the biggest one of all. "What will happen when *Baba* finds out?"

Hui Fen hesitated. Wei Sheng was right. If *Baba* found out she opened the door when no adults were home he would be angry. And of course Aunty would tell him. She was *such* a worrier.

But Hui Fen was already nine years old. Her parents would treat her like a baby forever if she let them. Maybe if she started to *act* like an adult, they would start to treat her like one.

Besides, it was just a monk. He had probably come to beg for money. They didn't have any money, but maybe he would tell them a good story. Hui Fen liked monks. They told the best stories if they were in the right mood.

She opened the door and smiled. "Hello."

The monk smiled back. He was very handsome. He had the grayest eyes Hui Fen had ever seen. "Hello, Hui Fen."

"Who're you?"

"I know your father." The monk's face twitched but his eyes did not leave Hui Fen's.

"He's not here." For reasons Hui Fen did not grasp, those gray eyes suddenly reminded her of a cat watching a mouse. She took a backward step.

"I know." The monk stepped forward, keeping the distance between them the same.

Hui Fen took another step back. "I'll tell him you were here. Just tell me your name and I'll tell my father. I won't forget. I have a good memory."

Still smiling, the monk took another step. Now he was standing in their common room. Still those gray eyes did not leave hers. "He will know I was here. Soon the whole world will see the coming of the Thunder God and his disciple."

Hui Fen's eyes drifted up. Something was wrong with the monk's forehead. It looked strange, like someone had drawn a spider web on it. Not only that, it was pushed in. It was like a giant had pressed the monk's forehead with his giant's thumb and crushed it.

The monk's smile grew. "Are you looking at my injury, child? I got this the day I met your father. Your father was the man who started me on my journey to greatness. Your father started all of it."

Hui Fen could not take her eyes from the monk's forehead. She thought of a boy who used to live in their ward. Last summer the boy fell from a tree and hit his head on the ground. He had died right there in the street while his mother screamed. After that, *Baba* had told Hui Fen she must always be careful. He said people died all the time from hitting their heads. Even a light hit could kill you.

This monk had hit his head. The hit hadn't been light, either. It was hard enough to smash his skull. How could a person live after that?

The answer was easy. He couldn't.

The monk was already dead.

Everyone knew sometimes the dead didn't rest. Sometimes they tried to stay here, in this world. But to do that they had to put someone else in their grave. The dead were always watching, always waiting for a chance to carry someone away. The more they waited, the angrier they became. If a spirit stayed hungry and angry for long enough, it became something even worse. It became a devil.

It wants to bury me and steal my place in this world. Or maybe it doesn't want me. Maybe it wants Wei Sheng.

Those thoughts were too much for Hui Fen. She turned to run toward her brother. She had to protect him, to make sure the devil didn't put him in the cold ground.

She took one step and screamed her brother's name. *"Wei Sheng!"*

Then a hand was over her mouth. An arm wrapped around her shoulders and pulled her back. There was a strange flying feeling as her feet left the floor.

Carrying me. The devil is carrying me back to its grave so it can take my place.

Hui Fen kicked and screamed. She struggled and tried to bite. Nothing worked. The grip around her grew tighter, stronger.

And still she fought.

Somewhere, in another world, Hui Fen heard a high, sharp scream. Then those awful arms let go of her, and there was terror as she realized she was falling. She hit the floor and cried out in pain.

Hui Fen looked up. The devil was in their house now. It was running right through their common room, its black robe flowing out behind it.

Aunty was there as well. Aunty was yelling at the devil and holding a broom out like a sword. That worried look she always had was gone. Her lips were pulled back in rage, making her look like an animal baring its teeth.

The devil lunged at Aunty. Aunty screamed and fell to the floor, her hands on her belly. Immediately she tried to sit up but it was like she had forgotten how. She kept her hands on her belly and flopped like a fish out of water.

Hui Fen looked around for Wei Sheng. She could not find him, and her panic grew. Finally she saw him huddling in a corner and crying.

Hui Fen got to her feet. She had to reach Wei Sheng, had to protect him from the devil.

Then those terrible hands were on her again, and again she was lifted up. This time she didn't have the chance to fight. Some kind of sack went over her head, covering her all the way down to her feet. One strong arm went around her chest, another around her legs. She tried to struggle and could not.

But she could scream.

Hui Fen opened her mouth and screamed as loudly as she could. She screamed until her ears felt like they would burst inside her head. She screamed for *Baba* and *Mama* and Aunty. She screamed at her brother, begged him to run.

The arms around her shifted, and a hand went over her mouth.

Hui Fen knew right away that more screaming was useless. No one would hear her now.

She heard other screams, though. She recognized this new voice as her mother's. *Mama* must have heard the noise and come out from her room.

The arms holding Hui Fen shifted again. She heard a man grunting with anger and a woman yelling. The thing holding her was fighting with someone, probably *Mama*. Then there was a loud *thud,* like someone hitting the floor. It was followed by a strangled cry.

The devil must have killed *Mama* and Aunty. Hui Fen felt tears spreading across her face and tasted salt in her mouth.

A hand went back over Hui Fen's mouth, and the devil began to walk. He was taking her back to his grave. He was going to put her in the ground and cover her with wet dirt until she couldn't breathe. And there was nothing she could do about it.

Still crying, Hui Fen closed her eyes and waited for the end.

31

"You don't have to understand the orders," Zhou said. He looked around again to make sure no one was in earshot. "You just have to follow the orders and trust that I know what *I'm* doing."

Officer Song frowned. "It's murder. A murder conviction gets you strangled or beheaded, nine times out of ten."

They were standing in front of the steps that led up to the Imperial Ministry. A moment ago Zhou's three Guards had led Ren Shu up those steps. Ren Shu was hooded and gagged, but that hadn't stopped him from screaming and fighting the whole way.

The screams had cut Zhou like daggers. They would echo in his ears for the rest of his life.

And that was all the more reason to see this drama through to the end. Otherwise Ren Shu would die for nothing.

"I don't know about this," Song said.

"Ten thousand coppers." Zhou wanted to cry as he spoke the figure. It was an obscene sum, but he would have to pay it. The only alternative was to kill Hai Tao himself. What did he know about such things?

"It's not some shop owner who's giving you trouble," Song said. "It's Hai Tao. He's high up there."

Zhou wanted to mutter a curse. Officer Song was the only candidate for this task, because he was the only person stupid enough to accept it.

But even he took convincing. "There are murders all the time in this city. They're almost never solved. Besides, no one will suspect a Guard. Just make sure there are no witnesses and you'll be fine."

"No. It's too risky."

Zhou decided to try another approach. He glanced around again and lowered his voice. "Hai Tao deserves to die."

Song took a step closer to Zhou. His eyes took on a conspiratorial glint. "Why?"

"Because," Zhou whispered. "He knew Lin was the killer all along."

"He *what?*"

"Quiet!" Zhou gave Song his deepest cringe and looked around yet again. "I can't tell you how I know, but I do. The bastard has been protecting Lin."

"But why? Why protect a killer of children?"

Zhou scoffed. "Who knows why these eunuchs behave the way they do? You know how they are, always scheming and plotting."

Song nodded, his face full of disgust. Like most men, he had a natural loathing for eunuchs. "Really, how do you know?"

"I said I can't tell you that. But I've been watching him for some time and I know he's been looking out for Lin. And you know what I think? I think that without his interference we'd have caught Lin a long time ago. Who knows? We might have prevented the last one or two murders."

"We should go to Governor Han." Song pointed at the Imperial Palace steps. "He'll have the lout tortured in front of the whole city."

"We can't. These eunuchs, they control the minds of the high officials somehow. Han is under Hai Tao's spell."

Song's mouth turned down in disgust. "Protecting a killer. Who could do such a thing?"

"So you'll do it?" Zhou hoped he didn't sound too eager.

"All right," Song said. "Twenty thousand coppers."

"You –" Zhou stopped himself. This was starting to look less like bartering and more like blackmail. But Hai Tao was a loose end he could not ignore. Besides, he had a moral obligation to end the terror. "All right. But you do it immediately. I mean today."

"Sure." Song grinned, clearly pleased at having swindled a rich mandarin. "I'll open his throat before midday. Where is he?"

"He's off duty right now but he's due back soon," Zhou said. "He usually cuts through the east alley on his way to the Ministry. You know the one I mean? There's an abandoned congee store at the end of it. You can wait for him there."

"I know it," Song said.

"Good. Let me know when it's done."

32

Thirty *li* beyond the city walls, in front of a shack barely the size of a wagon, Hai Tao watched the sky.

The clouds were heavy and dark. A few flecks of rain were already falling. Soon there would be a downpour.

Hai Tao's lips turned up in a thin smile. Of course there would be a downpour. The thunder was Heaven's gift to him, a signal that he was on the correct path. Now he was so close to his goal he could all but reach out and touch it. When he closed his eyes he could see it all. He saw the great wings above, pumping and sending out thick plumes of air. He saw the creature, ten times the height of a man, descending until its curved talons dug into the ground.

He saw the Thunder God.

The sky rumbled its affirmation.

Hai Tao turned and went into the shack. When he closed the door, the darkness around him was nearly total. The shack had two windows, but he kept them both covered with dark curtains. He didn't want some passerby seeing a candle and realizing this place wasn't as abandoned as it looked. Of course, the chances of that happening were slim. This shack was by a forgotten supply road that snaked through an empty piece of forest. Even better, it was perched atop a steep slope. From here Hai Tao had a commanding view of the road below, but it was almost impossible to see into the house from outside.

On the floor were a metal drill and a piece of wood. Hai Tao picked both objects up, placed the sharp end of the drill against the wood and twisted the handle in fast circles. Soon tendrils of smoke were curling into the air. He used the fire to light the wick of a candle.

The room was small, and with the candle Hai Tao could see everything. There was very little here. His satchel and cloak were hanging by the door. Against the far wall were a folded sleeping mat, a rotting chair and a chamber pot. In the center of the room was a dugout fireplace.

He glanced down into the dry fireplace. The girl was down there, whimpering and sometimes moving inside the bag. Hai Tao had already explained that if she screamed, terrible things would happen to her. He did not say what. It was more effective to let the mind conjure its own worst fears.

Hai Tao sat in the chair and considered the situation.

If Ming and Zhou hadn't discovered him yet, they would soon. Over the last few days Hai Tao had watched them draw closer and closer to the truth. It was only a matter of time until they found it. That was why Hai Tao had taken Ming's child today. There wasn't another moment to lose.

Yes, time was of the essence. Hai Tao couldn't afford to have Ming scratching his head, asking himself what to do next. He needed Ming out here. To help things along, he had left a clue in Ming's home. Sooner or later that clue would lead Ming to this house. Then the door to Hai Tao's future would finally open.

For Hai Tao, focusing on the future had always been a way to survive.

It was thinking about his future, about his reward, that had sustained Hai Tao after his mutilation. During his first years in the palace, before his destiny had revealed itself, life had been a daily torture. Hai Tao had spent those early years doing what most eunuchs did. He cleaned stables and shod horses and emptied privies. The work was bad, but the guards were worse. They hated eunuchs, and Hai Tao spent his days waiting for a guard – any guard – to set on him. He had contemplated suicide every day.

It was only when he was made a scribe and taught to read that things changed. He remembered that day in the Archives when he stumbled over a scroll someone had left on a table. His arms were aching from a beating he'd gotten for some infraction, and his eyes were scarlet, threatening tears. Then he saw the drawing of the being with blue skin. All pain and humiliation were forgotten as Hai Tao discovered Leigong, the god who came from on high and punished the wicked.

But why hadn't Leigong come to punish those who tormented Hai Tao? The answer had come to Hai Tao immediately, almost as though some invisible being had whispered it into his ear. The Thunder God *would* come, but only if summoned by someone worthy.

It was then that Hai Tao began to see that he was one of the few people in this world to have something special – a destiny. That understanding had sustained him, but he never stopped being a slave. As if to remind him of his station, his masters still made him work in the kitchen with the other servants. He hated preparing slop for the mandarins and the other pigs. He hated that he degraded himself by doing what so many workers did: swiping rare, forbidden foods and delighting in tasting them. Those sad little pleasures were traits of the mediocrity he was fighting so hard to shed.

But he had persevered, and now his time had finally come. Before his death he would have the only thing he wanted in this world. He would have the sublime honor of laying eyes upon Leigong, the Thunder God.

Hai Tao walked to his sleeping mat. The object resting on the mat was a bit longer than his arm. It had a thin wooden handle which had turned black years ago. At one end of the handle was a thick piece of metal about the size of a brick. The object was heavy, clumsy. Only a powerful person could wield it effectively.

Hai Tao picked the hammer up and brought it back to the chair. He sat down with the hammer across his legs. Its weight always gave him comfort.

It had gone quiet outside, but Hai Tao knew that would not last long. There was something underneath the silence. It was a gathering energy, a growing power that tickled the hair on his arms. Soon the sky would be smashed by a storm stronger than any this world had ever seen. The skies would part like an ocean, giving way to a glorious being called to this world by Hai Tao's sacrifices.

With his hands resting on the hammer, Hai Tao sat back and waited.

33

Ming and Dragon hurried through the Imperial Ministry. As usual, busy-looking mandarins were rushing through the corridors. A few cast glances at the strange duo but none stopped to ask them their business. That was fortunate. Ming and Dragon had no right to be in this building without an escort.

Talking their way through the front door had been easy, and Ming had Dragon to thank for that. The young Gold Bird Guards had recognized the famous thief catcher right away, and they were eager to believe his story about an important meeting with the Governor. They had all but fallen over each other to open the door.

But could Dragon get them into Han's office? Ming wasn't so sure. Offices like that were guarded. If the Guards were experienced men then Dragon's fame would be worth nothing. If the Guards were younger, who knew?

Ming's spirits rose when they rounded the next corner. Only one Guard was outside the Governor's office, and he looked too young to grow a beard. The boy was sitting at a desk and staring at the wall across from him.

Dragon spoke into Ming's ear as they walked. "Chin up, shoulders squared. We belong here. Seeing the Governor is just another dull part of our day."

"Yes." Ming had been thinking the same thing.

They walked in lockstep and stopped in front of the Guard's desk.

The Guard looked up, shrank from Dragon slightly and said, "Yes?"

Ming said, "We are here to see Governor Han."

The Guard glanced at the door. "He's not taking visitors. What is this about?"

Dragon stepped forward and glared. "It's about you letting us in."

The Guard's face went pale at the sound of Dragon's voice, but he did not drop his eyes. "I'm sorry. No unscheduled callers today. Express wishes of Governor Han."

As Ming searched for a response, the door to Han's office opened and a short man of about seventy stepped out.

Ming had heard enough about Governor Han to know this was the man himself. There wasn't much to him at first glance. He was a head shorter than most men, and he was dressed like a street merchant. But he moved like someone used to being the most powerful man in the room.

The Snake stopped and stared at his visitors. "What's this, then?"

The Guard jumped to his feet. "I didn't let them in, Sir. They wanted admission but I didn't give it to them and I wasn't going to."

"That's true, Governor," Ming said. "This man swore he would cut our stomachs open if we took another step toward your door." Ming gave the boy a look that was half anger, half terror. The boy looked back at Ming with a puppy's gratitude.

"I'm here now," Han said. "What is it?"

Dragon bowed. "My name is Li Jian Guo. I am a thief catcher here in the city."

"The half-blooded cavalryman," Han said. "I know the name."

Dragon said, "If it's not too forward, may we speak in your office? This is a delicate matter and it's very urgent."

Han thought for a moment, and then nodded. "I certainly hope it is, gentlemen. Be quick."

From behind them, a familiar voice said, "Ming?"

Ming and Dragon both turned. Zhou was standing in the hallway, his arms full of documents.

Ming couldn't believe his luck. "Zhou, thank the gods you're here. We know who has really been killing the children!"

Governor Han stepped forward. "Not out here." He glanced at the Guard, who was studying a scroll as though it were the most fascinating document in creation. "My office – all three of you." He pointed at the Guard. "You. Summon some Guards. Better yet, find the three who helped Zhou make his arrest this morning. Have them wait outside."

The Governor entered his office and the three men followed him. Han sat behind his desk. There was only one chair opposite him. Zhou took it without comment, leaving Ming and Dragon to stand.

Han looked at Zhou first. "You know these men."

"Yes, Sir. They are independent thief catchers. With the government's approval I hired them to assist in the apprehension of the killer."

Han's narrow eyes studied Dragon. Then they moved to Ming and did the same thing. "They don't look like much."

"They're very capable," Zhou said. "Dragon was a cavalry officer in the Army of Divine Strategy for – how many years?"

"Nineteen," Dragon said.

"Nineteen. Furthermore, his record as a thief catcher is flawless. Ming here was in the Gold Bird Guard for ten years. Sir, I assure you they're beyond reproach."

Han turned to Ming. "In that case let us hear your news. Since you're beyond reproach."

Ming decided to be direct. There was no patience in Han's voice. "With apologies, Governor, you executed the wrong man for the child killings. Lin was innocent." He turned to Zhou. "The real killer is your eunuch, Hai Tao. I'm sorry, Zhou."

"You can't be serious," Zhou gasped.

Han silenced Zhou by raising one finger, all the while keeping his eyes on Ming. "What are you basing that on?"

"Several things. In every letter, the killer accused his victim's parent of a crime. Those crimes were very sensitive secrets. A person could only discover all those secrets in the Imperial Archives."

Han gave a small shake of his head. "We have already considered this. Even if you are correct we still have countless suspects to consider. Thousands of people can access those Archives."

"True," Ming said. "But there is also the case of Meng Chun, the pub owner. There was nothing in the Archives about her, so how did the madman discover her secrets?" Ming knew he sounded too triumphant, but he couldn't help himself. He and Dragon had unraveled the mystery, and now they were explaining it to those who could not.

And still the Snake refused to look impressed. "So how did the eunuch learn Meng Chun's secrets?"

"Meng Chun lived in Zhou's ward, and Zhou had already been investigating her. It was for – what was it, Zhou? Tax issues? Regardless, Zhou told Dragon and me he'd had Hai Tao turn Meng Chun's pub upside down looking for evidence of criminal activity. Hai Tao claimed he had found nothing, but clearly he was lying. He learned about Meng Chun's crime and took matters into his own hands. That is the key. I can think of no other person who had access to the Archives and to Meng Chun's past."

As Ming spoke, it occurred to him he could be getting Zhou in trouble. The Governor might take a dim view of a mandarin having his assistant break into a citizen's home. Ming *had* to tell Han everything, though. That was the only way to convince him. Besides, they had solved this mystery for Han, so surely he would let some minor transgressions pass. Wouldn't he?

"All right," Han said. "I see the relevance."

Zhou ran a hand through his hair. "That's incredible, Ming. As Governor Han said, recently I also came to see the importance of the Archives."

"I'm sure you did." Ming smiled a little.

"I did. And I am happy to report that by a stroke of luck I have found the real killer. It is not Hai Tao."

Ming said, "How –"

"Quiet!" Han snapped. "Let him finish."

Zhou cleared his throat. "As I said, it was only luck. After we parted company last night it came to me that someone could use the Archives as a way of spying on wealthy families. Then I remembered that over the last few weeks I had often noticed a young man lingering in the Archives. Every time I saw him, he was in the criminal complaints section. The young man always seemed to behave rather, eh, strangely. I wondered, could *he* have something to do with the murders?"

"Wait," Ming said. He turned to Governor Han. "I'm sorry to interrupt again. May I ask a question?"

Han nodded.

Ming tried to collect his thoughts. "Zhou, you're saying all of this happened last night? You had these epiphanies and went directly to the Archives on the hope this young man might happen to be there at the same time?" Ming could hardly believe it. Zhou was the most ordered and efficient man he knew. He was not the kind of person to waste time following up on such a weak premise.

"That's right." Zhou offered the others an embarrassed smile. "I know it was a desperate step, but this investigation has been so…so frustrating. I was there for quite some time, keeping an eye on the criminal complaints shelves and pretending to work. Just as I was about to give up, fortune intervened. You wouldn't believe what I saw!" Zhou paused dramatically and drew in a deep breath. "That very same young man appeared! He walked right up to the shelves and slipped a file into his satchel. Then he hurried away. I reported this to Governor Han and he authorized me to search the man's home. The search turned up a file on Lei Lei's father. We even found a carving of Leigong!"

"So who is your killer?" Dragon asked. The big man had been quiet for so long that his voice made the others jump.

"An imperial exam candidate," Zhou said. "His name is Wang Ren Shu. I don't know much about this young man yet, but I assure you we will learn all there is to know about him within a day or two."

"Did this man know Meng Chun?" Dragon asked. "How did he find out about her?"

"As I said I know next to nothing about the boy." Zhou indicated a scroll resting on Han's desk. "This document represents all the information we have about him at the moment. However, I am sure interrogation will tell us how he learned about Meng Chun."

"But what about the purple fruit we found?" Ming asked. This entire meeting was beginning to feel like a dream. Ming was quite certain Hai Tao was the killer, and yet Zhou had produced his own culprit for the very same crimes. "Did this Ren Shu dine at an imperial banquet? Did he work in the palace kitchen?"

Han turned to Zhou. "What is he talking about?"

"A...theory. It –"

Dragon said, "It was in a letter we drafted for you earlier in the week, Governor. Zhou was supposed to give it to you for us."

Han shuffled through some papers on his desk and found one that looked new. "This letter?"

Ming squinted at it. "It doesn't appear to be. That is not my handwriting."

Han held out the letter. "Take a closer look, then."

Ming read only half the letter before looking up. "Zhou, what is this?"

Dragon pointed at the letter in the Ming's hand. "What does it say?"

Ming looked back down at the letter. "This is similar to the letter we gave Zhou, but it's not ours. It is missing a great deal of information that was in the original."

Han snatched the letter back. "What original?"

"The original letter we wrote," Ming said. "It detailed our investigation and explained why Lin could not have been the killer." He pointed at the letter Han was holding. "But that is not it. I have never seen that letter before."

Zhou laced his fingers and placed them in his lap. "I'm sorry, Ming. I felt it was prudent to summarize your letter and do away with its inconsistencies."

"What inconsistencies? You didn't mention any to us before."

"Events were transpiring so quickly," Zhou said. "I didn't have time to review the letter with you in detail. It was only later, before I gave the letter to Governor Han, that I realized it contained several hopeful assumptions."

"But you knew the letter's contents when we gave it to you," Ming said. "You knew all of it and you endorsed it. What could have made you change your mind?"

Dragon was nodding as Ming spoke. "And if you *had* changed your mind, why did you not tell us?"

Zhou offered them another smile. "Forgive me, my friends. As I said, things were happening quickly and I did not have the time to speak with you about my doubts. And Dragon, a man in my position has to be careful. I cannot walk into Governor Han's office and make incorrect assertions about a case like this. If I were wrong I would look like a fool."

Dragon made a sound and turned away. Ming had to suppress a cringe. Showing one's back to a man like Governor Han was an act of terrible disrespect.

A heavy silence settled over the room. Even Han had nothing to say.

Then, slowly, Dragon turned back to the others and looked at Zhou. "You." His voice was so low the others strained to hear it. "You conniving bastard."

Zhou recoiled as though he had been slapped. "What did you say?"

Dragon looked at Zhou with disbelief. "You deliberately made the letter weak, didn't you? You undermined it. You *wanted* to see Lin executed."

Zhou craned his neck to look up at Dragon. "Why would I do such a thing? I risked my *career* speaking up for Lin."

"It helped you." Dragon appeared to be working out his thoughts as he spoke. "You made yourself look intelligent and you made everyone else look like fools at the same time."

"Nonsense. It is my duty to serve the city and the Emperor as well as I can. Besides, if I had saved Lin's life I would have looked very good to my superiors."

"It wasn't enough to look good." Dragon was standing over Zhou's chair and looking down at him now. "You also needed your enemies to look bad. If you could make them appear responsible for an innocent man's death, you would disgrace them for life. They would never recover from that, would they? And when it was all over you would be the only man who had the fortitude to speak the truth. You would be a rising star."

Ming was getting scared. Dragon's blood was up, and he was saying dangerous things. Ming needed to calm his friend before he went any further.

Instead, Ming looked at the letter on Han's desk. Their original letter had been a scathing indictment of the case against Lin. It provided a description of the man seen lurking near Chang's home. It made mention of the strange food near the temple. It exposed Blossom and Toad as opportunists and known gangsters.

But Zhou's letter was just a long lecture about morality and government responsibility. Its only valid point was that the authorities should not rush to conclusions. All the hard evidence that would have saved Lin was absent from it.

Ming's confusion vanished like fog under the morning sun. Dragon was speaking the simple truth: Zhou had betrayed them. "Dragon is right."

Zhou looked hurt. "How can you say that, Ming? We've known each other since we were children. I helped you get a tutoring position after you left the Gold Bird Guard."

"That is not –"

Han slapped his hand down on the desk. "Enough! Ming, what else was in the letter you wrote? Give me every detail."

In a voice that did not feel like his own, Ming explained every part of the original letter to Governor Han. He spoke slowly, careful not to leave anything out. Finally he said, "I do not believe you could have read our letter and concluded that Lin was the killer."

Zhou's face was expressionless as he listened to Ming's speech. "Ming, you presented mere theories as hard evidence. That fruit could have come from anywhere. And we have no idea whom that witness – that *vagrant* – saw outside Chang's home. How can we be sure it was actually the killer? It was all flawed so I kept it out. It was my prerogative as your employer to use your contributions however I wanted to."

Ming took a step back. He was suddenly afraid he might strike Zhou. "That's not what you said yesterday. You believed our theories completely."

Dragon turned to Han. "Sir, I think it's clear that Zhou has been sabotaging us. This man has no scruples and he's willing to do anything to achieve his goals. He'll see ten more children beaten to death if it helps him become the next Commandant."

"Outrageous!" Zhou jumped to his feet. For the first time his face showed real anger. "I'll see you strangled for saying that!"

"Let's bring Hai Tao in here," Ming said. "We'll have him account for himself."

Zhou's anger vanished as quickly as it had come. He chuckled and shook his head, as though he couldn't believe the things he had to deal with at work. "It was a mistake to hire you, Ming. I should have remembered your past. I should have remembered you left the Gold Bird Guard because you were unfit for duty."

Han said, "What do you mean?"

Zhou smoothed out his robe and sat down again. "Governor, Ming left the Gold Bird Guard because he was mentally incompetent. He could not handle the strain of his work."

"That is not true." Ming tried to keep his voice steady. There would be time to marvel at Zhou's wickedness later. Right now he needed to maintain control of his faculties. "My wife got sick. She is dying, in fact."

"I'm sorry, Ming," Zhou said sadly. "I can't protect you here – not when you're threatening to destroy the whole investigation. "

Han placed his hands on his desk and leaned forward. "Tell me how this man is mentally incompetent."

"I am not!" Ming tried to say more but he suddenly felt unable to draw breath. When he did manage to take in air his chest felt full, as though a heavy stone was inside it.

Zhou said, "Governor, ever since he was young, Ming has endured spells. They are not brought on by any malady a physician can find. They come without warning and they stop him from performing even the most basic functions. They got so extreme he had to retire from the Gold Bird

Guard, even though he knew it might bankrupt his family. I tell you he is unfit."

Ming cleared his throat and wiped his mouth with the back of his hand. He saw Governor Han staring at him and realized he looked as unstable as Zhou said he was. He had to say something, anything that would expose Zhou. But still he could not speak. That stone in his chest was growing heavier with every strained breath.

"If all of that is true," Dragon said, "then why did you hire Ming? Why did you appoint this mentally incompetent man to help you solve the most severe crimes in living memory?"

"I never doubted his *intelligence,*" Zhou said patiently. "As a matter of fact Ming is one of the smartest men I know. I also thought that after he left law enforcement he had managed to…eh…calm down a bit. I didn't believe that merely advising in an investigation would overburden him. That was a tragic misjudgment and I'm sorry."

"You're lying," Ming managed. He tried to say more but his throat seemed to close.

Governor Han leaned back in his chair. "Zhou has shown poor judgment, but I do not believe his actions were malicious. It is my opinion that he has acted in good faith."

"That can't be your assessment," Ming said. How could Han display such willful blindness? Didn't men like him survive by sniffing out treachery? At least the shock of Han's statement had one benefit. It shattered Ming's fit the way hard slap to the face would have. "This is madness."

Han's level gaze settled on Ming. "Are you questioning my intelligence?"

"No. I am just disagreeing with you, Sir."

"Zhou was wise to be careful when he presented that letter to me." Han sounded like a patient father explaining the ways of the world to his confused son. "No intelligent mandarin would attach his name to a letter that cited flawed evidence. It is clear to me he was being prudent. Nothing more."

Zhou looked weary. "Ming, despite this incident I want you to know I still consider you a close friend. I will always be there if you need me."

Ming bit his lip. He wanted to shout a curse, but Zhou was probably hoping for that. Instead he bowed. "I thank you for your time and consideration, Governor Han." He turned to leave.

Dragon raised his arm to stop Ming. "What are you doing? Are you going to let this man win?"

"No. But there is nothing else to say right now."

"Ming, a murderer of children *works right here in this fucking building!*"

Governor Han looked at the door and shouted, "Guard!"

The door swung open. The boy with the eternally terrified eyes entered the office and bowed. "Sir?"

"Have the other three Guards arrived?"

"Yes, Sir. They're waiting outside."

"Send them in."

The boy turned back toward the hallway and said something Ming could not hear. Three large Guards materialized in the doorway.

Han said, "Escort these men out of my office." He pointed at Dragon. "If this one resists, kill him."

The three Guards moved into the office and formed a rough ring around Dragon.

The Guard closest to Ming was uglier than a bull and had a giant forehead. "Out."

Dragon swept his gaze over the three Guards, and for just a moment his arms tensed. Then he turned to Zhou. "I should have seen this coming. You feel you have to protect the eunuch because you don't want to lose face. You can't have the city knowing your assistant has been kidnapping children and beating them to death."

One of the Guards put a hand on Dragon's shoulder. "*Let's go.*"

"All right." Dragon pushed the man's hand away. He headed for the door with the Guards close behind. "Who did you set up for the murders, Zhou? It's not enough that you had Lin executed? You have to claim another victim?"

"I know nothing at all about the young man we arrested," Zhou said. "But I am sure he is a monster."

The ugly Guard stopped and looked at Dragon. "You believe Mandarin Zhou is lying?"

Han walked out from behind his desk. "You're not here to conduct an interview. My patience for people overstepping their bounds is exhausted. If you don't take these men out of my office, I'll have you strangled for disobeying orders."

Ming headed for the door. He had no doubt Han's threat was real, and he did not want to get a Guard killed.

But the Guard stayed put. He gestured toward Ming and Dragon. "Governor, I believe these two men are right. I have a very strong reason to believe it."

"You have two choices," Han said. "First, take these men out and leave with your life. Second, speak your mind. But I'm warning you. If I am not completely convinced you are right, you'll be dead by nightfall."

Without hesitation the Guard said, "Mandarin Zhou knew the man we arrested this morning. But he acted as though he did not."

"That is not true," Zhou said. "I had never met the accused before today."

"Then why did he call you by your name?" the Guard asked.

Han said, "What are you talking about?"

The Guard shifted on his feet. He was clearly uncomfortable speaking with officials. "It happened as we entered Wang Ren Shu's room this morning, Sir. Ren Shu said 'Zhou, what are you doing?' He already knew Zhou's name."

Han turned to Zhou. "Well?"

Zhou said, "I must have introduced myself without thinking of it when we opened the door. Either that or this Guard misheard the accused."

"Which is it?" Han asked. "Did you introduce yourself or did the Guard mishear?"

"The Guard misheard me. He must have."

Han looked at the other two Guards. "Did you hear Mandarin Zhou introduce himself to the suspect?"

One of the Guards shrugged his shoulders. "I wasn't listening to the suspect, Sir."

The other shook his head. "I don't think he did, Sir."

Han went back behind his desk. "Zhou, you stay. The rest of you get out of my office now. Ming and Dragon, go home. Chances are I'll be summoning the both of you back here soon to discuss this."

Dragon headed for the door before the Guards could touch him. "You're done for, Zhou."

Han pointed a thin finger at the door. "Out!"

Ming looked at Zhou and realized right away that the guard's revelation had broken him. All of Zhou's steady confidence was gone, replaced by a guilt that was almost childlike. Ming felt a sudden wave of remorse for the wretched man. It was all too much right now, and Ming had to look away.

Ming bowed to Governor Han again. Then he followed Dragon out of the room.

34

Hai Tao sat at the edge of the dugout fireplace with his feet hanging in the pit. He drummed his fingers against the faded dirt floor. He did it until his hand ached, until the tips of his fingers were raw and sore. Every bit of his soul screamed at him to look outside, to check the skies again. But that was a bad idea. He had only checked a moment ago, and not enough time had passed for any meaningful change. Another look now would only compound his torture.

He decided to check again.

He stood up, pulled a curtain back and looked out the window. The clouds were still heavy and dark, but they were only producing sporadic drops of rain. Where was the downpour? Where was the bellowing thunder?

None of this was right. The sky was supposed to burst open and flood the world. The thunder was supposed to shake the very ground. That was to be Heaven's signal that all was ready for Leigong's arrival. Only then could Hai Tao complete his sacrifice.

He must have done something wrong. At some point along the way he must have blundered. That was why the thunder hadn't come. But *how* had he blundered? He hadn't strayed from his plan once.

Whatever the problem was, he had to address it soon.

Hai Tao slammed his fist against the floor. He had spent years climbing a mountain and now he was stumbling just as the summit came into view.

What *was* it?

From down in the fireplace, the girl whimpered. Hai Tao looked down at her and snarled. Her voice had the same grate Ming's did. He opened his mouth to hiss a threat…and paused.

Come to think of it, the girl didn't just sound like her father. She rather looked like Ming as well. She probably shared quite a few other qualities with him.

Hai Tao stared at the sack. He thought of what was inside it. This time it wasn't just another brat he had taken to punish the parents. This was the child of Ming, of the man who had started everything.

The girl in the fireplace didn't know that. She had no idea why it was here. She probably just thought a bad man had taken her because bad men did such things. That was not true, though. *Ming* was responsible for the girl's coming death, not Hai Tao. Perhaps she needed to know that. Perhaps Hai Tao's final act had to include a spoken reckoning with his past.

Hai Tao kept his eyes trained on the shapeless form in his fireplace. Yes. He needed to speak his grievance out loud before he made his final sacrifice. And who better to witness those words than the sacrifice herself?

Hai Tao hopped into the fireplace and pulled the sack down around the girl's thin shoulders. Her eyes were red with tears. Sweat had matted her hair against her skull. She looked around, trying to take in her surroundings. Then she saw Hai Tao and screamed into her gag.

Hai Tao felt better when he heard the scream. "Child, do you know who I am?"

The only answer was another muffled scream.

"I am a eunuch. Do you know what that is?"

This time the girl nodded.

"Your father knows me. He is the one who made me this way." Hai Tao saw the girl's surprise and laughed. "No, he didn't cut me. Someone else took off my dirty thing. But your father was the one who made that happen. He sent me to the man with the knife. I will tell you why."

Hai Tao swallowed hard. He had never spoken of his past out loud before. "It goes back to before I lost my dirty thing. When I was eleven years old my father killed my mama. He accused her of being unfaithful and then he stabbed her in her belly. But he wasn't punished for his crime. Do you understand me, child?"

The girl nodded. Hai Tao suspected she didn't understand everything, but she appeared to grasp enough.

"My mother wasn't – she didn't stray from my father. *He* was the one who strayed. He found someone else and he wanted to marry her. That *bitch!*"

The child cried into her gag and turned away.

"Look at me," Hai Tao said softly. He brushed the girl's chin with the tip of his index finger. "Look at me or bad things will happen."

The girl turned back but she did not meet Hai Tao's eye. That was good enough.

"Before my father killed my mama he was an important man in the city. But after his disgrace, he lost everything. He ended up bringing us out here, to this place." Hai Tao swept his arm at the house around them. "My father was a coward and he let his new woman control the household. She beat me and told me I was nothing. She complained to my father that I was weak, that my mother had ruined me. She said I was worthless because of her."

Hai Tao leaned forward and looked into the girl's red eyes. He tapped himself on the chest. "But I am not worthless. Do you believe me?"

Another nod.

"By the time I was twelve, my father was frail and sick. But not me. I was big for my age, so I knew my plan would work." Hai Tao smiled. Remembering this part of his past was easier. He did it every day and it always brought him joy. "All I needed was a rock. I did it to my father first, when he was asleep. He woke up and he even tried to fight me, but it was easy to beat the strength from him. I don't know how long I kept hitting him after he was dead. A long time, I think."

From outside, somewhere past the mountains, Hai Tao heard rumbling. It sounded like a giant stomping his foot on the ground a thousand *li* away. The sound brought Hai Tao sweet relief. Heaven approved. His plan was working.

"I did my father first on purpose, you see. I wanted that bitch to watch. I wanted her to know that she had lost, that she could never break me. But when it was her turn she came at me with a knife. Can you believe it? She actually thought she could *kill* me!" Hai Tao laughed.

Another rumble in the distance. It sounded closer, but Hai Tao could not be sure.

"I took the knife from her. She didn't even cut me once. Then I started on her with the rock. I remember the sound of her skull cracking. I didn't stop until I saw the gray brains in her head."

Thick tears were streaming down the girl's face now. She tried to blink them away with no success. Hai Tao wiped her face with the back of his hand.

"Do you know what I did then?"

No answer.

Hai Tao smiled again and leaned forward. "I did it to myself." He traced a finger along the dent in his forehead. "I managed to hit myself four times, right here. Four times and I did this. Maybe now you can imagine how strong I am."

Hai Tao was not surprised to see doubt on the girl's face. After all, he was wearing a baggy cloak. It was almost as loose as his city official's robe, and it made him look slight.

Removal of that cloak would tell a different story. A lifetime of manual labor had left Hai Tao lean and roped with muscle. Even as an adult he was growing stronger all the time. When Hai Tao was assigned to a bridge building project last month, he had become a hero to his fellow workers. The other men all struggled to carry giant sacks of sand to the building site. They could only carry one sack at a time and even then they needed frequent rest. Hai Tao had carried a sack over each shoulder on every trip, baring his teeth with the strain. As soon as he dropped his burden he turned around and went back for more, ignoring the cheers from his weaker comrades.

"I had a simple plan for getting away with those murders," Hai Tao said. "I told the authorities it was thieves. It worked. After that I was ready to show the world that my mama had never strayed from my papa. That should have worked too. But there was one factor I did not foresee – your father."

When Hai Tao said *your father* the girl's eyes lit up. She looked around the room, as if hoping Ming would appear from nothing and save her.

"Your father was one of the men who found me here. He took me in. He sheltered me in his barracks and nursed me back to health. After that he let me stay there with him for a while. I earned my keep, however. Don't think I did not. Every day I cleaned the barracks and brought the men their food. After living with my father and the whore for so long, I believed I had found a paradise. I hadn't felt that safe since before my mother died. But Ming said I could not stay there forever, so he turned me over to the government. I begged him to let me stay. He said I did not have to worry. They could help me, he said. And they did. Their calculated cruelty showed me my destiny.

"You see, there was a shortage of eunuchs at the time. Usually they castrate boys when they're five years old. But they were desperate for more servants, so they made an exception with me. I was thirteen when they cut me."

Hai Tao stopped. Even now he could feel the blade. The man who did it had been kind. He told Hai Tao to look away, because the ones who didn't watch had a better chance of surviving. When the man cut him it felt like something was crushing him down there, was grinding the flesh from his body. The pain seemed to go on for an eternity, and then his vision went gray. He woke up two days later with dried blood on his crotch and pain that went from his stomach to his toes.

"So you see it is thanks to your father that I am here – that we are both here. He started it all and very soon he will end it. It has to be that way."

Thinking about Ming always brought Hai Tao a strange mix of loathing and relief. Ming was a cowardly wretch who had abandoned a child. On the other hand, that was Hai Tao's first step toward becoming a disciple of the Thunder God. The removal of his dirty thing had been his sacrifice.

Hai Tao saw what those things did to the men who owned them. They controlled men's brains, made them lusty and irrational. Men followed their things around like dogs trailing their masters.

But not Hai Tao. He was free of the nasty thoughts that enslaved ordinary men. He was free to become something better: the punisher of hidden sins. It was only after he felt the blade that he became an agent of Heaven.

So in a strange way, Hai Tao knew he should be grateful to Ming for putting him on this path. But Ming hadn't known the greatness he was spawning. Ming had only known he was turning away from a boy who needed help. Ming had only known he was giving a child over to a life of terror. For all of that, he deserved to pay.

The girl was staring at Hai Tao with a fear even he wasn't used to seeing. Hai Tao guessed he must have been scowling. He calmed himself. "Your father is to blame for this, not me."

Hai Tao put the sack back over the girl's head and hopped out of the fireplace. He opened the door and walked outside. He felt better, as though his body had grown lighter.

The sky rumbled. This time it was louder. Closer. He had corrected his mistake.

Hai Tao closed his eyes, felt the wet air blow against his face. Soon it would rain, and then there would be thunder. The great storm was about to start. Hai Tao was sure of it.

Sometime during that storm, Ming would arrive. Then the girl would die, and Hai Tao would finally reap the reward he had pursued for ten years. He would finally lay eyes on the Thunder God.

35

By the time Ming and Dragon were walking down the Imperial Ministry's front steps it was mid-afternoon. A thick sheet of cloud had formed overhead, making it look more like dusk.

When they reached the bottom of the steps Ming stopped. He stood mute, his arms hanging at his sides. He waited for some kind of emotion to form, but nothing came.

His closest friend had used him, had probably been using him since the start of this drama. And Ming had let it happen. He had allowed himself to be led by the nose like some beast of burden. It was staggering. How could he ever trust his own judgment again?

Dragon said something.

"What?"

"I said, what do you think will happen to Zhou?"

"I don't know," Ming said. "It worries me that Han threw us out. If we had been allowed to stay we could have pressed our argument further. Then Zhou would almost certainly have been dismissed. He would probably end up getting exiled or worse. But now that he's alone with Han? He could talk his way out of it. Even if he can't make Han swallow his lies the two of them might cut some kind of deal."

"No. There's no way Han will side with Zhou after all that. The Guard proved Zhou a liar. They'll beat him and dismiss him for sure. And you're right. He could get worse than that." A dark smile spread across Dragon's face.

"All of that might well happen. But even if it does I won't feel like we've had a victory."

"I will," Dragon said. "And I believe Zhou is finished. But let us at least consider the worst possible scenario. What if Han sides with Zhou and refuses to arrest Hai Tao? What do we do then?"

"Then we will kill Hai Tao ourselves."

"Yes," Dragon said. "I was thinking the same thing."

"How?"

"I was in the cavalry and you were in the Gold Bird Guard. It won't be hard."

"But we can't just rush into the Imperial Ministry and stab him. I have two children who depend on me." Before Ming could stop it, another thought entered his mind. *Soon they won't have a mother and they'll need me even more.*

"Come on," Dragon said. "We need to find somewhere quiet to talk."

"Han told us to head home and wait to be summoned. Let's go to my house."

They started walking. For a long time neither of them spoke.

It was Dragon who finally broke the silence. "Hai Tao's going to hear about this. He'll know we've found him out and he'll be on his guard."

A fat drop of rain hit Ming on the cheek. That sheet of cloud overhead was getting darker. It looked like they were in for quite a storm. "You're right. Has it occurred to you that he may come after us first?"

"Let him try it." Dragon looked straight ahead as he spoke. "Let him just come and try it."

"It would certainly make things easier. That way you could just kill him with your bare hands."

"I don't think he'll come to us. We won't be that lucky." Dragon put up a forearm to shield his face. The raindrops were coming faster now.

"No, we probably won't. My home's not far. Let's hurry up and get there before we're soaked."

• • •

Ming knew something was wrong as soon as they turned onto his street.

At least twenty people were milling around in front of his home. Five Gold Bird Guards were among them. Even from forty paces away Ming could hear everyone talking in fast, high-pitched voices.

Ming broke into a run, with Dragon close behind.

As Ming approached, he saw a Guard he recognized. The man was wearing an officer's uniform and giving orders to two younger Guards. His name was Kuo.

Ming said, "What's going on, Kuo?"

Kuo finished speaking to his subordinates and turned to Ming. "Your daughter is missing."

Ming and Dragon pushed through the throng of people and entered the house. Li Juan and Li Hua were sitting on the common room's bench. Wei Sheng sat on the floor, his face buried in his forearms and his back against the wall. When he heard the door open he looked up, saw who was there and put his head down again.

The two women stood up and rushed over to Ming.

Ming's sister-in-law spoke first. "I was out back in the privy. He must have waited until –"

"Where is she?"

"Ming –"

"Where is my *daughter*?"

Li Juan put a thin hand on Ming's arm and looked up at him. Her eyes were red, but they were clear. "She's gone. A man came here and took her."

Dragon said, "Did either of you see anything that might help us? Any information could be of use."

Li Juan took a rattling breath. "I was sleeping in the back room. That man came for my child and I was right there in the next room. I came out when I heard the noise and he shoved me to the floor. I didn't see his face."

Ming could see that Li Juan's self-control was strained to its limit, like an overloaded cart on the verge of collapse. That she could maintain even this level of calm was remarkable. Ming had to follow her example. "How about you, Li Hua? What can you tell us?"

"It wasn't long ago." Li Hua's voice was steady but barely audible. "The children were sitting in the common room and playing a game. I went out to the privy. When I came back that...man was in the house."

Ming tried to ask another question but his mouth refused to work.

Fortunately Dragon was there to speak for him. "Can you describe him?"

The corners of Li Hua's mouth began to tremble. "No. I looked in his eyes, but when I try to remember I just see a face made of shadow. I don't know how that is possible. How can you look right at a man and just –"

"Tall," said a new voice.

Ming turned.

Wei Sheng was standing and looking up at Ming. "Tall and skinny. He was wearing a cloak. It was just like the ones the monks wear in the market. His forehead had a strange shape, like it was broken."

"That's good," Dragon said. "That's very good. Did you see which way he went when he left your house?"

"No." Wei Sheng spoke in a strange, adult way that Ming did not like. "I didn't." He walked back to the wall, sat down and buried his face in his forearms again.

Li Juan had clearly noticed the change in her son's voice as well. She watched him sitting in the corner, her thin face set with concern. Finally she turned to Ming. "It was him, wasn't it? It was the man who has been taking the children."

Dragon spoke first. "It was. They executed the wrong man. A moment ago we were discussing the possibility that the *right* man might attack one of us, but I never thought…" He looked around the room and his face turned pale.

"Wait," Li Hua said. "There's something else. With everything that's been going on I forgot all about it. I found this by the fireplace. He must have dropped it." She held out a book to Ming. It looked old, and it was small enough to fit in her hand.

Ming took the book from his sister-in-law. He squinted at it and turned it over in his hands. Its size and weight felt familiar right away. Even its smell was familiar. "I've seen this before." Ming felt like he had rediscovered an old toy from his childhood. "I haven't seen this in years, but it's *mine.*"

"Then Hai Tao didn't leave it here by accident," Dragon said. "We were meant to see this."

Ming didn't answer. He flipped through the book – back to front and front to back. Back to front, front to back. Finally he stopped at a random page. It showed a crude drawing of two large, muscled soldiers. Both had the bodies of men, but one had the head of a horse and the other had the head of an ox.

Dragon squinted at the drawing. "Ox Head and Horse Face. The guardians of the underworld. What is this?"

"This belonged to me once," Ming said. "It's a book about the gods. I used to read it a lot, back when I was new in the Gold Bird Guard. I loved these stories. I must have read through this book a dozen times. But I haven't seen it in years. Not since before the children were born, even."

Li Hua was looking at the book as though it contained curses from the underworld. "What does it mean?"

"It means…" Ming stopped. It was just too strange to see this relic from his past. "I don't know. I don't know where this could have come from or why it's here."

Li Juan put her hand on Ming's forearm again. She clutched him tight, digging her fingernails into his skin. Ming could feel the barely controlled panic in her grip. "Ming, Dragon is right. This is too strange to be an accident. It's a message from the man who took Hui Fen. It's a message and you're meant to figure it out. So think. Ming, stay calm and *think.*"

"There's no time. We –"

"No, Ming." Li Juan's voice was harder now. The dying woman who spent her days and nights in bed was gone. Her face was full of the strength Ming remembered from the early years of their marriage. "If you rush you will panic. You have to slow down. Sit if you need to. Just figure it out."

Ming sat on the bench. He looked down at the book in his hands. It was beginning to feel less like a childhood toy and more like a weapon used in a secret, sinister crime. But why would a book bring him that kind of dread? Was it only because it came from the man who had taken his daughter? Or was it something else?

Ming flipped through the pages. Back to front. Front to back. Back to front. He began to flip through them again – and came to a stop. He looked up at the others. "I don't believe it."

Even Dragon's calm was starting to look fragile. "What is it, Ming?"

"I know where he is. I know where he's taken Hui Fen."

Ming's sister-in-law said, "Where –"

Li Juan raised her hands. "No! You don't need to tell us now. Just go. Go and bring her back."

Ming opened his storage chest. Inside were the belt and dagger he had carried when he was with the Gold Bird Guard. He put on the belt and sheathed his dagger.

Dragon said, "I'm going with you."

"Thank you."

Li Juan brushed Ming's face lightly with the tips of her fingers. Her fire was gone and she looked sick again. "Bring her back."

"I will."

• • •

By the time Ming and Dragon left the house, the number of Gold Bird Guards standing on the street had grown to more than a dozen. Most of the civilians had retreated indoors; the rain was picking up.

One of the older Guards stepped forward. He was wearing an officer's armor, and he was going bald on top. "Ming De Wei?"

"Yes."

"Governor Han wants you in his office right away." The officer pointed at Dragon. "You as well, Li Jian Guo."

"Sorry," Dragon said. "Later."

The officer gave them a scowl clearly meant to discourage argument. "This is a summons from Governor Han. There is no *later.*"

"This time there is," Ming said. He and Dragon started walking. "Just tell him you couldn't find us."

The officer caught up to Ming and stood in his way. Several of his men saw confrontation and hurried over. "You're coming with us."

Ming stopped. "No."

The officer grunted an order. It was followed by the sound of swords being unsheathed.

Ming said, "Did you hear the other men talking about my daughter? Do you know what happened to her?"

"Your family is not my concern."

Dragon grasped the hilt of his sword. "Go, Ming. They won't stop you."

His eyes still on the balding officer, Ming raised his voice and called back over his shoulder. "Officer Kuo."

Kuo walked over to them, looking like a man who had drawn latrine duty. No Guard would want any part of a conflict like this. "Yes?"

"Kuo, I'm sorry to bring you into this," Ming said. "I know where my daughter is. She's been taken to a place well outside the city walls. This man won't let me go to her. I need you to convince him."

"If you're right then we should go to the Imperial Ministry and report it. You can head out there with an army at your back."

"I don't have time for that. I have to go *now.*"

Kuo went silent and looked up at the falling raindrops.

As Kuo thought, Ming glanced to his right. Only one Guard was there, and he was busy feeding scraps of meat to an old mongrel dog. Ming decided that if Kuo refused to help, he would run. He could knock the lone Guard over and be halfway down the road before anyone had time to react. Perhaps Dragon could occupy the other Guards long enough to enable Ming's escape.

Kuo looked hard at Ming. "Tell me this is a matter of life or death for your daughter."

"It is."

Kuo sighed. He looked at the other officer and gestured toward a vacant area across the street. "A word, Officer?"

The officer scowled again, but he allowed himself to be led away.

Dragon waited until the Guards were out of earshot. "You could run right now, Ming. I'll hold them for as long as I can."

"Let's wait and see."

Ming watched the Guards. He could not hear them over the rain, but Kuo appeared to be repeating the same thing again and again. The bald Guard stood with his arms crossed and his head turned away. Kuo began to gesture as he spoke, but he still got no reaction. He looked like a lunatic appealing for help from a statue. Then, just as Ming was thinking he might have to run after all, the bald man gave Kuo a curt nod.

The two Guards approached Ming together.

Kuo smiled. "I told officer Wen here there's been a small misunderstanding. You look a bit like Ming but you're not him. He's going to wait here with his men until Ming shows up."

Officer Wen spat in the dirt.

"Thank you," Ming said. "Both of you."

As Ming turned to leave, Kuo stepped in front of him. "Ming, I can go with you. I'm sure my men will come as well. They'll be eager to help."

"A kind offer," Dragon said. "But we have to decline."

"I was making the offer to him." Kuo looked a little hurt by the refusal. "Not you."

"Dragon's right," Ming said. "If we go out there with a large group, Hai Tao will see us coming."

"All right, I understand," Kuo said. "But from what you said I gather this place is a good ways away?"

"Yes. A very good ways, as I recall." *If I can even find it after all these years.*

"In that case you'll need horses. Maybe you can't accept all of our help, Ming, but let us do this for you."

"All right." Ming had been planning to rent horses from a livery but this would save them time. "And thank you again."

Kuo pointed past Ming's shoulder. "Go to the west gate. Wait outside and I'll bring you two fresh horses. And you might want to hurry, just in case Officer Wen recognizes you after all."

• • •

Ming was pacing back and forth through the rain, his hands clasped behind his back. He looked down the road that ran parallel to the city wall. Kuo still hadn't shown. "This is taking too long."

Dragon had taken shelter under a small tree. His eyes followed Ming as he paced. "He's coming. Ming, you need to be sure about this. You need to be *certain* we're going to the right place."

Ming looked up, saw that Kuo had not arrived yet, and resumed pacing. "I'm certain."

"Because if you're wrong then that's it. We're not going to save your daughter."

Ming stopped and looked at Dragon. "I'm not wrong. It's him. He has a new name and he's grown like a weed, but it's him."

Dragon wiped a forearm across his face. The tree wasn't giving him much cover from the building rain. "What do you mean?"

"I knew the killer was after me because I was the Sorcerer. But I never thought it could be *him.*" Ming wanted to throw his fist against the wall. "I can't believe I didn't see it. How many times have I looked *right at him* without realizing who he was?"

"Ming –"

"Where are those *horses?*"

"They'll be here. Tell me what you're talking about."

Ming joined Dragon under the tree. "Got any water?"

Dragon opened his satchel and produced a black jug.

Ming took a long gulp of water. "That book of the gods we found on my floor – I had it when I was in the Gold Bird Guard. The last time I saw it was when I gave it to a boy I sent off to the orphanage."

"That boy you found in the shack," Dragon said quietly. "It was Hai Tao."

"I never would have known it if I hadn't seen that damn book. I was blind."

"Why didn't you recognize him from the injury on his head?"

. "He was bandaged the whole time he was with us in the barracks, Dragon." Ming put his hands over his face. "All those children. All that death because of a choice I made."

"Ming, did you know they would castrate him?"

"No." Then, a little louder: "No. He was a teenager by then. Bastards should have known better. But I sent him away when I could have helped him. I warped his mind."

"You didn't make him insane, Ming. The cutting did that. Or maybe something was wrong with his mind all along. From what you're telling me, it seems likely he killed his parents. That happened before you even met him."

"Perhaps he *was* always insane," Ming said. "But my actions still had a hand in his fate. My crimes are coming back to me now, Dragon. This one, along with all the things I did as the Sorcerer."

Dragon did not argue the point.

From the east, the rumbling of hooves.

Ming turned. Kuo was riding toward them on a small black horse. He was pulling a second horse next to him. When he stopped he was out of breath. "I'm sorry that took so long. The stable master required some coaxing."

"How much did you give him?" Ming asked. "I'll pay you back."

"No bribes." Kuo hopped down from the horse and handed the reins to Ming. "Just bring them back. If these horses disappear I'll probably be flogged."

"Thank you," Ming said. "We'll bring them back."

Kuo nodded. "Soon as you can."

As Kuo turned and jogged away through the rain, Ming and Dragon mounted their horses.

36

It was only dusk, but the storm was bringing an early blackness to the sky. In that blackness Hai Tao could just make out the long drops of rain cutting through the air. He could feel wind pushing the hair back from his temples.

And in the distance he heard the rumbling of thunder.

Hai Tao brushed his fingers over the dent in his head. When the air was wet the pain became incredible. It felt like his skull was splitting along the mended cracks of his old injury. But the pain was good. It reminded him of all he had paid in his journey.

Soon it would happen. By now Ming must have figured out the book's significance, and that meant he was coming.

Hai Tao twisted his torso back and forth. He shook his legs and made his muscles loose. Every part of his body felt limber, strong. Ming, on the other hand, was no longer a warrior. He had grown soft and weak in his retirement. The coming fight would be no challenge for Hai Tao. He would incapacitate Ming quickly, but he would not kill him. Instead he would bind Ming's hands and feet.

Then he would make Ming watch.

Hai Tao would make Ming watch him pull the girl from the fireplace and lay her on the floor. He would make Ming watch as he struck the girl with his hammer until she went limp. He would strike and strike until the girl's face was so much mush and splintered bone.

When that was done Hai Tao would cut the bonds from Ming's hands, sit on the floor and wait. Sooner or later Ming's shock would wear off. And then Ming would be free to do as he pleased.

Hai Tao often wondered how Ming would kill him. In his estimation Ming was most likely to use the hammer. After all, the hammer would be within reach, and in his rage Ming would probably seize the first weapon he saw.

But that was just a guess. Perhaps Ming would stab him or strangle him. If Ming could control his faculties, he might devise some kind of fantastic torture. It didn't matter. What mattered was that Hai Tao would die by Ming's hand.

And then, with his journey complete, Hai Tao would be reborn as the Thunder God's true disciple.

Hai Tao would watch Leigong descend through the clouds on blue webbed wings. He would hear Ming's screams as the Thunder God hovered above the treetops, holding Ming high overhead. He would watch as the Thunder God cast down the sinner who had slunk in the shadows for so long. The sound of Ming's skull breaking would be like a melon splitting against a rock.

As Hai Tao turned and entered his shack, a line of lightning cut the sky. The thunder followed.

37

Ming kicked the flank of his horse hard enough to hurt his own foot. "Come on!"

The horse grunted and picked up speed. Ming kicked it again.

"Ming! Ming!"

Dragon's voice was barely audible over the storm. Ming ignored it.

"Ming!"

Ming stopped his horse and turned around. "What?"

Dragon was fifty paces behind him. He closed the distance easily and drew to a smooth stop next to Ming. "We've been riding at top speed for too long. Your horse needs to rest. Not only that, you're riding through a storm. If you don't slow down you're going to fall."

Ming yanked on his reins and kicked his horse's flank again. The animal responded with a snort and a beat of its hoof.

Dragon put his hand on Ming's horse. "See? It needs to stop."

"We don't have time for this." Ming had to turn away as he spoke. The wind was throwing rain in his face and stinging his eyes. "I'll replace the damn horse if I have to. I don't need you to–"

"There's something else," Dragon said patiently. "We must be getting close. If we're not careful we'll ride right by the house without even knowing it. Then we'll have no chance of saving Hui Fen."

"We haven't been riding that long. We don't need to start looking for the right spot yet."

"I don't think you realize how fast we've been going. These horses are used to hard running and they're at the limits of their endurance. I was in the cavalry for most of my life, Ming. You need to trust me."

Ming opened his mouth to argue, but then he caught sight of the city walls. Those walls were massive things, three times the height of a man, but now they were tiny slivers of black in the distance. Dragon was right. They had been going faster than Ming had thought. He was correct about something else, too. If they passed by the right house, Hui Fen was doomed. "All right. I'll slow down."

Dragon wagged his finger. "Not good enough. Give me your reins. I'm going to lead your horse."

"No."

"If you ride ahead you're going to pick up speed without noticing it. As panic sets in you'll start riding faster and faster. Before you know it you'll be flying again. Let me set the pace."

"No," Ming repeated. He was beginning to think he should leave Dragon behind.

Dragon held out his hand, palm up. "Trust me. I'll guide the horses. You watch the houses. Take a good look at every one we pass. Look at each house until you're sure it's not the one we want. Don't worry, Ming. We're going to save her."

Ming put his reins in Dragon's hand. "It's time to go."

"It is. Keep your eyes open."

They began to move again. Dragon set the pace at a quick trot, but to Ming it felt like crawling speed. It was maddening. He wanted to slap Dragon's horse on the rump and shout *go!*

"Ming." Dragon did not turn around as he spoke. "Stop being frustrated with me and keep watch for the right house."

Ming muttered something and scanned the side of the road. How long until full dark? He prayed that dusk was farther away than it seemed. If they didn't spot the right place before the light died, they would have no chance of finding it until morning.

Ming wiped rainwater from his face and squinted at the houses. He saw one sad ramshackle another. They all looked the same and not one gave Ming a spark of recognition.

In what felt like just a few moments, the sky had grown almost black. Sick panic stirred inside Ming. He felt like he was standing on a riverbank and watching the current pull his daughter away, powerless to stop her death. And still the black consumed more of the sky, like a living thing that meant to kill his child.

When Ming first saw the little shack he felt no excitement. It was just another decrepit structure, this one overlooking the road from a high slope. But Dragon had told Ming to pay close attention to every building, so he did.

The first thing Ming recognized was the walkway that led from the road up to the house. It was a narrow, ugly thing – little more than a dirt path fading into brown weeds. After that other details began to look familiar. The right side of the roof was sagged, giving the house a strange, slanted appearance. Statues of lions sat on either side of the front door. They were so old they looked like little more than oddly shaped stones. But Ming recognized them. He looked at the lion on the left side of the door, already knowing what he would see. One of its front legs was missing.

Ming shouted, "Stop!"

Immediately Dragon pulled on the reins and looked back at Ming. "That's it?"

Ming nodded. He was furious with himself for yelling. How loud had he been? Had the storm masked his voice?

Dragon put a hand over his face to stop the driving rain and looked up at the house. "You're sure?"

Ming nodded again.

"All right. I trust you're not going to shout again?"

"I won't." Ming looked down the road. Fifty paces ahead there was another abandoned building. The front wall had collapsed, ages ago by the look of it. "Let's leave the horses there and double back."

"Perfect."

When the horses were tied, Ming turned back and looked up at the old shack. He could barely discern its outline against the black sky. Full night had finally come.

Dragon used a hand to shield his eyes from the rain. "What is our plan?"

Ming kept staring. There was no firelight visible through the shack's window, no sign of anyone inside. All the same he felt certain Hai Tao was there, waiting for them. "We keep it simple. We climb up the slope as quietly as we can so he doesn't know we're coming. The rain and the darkness should give us plenty of cover. As I recall there is a back door. I'll go in through the front and you go in through the back. Get in position. When you hear me kick in the front door, you break in. Are you ready?"

Dragon nodded, his eyes never leaving the house.

Ming drew his dagger. "In case I can't say this to you later, thank you. Thank you for risking your life to save my daughter."

"You're welcome. Come on. We shouldn't waste time."

"Then let's go."

• • •

The girl was making too much noise. She wasn't just crying, either. She was also struggling, probably trying to get loose. Hai Tao had tried more threats, but they weren't working. Chances were the girl was too hysterical to even hear them.

Hai Tao couldn't have this right now. He was focusing on the road below, waiting for a sign that Ming had come. Being on the lookout for Ming was already a difficult task, thanks to the rain and the darkness. The girl's distractions were making it that much harder.

Well, talking might not work, but Hai Tao had another way to keep the girl quiet. He just needed to show her his face. After looking into Hai Tao's eyes, the little brat wouldn't dare make another sound.

Hai Tao jumped down into the fireplace, opened the sack and got a nasty shock. The girl had worked free of the bonds on her wrists, and now she was tugging at the ones on her ankles. At least the gag was still over her mouth. Hai Tao was fortunate the girl was too stupid to remove that gag and scream for help.

Putting the bonds back on should have been easy, but the girl was struggling like an injured animal. She thrashed and kicked, putting her entire body behind every movement. Each time Hai Tao got a strong grip on an arm or a leg, it wriggled loose.

"Quiet," Hai Tao growled. "Quiet or you'll get some real pain."

The girl buried a nail into Hai Tao's forearm and dragged her hand down. Hai Tao felt sharp pain and then wet warmth. He looked down and saw blood spreading from a thin line on his arm.

"Quiet!"

The girl thrashed even more.

Hai Tao clenched his teeth and bit back a scream. Showing his face should have been enough, but it was only making the girl fight more. Why wouldn't she just *obey* him?

Finally he managed to pin the girl's shoulders to the floor. He put his knees on her shoulders so his hands were free. After that, grasping the wrists was easy. He began to tie the bonds...and stopped.

Had he just heard something? Probably not. He had been so focused on restraining the girl he couldn't have noticed any other noises. Besides, the storm had rendered him almost deaf to the world beyond his window. Logic said it was nothing.

But this was not an ordinary night. This was a night when every precaution was to be taken. Hai Tao remained still, his ear cocked toward the black window.

At first he only heard the heavy whisper of rain. He was about to turn his attention back to tying the girl's bonds when he heard something else. It sounded like splashing in the mud on the road below. The rain masked most of it, but that high and sharp *splat splat splat* still reached his ears. It sounded like footsteps, but it was too fast and heavy to be human.

Horses.

It had to Ming. Who else would be riding in this weather?

Hai Tao turned back to the girl and finished tying her wrists. Then he re-tied her ankles and tightened the gag.

One last tug on each restraint was enough to reassure him. The girl wasn't going anywhere.

Hai Tao climbed out of the fireplace and stared out the window. He saw only darkness shifting in the rain, but his eyes had not adjusted to that darkness yet. He waited, motionless. Slowly, he began to make out a shape on the road below. It was a man on horseback. The man was just sitting there in the rain, so it had to be Ming.

Then Hai Tao got a nasty shock. Ming wasn't alone! Just barely, Hai Tao could see another man on horseback slightly behind Ming. Hai Tao rubbed his eyes and tried to focus. The second man was big. In fact he was so large he made his horse look like a donkey.

It could only be Dragon.

Hai Tao cursed. He had expected Ming to come alone. Every time he pictured this confrontation he had imagined only three players: himself, Ming, and the child. He saw now he had made a foolish assumption. Of course Ming was too cowardly to come out here on his own. Of course he would ask that big savage to come with him.

For the first time in years, Hai Tao felt real panic. They were two and he was one. He was facing a disadvantage for which he had not prepared. They were about to come for him and he didn't know what to do.

Hai Tao looked out the window again. The figures were gone, and more panic welled up in him. Maybe they were already creeping up to the house. Maybe they were about to kick his door in.

He squinted through the rain and felt desperate relief. They had just moved up the road to the next abandoned building. They appeared to be tying their horses. That meant Hai Tao had time.

Hai Tao forced himself to remain calm. Heaven had seen fit to give him a final test. So be it. He would overcome it. How?

Hai Tao looked out the window again. They were moving toward the house now, low and silent. In the driving rain, they looked like spirits sneaking into the living world.

When they were one hundred paces from the house they separated. The larger shape circled around toward the rear of the house. The smaller one moved toward the front. They probably meant to enter the house through both the front and the back.

Hai Tao smiled. They believed they had the element of surprise, so they intended to trap him here. But Hai Tao knew they were coming, which meant they were the ones in for a surprise.

Best to deal with Dragon first. The area behind his house was thick with trees, so ambushing him would not be hard. After Dragon was dead Hai Tao could turn his full attention to Ming.

Silent as a ghost, Hai Tao removed his shirt and dropped it on the floor. He did not want Dragon to grab two handfuls of his clothing and throw him to the ground. He put out the lantern, picked up his hammer and slipped out through the back.

The storm had transformed the world outside. The falling rain and rising mist made the forest look like a place made of shadows. Hai Tao thought that if he reached out and tried to touch a tree, his fingers would pass through it, leaving a wispy trail of smoke. He had stepped from his home into the underworld.

Hai Tao pushed those thoughts away. Time was short. He needed to decide where he should lie in wait for Dragon.

And right away he saw the ideal spot for an ambush: a wide tree that offered excellent concealment. Dragon would not see him hiding there.

The slope behind Hai Tao's home was so steep a fall could end a person's life. Hai Tao needed to hurry, but he would also have to be careful. As Hai Tao descended he slipped once and stepped on the ground hard. He stopped, made his body completely still. He didn't even dare breathe. How much noise had he made? To his ears he had been louder than a scream.

But then, maybe it had only felt that way. Maybe the rain had masked all of it. He kept his ear trained and listened to the night. He waited for Dragon to call out, to yell 'he's here!' He only heard the same deafening whisper of rain.

Hai Tao knelt down low. He kept his grip on the hammer tight, and he waited.

• • •

Dragon stood at the bottom of the hill behind the shack. From down here he could just make out the old structure's rear wall. It was only fifty or sixty paces away, but the weather and the darkness made it look much farther.

Dragon unsheathed his sword, wincing at the loud scrape of metal on scabbard. His mind screamed that he needed to run up the hill, but he restrained himself. Elephants were lighter on their feet than he was. If Dragon went too fast Hai Tao would surely hear him. Besides, the slope was steep and soaked with rain.

An ugly thought occurred to Dragon: he and Ming had acted in haste, and in doing so they had made several mistakes. They had the advantage of numbers, but by separating they had sacrificed that advantage. Even worse, they had assumed Hai Tao didn't know they were here. But that wasn't logical. After all, Hai Tao had left the book for Ming, and that meant he expected an attack. Of course he would be on the lookout for his enemies.

Mistakes. Too many damn foolish mistakes.

Dragon's eyes passed over the trees. Back here there were a hundred good spots for an ambush. The rain shook the leaves, bringing a slow, eerie movement to the forest that Dragon did not like. Had the night been clear, he could have waited and listened for rustling, perhaps a twig breaking. Instead the storm had rendered him deaf. He could hear nothing above the rain.

He looked up at the house again. The house seemed to look back.

It was a strange feeling, being out here in a storm and hunting a monster. Dragon had killed six men in the cavalry and one more as a thief catcher…but he had never crawled through the dark and stalked his enemy. This was a foreign experience, and it brought a tight fear to his chest. It reminded him of the first time he rode into battle.

Dragon planted his foot on the hill. Rain had made the ground loose and he slipped back. He pushed down a little harder, giving himself better footing. With another admonishment to take it slow, he started to climb.

He was halfway up the hill when the darkness in front of him shifted. A black form rushed at him, making him think the night had come alive and meant to claim him.

Dragon looked up to see something long and thin coming down at him in a short, fast arc. Without thinking he shifted his weight to the right. There was terrible pain in the left side of his head, as though someone had driven a nail into his skull. More pain followed, this time in his left shoulder. He had the dim idea that someone had stabbed him there. Dragon heard something hit the ground and realized he had dropped his weapon.

A terrible ringing sound filled Dragon's ears. It was so loud it drowned out the storm. His entire head was growing numb. Everything around him began to seem far away and unimportant.

Dragon felt his forehead. He pulled his hand away and saw black liquid on the tips of his fingers.

Not black. Red. It's blood. Why is there blood?

He looked up. Someone was stumbling past him down the hill. He looked like he was trying to stop. The man righted himself, turned back toward Dragon, and raised that long, thin object again. Dragon thought dimly that it might be an axe.

The object came down. One thought exploded in Dragon's mind: *Hai Tao!*

As Dragon threw up his hands to stop the attack, pain screamed into his left shoulder. He tried to catch the weapon that was coming at him, but he only managed to slow it down. The weapon pushed through his hands and glanced off the side of his face.

Dragon gritted his teeth and tried to shake off the pain. He pivoted on his right foot to put some distance between himself and Hai Tao. As he prepared to fight he took an instant to assess his adversary.

The madman wore no shirt. Dragon realized for the first time that those loose officials' robes concealed a lot. Hai Tao wasn't as large as Dragon, but he was all sinew and hard muscle. He looked like a peasant weaned on hunger and hard labor. Dragon saw a body filled with lithe, cruel strength.

Hai Tao lifted the weapon high over his head. Dragon saw that it wasn't an axe – the head was too round. It was a hammer.

As the weapon came down Dragon backed away. Had the ground been dry he could have dodged the blow with little trouble. Instead his back foot slipped and the hammer glanced off his chest, sending another wave of pain through his body. It was worst in his left shoulder, and he guessed something there was broken.

Should have thought to wear armor.

Dragon shifted his weight forward and grabbed the hammer when its head was still planted in the ground. Hai Tao tried to yank the hammer away but Dragon had both hands around it. Hai Tao only succeeded in pulling both Dragon and the hammer closer to himself. How much strength did it take to drag a man of Dragon's size across the ground like that?

The rain had made the hammer's handle slick. Every time Dragon thought he had the weapon it slid in his grip again. He felt long fingers trying to slide between his hands and the handle. Those fingers felt thin, but they were stronger than metal wires.

The hammer began to slip from Dragon's fingers.

Dragon felt Hai Tao's breath hitting him in the face. He gauged the distance and snapped his head forward. The top of his forehead connected with something hard, and he heard an ugly *crunch.* It was followed by a high, shocked cry of pain.

Dragon yanked the hammer from Hai Tao. He took only an instant to adjust his grip, and then he swung the weapon out in a horizontal arc. The pain in his shoulder made it hard to muster a proper attack, but he put everything he had behind it. The hammer glanced against something, probably an arm, and he heard another cry of pain.

Hai Tao stumbled back, but immediately steadied himself and came forward again. He lowered his shoulders and charged at Dragon's midsection.

It was perfect. By coming in low like that, Hai Tao exposed himself to a blow against the back of his head.

Ignoring the pain in his shoulder, Dragon raised the hammer high, like an executioner readying his axe. Just as Dragon brought the weapon down, something impossible happened. Hai Tao's body changed direction and he charged up, leading with his head.

Dragon had time for one fragmented thought: *my turn for a head butt*. Then the world exploded in white pain.

Hands were at the hammer again. Hai Tao was tugging at the weapon with an animal's fury. Dragon tried to hold on, but the pain in his shoulder was fire.

Lightning flashed overhead, covering Hai Tao's face in a queer, blue light. Dragon saw a demon, its eyes white from the lightning glow, its face bloody and grinning.

Dragon planted his feet on the ground. He summoned all the strength he had left and yanked at the hammer. It suddenly felt lighter – he was the only one holding it now.

Dragon brought the weapon back, waist high. There was a terrible moment when he was certain the wet handle would slip from his hands and the hammer would fly into the darkness. Then he swung the weapon out as hard as he could, connecting with Hai Tao's rib cage.

Dragon heard a loud *snap*, like twigs breaking. Hai Tao howled in pain and wrapped both hands around the hammer. He almost pulled it away but Dragon held on. They held the weapon horizontally between them, each man trying to wrest it from the other's fingers.

Hai Tao began to circle left, trying to move to Dragon to his own left. Dragon pushed back, but his shoulder was nearly useless. He took a step to his left. He planted his feet and pushed with his legs, but the pain in his shoulder seemed to suck his power away. He took another step left.

Suddenly Hai Tao was taller. Dragon saw why. His enemy had circled their bodies so that he was on a higher part of the hill and Dragon was lower down. Now Dragon had to push up with all his strength, while Hai Tao could simply lean down and use his own bodyweight.

In the darkness, Dragon saw the madman grinning at him with insane triumph.

Dragon's rear foot slid back on the wet ground. He saw with numb dismay that it was only a matter of time until his weary shoulder gave out and he went sprawling down the hill.

But he didn't have to fall alone.

With one hand, Dragon released the hammer and hooked his fingers around the back of Hai Tao's neck. The triumph on Hai Tao's face turned into confusion. Then, as understanding set in, confusion became terror.

With his other hand Dragon punched the eunuch in the face, hard. Then he tried to wrap that hand around Hai Tao's neck as well. If he could get both hands on Hai Tao they would fall to their deaths together. But Hai Tao was fighting him now, leaning back and trying to shake free of Dragon's grip. The eunuch let go of the hammer and tried to pry Dragon's fingers loose. But Dragon did not let go.

Still ignoring the pain in his shoulder, Dragon lunged up with his other hand and wrapped it around the back of Hai Tao's neck. Now he was free to pull back with all his strength. He grinned at the madman. "Coming with me, Hai Tao?"

Dragon dug his heels in and continued to pull. He could feel them getting closer to the tipping point.

Then Hai Tao whipped his body to the side and grabbed hold of a tree. The sudden movement was too much for Dragon's weakened body, and just like that he lost his grip on Hai Tao's neck.

As Dragon fell back he reached out, tried to grasp Hai Tao's arm and missed.

Then Dragon was falling, falling backward down the hill and unable to protect himself. He tried to spin his body around and at the same time he brought his hands up to cover his head.

His wounded shoulder crunched against the ground, making him scream in pain. As he picked up speed the forest spun and jumped around him. He caught sight of a thick and slanted tree trunk at the bottom of the hill – directly in his path.

The tree trunk was filling his vision and rushing toward him. Dragon imagined an ancient, gnarled fiend reaching out for its wounded prey.

When he struck the trunk he felt a deep, heavy blow that rocked his entire body.

Skull. I broke my skull.

Dragon came to a rest at the bottom of the hill. He managed to turn onto his back. He did not want to die with his face in the dirt. He felt raindrops, cold and clean, running down his face.

And then the darkness took him.

• • •

Ming watched Dragon disappear around the far side of the hill. Then he turned his eyes to the shack. It was little more than a blur behind the thick sheets of rain, but Ming could see the broken roof slanted down at a wild angle, the weeds crawling up both sides of the crumbling porch. It looked like something from a child's nightmare – some broken hovel in which a troll boils its victims alive.

Ming drew his dagger and started to creep up the hill. The rain had turned the dirt path into a river of mud, and with every step Ming felt the earth slide underfoot. He kept his shoulders low to the ground. That made moving easier but the danger of falling was always there, like a demon lingering over his shoulder.

When Ming was fifteen paces from the shack, he stopped. There was still no light in the window, still no sign of anyone living there. But someone *was* there. Hui Fen was in there right now, lying on the floor of that dark and filthy hovel.

Above the roaring storm, Ming heard a high, terrified whimper.

His control broke. He slammed up the path, making loud splashes with every step. Twice his feet slipped and he almost went tumbling backward to injury, but he did not slow down.

Then he was standing at the front door.

From up close the shack looked just as it had ten years ago. Ming remembered the door with the cracked boards and the wood so rotten it was almost black. The porch still had an ugly brown stain, and Ming supposed no one had ever cleaned the blood that spilled there so many years ago.

Ming shoved the door open. He raised his weapon and charged into the shack, ready for anything.

But the shack's only room was black and empty. There was no light, no sound at all. The air tasted thick and musty, as though no one had disturbed it in years.

They had come to the wrong place. The crying Ming had heard was his imagination. They had wasted precious time because Ming panicked and led them to nowhere.

The silence screamed at him.

Ming's lungs and chest suddenly felt too tight. He tried to breathe and could not. He clutched his chest with one hand and groped for a wall with the other. His hand found nothing, and the world spun away. He doubled over and tried to vomit.

From somewhere in that black room, he heard a child's cries.

The world came rushing back at him. "Hui Fen! Hui Fen!"

The only answer was another cry.

Light. I need light.

Ming put his hands out and walked forward, forcing himself to go slowly. Soon his fingers touched a wall. He moved his hands along the wall, waiting to feel a torch or a candle. Finally he had some good fortune when his foot kicked something heavy and metallic. When he knelt down and felt the object his foot had struck, he knew it was a lantern.

He lit the lantern. It bathed the room in a dull, yellow light.

Ming looked around. Even with the lantern burning the room was dim, as though the walls themselves had absorbed the years of darkness. There was no furniture save an old chair, no firewood or cooking tools.

No one has come here in a decade. I have entered a tomb. I think I hear my daughter crying but she is not here. I hear her cries because I am losing my mind.

Then Ming saw a sleeping mat and a satchel in a far corner. Both objects were worn, but they looked new enough to stand out in this ancient place. Next to the sleeping mat were several pieces of thick, sturdy looking rope. The rope looked new, expensive.

So someone did live here.

But where was Hui Fen? Where was his daughter? There was no spot in this room where Hai Tao could have hidden a child.

Ming took a step forward, but when he tried to put his foot down he could not find the floor. He felt a sickening, terrifying lurch as he fell forward. It was like stepping off the edge of an invisible cliff. Just in time, Ming managed throw his weight backward.

After he regained his balance, Ming held the lantern out and looked down at the floor. The dugout fireplace! In his panic he had forgotten all about it.

Ming looked into the pit and let out a high, strangled cry. Hui Fen was on the fireplace floor. Her hands were tied and her mouth was gagged, but she appeared unhurt. The bottom half of her body was in a crumpled brown sack. She looked like she had been working her way out of it.

Hui Fen looked up at him and screamed into her gag. Ming put the lantern down and half jumped, half fell into the old fireplace. He was certain that if he did not grasp his daughter right now, the ground would open and swallow her up.

Ming did not dare try to cut Hui Fen's bonds. His hands were shaking too violently. Instead he dropped his knife and began to work at the bonds with his fingers. With more determination than skill, Ming freed Hui Fen's hands and feet. He left the gag on in case she started screaming and whispered, "Are you hurt?"

Hui Fen shook her head.

"I have to go –"

Hui Fen thrashed and screamed into the gag.

As gently as he could, Ming put a hand over his daughter's mouth. "That man is still out there. I have to deal with him."

Hui Fen went quiet, but the terror was still in her face.

"Is he close by?"

Hui Fen nodded at the back door.

"He went out that way?"

A nod.

"Just a moment ago?"

Another nod.

Ming wrapped his fingers around the gag. "I'm going to take this off, but I need you to keep your voice low. I know you can do that. Tell me – did he know we were coming?" Slowly, he pulled the gag down.

"I think so." Hui Fen's voice was calmer than Ming had thought possible. "I couldn't see what he was doing but just now he got quiet, like he was waiting for something."

"Listen to me," Ming said. "I have to go out back and find that man. But that means you have to be alone just a bit longer. Can you do that?"

Hui Fen nodded again.

"Go outside. Wait right by the front door and count to two hundred. Can you count that high?"

"Yes."

Ming said, "If you get to two hundred and I don't come back, run."

Hui Fen's tight composure began to crack again. "Run? Alone in the dark?"

"Yes," Ming said. *Because if I don't come back soon I'll be dead.* "When you're outside you'll see the city walls. Even in the storm you'll see the torches. Just walk toward the torches and you'll reach the city. Remember to stay on the road." The words didn't sound real to Ming. He was telling his nine-year-old daughter she may have to walk alone down an empty road at night. "Can you do that?"

"I think so."

Ming lifted Hui Fen out of the fireplace. Then took her head in his hands and kissed her on the cheek. "Good girl. But don't worry. I'll be back soon and we'll go home together."

Hui Fen opened the front door. She stepped into the storm and closed the door gently behind her.

The thought came to Ming again. *I just sent my nine-year-old daughter into a dark storm by herself.*

As Ming climbed out of the fireplace, the shack's back door exploded inward with a fantastic *crack!* Ming took a backward step and shielded his face.

Then he straightened up and looked.

The person in the doorway was outside the lantern's weak circle of light, but Ming could see it was not Dragon. This figure was tall and broad across the shoulders, but much slimmer than Dragon.

The man stepped into the light.

Not a man, Ming thought. *Something else.*

Hai Tao looked like he had been mauled by an animal. His nose was pressed back at a strange angle, and his face was bleeding from a series of gashes. The blood mixed with smears of grime, covering most of his face. His eyes, somehow bright and dull at the same time, gleamed at Ming from behind his mask of filth.

Ming thought of Dragon. Hai Tao had clearly been in a terrible fight, but he was here and Dragon was not. That meant Dragon was dead. Dragon, who had ridden into blackness to save Ming's child, was lying dead in the rain.

Ming would mourn his friend later. Right now he had to kill Hai Tao.

Just as Dragon had, Ming marveled at Hai Tao's build. In his official's robe the eunuch had always appeared tall and slight. Now he looked like a veteran soldier who spent his days fighting in the wilderness.

Hai Tao was holding a long hammer in his right hand. Ming looked at it and realized his own weapon was still down in the fireplace.

Ming said, "Hello, Rabbit."

Hai Tao smiled. One of his teeth was missing. Another had been broken off at the middle. "You finally remembered me."

"I can't believe I didn't see it before." Ming tried not to look at Hai Tao's hammer. He did not want the eunuch to notice only one of them was armed.

Hai Tao's grin widened. "Fooled you. Fooled all of you. You never thought an orphan like me could turn into this. Never thought I could outwit the government and terrorize the whole city."

Ming needed to close the distance between himself and Hai Tao. He picked up the lantern and held it close to Hai Tao's face. He expected to see the hammer come up, but the madman did not move.

"It really is you." Ming forgot about the danger as disbelief took hold of him. "You used to be a little scrap of a boy who flinched at his own shadow. Now look at you."

"You shouldn't be surprised by my transformation." Hai Tao stepped back from the lantern's glow. The top half of his face was masked by shadow again. "You brought it about."

"I didn't know they...I didn't think they would castrate you."

"But you knew it *could* happen!" Hai Tao sounded like a quick-witted scholar refuting a flawed argument. "Everyone knows they castrate orphans all the time, so you knew it might happen to me as well. You knew it and you sent me to them anyway."

Ming slid his foot forward. "You cannot blame me for everything. You started down this road when you murdered your parents."

Hai Tao's face twisted into a scowl. "Don't you call them my parents. The dead bitch you found here wasn't my mother. My father killed my real mother. Stabbed her in the belly and then lied to the authorities about it. I told you my mother wasn't unfaithful. You remember."

"I do. I'm sorry about what happened to your mother. It must have been hard for you."

"Oh, it was." Hai Tao adjusted his grip on the hammer, as though testing its weight. "But now it's all right. It's all right because that was my first step."

"Your first step toward what?"

"Toward discovering the Thunder God," Hai Tao whispered. His voice was thick with awe. "Toward becoming his holy disciple."

"So that's why you killed," Ming said. "You were making sacrifices to Leigong."

Hai Tao nodded.

"And me? You've been watching me for years, haven't you? Learning about my secret work."

Another grotesque smile. "It was easy to keep an eye on you from the shadows. You're so predictable, Ming. Of course a man like you would become the Sorcerer."

"You see a lot." Ming slid his foot forward again. The sound of his boot scraping the dirt floor felt very loud.

"But *you* see nothing," Hai Tao said. "You still don't know the final step. My sacrifice."

"You want me to kill you? Happily."

"How? You don't even have a weapon."

"Give me the hammer and I'll do it right now."

"You'll kill me soon enough. But first I must see to your daughter." Faster than a striking cobra, Hai Tao threw his fist out and smashed it into Ming's right eye.

Ming put his hands to his face and stumbled backward. Then something heavy slammed into his side. There was a queer feeling of weightlessness, of falling farther than was possible in this little house. Even then, Ming held on to one thought. *He said he will see to my daughter. He is chasing after my child right now.*

Ming hit the floor shoulder first. The impact made his bones rattle, made his teeth crack painfully together. He felt dizzy, sick. A tiny voice whispered into his mind: *I am in shock.* He tried to fight that shock and pull himself back into reality, but the room refused to stop spinning.

From a world away came a loud *bang,* like one piece of wood hitting another. It almost sounded like…

Like a door slamming closed!

Ming sat up. He put his palms against his temples and forced the room to be still. There was no more time for shock. Hai Tao had run out of the shack, had gone out in search of Hui Fen. Had she already counted to two hundred and started running? Or was she still right outside the front door?

Ming wiped blood from his eyes and looked around. The first thing he recognized was the hemp sack on the floor. So that was why he had seemed to fall forever. Hai Tao had knocked him into the dugout fireplace.

Ming saw his dagger and grabbed it. Then he gritted his teeth, held the edge of the fireplace and pulled himself up. The room began a sickening rocking motion, like a boat in rough waters.

As Ming pulled himself out of the fireplace, pain tore into his left knee. He got to his feet and tried to stand. The pain drilled into his knee again, deeper than before.

Dislocated. Maybe broken.

Ming lurched to the door, trying to forget the pain. He pushed the door open and rainwater hit him in the face like a slap. That brought more pain, this time through to the back of his skull. Perhaps his nose was broken too.

Ming stepped out of the shack and looked around. There was no sign of Hai Tao or Hui Fen. Ming saw shadows, rain and nothing else. There was no forest between here and the road, no spot where a person could hide. It was as though Hai Tao had vanished.

But Hai Tao had to be close. Hui Fen had to be close as well.

Ming began to work his way down the slope's muddy path. The task filled his knee with black agony. He felt his leg wanting to give out and let him fall. To make things worse, the rain was stronger now. It came down on him relentlessly, blinding him and making his feet slip. Just as the dark had felt like some living thing come to blind him, the storm seemed like a creature sent from above to cast him down.

He reached the road. Somewhere to his left, he heard a heavy rustling noise. It sounded like an animal scurrying through tall grass. After that came a fast, sharp cry.

And then silence.

Ming spun to his left and dashed down the road. More pain blossomed in his knee, and he imagined of two pieces of bone pressing against each other beneath his skin. He ran harder.

Shapes emerged in the blackness ahead. After three more steps Ming recognized Hai Tao and Hui Fen. Hai Tao was standing in the middle of the road, the hammer still in his hand. Hui Fen was huddled at his feet. She appeared unhurt, but from where Ming was he could not be sure.

Hai Tao saw Ming coming and raised the hammer to waist level. "Not another step."

Ming slid to a stop. He tried to think of a strategy and could not.

"She was hiding out here," Hai Tao said. "You told her to run through a dark storm? By herself? Not very wise, but then you never were good at caring for the weak."

Ming took a step forward. "Let her go."

Overhead, lightning forked across the night. Hai Tao looked up and held his long arms out at his sides. Then a blast of thunder seemed to split the sky in half.

Hai Tao yelled something, but it was lost in the storm. With both hands he raised the hammer high above his head.

Ming lowered his shoulders and threw himself forward with his good leg. The ground underfoot was slick but he kept his balance. He heard a cry of surprise from Hai Tao and hoped he had caught the madman off guard.

Ming's shoulder hit Hai Tao's midsection. Both men yelled out in pain as their injured bodies collided. Ming kept driving forward with his legs. He managed to push Hai Tao back a few steps, but then Hai Tao shifted his weight and brought them both to a dead halt.

Ming wrapped his arms around Hai Tao's midsection. "Hui Fen! Run! Now!" He heard footsteps and hoped Hui Fen had done as she was told.

Ming stabbed out blindly with his knife. It hit something hard and he heard a scream. Then Ming planted his free hand on Hai Tao's stomach and shoved, sending the eunuch stumbling back. He felt a surge of desperate panic as the knife slipped from his fingers. When he looked up he saw the knife handle protruding from Hai Tao's left side, just above the waist. The blade was buried up to its hilt.

With one hand Hai Tao probed the knife in his side. He felt the handle and released a tight hiss of pain. To Ming's disappointment, he seemed aware and in control. He even had the presence of mind to hold on to the hammer.

Hai Tao said, "Thinking you've won? Thinking you can finish me?" He yanked the knife from his body and threw it into the darkness.

Hai Tao tried to run after Hui Fen but this time Ming was ready. He stepped in front of Hai Tao and grasped the hammer with both hands. Hai Tao bared his teeth and tried to pull the hammer away but now there was less strength in his arms. The madman must have already lost a great deal of blood. He glared at Ming with desperate, cheated rage.

Ming let go of the hammer and hit Hai Tao in the face with a hard, short punch. Hai Tao screamed and staggered back. Ming threw out his fist again, this time connecting with Hai Tao's jaw. He heard a dull crack, felt pain in his hand, and knew a bone had been broken. Whether it was in Hai Tao's face or his own hand he did not know.

Ming moved forward and shoved Hai Tao with both hands. Hai Tao dropped the hammer and grabbed Ming's tunic. They fell to the ground together, Hai Tao on his back and Ming on top of Hai Tao.

Ming immediately pressed down with all his weight. Hai Tao writhed and fought, but his power was gone. He looked at Ming and said, "Let me up." Even now there was hubris in his voice.

Ming saw the hammer lying in the mud. He reached out, grabbed it. He placed the length of the handle against Hai Tao's throat and pushed down with all the strength he had left.

Hai Tao's mouth went wide and his tongue began to wag back and forth like some grotesque animal. He gagged and retched. His eyes bulged out so far they looked ready to burst into mush. He pushed weakly at the handle.

Ming pressed down harder.

In the darkness behind Hai Tao, a shape materialized. "Hui Fen," Ming breathed. "Hui Fen, don't watch. Turn away."

Hui Fen lingered for a moment, and then stepped back into the shadows. Ming hoped she had obeyed him, but a part of him could feel her watching from the darkness.

Hai Tao's mouth was still pulled back into a rictus of pain, but his eyes were on Ming. They were clear, aware. Ming tried to look away, but Hai Tao held him with his gaze, willed him to watch.

And Ming did watch. He pushed down harder and he watched. For an eternity he looked down at the dying man, watched as his face trembled, as it went from red to purple. Finally Hai Tao's eyes grew foggy and rolled back into his head.

Time passed. Ming did not know how much. He placed two fingers on Hai Tao's neck. There was no pulse.

As Ming climbed off the dead man his pain came raging back. He felt it in his face, his arms, his shoulder. He was certain his left knee had shattered into pieces.

Hui Fen stepped out of the darkness. Ming opened his mouth to scream, to warn his daughter away. She needed to run, run back to the city as fast as she could. The predators of the black forest were nothing next to this monster that meant to beat the life from her. Instead all he managed to say was, "Hui Fen. Are you all right?"

Hui Fen only stared.

When Ming tried to stand his knee gave out. He fell onto his back next to Hai Tao. They lay side by side like lovers on the wet ground.

Overhead another fork of lightning cut across the sky. It was followed by a crash of thunder so powerful it shook the puddles around Ming's head. The rain grew stronger.

As Ming felt the water wash over him, he thought of gods and sacrifice. Many people sent offerings to the gods, hoping to curry favor with Heaven. And tonight, Ming had thwarted one of those sacrifices. Had he angered the Thunder God by cheating him of his prize? If he had, what would the consequences be?

Ming closed his eyes and fell asleep on the road, with gods and demons still haunting his thoughts.

• • •

When Ming awoke the rain had stopped, and light was touching the edges of the sky.

He sat up in a panic. Where was Hui Fen?

"Baba."

Ming turned toward the voice. Hui Fen was standing just a few paces behind him. Her skin was splotched with grime and her hair was in clumps, but she looked dry. "Hui Fen. You're not all wet."

"I had shelter. I tried to drag you there but you were too heavy. I had to leave you here."

"You did the right thing." That was true, but Ming had to suppress a shudder. He imagined his daughter hiding up in that dreadful little shack, taking shelter in the home of a man who had meant to kill her. "I'm sorry you had to go back up there."

"I didn't." Hui Fen pointed. "There's another old building down the road. I sat in there with the horses. Are they yours?"

"Yes. Well, I borrowed them." Ming wanted to say more, but he was distracted by a stir of unease. His daughter's voice was flat and detached in a way he did not like. Hadn't he noticed a similar change in his son only yesterday? He extended his hand. "Hui Fen. Come here."

Hui Fen did not move.

Ming's mind was still foggy, and he needed a moment to understand. Hai Tao's body was right next to him. "Right." He struggled to his feet, wincing as a hundred blades pushed into his body. At least his knee was bearing some weight. "Are you hurt?"

"No."

"How long was I out?"

"I don't know. A long time."

"Turn around. I don't want you to see this." After Hui Fen turned away, Ming looked down at Hai Tao. The dead man's face was the color of rotten grapes. His mouth was still pulled back, exposing rows of broken and bloodied teeth.

Ming searched Hai Tao's face. He looked for something to remind him of the boy he had known years ago. He wanted to see that some part of Rabbit had survived, that the madman hadn't consumed him completely.

But all he saw was a leering corpse.

Ming took Hai Tao's hands and began dragging his body off the road. Normally that would have been a simple task, but his injuries slowed him terribly. After a long struggle he dropped the upper half of Hai Tao's body into the brush. He kicked at Hai Tao's legs until they disappeared from the road as well. It was a fitting end. Let the animals have him.

Then Ming knelt down and picked up the hammer. That went into the brush as well.

"Can we go now?"

Ming turned to see Hui Fen looking at him. He considered reprimanding her for watching him after he had told her not to, and then decided against it. "Not quite yet."

"Why not?" Hui Fen's weird calm was suddenly gone, and her voice was edging toward panic.

As gently as he could, Ming placed a hand on his daughter's shoulder. "First I have to see about a friend. Come with me."

• • •

As soon as they circled around to the rear of the shack, they saw Dragon's body. He was some twenty paces away, lying face up at the bottom of a steep hill. The giant was resting against a tree stump, and Ming supposed his friend had died from a fall.

Ming pointed a finger at his daughter. "Wait for me on the road. Do *not* follow me."

Hui Fen turned away, trudged back to the road and sat on a large tree stump.

Ming began to pick his way through the forest. The ground was still slippery from the storm, and he had to hold the trees for balance. Again his injuries turned a simple task into a brutal trial. Twice he slipped and felt pain charging through every part of his body. By the time he reached Dragon his knee was screaming and his face was covered in sweat.

Ming knelt down next to his friend. Dragon's knuckles were caked with blood. Even the heavy rain had failed to wash it away. He had died fighting. Knowing that gave Ming comfort but it was weak, like a thin gruel.

Ming put a hand on Dragon's arm. "We did it. We saved Hui Fen and we killed Hai Tao. Thank you, friend."

Dragon's eyes opened. "Ming. Am I dead?"

Ming grasped Dragon's shoulders and tried to bring him to a sitting position, but Dragon grunted in pain.

"Wait." Dragon's voice had the dry, rusted creak of a very sick man. "If I move too fast, my bones might well shatter inside my skin."

"All right." Ming tried to say more, but his mouth produced no sounds. He wet his lips and tried again. "Dragon, what happened?"

"I died," Dragon said in that same rusted voice. His eyes, cloudy but aware, found Ming's. "Ming, I died. That madman got free of me and I fell down this hill. My skull broke. I was sure of it."

"Perhaps," Ming said, "your skull is thicker than even you realized."

Dragon let out a weak laugh that turned into a series of deep, wracking coughs. "Help me sit, Ming."

"You're sure?"

"I'm sure."

With the care of a person handling a newborn baby, Ming placed his hands on Dragon's shoulders again. Dragon propped himself up on his elbows, his teeth clenching so hard that Ming could hear them grinding against each other. He tried to rise to a full sitting position and nearly made it. But the pain was too much, and soon he was back on his elbows again.

Then another pair of hands, these much smaller than Ming's, were pulling at Dragon's shoulders. Ming could hear his daughter's pants of effort as she helped the injured man. Dragon set his jaw and threw his weight forward. A low scream churned behind those clenched teeth.

And then Dragon was sitting up. His shoulders were slumped and tears had cut paths through the grime on his face, but he was sitting up.

Dragon locked eyes with Hui Fen, and the pain in his face gave way to disbelieving wonder. He reached for the child, but then withdrew his hand.

"Hui Fen," Dragon said slowly. "You're unhurt?"

Hui Fen nodded.

Dragon said, "If you're alive, then speak."

Hui Fen did not speak. Instead, she threw her arms around Dragon and buried her face in the hollow of his shoulder. They stayed that way for a long time, two people who by all rights should have died in the driving rain.

Then Dragon burst into tears.

• • •

The three of them stood on the muddy road, the day's silence heavy and thick. Ming's knee was a storm of pain, and his body screamed from an untold number of bruises and gashes. He wondered dimly if he would ever be the same after this crucible, and cast the thought aside. He most certainly would never be the same.

None of them would be.

Unable to help himself, Ming stole another glance at Dragon. It really was a wonder that the man could still breathe, let alone stand. His left eye had swollen to twice its normal size and turned a dark, angry purple. Dried blood was caked under his nose, which still leaked fresh blood in slow and steady streams.

And yet here he stood, here they *all* stood, battered but living. The miracle was so great Ming could scarcely believe it was real.

It was Hui Fen who finally spoke. "What now?"

Ming said, "Can the two of you ride?"

Hui Fen nodded. Dragon touched his ribs and winced, but then he nodded as well.

"All right," Ming said. "Then let's go get those horses."

38

It was well past midday when Ming pushed open the door to Dragon's small home. They stood in the doorway, swaying like carousers after a night of hard drinking.

They had brought Hui Fen home before coming here, and now both men were at the limit of their endurance. Dragon had one arm draped over Ming's shoulders, forcing Ming to put all that weight on his one good leg. To Ming, supporting the wounded giant felt like hauling a load of bricks up a steep mountain.

Ming spotted a sleeping mat against the far wall. "There."

The men started forward, both of them grunting from the pain and the effort. Slowly, slowly, Ming lowered Dragon onto the mat.

Dragon rested his head on the floor. His left eye was now swollen shut entirely, and his right eye was but a white slit in his purple black face. The left side of his jaw looked broken in a way that reminded Ming grotesquely of Hai Tao.

"Ming," Dragon said. His voice was stronger now, but it still had a rasp that Ming did not like. "Stop looking at me like a doting mother. I'll be all right."

"I know that." In truth, Ming knew no such thing.

"I mean it," Dragon said. "I've got broken ribs and a broken shoulder, and my head will probably throb for weeks. But I'll recover. I've come back from injuries before."

"None as bad as these," Ming said.

"No," Dragon agreed. "None as bad as these. No matter. After two moons or three or ten, I'll be the man I was."

"I'll bring you food and drink every day," Ming said. It felt like a shabby promise to make after Dragon's sacrifice, but he could think of nothing else to say. "And anything else you need. Once you're back on your feet, I'll –"

"Once I'm back on my feet I'm going to leave this city," Dragon said.

Ming studied Dragon's face. "You're certain?"

"I'm certain. I'll head west, I think. Out to the area where I was born."

"And you'll remain a thief catcher?"

With an effort, Dragon nodded. "It can be tiresome work, but I've lost my stomach for life in the capital."

"Dragon." Ming felt tears pressing at the backs of his eyes. "Thank you. I can never repay you for what you did for me. For my family."

"No," Dragon said. "No, I suppose you can't."

Ming swallowed. "But I will be in your debt until I die. For as long as I draw breath, I will be ready to lay my life down for you."

"That was beautifully said, Ming."

Ming and Dragon considered that remark for a long moment. Then they both burst out laughing.

39

It's strange, Ming thought. *Just four moons ago I killed the most feared criminal in the city's history. I saved my daughter when she was a heartbeat from death. I've been through all that and more, but this little bald man who picks his nose still terrifies me.*

These thoughts passed through Ming's mind as he sat in Governor Han's office and tried to look calm. He knew he was doing a poor job of it. He just did not like being alone with the Snake. He kept worrying he might say the wrong thing and pay for it with his head. Being here felt like climbing a steep mountain without a rope.

Ming hadn't seen Han since he and Dragon stormed out of this office last summer. After returning from Hai Tao's shack, Ming had been too tired and weak to report it all to the government. Instead he told everything to Kuo, the man who had secured their horses. Giving Kuo such sensitive information was risky, but Ming's old comrade had proven trustworthy again. He reported the news directly to Han and then kept it to himself. That Kuo still lived was proof of his discretion.

A few weeks after Hai Tao's death, Kuo had called on Ming with some news. He told Ming the government had found the shack and sent its own people out to investigate. Apparently they saw enough to convince them Hai Tao was their killer. That was fortunate. If the authorities hadn't believed Hai Tao was the culprit, Ming and Dragon would have stood accused of killing a civil servant.

Han finished picking his nose and brushed his hands. "How is your wife's health?"

"She is deteriorating quickly."

"I am sorry to hear it."

"Thank you." Ming shifted in his chair. "It's difficult for my children."

"Of course. And you? How are you coping with your injuries?"

"The pain has been manageable," Ming said mildly. That was a fiction, but he saw no need to tell Han the truth. Besides, he could never make another person understand the agony of his convalescence. As it turned out, Ming's recovery had been nearly as grueling as Dragon's.

The first week after killing Hai Tao had been the worst. Ming had awoken every night, certain some unseen demon was torturing him. When he did manage sleep he dreamed of long, crooked teeth burrowing into his knee. Every morning his tunic was soaked and stinking with sweat. Bringing food and drink to Dragon was always a trial of torment, but Ming had made the trip every day until his friend was mobile again.

Recovery had been steady but slow, like hauling a load of stones across a desert. He marked his progress with achievements that had once seemed trivial. He was still proud of the first time he managed to walk across his room without leaning against the wall. He considered his first night of uninterrupted sleep a dazzling victory. These days the only real bother was his knee. He still had a slight limp, which he expected to remain for the rest of his life.

Governor Han said, "Ming, you know why I've summoned you."

"You want to talk about the murders." Ming had not been told why Han waited four moons to speak with him, but he could guess. Likely the government had been too busy scrambling to conceal the scandal of their insane eunuch. In that they had been remarkably successful. Ren Shu had been released quietly. Ming heard the young man had since passed the Imperial Exams and received a posting far from the capital. Hai Tao was a eunuch and therefore property of the state, so no one had to explain his disappearance. Dragon had left the capital and headed west, just as he had planned. All in all, things were wrapped up quite nicely. The Sorcerer couldn't have done it better.

The only loose ends left were Ming and Zhou.

"Correct," Han said. "More to the point, I want to make sure that *you* don't talk about the murders. Things are finally under control, Ming. Gossip could change all of that very quickly."

"I understand."

Han leaned forward. "Ming, I need you to stay silent about this for the rest of your life."

Ming was confused. The Snake didn't need to ask anyone for silence. He had countless ways of shutting a person up.

"You're wondering why I don't just kill you." A dangerous look flashed in the Snake's eyes. "I could do that, and I will if I have to. But I see a better way for this to end."

"You do?"

"You return to Gold Bird Guard. Work for us again."

"A bribe," Ming said.

"No." Han did not look offended by the accusation. "You have shown your worth. You discovered the real killer's identity while the rest of us chased our tails. You and your friend Dragon rode out yourselves and killed that man. You even managed to save your daughter. You are qualified to be a Guard and you know it."

"All the same it's a bribe. At least partially."

Han shrugged. "Perhaps it is, but I wouldn't offer you the position if I didn't want you in it. If you take the job – and agree to stay silent – I can end this crisis and have a competent officer in the Gold Bird Guard."

"I can't be in the Guard again," Ming said. "With my knee I couldn't chase down an old woman."

Han made a sharp, hollow bark that may have been laughter. "I can see that. But you can investigate, can't you? You can interview witnesses and help us track down the more elusive criminals. You've shown a talent for those things. We'll give you the best salary you've ever gotten in your life, and we will never ask you to resume your role as the Sorcerer."

Ming was not surprised to learn that Han knew his old identity. Likely the old man had been looking into his past for some time. "Interview and investigation. Nothing more."

"That's right. No danger and certainly no concealing misdeeds."

Ming couldn't suppress his amusement. A few moons ago his wife had predicted his return to the Gold Bird Guard. You could count on some people to be right almost all the time. "I'll do it. But I reserve the right to resign any time I wish."

Han grinned, exposing his yellow teeth. "Wonderful!" For the first time since Ming had met him, the Snake looked genuinely pleased. "You'll start tomorrow."

"I have another condition."

Han's face revealed the smallest hint of surprise. "Oh?"

"I want you to exonerate Lin."

"Lin is already dead."

"And everyone believes he was a monster," Ming said. "He does not deserve that."

"How do you suggest we clear his name without looking like incompetents?"

Ming had anticipated the question. "Toad and Blossom. Just tell the truth and say they framed Lin for the murders. If you're still worried about looking foolish, embellish on their plot. Say they planted more evidence than just the bracelet. The people who knew those two won't have any trouble believing your story. The rest of the city can be convinced."

"If we exonerate Lin, people will think the real killer is still alive," Han said. "Panic will return to the city."

Ming was ready for that point as well. "Again, Toad and Blossom are the solution. They killed the children. They did it for evil reasons that decent people cannot fathom. That's just one idea, mind you. After you exonerate Lin you'll have a myriad of truths you can fashion."

Han grunted. "You're trying my patience."

"It's part of my price. And it's the right thing to do." Ming felt sweat tickling his chest. He was demanding a lot and he didn't have a bit of leverage.

Han looked up at the ceiling. He stayed so still for so long that it looked like he had died right there in his chair. Finally he looked back at Ming. "All right. Half the damn city thinks he's innocent anyway."

"And what about Zhou?" Ever since Hai Tao's death, Ming had heard nothing from his one-time friend. Zhou had simply disappeared. But Ming suspected the government had him locked away somewhere.

"He'll be dealt with," Han said.

"How? The punishment of a mandarin will raise questions."

That same dangerous look flashed in the Snake's eyes. "No one does what he did and gets away with it. We have ways of handling these things."

40

Three days later, Ming learned what those ways were.

Some two hundred people stood around the willow tree at the edge of the West Market. It was a large crowd for an execution, but the government had anticipated that. Security was high.

Ming stood at the front of the crowd, and thanks to his Gold Bird Guard uniform no one shouted at him to move. He had forgotten how differently people treated him when he was in his armor.

A stone about the height of a man's knee sat under the willow tree's long branches. The stone's natural color was slate gray, but over the years countless stains had turned most of it a deep, ugly brown. Hundreds of scars were slashed across the stone's rough surface.

Excited whispers began to bubble up from the spectators. Ming turned and saw six Gold Bird Guards approaching the willow tree. A horse-drawn cart followed. The cart had four walls and a roof so no one could look inside. Behind the cart were six more Guards.

The cart stopped at the edge of the clearing. When a Guard opened its door and dragged the prisoner into the sunlight, a collective gasp rose from the crowd.

Ming took a step back. He turned away and rubbed his eyes. His mind was playing tricks on him. That was the only explanation for what he had seen.

You didn't see what you thought you saw. You couldn't *have. Just relax, turn back and take a longer look this time. You'll see there's nothing to worry about.*

Ming took a slow breath, calmed himself and looked again. He saw the same thing, and panic welled up inside him.

The prisoner wasn't Zhou. The man being led through the clearing had Zhou's height and build, but that was where the similarities ended. Zhou was prim and plump, but this man was just a skeleton with skin stretched over its bones. He looked like the vagrants who lived beyond the city walls, the ones who kept death at arm's length by begging and stealing. The gag over his mouth and the wooden handcuffs on his wrists made him look all the more wretched.

Ming looked around for the man in charge of the execution. He had to tell him they were about to kill the wrong person. The right man had slipped away, had used his uncanny guile to steal back his freedom. Perhaps he had tricked a Guard into letting him go. Perhaps he had blackmailed an official and gotten out that way. The possibilities were endless. These people had no idea of who they were dealing with.

Then the prisoner tilted his head in a way Ming recognized, and the illusion vanished. It really was Zhou. Hunger and other unknown terrors had broken him down to almost nothing, but it was Zhou.

As the Guards led Zhou into the clearing, a mandarin in a green robe unrolled a scroll and read about treason. He called Zhou a criminal, a traitor who sought to undermine his king. Ming did not hear mention of any specific crimes.

Every time the mandarin attacked Zhou, the crowd's hostility grew. A few people began shouting at them to get on with it, to cut the bastard's head off. Zhou did not react to any of it. He just stood with his head hanging down between his shoulders. Ming got the sense his old friend did not understand what was happening to him. Or maybe he was too beaten down to care.

It was all too much and Ming had to turn away. When he looked back at the clearing he suffered a jolt of shock. Zhou was staring at him. He seemed to be studying Ming, like a man trying to place a familiar face.

Ming did not know how to respond, so he just stared back at the pitiful man.

One of the Guards placed a hand on Zhou's arm and pulled him toward the cutting stone. Zhou followed, his eyes still on Ming. As Zhou was turned away, Ming thought he saw a spark of recognition in his old friend's face. But he was not sure.

Zhou looked down at the stone. His puzzled expression did not change. One of the Guards spoke into Zhou's ear. Ming could not hear it, but it looked like the Guard said "kneel."

It was as though the Guard had cast a spell that restored Zhou's mind. Zhou blinked hard and looked at the stone again. His eyes went wide and he screamed into his gag. The Guard repeated his order to kneel. Zhou's only reaction was to scream again and try to break free of the man's grip.

The Guard cursed. He kicked the back of Zhou's knee, sending him to the ground and drawing cheers from the crowd. The Guard placed both hands on Zhou's shoulders. With little effort he forced Zhou down until his head was against the stone.

Another Gold Bird Guard stepped into the clearing. He was much older than the other Guards, and he had a slightly foreign look about him. He was holding a short, thick sword in his right hand. As he walked toward Zhou he took two practice swipes with his weapon. Ming could hear the blade cutting the air.

The executioner stood over Zhou. He placed the edge of his sword gently against Zhou's neck, as though checking for the right place to strike.

Every eye was on the blade as it rose high above the Guard's head. When the blade's tip pointed at the sky, it froze in place for an extra beat. Somewhere, a woman screamed.

Then the blade came down and the crowd erupted into cheers.

41

Winter came early that year. Ming and his family stayed indoors as much as they could, but there was no escaping the cold. Nights were the worst. The wind was like a living thing, probing the outside of their house for cracks in the walls. Their dugout fireplace provided some relief, especially now that Ming could afford to keep it fully stocked. But it was never enough.

Ming sat in the back bedroom, keeping Li Juan company as she napped. He could hear the children playing on the other side of the thin door. Presently he heard a loud crash followed by muffled laughter. Ming guessed his armor was lying in a heap on the floor now.

Li Juan opened her eyes and put her hand over Ming's. "Tell them to quiet down."

Ming turned toward the common room. "Stop it, you two!"

Protests of innocence floated back to them.

Li Juan shifted in her bed and winced. "Hui Fen seems well."

"She does, and I am grateful for it." Ming wondered if his answer sounded as hollow as it felt. It was true that their daughter did appear better than he had dreamed possible. There had been nightmares during the first few weeks, bouts of screaming that lasted until sunrise. But after that Hui Fen started to behave as though nothing had happened. She was as cheerful and mischievous as she had ever been.

Hui Fen's cheer bothered Ming. He almost would have preferred to see their daughter more distraught. After all, she *must* have sustained some kind of trauma from the horror of that night. Had she shown evidence of that trauma, Ming could feel she was at least addressing it. Instead she was just burying it, and that was troubling. Could a person really pretend that pain and fear did not exist…or would that reaction just cause those feelings to build until they became too much to bear?

Li Juan said something, but it was a whisper that Ming could not hear. "What?"

Li Juan took a shallow breath and let it out slowly. "I said you saved her. She'll never forget that and neither will I."

"I want her to forget it."

"And I'm so glad things are going well for you in the Gold Bird Guard." Li Juan never spoke of their daughter's ordeal for long. She always just mentioned it briefly, as if to remind herself that it was really over. "Now you'll be able to provide for the children."

"If the boredom doesn't drive me mad." Ming worked in a small office in the basement of the Imperial Ministry. He spent his days interviewing suspects and witnesses. Since people were always brought to Ming for interviews, there were days when he never saw the sun. Sometimes the stillness of that little room grew oppressive. There had been times – not many but some – when that stillness became too much. During those times Ming could feel his heart gallop and his chest constrict. At least now when a fit came he could close his office door, sit in the dark and wait for it to pass.

Li Juan was looking up at Ming. "Are you going to miss me?"

"Of course I will," Ming whispered. Almost without noticing he added, "More than I can ever say."

"I'm going to miss you, too." Li Juan closed her eyes. "Wherever I go after I leave here, I'll miss you."

Ming squeezed his wife's hand. *Just stay with me another month or two. I'm not ready yet, so just another month or two. Please.*

42

She left them two weeks later.

Ming walked out of the cemetery with his children and sister-in-law. As they made their way along the street Ming pulled the children close. Their clothing was thick and new, but Ming could feel them shivering against him. The day had brought fog, snow and a wind that bit.

Ming could still hear the paid mourners wailing back in the cemetery. He had hired them, but now he wished they would stop. Those false cries seemed to follow him onto the street, to remind him that the funeral was just the start of his grief.

They turned a corner and the crying fell away.

As they made their way down the street, Wei Sheng wrapped his arms around Ming's waist. The boy had been clinging to him like that all morning. Ming wanted to comfort his son but he didn't know what to say. Instead he just pulled him closer.

Ming looked down at Hui Fen. He always found it easier to communicate with his daughter. That was natural since she was older, but Ming suspected it would always be that way. "How are you doing?"

Hui Fen kept looking forward as she walked. "I was just thinking about the night I was in that crazy man's house."

Ming raised his eyebrows. His daughter had never spoken of that before. "I think about it every day."

Somewhere to his right, Ming heard a disapproving grunt from his sister-in-law. Li Hua believed the experience was best never mentioned again.

They turned another corner and started down a wider street. Normally this street was teeming with people, but the cold had driven everyone indoors. The stores were closed and quiet. Ming was grateful for that. His family needed privacy today.

Hui Fen said, "When we rode home from that place, I was so happy to be alive. I wasn't scared or angry. I just thanked the gods and my ancestors that I wasn't dead. I didn't care about anything else because being alive was the only important thing."

"I felt the same way when we got you out of there," Ming said.

"I was happy because I knew that if I was alive, everything else would be all right. But now Mama is dead and nothing will be all right for her ever again." Hui Fen sniffed and rubbed a sleeve across her eyes.

"Tell me this," Ming said. "On your mother's last day, what do you suppose she was thinking? Was she sorry that she was dying, or was she happy knowing you were safe?"

Hui Fen was quiet for a long time. The only sound was their feet crunching in the snow. They made a final turn and their home came into view.

Hui Fen looked up at Ming. "I think she was sad to be dying, but she was also glad because I was safe."

"More than glad," Ming said. "She was happier and more relieved than she had ever been in her life. And no matter what else she was thinking about, that mattered to her most of all."

They stopped in front of their house. Li Hua and Wei Sheng went inside right away, but Hui Fen sat down on their front step. Ming sat next to her. She leaned against him, and he put an arm around her shoulders.

They watched the snow drift down through the fog. A few people rushed past, holding their clothes tight against their bodies to fight the cold. The fog made them look dim and distant. Ming felt like he and Hui Fen were the only living people in a city of ghosts.

Hui Fen pushed closer against him. "You're right. Knowing I was safe made her happy."

"Try to remember that," Ming said. "When I remember it I feel better."

"It makes me feel better too, but it's not enough."

"No," Ming said. "It's not."

The End

Thank you for reading *Dynasty of Shadows*.

Join my mailing list for a **free** copy of my novel, *Jin Village*.

Visit www.vincentstoia.com to sign up.

And while I have your attention, please give me a review!

Reviews are immensely helpful to authors. If you enjoyed *Dynasty of Shadows*, I would greatly appreciate a brief review. A sentence or two would do just fine. Thank you!

Continue to the next page for an excerpt of *Jin Village*.

Jin Village by Vincent Stoia

American historian Malcolm Wang is embarking on the adventure of his life, leading a team of archaeologists deep into the mountains of rural China. There, they will excavate the ruins of Jin Village, a tiny hamlet that has not seen a human visitor in a century.

But Jin Village is more than just a collection of overgrown stones. There are forces here, relics of a forgotten past that will fight – and kill – to survive. One by one, the archaeologists begin to disappear.

The survivors find themselves isolated and hunted by a being they do not understand. In this place of ancient myth and magic, the trappings of the modern world mean nothing. If Malcolm and his people are to survive, they must delve deep into the past of Jin Village, and confront its terrifying secret.

Preview: Chapter 1

Zhou already knew it was going to be a terrible day. He had awakened with that feeling, and it persisted through the morning. By the time the sun got higher and Zhou began setting up floodlights around the tiny forest clearing, his discomfort had evolved into a steady, rumbling dread. So he was already in poor spirits when he found the white girl's body.

Forgotten cigarette dangling from the corner of his mouth, Zhou stared at the corpse. *Her,* he thought. *Don't think of the girl as a* corpse.

Only part of the young woman's body was visible. Everything below her midsection was covered in brush, fallen leaves and miscellaneous forest debris. Most of her neck was missing, and although he hated to admit it, this relieved Zhou. The girl had clearly been mauled by some kind of animal (Zhou reminded himself to get that rifle from his truck), so nobody could suspect him of murder.

He ran for the satellite phone.

• • •

"Who is this again?" The voice on the other end of the sat phone was weak and grainy, but still managed to sound obnoxious. She had a Shanghai accent. Zhou didn't like people from Shanghai. Bunch of snobs.

"This is Zhou Muoya. I am at the Jin Village dig site in the Shaanxi Province. It's…maybe forty kilometers north of Han Village. I have found a dead body."

More static coming through his sat phone. Zhou frowned and looked up at the Jade Mountains, looming high over this tiny forest clearing. Why had he accepted this job, anyway? What was he thinking when he agreed to come to one of China's most isolated places, and by himself at that? He said, "Can you repeat that, please?"

This time the woman's voice was clear, and so was her irritation. Yes, she was from Shanghai. Definitely. "I said, why don't you alert the local authorities?"

Gee, thanks lady. I never thought of that. "There's no cell phone reception out here. I can only contact your office. I need you to get in touch with the local police, have them send someone."

"I'll contact the local police," said Miss Shanghai. "Have them send someone."

Zhou sighed. He gave her the dig site coordinates. "Tell them to come by boat if they can. The Han River runs right by this place."

More static, none of it intelligible.

"What?"

"I said, that's not up to me. The authorities know the area, so they'll decide how to get there."

Zhou used his free hand to rub his temple. "If they come over land they'll need off-road vehicles and they'll need to know the correct routes. I am in a forest clearing that's only a few hundred square meters. I've got the Jade Mountains to the west, the Han River to the east and trees everywhere else. You see my point?"

There was a pause, and Zhou felt immense satisfaction. So there!

"All right," said his new friend. "I'll pass along what you said."

"There's one more thing." Zhou looked in the direction of the young woman's body and wondered if he should cover her with a blanket. "The dead person is a foreigner. I'm pretty sure I know who she is. She was the first of a team that's scheduled to excavate the Jin Village ruins next month. They told me a foreigner might be here when I arrived, but I didn't think anything of it when she didn't show. They said 'might.'" Zhou wondered if that sounded suspicious.

"Do you know her name?"

Zhou thought for a long time. English names all sounded the same to him. "Jennifer, I think. Jennifer Cranmer."

"All right. I'll contact local police. Check back with me for an update in…say, an hour."

I'll look forward to it, Zhou thought. They said their goodbyes and hung up.

A heavy silence descended. Even the birds grew quiet. Zhou considered sitting under a tree for the next hour. He could just smoke and relax and wait until it was time to call back. But they weren't paying him to be lazy. Besides, given time to think, his mind would go back to all the colorful stories he'd heard about tiny Jin Village.

It would be better to work, to keep his mind off those damn ghost stories. He decided to finish the floodlights. That would keep him occupied until he called Miss Shanghai back.

But first, Zhou walked to the truck and took out his rifle.

About the Author

Vinnie is a novelist and a screenwriter. He grew up in Boston, but he has spent more than fifteen years abroad. He has lived in Australia, Taiwan and Japan. Most of Vinnie's prose is horror. As a screenwriter, he tends to write comedies. Horror and comedy may seem like a strange combination to some, but Vinnie respectfully disagrees. After all, both genres come from dark places.

Vinnie spends his free time studying Chinese, listening to podcasts and arguing about obscure horror movies that no sane person would ever watch.

Made in United States
North Haven, CT
16 January 2024